NEW FOLKS' HOME

NEW FOLKS'
HOME

AND OTHER STORIES

The Complete Short Fiction
of Clifford D. Simak,
Volume Six

Introduction by David W. Wixon

OPEN ROAD

INTEGRATED MEDIA
NEW YORK

"New Folks' Home" © 1963 by The Conde Nast Publications, Inc. © 1991 by the Estate of Clifford D. Simak. Original appearance in *Analog Science Fact-Science Fiction*, v. 71, no. 5, July, 1963.

"The Questing of Foster Adams" © 1953 by King-Size Publications, Inc. © 1981 by Clifford D. Simak. Originally published in *Fantastic Universe*, v. 1, no. 2, Aug.-Sept., 1953.

"Hermit of Mars" © 1939 by Street & Smith Publications, Inc. © 1967 by Clifford D. Simak. Originally published in *Astounding Science-Fiction*, v. 23, no. 4, June, 1939.

"Worlds Without End" © 1956 by Columbia Publications, Inc. © 1984 by Clifford D. Simak. Originally published in *Future Science Fiction*, no. 31, Winter 1956-1957.

"Barb Wire Brings Bullets!" © 1945 by Fictioneers, Inc. © 1973 by Clifford D. Simak. Originally published in *Ace-High Western Stories*, v. 10, no. 3, Nov., 1945.

"Second Childhood" © 1950 by World Editions, Inc. © 1978 by Clifford D. Simak. Originally published in *Galaxy Science Fiction*, v. 1, no. 5, Feb., 1951.

"You'll Never Go Home Again" © 1951 by Ziff-Davis Publishing Company. © 1979 by Clifford D. Simak. Originally published in *Fantastic Adventures*, v. 13, no. 7, July, 1951. Subsequently reprinted under title "Beachhead."

"Sunspot Purge" © 1940 by Street & Smith Publications, Inc. © 1968 by Clifford D. Simak. Originally published in *Astounding Science-Fiction*, v. 26, no. 3, Nov., 1940.

"Drop Dead" © 1956 by Galaxy Publishing Corp. © 1984 by Clifford D. Simak. Originally published in *Galaxy Science Fiction*, v. 12, no. 3, July, 1956.

"Worrywart" © 1953 by Galaxy Publishing Corp. © 1981 by Clifford D. Simak. Originally published in *Galaxy Science Fiction*, v. 6, no. 6, Sept., 1953.

Introduction copyright © 2015 by David W. Wixon

Cover design by Jason Gabbert

978-1-5040-6032-5

Published in 2020 by Open Road Integrated Media, Inc.
180 Maiden Lane
New York, NY 10038
www.openroadmedia.com

CONTENTS

INTRODUCTION:
THE NAMES IN SIMAK

"The night was as black as a stack of cats."
  —*Clifford D. Simak in "A Death in the House"*

Those who have read more than the occasional piece of Clifford D. Simak's fiction—and done so with some attention—may have noticed two things about the names of his characters. One is that Cliff repeats names, or portions of names, and uses them over and over despite any relationship among them. Characters in several stories (including "How-2" and "Eternity Lost," for instance) are named Anson Lee, and he uses Anson as a first name in his novel *Why Call Them Back from Heaven?* I have found nothing in Cliff's past life to indicate that the name was based on someone he might have known. Nor is that true with regard to the name Horton, which appears in at least four of Cliff's novels—sometimes as a first name, sometimes last (see *Ring Around the Sun, Shakespeare's Planet, Out of Their Minds,* and *The Werewolf Principle*).

Not so with Parker. Again, Cliff sometimes uses it as a first name, sometimes last (as in Thomas Parker in "The Whistling Well"). But Parker was the maiden name of Cliff's maternal grandmother, a person who clearly had a special place in his life. (Her first name was Ellen, which Cliff named his only daughter and used in "Over the River and Through the Woods": He clearly modeled the protagonist, Ellen Forbes, after his grandmother.)

And the name Carson, which turns up frequently in the earlier Simak stories, is that of his brother.

Other character names seem to have been taken from place names familiar to Cliff—in particular the name Grant, which was the name of the Wisconsin county in which he was born. (In what may have been a piece of whimsy, in one of his never-published stories Cliff had a character named Grant Sheridan.) And quite a number of his characters bore names clearly derived from towns in areas where Cliff had lived: Fennimore, Wisconsin, and Navarre, Minnesota.

The second thing about the character names used by Clifford Simak is that they are, almost uniformly, the sort that would be labeled "white bread" in today's parlance. That is, they are names commonly found in the midwestern United States: names such as Wallace, Webster, Carter, Blaine, Foster, Sutton . . .

No great mystery here: When asked once, Cliff said it meant nothing; he was simply not interested in picking names that might have particular meanings; when writing a passage that called for a name, he simply reached out for whatever came into his head.

That same lack of intent apparently came into play when Cliff was creating titles for his stories: Many of the stories he sold had their names changed by editors, and in only a few of those cases did he bother to change it back for reprints ("Skirmish" was originally printed as "Bathe Your Bearings in Blood," but Cliff reclaimed the original title in later appearances).

And that trait carried over when Cliff, as successful authors do, signed contracts for still-unwritten novels: *Cemetery World* was contracted for under the name *Aesop and Pilgrim*; *A Choice of Gods* under the name *August 1, 2185*; and *Out of Their Minds* as *The Horse*.

Two aspects of the names Cliff used will certainly be familiar to his readers. First, many—though not all—of his robots bore biblical names: Nicodemus, Ezekiel, Gideon, Abraham. Second, many place names from his own past appear over and over again:

Bridgeport, Woodman, Willow Bend, and above all, Millville, the little town that was closest to the Simak farm.

And yet, Clifford Simak was clearly capable of creativity in the field of names. For instance, in his novel *The Goblin Reservation*, when crafting names for solar systems, he came up with Headache No. 2, Misery IV, and the Slaughter Suns—and he used the Coonskin Systems several times. More often, when he needed to name a solar system in a story, he often simply chose names of stars familiar to the average reader: Polaris, Centaurus, Canopus, or Arcturus.

As Cliff said, the Millville of so many of his stories was really not the Millville of his youth—just as the hollows, ridges, and woods in his stories are deeper, higher, darker, and thicker than the real things. For Cliff, after all, was a user of his own imagination. And he used his imagination to transform what was familiar to him into something more wonderful. I have a mental picture of that farm boy walking through his so-familiar environment, playing a boy's game of populating it with creatures out of his head. . . . And he never stopped that game.

More than any of the other names Cliff Simak used in his stories, the one I'm most curious about is Myrt, which I presume is a shortened form of Myrtle, a female name that was popular around 1900. When he tapped the name in his stories, he generally applied it to a person who did not even appear in the story but was referred to as being elsewhere—such as Aunt Myrt in "Buckets of Diamonds"—but he also bestowed it on the gigantic computer that was supposed to create the dreams in "Worlds Without End."

Was there a Myrt, or an Aunt Myrt, somewhere in Cliff Simak's background?

David W. Wixon

NEW FOLKS' HOME

In early 1963, Clifford Simak sent his agent a story named "Failure," and I think this is that story. It was published in the July 1963 issue of Analog Science Fiction and Fact, *part of that magazine's short-lived experiment with the "bedsheet" format. It's a story about a man all alone, to whom something—something else—reaches out, to give a kind of salvation.*

It is a story told to beat back the sadness of thinking of all the lives that end in loneliness and despair. . . .

—dww

The house was an absurdity. What is more, it was out of place. And it had no right to be there, Frederick Gray told himself. For this was his country, his and old Ben Lovell's. They had discovered it almost forty years before and had come here ever since and in all that time there had been no one else.

He knelt in the canoe and stroked idly with the paddle to keep the craft in place, with the bright, brown autumn water flowing past, bearing on its surface little curls of foam from the waterfall a half a mile ahead. He had heard the faint thunder of the falls when he had parked the car and lowered the canoe from its top and for the past hour he'd traveled toward it, listening to it and storing the sound of it away, as he was storing everything away, for this, he knew, was the last trip to this place he would ever make.

They could have waited, he told himself, with a strange mellow bitterness. They could have waited until he had made the trip. For it was all spoiled now. No longer could he ever think upon this stream without the house intruding. Not as he had known the stream for almost forty years, but now always with the house.

No one had ever lived here. No one would want to live here. No one ever came here. It had been his and Ben's alone.

But the house stood there, upon the little knoll above the flowing stream, framed in all its shiny whiteness against the greenness of the pines, and with a path leading from his old camping place up to where it sat.

He wielded the paddle savagely and drove the canoe to the shore. It grounded on the gravel and he stepped out and hauled it up the beach, where it would be safe from the tugging current.

Then he straightened and stared up at the house.

How would he tell Ben, he wondered. Or should he try to tell him? Might it not be better, when he talked with Ben, to disregard the house? You could not tell a man, lying in a hospital from which he had small chance of ever going home, that someone had robbed him of a segment of his past. For when a man is near the end, thought Gray, his past is somehow precious. And that, Gray admitted to himself, was the reason he himself resented the house upon the knoll.

Although, perhaps, he thought, he would not have resented it so much if it had not been so ridiculous. For it was not the kind of house for a place like this. If it had been a rustic structure, built of natural wood, with a great rock chimney, all built low against the ground, it would not have been so bad. For then it would have fitted, or would have tried to fit.

But this stark white structure, gleaming with the newness of its paint, was unforgivable. It was the sort of place that some junior executive might have built in some fashionable development, where all the other houses, sitting on the barren acres, would be of the same sleek architecture. There it would be quite all right and acceptable, but in this place of rock and pine it was an absurdity and an insult.

He bent stiffly and tugged the canoe farther up the beach. He lifted out his cased rod and laid it on the ground. He found the creel and strapped it on, and slung the pair of waders across his shoulders.

Then, picking up the rod, he made his way slowly up the path. For it was only dignified and proper that he make his presence known to these people on the knoll. It would not be right to go stalking past them, up the river, without an explanation. But he would be very sure not to say anything that might imply he was asking their permission. Rather it might be quite fitting, he told himself, to make very clear to them the prior right that he held and to inform them stiffly that this would be the last time he was coming and that he would bother them no further.

The way was steep. It had seemed of late, he thought, that all little slopes were steep. His breath was shorter now and his breathing shallow and his knees were stiff and his muscles ached from kneeling and paddling the canoe.

Maybe it had been foolish to try the trip alone. With Ben it would have been all right, for there would have been the two of them, the one to help the other. He had told no one that he planned the trip, for if he had they would have attempted to dissuade him—or what might have been far worse, offered to go along with him. They would have pointed out that no man of almost seventy should try such a trip alone. Although, actually, it was not much of a trip, at all. Just a few hours drive up from the city to the little town of Pineview and then four miles down the old logging road until he reached the river. And from there an hour of paddling up the river to the falls and the olden camping place just downstream from the falls.

Halfway up the slope he stopped to catch his breath and rest. From there he could see the falls, the white rush of the water and the little cloud of mist that, when the sun was right, held captive rainbows in it.

He stood looking at it all—the darkness of the pines, the barren face of rocky gorge, the flaming crimson and the goldenness of the hardwood trees, now turned into autumn bonfires by the touch of early frost.

How many times, he wondered—how many times had Ben and he fished above the falls? How many campfires had they lighted? How many times had they traveled up and down the river?

It had been a good life, a good way to spend their time together, two stodgy professors from a stodgy downstate college. But all things approach an end; nothing lasts forever. For Ben it had already ended. And after this one trip, it would be the end for him.

He stood and wondered once again, with a twinge of doubt, if he had made the right decision. The people at Wood's Rest seemed kind and competent and had shown him that he would be with the kind of people he could understand—retired teachers and ancient bankers and others from the genteel walks of life. But despite all this, the doubt kept creeping in.

It would have been so different, he thought, if only Clyde had lived. They had been closer than most sons and fathers. But now he had no one. Martha had been gone for many years and now Clyde was gone as well and there were no others.

On the face of it, from every practical consideration, Wood's Rest was the answer. He would be taken care of and he could live the kind of life, or at least an approximation of the kind of life, to which he was accustomed. It was all right now to keep on alone, but the time was coming when he would need someone. And Wood's Rest, while perhaps not the perfect answer, was at least an answer. A man must look ahead, he told himself, and that was why he had made the arrangements with Wood's Rest.

He was breathing easier now and he went on up the path until he reached the little patch of level ground that lay before the house.

The house was new, he saw, newer than he had thought at first. From where he stood he imagined that he could smell the newness of the paint.

And how, he wondered, had the materials which had been used to build it been gotten to the site? There was no sign of any road. It might, he thought, have been trucked down the ancient logging road and brought up the river from where he had left his car. But if that had been the case, the logging road would have shown the signs of recent travel, and it hadn't. It still was no more than a rutted track, its center overgrown with grass, that snaked its way through a tunnel of encroaching second growth. And if it had been brought by boat, there should have been a skidway or a road leading from the river to the site, and there was nothing but the faint, scarcely worn path up which he'd made his way. There would not have been time, he knew, for the wilderness and weather to have wiped out the traces, for he and Ben had been here fishing in the spring and at that time there had been no house.

Slowly he crossed the level place and the patio that looked out upon the river and the falls. He reached the door and pressed the button and far in the house he could hear the sound of ringing. He waited and no one came. He pressed the bell again. He heard the ringing from within the house and listened for the sound of footsteps coming to the door, but there were no footsteps. He raised his hand and knocked upon the door and at the knock the door came open and swung wide into the hall.

He stood abashed at this invasion of another's privacy. He debated for a moment whether he should reach in and close the door and quietly go away. But that, he told himself, had a sense of sneaking that he did not like.

"Hello!" he called. "Is anybody home?"

He would explain, when someone came, that he had merely knocked upon the door, that he had not opened it.

But no one came.

For a moment he stood undecided, then stepped inside the hall to grasp the doorknob and pull it shut.

In that instant he saw the living room, newly carpeted and filled with furniture. Someone was living here, he thought, but they were not at home. They had gone somewhere for a little while and had not locked the door. Although, come to think of it, no one up here ever locked a door. There was no need to lock them.

He would forget it, he promised himself, forget this house, this blot upon the land, and spend his day fishing and in the afternoon go back downriver to the car and home. He would not let his day be spoiled.

Sturdily, he set out, tramping along the ridge that took him above the falls and to that stretch of water that he knew so well.

The day was calm and clear. The sun was shining brightly, but there was still a touch of chill. However, it was only ten o'clock. By noon it would be warm.

He jogged along, quite happily, and by the time he donned the waders and stepped into the water, a mile above the falls, the house no longer mattered.

It was early in the afternoon that the accident occurred.

He had waded ashore and found a medium-sized boulder that would serve as a chair while he ate the lunch he'd brought. He had laid the rod down carefully on the shingle of the little beach and had admired the three trout of keeping size that rested in the creel. And had noted, as he unwrapped his sandwich, that the sky was clouding over.

Perhaps, he told himself, he should start home a bit sooner than he had planned. There was no point in waiting if there were a chance the weather would turn bad. He had put in three good hours upon the stream and should be satisfied.

He finished the sandwich and sat quietly on the boulder, staring at the smooth flow of the water against the rampart of the pines that grew on the farther bank. It was a scene, he told himself, that he should fix into his memory, to keep and hold forever. It would be something to think upon in the days to come when there were no fishing trips.

He decided that he'd take another half hour before he left the stream. He'd fish down to the point where the fallen tree lay halfway across the water. There should be trout in there, underneath the tree, hiding there and waiting.

He got up stiffly and picked up the rod and creel and stepped into the stream. His foot slipped on a mossy boulder hidden by the water and he was thrown forward. A sharp pain slashed through his ankle and he hit the shallow water and lay there for a moment before he could move to right himself.

His foot, the one that had slipped, was caught between two chunks of rock, wedged into a crevice in the stream bed. Caught and twisted and throbbing with a steady and persistent pain.

His teeth clenched against an outcry, he slowly worked the foot free and dragged himself back onto the shore.

He tried to stand and found that the twisted ankle would not bear his weight. It turned under him when he tried and a red-hot streak of pain went shooting through his leg.

He sat down and carefully worked off his waders. The ankle already was becoming swollen and had a red and angry look.

He sat upon the shingle of the beach and carefully considered all that he must do.

He could not walk, so he would have to crawl. He'd leave the waders and the rod and creel, for he could not be encumbered by them. Once he got to the canoe, he could make it down the river to where he'd parked his car. But when he got there, he'd have to leave the canoe behind as well, for he could never load it on top of the car.

Once he was in the car, he would be all right, for he could manage driving. He tried to remember it there were a doctor at Pineview. It seemed to him there was, but he could not be sure. But, in any case, he could arrange for someone to come back and pick up the rod and the canoe. Foolish, maybe, he thought, but he could not give up the rod. If it wasn't picked up soon, the porcupines would find and ruin it. And he could not allow a thing like that to happen. For the rod was a part of him.

He laid the three—the waders, the creel and rod—in a pile beside the river where they could be spotted easily by anyone who might be willing to come back for them. He looked for the last time at the river and began the crawl.

It was a slow and painful business. Try as he might, he could not protect the ankle from bumps along the way and every bump sent waves of pain surging through his body.

He considered fashioning a crutch, but gave it up as a bad idea when he realized that the only tool he had was a pocket knife, and not too sharp a one.

Slowly he inched his way along, making frequent stops to rest. He could see, when he examined it, that the ankle was more swollen than before and the redness of it was beginning to turn purple.

And suddenly the frightening realization came, somewhat belatedly, that he was on his own. No one knew that he was here, for he had told no one. It would be days, if he failed to make it, before anyone would think to hunt for him.

It was a foolish thought. For he could make it easily. The hardest part came first and that was for the best. Once he reached the beached canoe, he would have it made.

If only he could keep crawling longer. If he didn't have to rest so often. There had been a day when he could have made it without a single rest. But a man got old and weak, he thought. Weaker than he knew.

It was during one of his rests that he heard the rising wind whining in the treetops. It had a lonesome sound and was a little frightening. The sky, he saw, was entirely clouded over and a sort of ghostly twilight had settled on the land.

He tried to crawl the faster, spurred on by a vague uneasiness. But he only tired the quicker and banged the injured ankle cruelly. He settled down again to a slower pace.

He had passed the fall line and had the advantage of a slightly downhill slope when the first drop of rain spattered on his outstretched hand.

And a moment after that the rain came in gusty sweeps of ice savagery.

He was soaked in the first few minutes and the wind was cold. The twilight deepened and the pines moaned in the rising gale and little rivulets of water ran along the ground.

Doggedly, he kept at his crawling. His teeth tried to chatter as the chill seeped in, but he kept his mouth clamped shut to stop the chattering.

He was better than halfway back to the canoe, but now the way seemed long. He was chilled to the bone and as the rain still came down it seemed to bear with it a great load of weariness.

The house, he thought. I can find shelter at the house. They will let me in.

Not daring to admit that his earlier objective, to reach the canoe and float down the river to where he'd left his car, had now become impossible and unthinkable.

Ahead, through the murkiness of the storm, he saw the glow of light. That would be the house, he thought. They—whoever they might be—were now at home and had turned on the lights.

It took longer than he had thought it would, but he reached the house with what seemed to be the last shred of his strength. He crawled across the patio and managed to pull himself erect beside the door, leaning on the house, bracing on one leg. He thumbed the button and heard the ringing of the bell inside and waited for the footsteps.

There weren't any footsteps.

And it wasn't right, he told himself. There were lights within the house and there should be people there. And if that were the case, why should he get no answer?

Behind him the moaning in the pines seemed deeper and more fearsome and there was no doubt that it had grown darker. The rain still came hissing down in its chilling fury.

He balled his fist and pounded on the door and as it had that morning, the door swung open, to let the light spill out across the patio.

"Hello, in there!" he shouted. "Is anybody home?"

There was no answer and no stir, no sign of anything at all.

Hopping painfully, he crossed the threshold and stood within the hall. He called again and yet again and there was no response.

His leg gave out and he slumped upon the floor, catching himself and breaking the fall with his outstretched hands. Slowly, he inched his way along, crawling toward the living room.

He turned at the faint noise which came from behind his back and he saw that the door was closing—closing of its own accord and with no hand upon it. He watched in fascination as it closed, firm against the casing. The snick of the lock as it settled was loud in the stillness of the house.

Queer, he thought, fuzzily. Queer how the door came open as if to invite one in. And then when one was in, calmly closed itself.

But it did not matter what the door might do, he thought. The important thing was that he was inside and that the cold ferocity of the storm was shut in the outer dark. Already the warmth of the house was enfolding him and some of the chill was gone.

Careful not to bump the dragging ankle, he snaked himself along the carpeting until he reached a chair. He hauled himself upward and around and sat down in it, settling back into the cushions, with the twisted ankle thrust out in front of him.

Now, finally, he was safe. Now the cold and rain could no longer reach him, and in time someone would show up who could help him with the ankle.

He wondered where they were, these people to whom the

house belonged. It was unlikely that they would stray far from it in a storm like this. And they must have been here not too long ago, because the lights were lit against the darkness of the storm.

He sat quietly, now only faintly aware of the dull throb of pain that was pulsing in the ankle. The house was warm and quiet and restful and he was glad for it.

Carefully he looked around, taking inventory.

There was a table in the dining room and it was set for dinner, with the steaming silver coffee pot and the gleaming china tureen and a covered platter. He could smell the coffee and there was food as well, of that he felt quite sure. But there was only one place set, as if one person only had been meant to dine.

A door opened into another room that seemed to be a study. There was a painting on the wall and a massive desk set beneath the painting. There were floor to ceiling bookcases, but there were no books in them.

And a second door led into a bedroom. There was a bed turned down and a pair of pajamas were folded on the pillow. The lamp on the bedside table had been lit. As if the bed were waiting for someone to sleep in it, all turned down and ready.

But there was a strangeness, a fantastic something about the house that he could not quite put his finger on. Like a case at law, he thought, where there was a certain quality that eluded one, always with the feeling that this certain quality might be the very key to the case itself.

He sat and thought about it, and suddenly he knew.

The house was furnished, but the house was waiting. One could sense a feeling of expectancy, as if this were a house that was waiting for a tenant. It was set and ready, it was equipped and furnished. But there was no one living here. It had an unlived-in smell to it and a vague sort of emptiness.

But that was foolishness, he told himself. Of course, there was someone living in it. Someone had turned on the lights, someone had cooked a dinner and set a place for one, someone had lit the bedside lamp and turned down the covers of the bed.

And yet, for all the evidence, he couldn't quite believe it. The house still persisted in its empty feeling.

He saw the trail of water he'd left in his crawl along the hall and across the carpeting to reach the chair. He saw the muddy handprints he'd left upon the wall where he had braced himself when he'd hobbled in.

It was no way to mess up a place, he thought. He'd do his best to explain it to the owner.

He sat and waited for the owner, nodding in the chair.

Seventy, he thought, or almost seventy, and this his last adventure. All his family gone and all his friends as well—all except old Ben, who was dying slowly and ungracefully in the alien and ungraceful atmosphere of a small hospital room.

He recalled that day of long ago when Ben and he had met, two young professors, Ben in astronomy and himself in law. They had been friends from the very first and it would be hard to have Ben go.

But perhaps he would not notice it, he thought, as much as he might have at one time. For he, himself, in another month, would be settled down at Wood's Rest. An old folks' home, he thought. Although now they didn't call them that. They called them fancy names like Wood's Rest, thinking that might take the sting away.

It didn't matter, though. There was no one left to whom it might matter now—except himself, of course. And he didn't care. Not very much, that is.

He snapped himself erect and looked at the mantle clock.

He'd dozed away, he thought, or been dreaming of the old days while no more than half awake. Almost an hour had passed since he'd last glanced at the clock and still the house was empty of anyone but he.

The dinner still was upon the table, but it would be cold by now. Perhaps, he thought, the coffee still might be a little warm.

He pushed forward in the chair and rose carefully to his feet. And the ankle screamed at him. He fell back into the chair and weak tears of pain ran out of his eyes and dribbled down his cheeks.

Not the coffee, he thought. I don't want the coffee. If I can just make it to the bed.

He pulled himself tenderly from the chair and crawled into the bedroom. By slow and painful maneuver, he stripped off his sodden clothing and got into the pajamas that had been folded on the pillow.

There was a bathroom off the bedroom and by hopping from bed to chair to dresser he finally reached it.

Something to kill the pain, he told himself. Aspirin would be of some little help if he could only find one.

There was a medicine cabinet above the basin and he jerked it open, but the shelves were empty.

After a time he made it back to the bed again and crawled beneath the covers, switching off the bedside light.

Lying stiff and straight, shivering with the effort of getting into bed, he wondered dully what would happen when the owner should return and find a stranger in the bed.

But he didn't care. He was beyond all caring. His head was large and fuzzy and he guessed he had a fever.

He lay quietly, waiting for sleep to come to him, his body fitting itself by slow degrees into the strangeness of the bed.

He did not even notice when the lights throughout the house went out.

He awoke to the morning sun, streaming through the windows. There was the odor of frying bacon and of brewing coffee. And a telephone was ringing, loudly and insistently.

He threw off the covers and was halfway out of bed to answer the telephone when he remembered that this was not his house, that this was not his bed, that the ringing phone could not possibly be for him.

He sat upon the edge of the bed, bewildered, as the memory of the day before came crashing in upon him.

Good Lord, he thought, a phone! There can't be a phone. Way out here, there can't.

But still it kept on ringing.

In just a little while, he thought, someone would come to answer it. The someone who was frying bacon would come and answer it. And when they did, they'd go past the open door and he would be able to see them and know to whom the house belonged.

He got out of bed. The floor beneath his feet was cold and there might be slippers somewhere, but he didn't know where to look for them.

He was out in the living room before he remembered that he had a twisted ankle.

Stopping in amazement, he looked down at it and it looked as it had always looked, no longer red or purple, and no longer swollen. And most important, not hurting any more. He could walk on it as if nothing had ever been the matter with it.

The phone standing on the table in the hall pealed aloud at him.

"I'll be damned," said Frederick Gray, staring at his ankle.

The phone brayed at him again.

He hurried to the table and snatched the handpiece off the cradle.

"Hello," he said.

"Dr. Frederick Gray, perhaps."

"You are right. I am Frederick Gray."

"I trust you had a restful night."

"A very restful one. And thank you very much."

"Your clothes were wet and beyond repair. We disposed of them. I hope that you don't mind. The contents of the pockets are on the dressing table. There is other clothing in the closet that I am sure will fit you."

"Why," said Frederick Gray, "that was very thoughtful of you. But would you mind telling me—"

"Not at all," the caller said, "but perhaps you'd better hurry out and get your breakfast. It will be getting cold."

The phone went dead.

"Just a minute," Gray yelled at it. "Just hold on a minute—"

But the buzz of an empty line kept sounding in his ear.

He hung up and went into the bedroom, where he found a pair of slippers tucked beneath the bed.

We hope you had a restful night. Your clothes were wet, so we disposed of them. We put the contents of the pockets on the dressing table.

And who in the world were we?

Where was everyone?

And what happened, when he slept, to repair the ankle?

He had been right the night before, he thought. It was an empty house. There was no one here. But in some manner which he could not fathom, it still was tenanted.

He washed his hands and face, but did not bother with a shave, although when he looked into the medicine cabinet, it was no longer empty. It now held shaving tackle, a toothbrush and a tube of paste, a hairbrush and a comb.

Breakfast was on the table in the dining room and there was only one place set. There were bacon and eggs, hash brown potatoes, tomato juice, toast and a pot of coffee.

But there was no sign of anyone who might have prepared the food or placed it on the table.

Could there be, he wondered, a staff of invisible servants in the house who took care of guests?

And the electricity, he wondered. Was there a private power plant? Perhaps one that was powered by the waterfall? And what about the phone? Could it be a radiophone? He wondered if a radiophone would look different from just an ordinary phone. He could not recall that he had ever seen one.

And who had been the caller?

He stood and looked at the waiting breakfast.

"Whoever you are," he said, aloud, "I thank you. I wish that I could see you. That you would speak to me."

No one spoke to him.

He sat down and ate the breakfast, not realizing until he put the food into his mouth how hungry he had been.

After breakfast he went into the bedroom and found the clothes hanging in the closet. Not fancy clothes, but the kind of outfit a fisherman would wear.

Coming out of the bedroom, he saw that the breakfast things had been cleared off the table.

He stepped outside into the sunshine and the day was beautiful. The storm had blown itself out sometime in the night.

Now that he was all right, he told himself, perhaps he'd better go upstream and bring down the rod and the other stuff he'd left. The rest of it didn't amount to much, but the rod was much too good to leave.

It all was there, piled where he had left it, neatly on the shore. He bent down and picked up the rod and stood facing the river, with it in his hand.

Why not? he asked himself. There was no hurry to get back. As long as he was here he might as well get in a bit of fishing. He'd not have another chance. He'd not come back again.

He laid the rod aside and sat down to pull on the waders. He emptied the fish he'd caught the day before out of the creel and strapped it on his shoulder.

And why just this morning? he asked himself. Why just another day? There was no reason to get back and he had a house to stay in. There was no reason he shouldn't stay a while and make a real vacation of it.

He stood aghast at how easily he accepted the situation, how ready he found himself to take advantage of it. The house was a thing of mystery, and yet not terrifying. There was nothing in the house, strange as it might be, that a man need be afraid of.

He picked up the rod and stepped into the stream and whipped out the line. On the fifth cast a trout struck. The day had started fine.

He fished to the first break of the rapids just above the falls, then clambered out on shore. He had five fish in the creel and two of them were large.

He could fish the rapids from the shore, he thought, but perhaps he shouldn't. He should be getting back for a good look at the house. He had to settle in his mind the truth about the power source and the telephone and there might be a lot of other things that needed looking into.

He glanced down at his watch and it was later than he thought. He untied the fly and reeled in the line and disjointed the rod, then set off down the trail.

By the middle of the afternoon, he had finished his inspection of the house.

There were no power and no telephone lines coming to the house and there was no private power plant. The house was conventionally wired for electricity, but there was no source that he could find. The telephone plugged into a jack in the hall and there were other jacks in the bedroom and the study.

But there was another item: The night before, as he sat in the living room, he could see into the study. He had seen the painting and the desk and the empty book shelves. But now the shelves were no longer empty. They fairly bulged with books and the kind of books that he would have chosen if he had put them there himself—a law library that would have been the envy of any practicing attorney, and with a special section that he first took to be a joke.

But when he looked at the phone directory, it had seemed somewhat less a joke.

For it was no such directory as any man had ever seen before. It listed names and numbers, but the addresses ranged the galaxy!

Besur, Yar, Mekbuda V–FE 6-8731

Beten, Varmo, Polaris III–GR 7-3214

Beto, Elm, Rasalgethi IX–ST 1-9186

Star names, he thought, and the planet numbers. They could be nothing else.

And if it were a joke, it was pointless and expensive.

Star names listed in the pages of the directory and those other star names upon the books in that special section in the study!

The obvious conclusion, he told himself, rather plaintively, was too outrageous to be given even slight consideration. It was outrageous and ridiculous and it made no sense and he would not entertain it. There must be other answers and the one he did not like to think about was that he'd gone insane.

There might be a way, he thought, that it could be settled.

He flipped the directory closed and then opened the front cover and there it was: TELEPHONE SERVICE CALLS. He lifted the receiver and dialed for INFORMATION.

There were two ringing sounds and then a voice said:

"Good evening, Dr. Gray. We are glad you called. We hope everything's all right. There isn't any trouble?"

"You know my name," said Gray. "How do you know my name?"

"Sir," said Information, "it is a point of pride with us that we know the name of each of our subscribers."

"But I'm not a subscriber. I'm only—"

"Oh, but you are," insisted Information. "As soon as you took possession of the house—"

"Possession! I did not—"

"But, Dr. Gray, we thought you knew. We should have told you at the start. We are very sorry. The house, you see, is yours."

"No," Gray said, weakly, "I did not understand."

"Yours," said Information, "so long as you may need it, so

long as you may want to keep it. The house and everything that's in it. Plus all the services, naturally, that you may require."

"But it can't be mine," said Gray. "I have done nothing that would make it mine. How can I own a house for which I've given nothing?"

"There might be," said Information, "certain services that, from time to time, you might be willing to perform. Nothing strenuous, of course, and not required, you understand. If you would be willing to perform them, we would be the ones who would stand in debt. But the house is yours no matter what you may elect to do."

"Services?" asked Gray. "There are few services, I am afraid, that I could perform."

"It does not really matter," Information told him. "We are very glad you called. Call us again any time you wish."

The connection clicked and he was left, standing foolishly with the receiver in his hand.

He put it back into the cradle and went to the living room, sitting in the chair he'd sat in when he'd found his way into the house the night before.

While he'd been busy in the hall with the telephone, someone—or something, or some strange procedure—had laid wood in the fireplace and had lit it and the brass wood carrier that stood beside the hearth was filled with other wood against the need of it.

He watched the fire creeping up the logs, flickering as it climbed, with the cold wind outside growling in the chimney.

An Old Folks' Home, he thought.

For if he'd heard aright, that was what it was.

And a better one, by far, than the one he had planned to enter.

There was no reason in the world why anyone should give this house to him. He had done nothing he could think of that entitled him to have it.

An Old Folks' Home, all to himself, and on his favorite trout stream.

It would be wonderful, he thought, if he only could accept it.

He hitched the chair around so he could face the fire. He had always liked a fire.

Such a pleasant place, he thought, and such thoughtful service. He wished that he could stay.

And what was there to stop him? No one would mind if he did not return. In a day or two he could make his way out to Pineview and mail a couple of letters that would fix it so no one would hunt for him.

But it was madness, he thought. What if he got sick? What if he fell and hurt himself? He could not reach a doctor and there would be no one to help him.

Then he thought of how he'd hunted for an aspirin and there had been no aspirin. And how he'd crawled into bed with a twisted, swollen ankle that had been all right when he got up in the morning.

He had no worry, he realized, about ever being sick.

There had been no aspirin tablet because there had been no need of any.

This house was not a house alone. It was more than just a house. It was a shelter and a servant and a doctor. It was a safe and antiseptic house and it was compassionate.

It gave you everything you wanted. It fulfilled your every need. It gave you fire and food and comfort and a sense of being cared for.

There were the books, he thought. The rows and stacks of books, the very kind of books by which he'd lived for years.

Dr. Frederick Gray, dean of the school of law. Filled with honor and importance until he got too old, until his wife and son had died and all his friends were gone or incapacitated. Now no longer dean, now no longer scholar, but an old man with a name that was buried in the past.

He rose slowly from the chair and went into the study. He put out his hand and rubbed the palm of it along the leathery spines of a row of books.

These were the friends, he told himself, the friends a man could count on. They always were in place and waiting for the time a man might need them.

He stopped in front of the section that had puzzled him at first, which he had thought of as a farfetched joke. But now he knew there was no joke.

He read the titles of a few of them: "Basic Statutes of Arcturus XXIV," "Comparison of the Legal Concepts of the Centaurian Systems," "Jurisprudence on Zubeneschamali III, VI and VII," "The Practical Law of Canopus XII." And many others with the strange names in their titles.

Perhaps, he thought, he would not have recognized the names so readily had it not been for Ben. For years he had listened to him talk about his work, reeling off many of these very names as if they might be places no farther off than just down the street a ways.

And maybe, thought Frederick Gray, they were not so far, at that. All he had to do to talk to men—no, not men, perhaps, but beings—in all of these strange places was to walk out into the hall and dial their numbers on the phone.

A telephone directory, he thought, with numbers for the stars, and on all these shelves law books from the stars.

Perhaps there were, on those other solar systems, nothing like a telephone or a telephone directory; perhaps, on those other planets there weren't any law books. But here on Earth, he told himself, the means of communication had to be a telephone, the means of information books upon the shelf. For all of it had to be a matter of translation, twisting the unfamiliar into something that was familiar and that one could use. And translation not for Earth alone, but for all those other beings on all those other planets. On each of a dozen planets there might be a different means of communication, but in the case of a call to him from any of those planets, no matter what means the creature of the planet might employ, the telephone would ring.

And the names of those other stars would be translations, too. For the creatures who lived upon the planets circling Polaris would not call their sun Polaris. But here on Earth it had to be Polaris, for that was the only way a human had to identify the star.

The language would have to be translated, too. The creatures he had talked with on the phone could not have spoken English, and yet it had been English when it had reached his ear. And his replies, he knew, must have reached that other party in some language other than the tongue that he had used.

He stood aghast at the very thought of it, wondering how he could abide such an explanation. And yet there was no choice. It was the only explanation that would fit the situation.

Somewhere a bell rang sharply and he turned from the shelves of books.

He waited for it to ring again, but it did not ring.

He walked into the living room and saw that dinner had been set upon the table and was waiting for him.

So that was what it had been, he thought. A bell to summon him to dinner.

After dinner, he went back to the living room to sit before the fire and fight the whole thing out. He assembled the facts and evidence in his old lawyer's mind and gave full consideration to all possibilities.

He touched the edge of wonder and shoved it to one side, he erased it carefully—for in his consideration of this house there was no room for wonder and no place for magic.

Was it no more than illusion? That was the first question one must ask. Was this really happening, or was he just imagining that it was happening? Was he, perhaps, in all reality, sitting underneath a tree or squatting on the river bank, mumbling at nothing, scratching symbols in the dirt with his fingernails, and living the fantasy of this house, this fire, this room?

It was hard to believe that this might be the case. For there were too many details. Imagination formed a hazy framework and let it go at that.

There were here too many details and there was no haziness and he could move and think of his own volition; he still was the master of himself.

And if it were not imagination, if he could rule out insanity, then this house and all that happened must be, indeed, the truth. And if it were the truth, then here was a house built or shaped or somehow put into being by some outside agency that was as yet unsuspected in the mind of humankind.

But, he asked himself, why would they want to do it? What could be the motive?

With a view, perhaps, of studying him as a representative specimen of the creature, Man? Or with the idea that somehow they could make some use of him?

The thought struck him—was he the only man? Might there be others like him? Men who kept very silent about what was happening, for fear that human interference might spoil this good thing that they had?

He rose slowly from the chair and went out in the hall. He picked up the phone directory and bought it back with him. He threw another log upon the fire and sat down in the chair, with the phone book in his lap.

First himself, he thought; he would see if he was listed.

He had no trouble finding it: Gray, Frederick, Helios III–SU 6-2649.

He flipped the pages and started from the front, running his finger slowly down the column.

The book was thin, but it took him quite a while, going carefully so that he would not miss another man from Earth. But there was no other listed; not from Earth, not from the solar system. He was the only one.

Loneliness, he wondered. Or should it be just a touch of pride. To be the only one in the entire solar system.

He took the directory back to the table in the hall and lying in the place where he had gotten it was another one.

He stared at it and wondered if there were two of them, if there had been two of them all along and he had never noticed.

He bent to look the closer at it and when he did he saw that it was not another directory, but a file of some sort, with his name printed across the top of it.

He laid the directory down and took up the file. It was a bulky and a heavy thing, with great sheaves of papers enclosed between the covers.

It had not been there, he was certain, when he'd gotten the directory. It had been placed there, as the food was placed upon the table, as the books had been stacked upon the shelves, as the clothing that would fit him had been hung within the closet. By some agency that was unobtrusive, if not invisible.

Placement by remote control, he wondered. Could it be that somewhere this house was duplicated and that in that house certain agencies that were quite visible—and in their term of reference logical and ordinary—might place the food and hang the clothes and that at the moment of the action the same things happened in this house?

And if that were the case, not only space was mastered, but time as well. For they—whoever they might be—could not have known about the books that should be placed upon the shelves until the occupant of this house had appeared upon the scene. They could not have known that it would be Frederick Gray, that it would be a man who had made the law his business, who would blunder on this house. They had set a trap—a trap?—and there would have been no way for them to know what quarry they might catch.

It had taken time to print, by whatever process, the books

upon the shelves. There would have been a searching for the proper books, and the translating and the editing. Was it possible, he wondered, that time could be so regulated that the finding and the translating and the editing, the printing and the place-ment, could have been compressed into no more than twenty-four hours as measured on the Earth? Could time be stretched out and, perhaps, foreshortened to accommodate the plans of those engineers who had built this house?

He flipped open the cover of the file and the printing on the first page struck him in the face.

SUMMARY & TRANSCRIPT
Valmatan vs. Mer El
Referral for Review Under Universal Law

Panel for Review:
Vanz Kamis, Rasalgethi VI
Eta Nonskic, Thuban XXVIII
Frederick Gray, Helios III

Frozen, he stared at it.

His hands began to tremble and he laid it down, carefully on the table top, as if it might be something that would shatter if he dropped it.

Under universal law, he thought. Three students of the law, three experts (?), from three different solar systems!

And the facts at issue, and the law, more than likely, from yet another system.

Certain little services, the voice on the phone had told him.

Certain little services. To pass judgment under laws and juris-prudence he had never heard of!

And those others, he wondered—had they heard of them?

Swiftly he bent and leafed through the phone book. He found Kamis, Vanz. Deliberately, he dialed the number.

A pleasant voice said: "Vanz Kamis is not present at the moment. Is there any message?"

And it was not right, thought Gray. He should not have phoned. There was no point in it.

"Hello," said the pleasant voice. "Are you there?"

"Yes, I am here," said Gray.

"Vanz Kamis is not home. Is there any message?"

"No," said Gray. "No, thanks. There isn't any message."

He should not have called, he thought. The act of phoning had been an act of weakness. This was a time when a man must rely upon himself. And he had to give an answer. It was not something that could be brushed off, it was not a thing that anyone could run from.

He got his cap and jacket from the closet in the hall and let himself outside.

A golden moon had risen, the lower half of it bearing on its face the dark silhouette of the jagged pines, growing on the ridge across the river. From somewhere in the forest an owl was muttering and down in the river a fish splashed as it jumped.

Here a man could think, Gray told himself. He stood and drew the freshness of the air deep into his lungs. Here on the earth that was his own. Better than in a house that was, at least by implication, the extension of many other worlds.

He went down the path to the landing where he had beached the canoe. The canoe was there and there was water in it from the storm of the night before. He tipped it on its edge so the water could run out.

To be reviewed, that first page had said, under universal law. And was there, he wondered, such a thing as universal law?

Law could be approached in many ways, he thought. As pure philosophy, as political theory, as a history of moral ideas, as a social system, or as a set of rules. But however it was viewed, however studied, no matter what the emphasis, it had one basic function, the providing of a framework that would solve all social conflict.

Law was no static thing; it must, and did, evolve. No matter how laggard it might be, still it followed in the footsteps of the society it served.

He grinned wryly in the darkness, staring at the foaming river, remembering how, for years, he had hammered on that viewpoint in seminar and lecture.

On one planet, given time and patience and the slow process of evolution, the law could be made to square with all social concepts and with the ordered knowledge of society at large.

But was there any chance to broaden this flexibility and this logic to include not one, but many planets. Did there exist somewhere a basis for a legal concept that would apply to society in the universal sense?

It could be true, he thought. Given wisdom and work, there was a bare chance of it.

And if this should be the case, then he might be of service, or more correctly, perhaps, the law of Earth might be of help. For Earth need not be ashamed of what it had to offer. The mind of Man had lent itself to law. For more than five thousand years there was a record of Man's concern with law and from that deep concern had come a legal evolution—or, more correctly, many evolutions. And in it might be found a point or two that could be incorporated in a universal code.

There was, throughout the universe, a common chemistry, and because of this there were those who thought that there was a common biochemistry as well.

Those other beings on those two other planets who had been named with him to review the issue set forth in the transcript could not be expected to be men, or even close to men. But given a common biochemistry, they would be basically the same sort of life as Man. They would be protoplasmic. They would make use of oxygen. The kind of things they were would be determined by nucleic acids. And their minds, while more than likely a far cry from a human mind, still would be based upon the same mechanism as the minds of Man.

If there were, he asked himself, a common chemistry and a common biochemistry, then did it not seem likely, as well, for there to exist a concept that would point toward common justice?

Not just yet, perhaps. But ten thousand years from now. Or a million years from now.

He started up the path again and his step was lighter than it had been for years, and the future brighter—not his future only, but the future of everything that was.

This was a thing he'd taught and preached for years—the hope that in some future time the law might represent some great and final truth.

It did a man's heart good, he thought, to find that there were others who felt the same as he, and who were at work on it.

No Old Folks' Home, he thought, and he was glad of that. For an Old Folks' Home was a dead end, and this was a bright beginning.

In a little while the phone would ring and there'd be a voice asking if he'd serve.

But he'd not wait for that. There was work to do—a great deal of work to do. There was the file to read and those strange books that he must study, and references that he would have to find and much thinking to be done.

He entered the house and shut the door behind him. He hung up his cap and coat.

Picking up the file, he went into the study and laid it on the desk.

He pulled out a drawer and took out pad and pencils and ranged them neatly, close at hand.

He sat down and entered upon the practice of interstellar law.

THE QUESTING
OF FOSTER ADAMS

Set, like many of his short works, in the vicinity of Clifford Simak's birthplace, this story is nonetheless uncharacteristic of his work, a conclusion that may be demonstrated by the fact that after being written, it was first sent to Weird Tales *(in May 1948), which was not a usual market for Simak stories. But after its apparent rejection, the tale was ultimately accepted by* Fantastic Universe *and appeared in the August-September 1948 issue.*

—dww

There can be no denial that the hobby of Foster Adams was a strange one. One must bear in mind that Foster Adams was a strange man. Whether Adams, himself, considered his research as a hobby or an occupation no one can ever say. It may have been a hobby or an obsession—or it may have been no more than the misdirection of a brilliant mind.

How he had come to take up his research, what deep-laid motive drove him to carry it out to its logical and deadly conclusion, I have no idea. Come to think of it, there is very little that I do know of Foster Adams. There is very little anyone knows.

I do not know where he was born nor who his parents were nor what became of them, although I always took it for granted they had died many years ago. I know nothing of his education except that it must have been extensive. I have no knowledge as to how or when or why he came into possession of the old Smith farm. Nor why he sought an answer to a question to which no man of this day and age would give more than passing notice, although there was a time not too many centuries removed when men must have spent much thought upon the matter.

That some deep compelling motive lay within his mind there can be no doubt. Certainly toward the end, when he had reason to believe the solution he sought might be within his grasp, he must have realized the danger of such knowledge.

Perhaps Foster Adams counted himself of stouter fiber than he really was or it may have been that in his most considered judgment, or even in his wildest imaginings, he never once came close to guessing what the answer really was. And this would seem most strange, for his questing was bolstered by many years of study.

I first heard of Foster Adams from an acquaintance in the history department at State University.

"Foster Adams is your man," he told me. "He lives down in your part of the country now. He probably has more historic insignificance packed inside his skull than any other living person."

It seemed strange to me, and I said so, that a professor of English history could not tell me about the eating habits of the English middle class in the fifteenth century, but he shook his head.

"I can tell you in a general way," he said, "but not down to the last crumb of barley bread as Foster Adams can."

When I asked who Adams was he couldn't tell me. He was not connected with any university, he had never published anything and he was not an authority, not a recognized authority, at any rate. But he did know what people had worn and eaten from Egypt down to the last century's turn—what tools they had used, what crops they raised, how they traveled—all the little trivial things that went to make up daily living down through the centuries.

"It's a hobby," my acquaintance said. And that's as close an explanation as I ever got from anyone.

The Smith farm is a stark weather-beaten place set upon a wind-scarred rocky ridge. It has no grace or character and no dignity. Notwithstanding what happened there of a late November night it even now fails to achieve a patina of terror or the somber greatness of dark happenings.

I still recall my first sight of it and the depression and melancholy that gripped me as I drove up the rocky road, winding up the hill to reach the ridge.

The house was grey, not with the greyness of old lumber, but with the flat, unhealthy grey of lumber that had known a coat of paint which long since has scaled and peeled and been dissolved in wind and weather. The barn's ridgepole sagged in the middle, for all the world like a swaybacked horse, and another building, which may have been a hoghouse, had fallen completely in upon itself. Seeing it for the first time I had the distinct impression that it had grown tired one day and simply given up.

At one time there had been an extensive orchard back of the house but now there were only ghosts of trees, strange humped things that stood in the sun like gnarled old men. A windmill sporting a buckled tower stood with bowed head above the dying orchard and the wind that never ceased to blow across the ridge flapped the great metal vane back and forth in a futile and nerve-grating monotony.

As I stopped the car I saw that the ravages of neglect reached even to the smallest item. Flower-beds struggled with encroaching weeds. The sloping doors that covered the outside stairway to the cellar were half rotted away and part of them had fallen in.

A shutter hung canted at one window, at another both shutters were missing and I saw where they had fallen to the ground, with grass and weeds growing through the interstices. The porch sagged, its posts canted dangerously, and the floor creaked and shifted underneath my feet as I walked to the door.

An old man, wearing a uniform so ancient that its black was turning green, opened the door in answer to my knock and never in my life have I seen a sight so incongruous. For this was an old worn-out Wisconsin farm and the man who stood in the door was straight out of Dickens.

I asked for Adams and the man held the door a little wider and asked me to come in. His voice croaked harshly and sent echoes sounding through the old high-ceilinged rooms.

The house was almost bare of furniture. There was a woodstove in the kitchen and a few old chairs and a table covered with a piece of greasy oilcloth. In what had been the wainscoted dining-room packing boxes were lined against the wall and stacks of books were piled here and there, apparently at random. The windows gaped upon the world with empty eyes, without a curtain to their name.

In the front parlor green windowshades were drawn and the room was dark with a darkness that was deeper than the dusk.

Foster Adams heaved his bulky body from a leather chair standing in one corner and came across the room to shake my hand. His handclasp was cold and flabby, indifferent if not bored.

"Not many find their way here," he said. "I am glad you came."

But I am sure he wasn't. I am sure he wished I hadn't bothered him by coming.

We sat there in the dusk behind the drawn shades and we talked in hushed voices, for the very room whispered not to speak aloud. Foster Adams, if no more could be said for him, had perfect manners. Prim, precise, even a little fussy—and disquieting.

It was queer, I thought, to hear the thin, high, cold and hostile whining of the wind at August noon against the sides and around the corners of the house. For there was no friendliness in hill or house. Whatever warmth they may have held had been leached away with the ruin of the acres and the callous abandonment of the buildings to wind and rain and sun.

Yes, Adams said, he could tell me the things I wished to know. And he told them to me without recourse to note or book, speaking as if he were drawing upon personal observation, as if he were talking of a time that was contemporaneous, as if he himself had lived in fifteenth-century England.

"Such things," he said, "have always interested me. What kind of petticoats a woman wore or the kind of herbs that went into the pot. And even more—" he lowered his voice a trifle—"even more, the way that men have died."

He sat motionless in his chair and it was as if he might be listening for something that he knew was there—rats in the cellar, perhaps, or crickets in the drapes.

"Men," he stated, "have died in many ways." He made it sound as if he were the first man who had ever thought or said it.

In the silence I heard the clumping tread of the old man-servant walking about in the dining-room just outside the door. Faintly from the orchard came the muted metallic thumping of the wind-tossed windmill vane.

Foster Adams rose abruptly from his chair. "It was nice seeing you," he said. "I hope you come again."

And that is exactly how it was. I was literally thrown out, told to go like a gawping schoolboy who has overstayed his welcome.

But I couldn't get the man out of my mind. There was a fascination about him that kept tugging at me to go back to the old grey farmhouse atop the bleak unfriendly ridge. Like a man who keeps going back to a certain cage in a zoo, to stand and stare and shiver at the sight of the beast it houses.

I finished my book, using Adams' information to good advantage, and sent it off to the publisher.

Then, one day, scarcely knowing what I was doing, never for a moment admitting to myself that I was doing it, I found myself once more among the tangled hills of the lower Wisconsin.

The old farmhouse looked just the same as it had before.

I had told myself that probably Adams had just moved in shortly before my visit and that, given time, he would fix up the place. A coat of paint most certainly would have helped. A fireplace would have done wonders to bring some cheer into the house. Flowers

and rock gardens and some terracing would have given its gaunt
lines a softer setting, while a poplar or two at the corners would
have broken the stark dreariness that reared against the sky.

But Adams had done nothing. The house was just the way I
remembered it.

He said that he was glad to see me but his handshake was still
a flabby gesture and he was as prim and straight as ever.

He sat in his deep leather chair and talked and I knew that if
he were glad to see me it was only because it gave him a chance to
hear his own voice. For he didn't talk to me, he didn't even look
at me. it was as if he were talking to himself and there were times
when I caught a querulousness in his voice as though he were
arguing with himself.

"There is a streak of cruelty," he said, "that runs through the
human race. You find it everywhere you look, on every page of
recorded history. Man is not satisfied with inflicting death alone,
he must inflict it with many painful frills.

"A boy pulls the wings off flies and ties tin cans to a dog's tail.
The Assyrians flayed screaming thousands while they were still
alive."

There was a feeling of mustiness in the house—a feeling, not
a smell. A sense of dusty time that had long since run through
the glass.

"The Aztecs," said Foster Adams, "cut out the hearts of their
living sacrifices with a blunt stone knife. The Saxons threw men
into the serpent pits or flayed them living and rubbed salt into the
quivering flesh as the pelt peeled off."

The talk sickened me—not the things he told me but the way he
talked of them, the smooth professional talk of a man who knows
his subject and views it objectively as something to be probed and
studied and catalogued as neatly as a merchant would invoice his
stock.

For to him, I realize now, the flayed men and the men in the serpent pits and the men who hung on crosses along the Roman roads were not flesh and blood but certain facts that someday might fall into a pattern under the persistent probing of his mind.

Not that he was callous. His interest was real and alive and personal—that his interest became acutely personal in his last few hours of sanity and life there can be small doubt.

He must have seen that his monologue disturbed me for he suddenly changed the subject and we talked of other things, of the country and the view from the hill, of the pleasant weather, for it was late October, and of the irritating curiosity of the natives concerning his reason for living at the farm and what he might be doing. I could see that he was disturbed by their actions.

More than a year elapsed before I saw Foster Adams again and then only by accidental circumstance.

Driving home from a brief visit to Chicago, a violent autumn storm caught me on the road just as night was lowering. Rain turned into ice, ice to snow. As the storm grew worse and the car was reduced to a mere crawl I realized that I could not continue much further and must soon seek shelter. And with this realization came another, that I was at that moment no more than two miles or so from the old Smith farm.

I found the side road that turned off the main highway and half an hour later came to the foot of the hill that ran to the ridge above. Knowing the car had no chance to make the slope I got out and walked, floundering in the wet and heavy snow, guided by a feeble beam of light from one of the farmhouse windows.

By daylight the wind on the hill had been merely vicious, a thin-flanked wind with a snarl between its teeth. Now it was filled with a terrible anger as it howled across the ridge and went booming down into the hollow.

Pausing to get my breath, I listened to it and heard the howling of a pack of hellish hounds, the screams of hunted harried victims, the slow wet whimpering gurgle of a cornered creature that foundered in a deep ravine.

I hurried on, ridden by senseless terror, and it was not until I was almost at the house that I realized I was running, driven by the throng of imagined horrors that pressed up the slope behind me.

I reached the porch and hung onto a canted post to regain my breath and beat back the illogical fear that had gathered in the dark. I was almost myself again when I knocked upon the door—and had to knock a second and a third time because the howling of the storm drowned out the sound of knuckles.

The old manservant let me in and it seemed to me that he moved more slowly on feet that dragged a little more than I had remembered, that he talked more thickly, as if a hand were at his throat.

Adams had changed too. He still was stiff and formal, almost distant, but he was prim no longer. He had not shaved for a day or two and his eyes were haggard and there was a sly nervousness about him that put me on edge.

He did not seem surprised to see me and when I mentioned the storm that had driven me to cover he passed over it with agreement that it was a dirty night. It was as if I lived just across the way and had dropped in for an hour or two.

There was no mention of anything to eat, no indication that he even suspected I hoped to spend the night.

Awkwardly, or at least awkwardly on my part, we talked of inconsequential things. Adams seemed wholly at ease although his face and hands were nervous.

Shortly the talk veered to his studies and I gathered from his words that he had dropped all other phases of his research to concentrate upon the punishments and tortures man had inflicted upon his fellows from the advent of historic time.

Hunched in his chair, staring at the wall, he called up the bloody sadism that had left a trail of blood and pain across the centuries, linking the old Egyptian king whose proudest title had been the Cracker of Foreheads to the man whose smoking revolver piled the dead knee-deep in Russian cellars.

He knew in detail how men had been staked out for the ants,

how others had been buried to the neck in desert sands, and he assured me most solemnly that the American Indian had been a past master at the art of burning, that the expert "questioners" of the Inquisition, in this respect at least, had been no more than quasi-efficient bunglers.

He talked of racks and quarterings, of hooks that ripped out a man's insides—and behind the hard cold words of erudition that he spoke I smelled the smoke and blood and heard the screams and the creaking of the ropes and the clanking of the chains.

But he did not, I am sure, know anything of this.

Then it came, the topic he had been leading up to, the quicksilver problem that slid within his brain, waiting to be grasped and solved—the end product of all the things he knew.

"But they all fall short of perfect," he said. "There is no such thing as a perfect torture, for always in the end the victim dies or gives in and the torture halts. There is no way of measuring what a man's resistance is. Sometimes you overdo it and he dies, other times you allow the victim to escape the full rigor of the execution for fear that he has reached the limit of endurance, which he hasn't."

"A perfect torture!" I said and I know my words must have been both a question and an exclamation point. For even then I didn't understand. Even then I couldn't understand why a man should be interested, even academically, in a perfect torture. Such interest seemed to verge on madness.

It was fantastic—sitting there in that old Wisconsin farmhouse with the first winter's storm raging against the windows, to hear a man talk calmly and learnedly about the technical problems of efficient torture past and present.

"Perhaps in hell," said Foster Adams, "but certainly not on earth. For human beings are crude things and the things they do are crude."

"Hell?" I asked him. "Do you believe in hell? A literal hell?"

He laughed at me and from the laugh I could not tell whether he did or not.

I looked at my watch and it was almost midnight. "I must be going now," I said. "The storm seems to have slackened a bit."

But I made no move to rise from my chair, for certainly, I thought, a hint as broad as that would get me an invitation for the night.

Adams said merely, "I'm sorry you must go. I had hoped you could stay another hour."

I was so angry as I trudged down the hill, back to the car, that I did not hear the feet behind me for some time. They must, I am sure, have followed me from the house but I did not hear them.

The storm had slackened and the wind was dying down and here and there the stars were shining through the scudding clouds.

I was halfway down the hill before I heard the footsteps, although thinking back upon it, I am certain that I had been hearing them for some time before I became aware of them. And hearing them, I knew they were made not by man but by some animal, for I could hear the click of hoofs and the cracking of hocks as they skidded on the ice that lay beneath the snow.

I stopped and swung around but there was nothing on the road behind me, although the footsteps kept coming on. But when they had drawn close they stopped and waited, only to start up again as soon as I went on, following me down the hill, letting me set the pace, keeping just out of sight.

A cow, I thought, although that seemed strange, for I was sure that Adams had no cow and cows as a rule do not wander down a road on a stormy night. And the hoofbeats too were not those of a cow.

I stopped several times and once I shouted at the thing that followed and after the third or fourth time I realized it no longer followed me.

Somehow I got the car turned around. Before I reached the main highway the machine bogged down three times but by dint of good luck and some profanity I got moving again. The highway was easier traveling and I reached home shortly after dawn.

Three days later I had a letter from Adams that was a half apology. He had been overworked, he said, and not quite himself. He hoped that I would overlook any eccentricity. But he did not mention his lack of hospitality. I presume that came under the heading of "eccentricity."

It was almost a year before I saw him again. By roundabout fashion I learned that his old manservant had died and that now he lived alone. I thought about him often, feeling that he must be lonely, for the servant had been, it seemed, his only human contact. But I was still a little put out by the snowstorm incident and I made no move to visit him again.

Then I got a second letter, really no more than a note. He indicated that he had something of interest to show me and that he would feel obliged if I would stop by the next time I happened to be in his section of the country. There was no word of the man-servant's death, no indication that Adams was lonely for human companionship, nothing to hint that his life was not exactly the same as it had been before. Terse, businesslike, the note made its point and that was all.

I waited a decent interval, for I was determined on two things—that I would demonstrate to my own satisfaction that the man had no hold upon me and that I would not rush off quickly at his summons. I felt the need to demonstrate toward him a certain degree of coolness for his shabby treatment of me that November night.

But finally I went and the house was the same as before except that it looked slightly shabbier and the cellar door had completely rotted and fallen in and another shutter or two had dropped from the windows.

Adams let me in and I was shocked at the change in him. He was unshaven and his beard was turning grey in spots. His hair hung down over his collar and his hands were unwashed with thick lines of black beneath broken fingernails. His collar and cuffs were ragged and his coat was threadbare. Splotches of dried egg had dribbled down his chin and spattered upon his shirt. He wore scuffed carpet slippers which made a swishing scraping noise as he walked along the hall.

He greeted me with the same aloofness as always and led me to the parlor, which seemed darker and mustier than ever before. Although his eyes were bright and his voice as firm as ever there was a fumbling attitude about him, a faint unsureness in his speech and manner.

He complimented me upon my novel and mentioned that he was gratified to see I had made good use of the information he had been able to supply me. But from the way he talked about it I felt sure he had not read the book.

"And now," he said, "I was wondering if you would mind looking over something *I* have written."

There was nothing I could do but indicate my willingness.

He shuffled to an old and battered rolltop desk. From it he took a heavy manuscript, tied with cord. "The facts are there," he said, "but I am poor at the tricks of writing. I wonder if you . . ."

He waited for me to say it and I did. "I'll look it over," I told him. "If I can be of any help I'll do it gladly."

I was about to ask him about the subject matter when he asked me if I had heard about his servant. I told him I had heard that the old man had died.

"That's all?" he asked.

"That's all," I said.

Adams sat down heavily in his chair. "He was found dead," he told me, "and I understood there have been some lurid stories making the rounds of the neighborhood."

I was about to reply when a sound froze me in the chair. Something was sniffing at the door that opened on the porch.

Adams must not have heard it—either that or he must have

heard it so often on previous occasions that he no longer paid attention to it, for he went on talking. "They found him out in the north pasture, at the end of the ridge. He was rather badly mangled."

"Mangled!" I whispered and I couldn't have spoken another word nor uttered it aloud had I been paid for it, for the creature was back at the door again, sniffing and snorting. At any moment I expected to hear the sound of nails clawing at the wood.

"Some animal must have got to him before he was found," said Adams.

I sat there, gooseflesh coming out on me, listening to the thing sniffing up and down the door crack. Once or twice it whined. But Adams still did not hear it or pretended not to hear it, for he went on talking, telling me about the manuscript.

"It's not completed," he said. "There is a final chapter, but I'll have the information soon and then I can finish it. There's just a little more research, just a little more. I am very, very close."

Now, for the first time, I saw it although I must have been staring at it ever since I came into the room—the thing upon the wall that was not the way it should be.

Now, for the first time, I saw it plainly and knew it for what it was—a crucifix turned upside down—turned upside down and nailed to the wall.

I stumbled to my feet, clutching the manuscript beneath my arm, muttering that I must go, that I had forgotten something, that I must go at once.

Behind me, as I left the room, I heard the shrill whimpering eagerness of the animal whining at the door, the sound of claws ripping at the wood, trying to get in.

My scalp was crawling and I know I must have run. Even now, thinking back on it, I have no apology to make. For the sounds at the door were sounds of fear deep graven in Man's soul, reaching back to the dim obscurity of the days when Man crouched in a cave and listened to the padding and snuffling and the whining of the things outside in the dark.

I reached the car and stood there, one hand on the door, ready to get in. Now that I had reached safety I suddenly was brave. I saw that the house was nothing more than an old farmhouse, that there was nothing in the world to be afraid of either in or out of it.

I opened the door, walked over and put one foot on the car's running-board. As I did I glanced downward and it was then I saw the tracks. Tracks like those a cow would make but smaller, more like the tracks of a goat perhaps. I wondered for a moment if Adams might keep goats and I knew instinctively that he didn't. Although it was entirely possible that some animals from adjoining farms might have broken through a fence and wandered here.

Now I saw that the barren trampled ground was a solid network of those cloven tracks and I remembered the night of the storm when something that sounded like a creature with hoofs had trailed me down the road.

I got into the car and slammed the door behind me and as if the sound of the slamming door were a signal a dog came around the corner of the house. He was big and black and sleek and as he walked I saw the muscles knotting and flowing beneath his shining hide. There was a sense of strength and speed about him as he slouched along.

He turned his head toward me and I saw his eyes. I shall not forget them—ever. They were filled with a terrible evil, an utter cynicism, and they were not a dog's eyes.

I stepped on the starter and put the accelerator to the boards. Ten miles later I finally stopped my shaking.

Home at last, I broke out a bottle and sat in the late autumn sunlight on the porch, drinking steadily and by myself, something I had never done before but have done often since that day.

When darkness fell, I went indoors and looked through Adams' manuscript, and it was the very thing that I had expected. It was a history of torture and of punishment, all the vast historic evidence of man's inhumanity to man. There were sketches and drawings and minute specifications concerning the construction and operation of every infernal machine the mind of man had been able to invent. The development of torture was traced with studious exactitude and each method was discussed in its many variations, with all the little trivial details of procedure carefully annotated.

And there were tortures listed that are very little known and almost never spoken of and scarcely fit to print.

Skimming through the pages I came to Chapter XLVIII and I saw that the writing ended there, that there was only the beginning of a paragraph upon the page.

It read—

But the ultimate torture, the torture that goes on and on, eternally, always just short of madness and of death, is found only in the depths of Hell and until now no mortal being has ever held the knowledge, prior to death, of the torments of the Pit . . .

I laid the manuscript on the table and reached for the bottle. But the bottle was empty and I hurled it across the room and it struck the fireplace and was smashed into flying shards that twinkled in the lamplight. I sat hunched in my chair and felt the hairy hands of Hell stretch out for me and not quite reach me and the perspiration ran down my body and my heart was in my throat.

For Adams knew—he either knew or meant to know. He had said that there was just a little research needed for him to complete the book, just a little information he still must get. And I remembered the tracks out in the yard and the dog with eyes that were not a dog's eyes and the creature, possibly the dog, that had been scratching at the door during my visit.

I sat there for a long time but finally I got out of the chair and went to my desk. From a drawer I took a gun that had been there for a long time and I checked its action and saw that it was loaded. Then I got out the car and drove like a madman down the night road toward a madman's retreat.

Scudding clouds covered the dying moon that lay above the western ridges when I reached the Smith farmhouse and the house itself reared up like a ghostly creation in the pre-dawn silence that lay across the hills.

Nothing stirred and there were no lighted windows. The wind came fresh and cold across the river valley and there was frost upon the fields. The porch boards creaked as I crossed them and knocked at the door—but there was no answer. I knocked again and yet again and there was still no answer, so I turned the knob and the door came softly open.

The moaning had been too soft and faint to hear through the door but it was there, waiting for me, when I came into the entryway that led into the kitchen.

It was a mewling rather than a moan, as if the tongue that made it belonged to a mindless creature. It sounded as if it had been much louder only a little time before, but now had dwindled through sheer physical exhaustion.

I found the gun in my pocket and my hand was shaking as I pulled it out. I wanted to run, I wanted very much to run. But I couldn't run, for I had to know. I had to know that whatever it might be was not as bad as I imagined it.

I slid into the kitchen and from there into the dining-room and the moaning began low and soared into a whimper, then rose to what would have been a scream if the creature that voiced it had had the strength to scream.

In the parlor I saw something on the floor and moved cautiously toward it. The thing upon the floor writhed and cowered and moaned and when it became aware of me it dragged itself toward me and I knew that it was begging, although it made no words, but begged with the heart-rending sounds that emanated from its mouth.

I backed against the wall, trying to get away, but it reached me and lifted up hooked claws and wrapped its arms around my knees. Its head tilted back to look at me and I saw the face of Foster Adams. The room was dark, for the blinds were tightly pulled as always and the first faint grey of dawn was just beginning to paint the dining-room windows.

I could not see the face too well and for that I always have been thankful. For the eyes were wider and whiter than I remembered them and the lips were pulled back in a frozen snarl of fear. There were flecks of foam upon the beard.

"Adams," I shouted at him. "Adams, what has happened?"

But there was no need to ask. I knew. Not what Adams knew—not the mind-shattering hell-raw facts that Adams knew—only that he had found the thing he sought. By reversed crucifix, by nails clawing at the door, by goat-tracks in the yard he had found the answer.

Nor did he answer me. His arms slipped from my legs and he fell upon the floor and lay very still and I knew that Foster Adams was beyond all answering.

Then, for the first time, I became aware of another in the room, a motionless blackness that stood in the deepest shadow.

For a moment I stood there above the sprawled body of Foster Adams and looked at the other in the room, not seeing him too well, for it was still quite dark. And he looked back at me. Still silent, I put the gun back into my pocket and turned around and left.

Behind me I heard the other walking across the floor. Hoofs crackled and hocks snapped and the rhythm of the footsteps told me that he walked not on four legs but on two.

HERMIT OF MARS

Clifford D. Simak received $125 for this story, and it was published in the June 1939 issue of Astounding Science Fiction. *It has features that lead one to think of "Masquerade" and "Madness from Mars," but I am always going to wonder if it was mere coincidence that led Cliff to use the names Kent Clark and Howard Carter in this story. . . .*

—dww

The sun plunged over the western rim of Skeleton Canal and instantly it was night. There was no twilight. Twilight was an impossible thing in the atmosphere of Mars, and the Martian night clamped down with frigid breath, and the stars danced out in the near-black sky, twinkling, dazzling stars that jigged a weird rigadoon in space.

Despite five years in the wilderness stretches of the Red Planet, Kent Clark still was fascinated by this sudden change from day to night. One minute sunlight—next minute starlight, the stars blazing out as if they were electric lights and someone had snapped the switch. Stars that were larger and more brilliant and gave more light than the stars seen from the planet Earth. Stars that seemed to swim in the swiftly cooling atmosphere. By midnight the atmosphere would be cooled to almost its minimum temperature, and then the stars would grow still and even more brilliant, like hard diamonds shining in the blackness of the sky, but they would be picturesque, showing their own natural colors, blue and white and red.

Outside the tiny quartz "igloo" the night wind keened among the pinnacles and buttresses and wind-eroded formations of the canal. On the wings of the wind, almost indistinguishable from the wind's own moaning, came the mournful howling of the Hounds, the great gaunt, shaggy beasts that haunted the deep canals and preyed on all living things except the Eaters.

Charley Wallace, squatting on the floor of the igloo, was scraping the last trace of flesh from the pelt of a Martian beaver. Kent watched the deft twist of his wrist, the flashing of the knife blade in the single tiny radium bulb which illuminated the igloo's interior.

Charley was an old-timer. Long ago the sudden goings and comings of Martian daylight and night had ceased to hold definite wonder for him. For twenty Martian years he had followed the trail of the Martian beaver, going farther and farther afield, penetrating deeper and deeper into the mazes of the even farther canals that spread like a network over the face of the planet.

His face was like old leather, wrinkled and brown above the white sweep of his long white beard. His body was pure steel and whang-hide. He knew all the turns and tricks, all the trails and paths. He was one of the old-time canal-men.

The heater grids glowed redly, utilizing the power stored in the seleno cells during the hours of daylight by the great sun-mirrors set outside the igloo. The atmosphere condensers chuckled softly. The electrolysis plant, used for the manufacture of water, squatted in its corner, silent now.

Charley carefully laid the pelt across his knees, stroked the deep brown fur with a wrinkled hand.

"Six of 'em," he said. His old eyes, blue as the sheen of ice, sparkled as he looked at Kent. "We'll make a haul this time, boy," he said. "Best huntin' I've seen in five years or more."

Kent nodded. "Sure will," he agreed.

The hunting had been good. Out only a month now and they had six pelts, more than many trappers and hunters were able to get during an entire year. The pelts would bring a thousand apiece—perhaps more—back at the Red Rock trading post. Most valuable fur in the entire Solar System, they would sell at three times that amount back in the London or New York fur marts. A wrap of them would cost a cool one hundred thousand.

Deep, rich, heavy fur. Kent shivered as he thought about it. The fur *had* to be heavy. Otherwise the beaver would never be able to exist. At night, the temperature plunged to 40 and 50 below, Centigrade, seldom reached above 20 below at high noon. Mars was cold! Here on the equator the temperature varied little, unlike the poles, where it might rise to 20 above during the summer when, for ten long months, the Sun never set, dropped to 100 or more below in the winter, when the Sun was unseen for equally as long.

He leaned back in his chair and gazed out through the quartz walls of the igloo. Far down the slope of the canal wall he saw the flickering lights of the Ghosts, those tenuous, wraith-like forms whose origin, true nature, and purpose were still the bone of bitter scientific contention.

The starlight threw strange lights and shadows on the twisted terrain of the canal. The naturally weird surface formations became a nightmare of strange, awe-impelling shapes, like pages snatched from the portfolio of a mad artist.

A black shape crossed a lighted ravine, slunk into the shadows.

"A Hound," said Kent.

Charley cursed in his whiskers.

"If them lopers keep hangin' around," he prophesied savagely, "we'll have some of their pelts to take out to Red Rock."

"They're mighty gun-shy," declared Kent. "Can't get near one of them."

"Yeah," said Charley, "but just try goin' out without a gun

and see what happens. 'Most as bad as the Eaters. Only difference is that the Hounds would just as soon eat a man, an' the Eaters would rather eat a man. They sure hanker after human flesh."

Another of the black shapes, slinking low, belly close to the ground, crossed the ravine.

"Another one," said Kent.

Something else was moving in the ravine, a figure that glinted in the starlight.

Kent leaned forward, choking back a cry. Then he was on his feet.

"A man," he shouted. "There's a man out there!"

Charley's chair overturned as he leaped up and stared through the quartz.

The space-armored figure was toiling up the slope that led to the igloo. In one hand the man carried a short blast rifle, and as they watched, the two trappers saw him halt and wheel about, the rifle leveled, ready for action, to stare back at the shadows into which the two Hounds had disappeared only a moment before.

A slight movement to the left and behind the man outside caught Kent's eye and spurred him into action.

He leaped across the igloo and jerked from its rack his quartz-treated space suit, started clambering into it.

"What's the trouble?" demanded Charley. "What the hell you doin'?"

"There's an Eater out there," shouted Kent. "I saw it just a minute ago."

He snapped down the helmet and reached for his rifle as Charley spun open the inner air-lock port. Swiftly Kent leaped through, heard the inner port being screwed shut as he swung open the outer door.

Cold bit through the suit and into his very bones as he stepped out into the Martian night. With a swift flip he turned on the chemical heat units and felt a glow of warmth sweep over him.

The man in the ravine below was trudging up the path toward the igloo.

Kent shouted at him.

"Come on! Fast as you can!"

The man halted at the shout, stared upward.

"Come on!" screamed Kent.

The spacesuit moved forward.

Kent, racing down the ravine, saw the silica-armored brute that lurched out of the shadows and sped toward the unsuspecting visitor.

Kent's rifle came to his shoulder. The sights lined on the ugly head of the Eater. His finger depressed the firing mechanism and the gun spat a tight column of destructive blue fire. The blast crumpled the Eater in mid-leap, flung him off his stride and to one side. But it did not kill him. His unlovely body, gleaming like a reddish mirror in the starlight, clawed upon its feet, stood swinging the gigantic head from side to side.

A shrill scream sounded in Kent's helmet phones, but he was too busy getting the sights of the weapon lined on the Eater again to pay it any attention.

Again the rifle spat and purred, the blue blast-flame impinging squarely on the silica-armored head. Bright sparks flew from the beast's head and then suddenly the head seemed to dissolve, melting down into a gob of blackened matter that glowed redly in places. The Eater slowly toppled sidewise and skidded ponderously down the slope to come to rest against a crimson boulder.

Kent signaled to the visitor.

"Come on," he shouted. "Quick about it! There may be more!"

Swiftly the man in the space suit came up the slope toward Kent.

"Thanks," he said as he drew abreast of the trapper.

"Get going, fellow," said Kent tersely. "It isn't safe to be out here at night."

He fell in behind the visitor as they hurried toward the open port of the airlock.

The visitor lifted the helmet and laid it on the table and in the dim light of the radium bulb Kent saw the face of a woman.

He stood silent, staring. A visit by a man to their igloo in this out-of-the way spot would have been unusual enough; that a woman should drop in on them seemed almost incredible.

"A woman," said Charley. "Dim my sights, it's a woman."

"Yes, I'm a woman," said the visitor, and her tone, while it held a hidden hint of culture, was sharp as a whip. It reminded one of the bite of the wind outside. Her eyebrows were naturally high arched, giving her an air of eternal question and now she fastened that questioning gaze on the old trapper.

"You are Charley Wallace, aren't you?" she asked.

Charley shifted from one foot to another, uncomfortable under that level stare. "That's me," he admitted, "but you have the advantage of me, ma'am."

She hesitated, as if uncertain what he meant and then she laughed, a laugh that seemed to come from deep in her throat, full and musical. "I'm Ann Smith," she said.

She watched them, eyes flickering from one to the other, but in them she saw no faintest hint of recognition, no start of surprise at the name.

"They told me at Red Rock I'd find you somewhere in Skeleton Canal," she explained.

"You was a-lookin' for us?" asked Charley.

She nodded. "They told me you knew every foot of this country."

Charley squared his shoulders, pawed at his beard. His eyes gleamed brightly. Here was talk he understood. "I know it as well as anyone," he admitted.

She wriggled her shoulders free of the spacesuit, let it slide, crumpling to the floor, and stepped out of it. Kent stored his own suit on the rack and, picking the girl's suit off the floor, placed it beside his own.

"Yes, ma'am," said Charley, "I've roamed these canals for over twenty Martian years and I know 'em as good as most. I wouldn't be afraid of gettin' lost."

Kent studied their visitor. She was dressed in trim sports attire, faultless in fashion, hinting of expensive shops. Her light brown, almost blond hair, was smartly coiffed.

"But why were you lookin' for us?" asked Charley.

"I was hoping you would do something for me," she told him.

"Now," Charley replied, "I'd be glad to do something for you. Anything I can do."

Kent, watching her face, thought he saw a flicker of anxiety flit across her features. But she did not hesitate. There was no faltering of words as she spoke.

"You know the way to Mad-Man's Canal?"

If she had slapped Charley across the face with her gloved hand the expression on his face could not have been more awe-struck and dumfounded.

He started to speak, stuttered, was silent.

"You can't mean," said Kent, softly, "that you want us to go into Mad-Man's Canal."

She whirled on him and it was as if he were an enemy. Her defenses were up. "That's exactly what I mean," she said and again there was that wind-like lash in her voice. "But I don't want you to go alone. I'll go with you."

She walked slowly to one of the two chairs in the igloo, dropped into it, crossed her knees, swung one booted foot impatiently.

In the silence Kent could hear the chuckling of the atmosphere condensers, the faint sputter of the heating grids.

"Ma'am," said Charley, "you sure must be jokin'. You don't really mean you want to go into Mad-Man's?"

She faced him with a level stare. "But I do," she declared. "I never was more serious in my life. There's someone there I have to see."

"Lady," protested the old trapper, "someone's been spoofin' you. There ain't nobody over in Mad-Man's. You couldn't find a canal-man in his right mind who'd go near the place."

"There is," she told him. "And probably you'll laugh at this, too, but I happen to know it to be the truth. The man I want to see is Harry, the Hermit."

Kent guffawed, softly, little more than a chuckle under his breath. But she heard and came up out of the chair.

"You're laughing," she said and the words were an accusation.

"Sit down," said Kent, "and let me tell you something. Something that no canal-man could admit, but something that every one of them know is the truth."

Slowly she sat down in the chair. Kent sat easily on the edge of the table.

"There isn't any such a person as Harry, the Hermit," he said. "It's just a myth. Just one of those stories that have grown up among the canal-men. Wild tales that they think up when they sit alone in the desolation of the Martian wilderness. Just figments of imagination they concoct to pass away the time. And then, when they go out with their furs, they tell these stories over the drinks at the trading posts and those they tell them to, tell them to the others—and so the tale is started. It goes from mouth to mouth. It gains strength as it goes, and each man improves upon it just a little, until in a year or two it is a full-blown legend. Something that the canal-men almost believe themselves, but know all the time is just a wild canal-tale."

"But I know," protested Ann. "I know there is such a man. I have to see him. I know he lives in Mad-Man's Canal."

"Listen," snapped Kent and the quiet casualness was gone from his words. "Harry, the Hermit, is everywhere. Go a few hundred miles from here and men will tell you he lives here in Skeleton Canal. Or he is down in the Big Eater system or he's up north in the Icy Hills. He is just an imaginary person, I tell you.

Like the Paul Bunyan of the old lumberjacks back on Earth. Like
Pecos Pete of the old American southwest. Like the fairies of the
old Irish stories. Some trapper thought him up one lonely night
and another trapper improved on him and a fellow dealing a stud
poker hand in some little town improved a little more until today
he is almost a real personage. Maybe he is real—real as a symbol
of a certain group of men—but for all practical purposes, he is
just a story, a fabrication of imagination."

The girl, he saw, was angry. She reached into the pocket of
her jacket and pulled out a flat case. Her hands trembled as she
opened it and took out a cigarette. She closed the case and tapped
the cigarette against her thumbnail. A pencil of metal, pulled
from the case, flared into flame.

She thrust the white cylinder between her lips and Kent
reached down and took it away.

"Not here," he said and smiled.

She flared at him. "Why not?" she asked.

"Atmosphere," he said. "Neither Charley nor I smoke. Can't
afford to. The condensers are small. We don't have too much current to run them. Two persons is the capacity of this igloo. Everything has to be figured down to scratch in this business. We need
all the air we get, without fouling it with tobacco smoke." He
handed her the cigarette.

In silence she put it back in the case, returned the case to her
pocket. "Sorry," she said. "I didn't know."

"Sorry I had to stop you," Kent told her.

She rose. "Perhaps I had better go," she said.

Charley's jaw went slack. "Go where?" he asked.

"My canal car," she said. "I left it about a mile from here.
Went past your place before I saw the light."

"But you can't spend the night in a car," protested Kent. "I'm
afraid you'll have to stay here."

"Sure," urged Charley, "we can't let you go. Sleeping in a car
is no picnic."

"We're harmless," Kent assured her.

She flushed. "I wasn't thinking of that," she said. "But you said two persons was the capacity of the igloo."

"It is," Kent agreed, "but we can manage. We'll cut down the heater current a little and step up the condensers. It may get a little chilly, but we can manage with air."

He turned to Charley. "How about a pot of coffee," he suggested.

Charley grinned, waggled his chin whiskers like a frolicsome billy goat. "I was just thinkin' about that myself," he said.

Ann set down the coffee cup and looked at them. "You see," she explained, "it's not just something I want to do myself. Not just some foolish whim of mine. It's something I've got to do. Something that may help someone else—someone who is very dear to me. I won't be able to sleep or eat or live, if I fail at least to try. You have to understand that I simply must go to Mad-Man's Canal and try to find Harry, the Hermit."

"But there ain't no Harry, the Hermit," protested Charley. He wiped the coffee off his beard and sighed. "Goodness knows, I wished there was, since you're so set on findin' him."

"But even if there isn't," said Ann, "I'd at least have to go and look. I couldn't go through life wondering if you might have been mistaken. Wondering if I should have given up so easily. If I go and try to find him and fail—why, then I've done everything I can, everything I could have expected myself to do. But if I don't I'll always wonder . . . there'll always be that doubt to torment me."

She looked from one face to the other.

"You surely understand," she pleaded.

Charley regarded her steadily, his blue eyes shining. "This thing kind of means a lot to you, don't it?" he said.

She nodded.

Kent's voice broke the spell. "You don't know what you're doing," he said. "You flew down from Landing City to Red Rock in a nice comfortable rocket ship, and now because you covered the hundred miles between here and Red Rock in a canal car, you think you're an old-timer."

He stared back at her hurt eyes.

"Well, you aren't," he declared.

"Now, lad," said Charley, "you needn't get so rough."

"Rough!" said Kent. "I'm not getting rough. I'm just telling her a few of the things she has to know. She came across the desert in the car and everything went swell. Now she thinks it's just as easy to travel the canals."

"No, I don't," she flared at him, but he went on mercilessly.

"The canal country is dangerous. There's all sorts of chances for crack-ups. There are all sorts of dangers. Every discomfort you can imagine. Crack your car against a boulder—and you peel off the quartz. Then the ozone gets in its work. It eats through the metal. Put a crack in your suit and the same thing happens. This atmosphere is poisonous to metal. So full of ozone that if you breathe much of it it starts to work on your lung tissues. Not so much danger of that up on the plateaus, where the air is thinner, but down here where there's more air, there's more ozone and it works just that much faster."

She tried to stop him, but he waved her into silence and went on:

"There are the Eaters. Hundreds of them. All with an insane appetite for human bones. They love the phosphate. Every one of them figuring how to get through a car or a spacesuit and at the food inside. You've never seen more than a couple of Eaters together at a time. But Charley and I have seen them by the thousands—great herds of them on their periodic migrations up and down the canyons. They've kept us penned in our igloo for days while they milled around outside, trying to reach us. And the Hounds, too, although they aren't so dangerous. And in the deeper places you find swarms of Ghosts. Funny things, the Ghosts. No physical harm from them. Maybe they don't even exist. Nobody knows what they are. But they are apt to drive you mad. Just looking at them, knowing they are watching all the time."

Impressive silence fell.

Charley wagged his beard.

"No place for a woman," he declared. "The canal ain't."

"I don't care," said Ann. "You're trying to frighten me, and I won't be frightened. I have to go to Mad-Man's Canal."

"Listen, lady," said Charley, "pick any other place—any other place at all—and I will take you there. But don't ask me to go into Mad-Man's."

"Why not?" she cried. "Why are you so afraid of Mad-Man's?"

She tried to find the answer in their faces but there was none.

Charley spoke slowly, apparently trying to choose his words with care. "Because," he said, "Mad-Man's is the deepest canal in this whole country. Far as I know, no man has ever been to the bottom of it and come out alive. Some have gone down part way and came back—mad and frothin' at the mouth, their eyes all glazed, babblin' crazy things. That's why they call it Mad-Man's."

"Now listen to me," and Ann. "I came all this way and I'm not turning back. If you won't take me, I'll go alone. I'll make it somehow—only you could make it so much easier for me. You know all the trails. You could get me there quicker. I'm prepared to pay you for it—pay you well."

"Lady," said Charley slowly, "we ain't guides. You couldn't give us money enough to make us go where we didn't want to go."

She pounded one small clenched fist on the table. "But I want to pay you," she said. "I'll insist on it."

Charley made a motion of his hand, as if sweeping away her words. "Not one cent," he said. "You can't buy our services. But we might do it anyhow. Just because I like your spunk."

She gasped. "You would?" she asked.

Neither one of them replied.

"Just take me to Mad-Man's," she pleaded. "I won't ask you

to take me down into the canal. Just point out the best way and then wait for me. I'll make it myself. All I want to know is how to get there."

Charley lifted the coffee pot, filled the cups again.

"Ma'am," he said, "I reckon we can go where you can go. I reckon we ain't allowin' you to go down into Mad-Man's all by yourself."

Dawn roared over the canal rim and flooded the land with sudden light and life. The blanket plants unfolded their broad furry leaves, spreading them in the sunshine. The traveller plants, lightly anchored to boulders and outcroppings, scurried frantically for places in the Sun. The canal suddenly became a mad flurry of plant life as the travellers, true plants but forced by environment to acquire the power of locomotion, quit the eastern wall, where they had travelled during the preceding day to keep pace with the sunlight, and rushed pell-mell for the western slope.

Kent tumbled out of the canal-car, rifle gripped in his hand. He blinked at the pale Sun that hung over the canal rim. His eyes swept the castellated horizon that closed in about them, took in the old familiar terrain typical of the Martian canals.

The canal was red—blood red shading to softest pink with the purple of early-morning shadow still hugging the eastern rim. A riot of red—the rusted bones of a dead planet. Tons of oxygen locked in those ramparts of bright red stone. Oxygen enough to make Mars livable—but locked forever in red oxide of iron.

Chimney and dome formations rose in tangled confusion with weathered pyramids and slender needles. A wild scene. Wild and lonesome and forbidding.

Kent swept the western horizon with his eyes. It was thirty miles or more to the rim, but in the thin atmosphere he could see with almost telescopic clearness the details of the scarp where the plateau broke and the land swung down in wild gyrations, frozen in red rock, to the floor of the canal where he stood.

Under the eastern rim, where the purple shadows still clung, flickered the watch-fires of the Ghosts, dim shapes from that distance. He shook his fist at them. Damn the Ghosts!

The slinking form of a Hound skulked down a ravine and disappeared. A beaver scuttled along a winding trail and popped into a burrow.

Slowly the night cold was rising from the land, dissipated by the rising Sun. The temperature would rise now until midafternoon, when it would stand at 15 or 20 below zero, Centigrade.

From a tangled confusion of red boulders leaped a silica-armored Eater. Like an avenging rocket he bore down on Kent. Almost wearily the trapper lifted his rifle, blasted the Eater with one fierce burst of blue energy.

Kent cursed under his breath.

"Can't waste power," he muttered. "Energy almost gone."

He tucked the rifle under his arm and glared at the tumbled Eater. The huge beast, falling in mid-leap, had plowed a deep furrow in the hard red soil.

Kent walked around the bulk of the car, stood looking at the uptilted second car that lay wedged between the huge boulders.

Charley climbed out through the open air lock and walked toward his partner. Inside his helmet he shook his head. "No good," he said. "She'll never run again."

Kent said nothing and Charley went on: "Whole side staved in. All of the quartz knocked off. Ozone's already got in its work. Plates softening."

"I suppose the mechanism is shot, too," said Kent.

"All shot to hell," said Charley.

They stood side by side, staring mournfully at the shattered machine.

"She was a good car, too," Charley pronounced, sadly.

"This," declared Kent, "is what comes of escorting a crazy dame all over the country."

Charley dismissed the matter. "I'm going to walk down the

canal a ways. See what the going is like from here on," he told
Kent.

"Be careful," the younger man warned him. "There's Eaters
around. I just shot one."

The old man moved rapidly down the canal floor, picking his
way between the scattered boulders and jagged outcroppings. In
a moment he was out of sight. Kent walked around the corner of
the undamaged car, saw Ann Smith just as she stepped from the
airlock.

"Good morning," she said.

He did not return the greeting. "Our car is a wreck," he said.
"We'll have to use yours from here on. It'll be a little cramped."

"A wreck?" she asked.

"Sure," he said. "That crash last night. When the bank caved
under the treads, it smashed the quartz, let the ozone at the
plates."

She frowned. "I'm sorry about that," she said. "Of course, it's
my fault. You wouldn't be here if it weren't for me."

Kent was merciless. "I hope," he sighed, "that this proves to
you travel in the canals is no pleasure jaunt."

She looked about them, shivered at the desolation.

"The Ghosts are the worst," she said. "Watching, always
watching—"

Before them, not more than a hundred feet away, one of the
Ghosts appeared, apparently writhing up out of a pile of jumbled
rocks. It twisted and reared upward, tenuous, unguessable, now
one shape, now another. For a moment it seemed to be a benign
old grandfather, with long sweeping beard, and then it turned
into something that was utterly and unnamably obscene and
then, as suddenly as it had come, it disappeared.

Ann shuddered. "Always watching," she said again. "Waiting
around corners. Ready to rise up and mock you."

"They get on your nerves," Kent agreed, "but there's no reason
to be afraid of them. They couldn't touch you. They may be noth-

ing more than mirage—figments of the imagination, like your Harry, the Hermit."

She swung about to face him. "How far are we from Mad-Man's?" she demanded.

Kent shrugged his shoulders. "I don't know," he said. "Maybe a few miles, maybe a hundred. We should be near, though."

From down the canal came Charley's halloo. "Mad-Man's," he shouted back to them. "Mad-Man's! Come and look at it!"

Mad-Man's Canal was a continuation of the canal the three had been travelling—but it was utterly different.

Suddenly the canal floor broke, dipped down sharply and plummeted into a deep blue pit of shadows. For miles the great depression extended, and on all sides the ground sloped steeply into the seemingly bottomless depths of the canyon.

"What is it, Charley?" asked Kent, and Charley waggled his beard behind the space-helmet.

"Can't say, lad," he declared, "but it sure is an awe-inspirin' sight. For twenty Martian years I've tramped these canals and I never seen the like of it."

"A volcanic crater?" suggested Ann.

"Maybe," agreed Charley, "but it don't look exactly like that either. Something happened here, though. Floor fell out of the bottom of the canal or somethin'."

"You can't see the bottom," said Ann. "Looks like a blue haze down there. Not exactly like shadows. More like fog or water."

"Ain't water," declared Charley. "You can bet your bottom dollar on that. If anyone ever found that much water on Mars they'd stake out a claim and make a fortune."

"Did you ever know anyone who tried to go down there, Charley?" asked Kent. "Ever talk to anyone who tried it?"

"No, lad, I never did. But I heard tell of some who tried. And they never were the same again. Somethin' happened to them down there. Somethin' that turned their minds."

Kent felt icy fingers on his spine. He stared down into the deep blue of Mad-Man's and strained his eyeballs, trying to pierce the veil that hid the bottom. But that was useless. If one wanted to find out what was down there, he'd have to travel down those steeply sloping walls, would have to take his courage in hand and essay what other men had tried and gone crazy for their pains.

"We can't use the car," he said suddenly and was surprised at his words.

Kent walked backward from the edge of the pit. What was happening to them? Why this calm acceptance of the fact they were going to go down into Mad-Man's? They didn't have to go. It wasn't too late yet to turn around and travel back the way they came. With only one car now, and many miles to travel, they would have to take it slow and easy, but they could make it. It was the sensible thing to do, held none of the rash foolhardiness involved in a descent into those blue depths before them.

He heard Charley's words, as if from a great distance.

"Sure, we'll have to walk. But we ought to be able to make it. Maybe we'll find air down there, air dense enough to breathe and not plumb full of ozone. Maybe there'll be some water, too."

"Charley," Kent shouted, "you don't know what you're saying! We can't—"

He stopped in mid-sentence and listened. Even as he talked, he had heard that first weird note from up the canal, a sound that he had heard many times before, the far-away rumble of running hoofs, the grating clash of stonelike body on stonelike body.

"The Eaters!" he shouted. "The Eaters are migrating."

He glanced swiftly about him. There was no way of escape. The walls of the canal had narrowed and closed in, rising sheer from the floor on either side of them, only a few miles away. There was no point of vantage where they could make a stand and hold off the horde that was thundering toward them. And even if there were, they had but little power left for their guns. In the long trek down the canal they had been forced to shoot time after time to protect their lives, and their energy supply for the weapons was running low.

"Let's get back to the car!" screamed Ann. She started to run. Kent sprinted after her, grabbed her and pulled her around.

"We'd never make it," he yelled at her. "Hear those hoofs! They're stampeding! They'll be here in a minute!"

Charley was yelling at them, pointing down into Mad-Man's. Kent nodded, agreeing. It was the only way to go. The only way left open for them. There was no place to hide, no place to stand and fight. Flight was the only answer—and flight took them straight into the jaws of Mad-Man's Canal.

Charley bellowed at them, his bright blue eyes gleaming with excitement. "Maybe we got a chance. If we can reach the shadows."

They plunged down, going at a run, fighting to keep their balance. Soft, crumbly rock shifted and broke under the impact of their steel-shod feet. A shower of rubble accompanied them, chuckling and clinking down the slope. The sun blinked out and they plunged into the deep shadows, fought to reduce their speed, slowed to a walk.

Kent looked back. Above him, on the level of the canal floor, he saw a fighting mass of Eaters, indescribable confusion there on the rim of the skyline, as the great silica-armored beasts fought against plunging into Mad-Man's. Those in front were rearing, shoving, striking savagely, battling against being shoved over the edge as those behind plowed into them. Some of them had toppled onto the slope, were sliding and clawing, striving to regain their feet. Others were doggedly crawling back up the slope.

The three below watched the struggle above them.

"Even them cussed Eaters are afraid to go into Mad-Man's," said Charley.

They were surrounded by Ghosts. Hundreds of them, wavering and floating, appearing and disappearing. In the blue shadows of the sunken world they seemed like wind-blown flames that rocked back and forth, flickering, glimmering, guttering. Assuming all kinds of forms, forms beautiful in their intricacy of design, forms angularly flat and ugly, gruesome and obscene and terrible.

And always there was that terrible sense of watching—of ghostly eyes watching and waiting—of hidden laughter and ghoulish design.

"Damn them," said Kent. He stubbed his toe and stumbled, righted himself.

"Damn them," he said again.

The air had become denser, with little ozone now. Half an hour before they had shut off their oxygen supply and snapped open the visors of their helmets. Still thin, pitifully thin by Earthly standards, the air was breathable and they needed to save what little oxygen might remain within their tanks.

Ann stumbled and fell against Kent. He steadied her until she regained her feet. He saw her shiver.

"If they only wouldn't watch us," she whispered to him. "They'll drive me mad. Watching us—no indication of friendliness or unfriendliness, no emotion at all. Just watching. If only they would go away—do something even!" Her whisper broke on a hysterical note.

Kent didn't answer. What was there to say? He felt a savage wave of anger at the Ghosts. If a man could only do something about them. You could shoot and kill the Eaters and the Hounds. But guns and hands meant nothing to these ghostly forms, these dancing, flickering things that seemed to have no being.

Charley, plodding ahead down the slope, suddenly stopped.

"There's something just ahead," he said. "I saw it move."

Kent moved up beside him and held his rifle ready. They stared into the blue shadows. "What did it look like?" Kent asked.

"Can't say, lad," Charley told him. "Just got a glimpse of it."

They waited. A rock loosened below them and they could hear it clatter down the slope.

"Funny lookin' jigger," Charley said.

Something was coming up the slope toward them, something that made a slithering sound as it came, and to their nostrils came a faint odor, a suggestion of a stench that made the hair crawl on the back of Kent's neck.

The thing emerged from the gloom ahead and froze the three with horror as it came. A thing that was infinitely more horrible in form than any reptilian monster that had ever crawled through the primal ooze of the new-spawned Earth, a thing that seemed to personify all the hate and evil that had ever, through long milleniums, lived and found its being on the aged planet Mars. A grisly death-head leered at them and drooling jaws opened, displaying fangs that dripped with loathsomeness.

Kent brought his rifle up as Ann's shriek rang in his ears, but Charley reached out and wrenched the weapon from his hand.

His voice came, cool and calm.

"It's no time to be shootin', lad," he said. "There's another one over there, just to our right and I think I see a couple more out just beyond."

"Give me that gun!" yelled Kent, but as he lunged to jerk it from Charley's grasp he saw, out of the tail of his eye, a dozen more of the things squatting just within the shadows.

"We better not rile them, son," said Charley softly. "They're a hell's brood and that's for sure."

He handed the rifle back to Kent and started backing up the slope, slow step by slow step.

Together the three of them backed slowly away, guns held at ready. In front of them, between them and the squatting monstrosities, a single Ghost suddenly materialized. A Ghost that did not waver but held straight and true, like a candle flame burning in the stillness of the night. Another Ghost appeared beside the first, and suddenly there were several more. The Ghosts floated slowly down the slope toward the death-head things, and as they moved they took on a deeper color, more substantiality, until they burned a deep and steady blue, solid columns of flame against the lighter blue of the eternal shadow.

Staring, scarcely believing, the three saw the gaping ghouls that had crept up the slope, turn and shuffle swiftly back, back into the mystery of the lower reaches of Mad-Man's.

Kent laughed nervously. "Saved by a Ghost," he said.

"Why, maybe they aren't so bad after all," said Ann and her voice was scarcely more than a whisper. "I wonder why they did it?"

"And how they did it," said Kent.

"Principally," said Charley, "why they did it. I never heard of any Ghost ever takin' any interest in a man, and I have trod these canals for twenty Martian years."

Kent expelled his breath. "And now," he said, "for Lord's sake, let's turn back. We won't find any hermit here. No man could live out a week here unless he had some specially trained Ghosts to guard him all the time. There isn't any use of going on and asking for trouble."

Charley looked at Ann. "It's your expedition, ma'am," he said.

She looked from one to the other and there was fear upon her face.

"I guess you're right," she said. "No one could live here. We won't find anyone here. I guess it must just have been a myth, after all." Her shoulders seemed to sag.

"We'll go on if you say the word," said Charley.

"Hell, yes," declared Kent, "but we're crazy to do it. I understand now why men came out of here stark crazy. A few more things like these we just seen and I'll be nuts myself."

"Look!" cried Ann. "Look at the Ghosts. They are trying to tell us something!"

It was true. The Ghosts, still flaming with their deep-blue color, had formed into a semicircle before them. One of them floated forward. His color flowed and changed until he took on a human form. His right hand pointed at them and then waved down the slope. They stared incredulously as the motion was repeated.

"Why," said Ann, "I do believe he's trying to tell us to go on."

"Dim my sight," shrieked Charley, "if that ain't what the critter is tryin' to tell us."

The other Ghosts spread out, encircled the three. The one with the manlike form floated down the slope, beckoning. The others closed in, as if to urge them forward.

"I guess," said Kent, "we go whether we want to or not."

Guarded by the circle of Ghosts they went down the slope. From outside the circle came strange and terrible noises, yammerings and hissings and other sounds that hinted at shambling obscenities, strange and terrible life forms which lived and fought and died here in the lower reaches of Mad-Man's.

The shadows deepened almost to darkness. The air became denser. The temperature rose swiftly.

They seemed to be walking on level ground.

"Maybe we've reached the bottom," suggested Kent.

The circle of Ghosts parted, spread out and the three stood by themselves. A wall of rock rose abruptly before them, and from a cave in its side streamed light, light originating in a half-dozen radium bulbs. A short distance to one side squatted a shadowy shape.

"A rocket ship!" exclaimed Kent.

The figure of a man, outlined against the light, appeared in the mouth of the cave.

"The hermit," cried Charley. "Harry, the Hermit. Blast my hindsight, if it ain't old Harry, himself."

Kent heard the girl's voice, beside him. "I was right! I was right! I knew he had to be here somewhere!"

The man walked toward them. He was a huge man, his shoulders square and his face was fringed in a golden-yellow beard. His jovial voice thundered a welcome to them.

At the sound of that voice Ann cried out, a cry that was half gladness, half disbelief. She took a slow step forward and then suddenly she was running toward the hermit.

She flung herself at him. "Uncle Howard!" she cried. "Uncle Howard!"

He flung his brawny arms around the space-armored girl, lifted her off the ground and set her down.

Ann turned to them. "This is my uncle, Howard Carter," she said. "You've heard of him. His best friends call him Mad-Man Carter, because of the things he does. But you aren't mad, really, are you, uncle?"

"Just at times," Carter boomed.

"He's always going off on expeditions," said the girl. "Always turning up in unexpected places. But he's a scientist for all of that, a really good scientist."

"I've heard of you, Dr. Carter," said Kent. "I'm glad to find you down here."

"You might have found worse," said Carter.

"Dim my sights," said Charley. "A human being living at the bottom of Mad-Man's!"

"Come on in," invited Carter. "I'll have you a cup of hot coffee in a minute."

Kent stretched out his legs, glad to get out of his spacesuit. He glanced around the room. It was huge and appeared to be a large cave chamber. Perhaps the cliffs that rimmed in Mad-Man's were honeycombed with caves and labyrinths, an ideal place in which to set up camp.

But this was something more than a camp. The room was well furnished, but its furnishings were a mad hodge-podge. Tables and chairs and heating grids, laboratory equipment and queer-appearing machines. One machine, standing in one corner, kept up an incessant chattering and clucking. In another corner, a mighty ball hung suspended in mid-air, halfway between the ceiling and the floor, and within it glowed a blaze of incandescence which it was impossible to gaze directly upon. Piled haphazardly about the room were bales and boxes of supplies.

Kent waved his hand at a pile of boxes. "Looks like you're planning on staying here for a while, Dr. Carter," he said.

The man with the fearsome yellow beard lifted a coffee pot off the stove and chuckled. His chuckle thundered in the room. "I may have to stay quite a while longer," he said, "although I doubt it. My work here is just about done." He poured steaming coffee into the cups. "Draw up your chairs," he invited.

He took his place at the end of the small table. "I imagine you are hungry," he said. "It's tiring work coming down into Mad-Man's. Almost five miles."

Charley lifted his cup to his mouth, drank deeply, wiped his whiskers carefully. "It's quite a little walk, I'll admit," he said. "For twenty Martian years I've trapped the canals and I never saw the like of it. What made it, Doc?"

Dr. Carter looked puzzled. "Oh," he said, "you mean what made Mad-Man's."

Charley nodded.

"I really don't know," said Carter. "I've been too busy on other things since I came here to try to find out. It's a unique depression in the surface of the planet, but as to why or how it came to be, I don't know. Although I could find out for you in a minute if you want to know. Funny I never thought of finding out for myself."

He glanced around the table and his eyes came to rest on Ann. "But there's something I do want to know," he said, "and that is how this precious niece of mine ferreted me out."

"But, Uncle Howard," protested Ann, "I didn't ferret you out. I wasn't looking for you at all. I didn't even know you were anywhere around. I thought you were off on one of your crazy expeditions again."

Charley choked on a mouthful of food. "What's that?" he

asked. "You weren't hunting for him?" He jerked his thumb at Dr. Carter.

Ann shook her head. "No," she said. "I was looking for Harry, the Hermit."

"Cripes," exploded Charley, "I thought we had found him. I thought your uncle here was the hermit. I thought you knew all along."

Dr. Howard Carter's fork clattered on his plate. "Now wait a minute," he roared. "What's all this talk about hermits?"

He eyed Ann sternly. "You didn't tell these men I was a hermit, did you."

"Hell," said Kent, "let's just admit there's no such a person as Harry, the Hermit. He's just a myth. I've told you so all along."

Ann explained. "It was this way. I was looking for Harry, the Hermit. Jim Bradley, the famous explorer, told me that if Harry, the Hermit, really existed, Mad-Man's was the place to look for him. He said Mad-Man's was the only place where a man could live for any length of time in any comfort. And he said he had reason to believe someone was living in Mad-Man's. So I started out to look."

"But," demanded her uncle, "why did you want to find this hermit? Just curiosity?"

Ann shook her head. "No, not curiosity," she said. "You see, uncle, it's dad. He's got into trouble again—"

"Trouble," snapped Carter. "Some more of his fool experiments, I suppose. What is it this time? Perpetual motion?"

"Not perpetual motion," said the girl. "This time he was successful. Too successful. He built a machine that had something to do with space-time, with the interdimensions. He tried to travel to another dimension. That was a month ago."

"And he isn't back yet," suggested Carter.

The girl glanced at him. "How did you know?" she demanded.

"Because I warned him that is what would happen if he went monkeying around with extra-dimensions."

"But what had the hermit to do with all this?" asked Kent.

"Bradley told me he thought that the Hermit really was Prof Belmont. You know, the great physicist. He disappeared a couple of years ago and never has been heard of since. Bradley thought he might be down here, conducting some sort of experiments. That might have given rise to the hermit legend."

Charley chuckled. "I heard stories about Harry, the Hermit, ten years ago," he said. "I judge, ma'am, from what you say, that they're just getting out to civilization. Nobody gave rise to those stories, they just grew."

Carter had shoved his plate to one side. Now he leaned forward, resting his arms on the tabletop. "Belmont did come here," he said. "But he's dead. The things out there killed him."

"Killed him!" Ann's face suddenly was white. "Are you sure of that?"

Carter nodded.

"He was the only man who could have helped Dad," the girl said tensely. "He was the only man who could have understood—"

"The Ghosts told me," said Carter. "There's no mistake. Belmont is dead."

Charley set down his coffee cup and stared at Carter. "You been talkin' with them Ghosts, mister?" he asked.

Carter nodded.

"Dim my sights," said Charley. "Who'd've thought them things could talk."

But Carter paid no attention. "Ann," he said, "maybe I can do something for you. Perhaps not myself. But the Ghosts can."

"The Ghosts?" asked Ann.

"Certainly, the Ghosts. What would anyone come here to study if not the Ghosts? There are thousands of them in Mad-Man's. That's what Belmont came here to do. When he didn't come back, and no one was able to locate him, I came out here secretly. I thought maybe he found something he didn't want the rest of the world to know, so I didn't leave any tracks for anyone else to follow."

"But how could the Ghosts help anyone?" asked Kent. "Apparently they are an entirely different order of being. They would have nothing in common with mankind. No sympathies."

Carter's beard jutted fiercely. "The Ghosts," he said, "are beings of force. Instead of protoplasm, they are constructed of definite force fields. They live independently of everything which we know as essential to life. And yet they are life. And intelligent life, at that. They are the true, dominant beings of Mars. At one time they weren't as they are now. They are a product of evolution. The Eaters evolved by taking on silica armor. The Hounds and beaver met conditions by learning to do with little food and even less water, grew heavy fur to protect them against the cold. It's all a matter of evolution.

"The Ghosts could solve many of the problems of the human race, could make the race godlike overnight. That is—if they wanted to. But they don't want to. They have no capacity for pity, no yearning to become benefactors. They are just indifferent. They watch the pitiful struggle of the human race here on Mars, and if they feel anything at all, it is a smug sort of humor. They don't pity us or hate us. They just don't care."

"But you," said Ann, "you made friends with them."

"Not friends," said her uncle. "We just had an understanding, an agreement. The Ghosts lack a sense of co-operation and responsibility. They have no sense for leadership. They are true individualists, but they know that these very lacks have stood in the way of progress. Their knowledge, great as it is, has lain dormant for thousands of years. They realize that under intelligent leadership they can go ahead and increase that knowledge, become a race of purely intellectual beings, the match of anything in the System, perhaps in the galaxy."

He paused for a moment, drummed his fingers on the table.

"I'm furnishing them that leadership," he declared.

"But what about dad?" asked Ann. "You and he never could get along, you hated one another, I know, but you can help him. You will help him, won't you?"

The scientist rose from the table, strode to the chattering, clucking machine at the other side of the room. "My communicator," he said. "A machine which enables me to talk with the Ghosts. Based on the radio, tuning in on the frequencies of the Ghosts' thought-waves. Through this machine comes every scrap of information which the Ghosts wish to relay to me. The thoughts were recorded on spools of fine wire. All I have to do to learn whatever has been transmitted over the machine is to put on a thought-translation helmet, run the spools of wire through it, and the thoughts impinge on my brain. I hear nothing, feel nothing—but I know. The thoughts of the Ghosts are impressed into my brain, become my thoughts."

Charley waggled his beard, excitement and wonder written on his features. "Then you know everything that's going on all over Mars," he said. "The Ghosts are everywhere, see everything."

"I know everything they think is important enough for me to know," Carter declared. "They can find out anything I might want to know."

"How do you talk to them?" asked Kent.

"Same process," said the scientist. "A helmet that broadcasts my thoughts to them."

He picked up a helmet and set it on his head. "I'm going to find out about your father," he told Ann.

"But he isn't in this space-time," objected Ann. "He's somewhere else."

Carter smiled. "The Ghosts know all about him," he said. "A few weeks ago they told me about a man lost outside of our space-time frame. It must have been your father. I didn't know."

He looked squarely at the girl. "Please believe me, Ann. If I had known who it was I would have done something."

The girl nodded, her eyes bright.

Silence fell upon the room. Finally Carter lifted the helmet from his head, set it back on the metal bench.

"Did you—did the Ghosts know anything about it?" asked the girl.

Her uncle nodded. "Ann," he said, "your father will be returned. No mortal man could get him back into his normal dimensions, but the Ghosts can. They have ways of doing things. Warping of world lines and twisting of inter-dimensional co-ordinates."

"You really mean that?" Ann asked. "This isn't just another of your practical jokes?"

The golden beard grinned broadly and then sobered. "Child," he said, "I don't joke about things like this. They are too important."

He looked about the room, as if expecting something, someone.

"Your father will be here any moment now," he declared.

"Here!" exclaimed Ann. "Here, in this room—"

Her voice broke off suddenly. The room had suddenly filled with Ghosts, and in their midst stood a man, a man with stooped shoulders and heavy-lensed glasses and lines of puzzlement upon his face. Like a puff of wind the Ghosts were gone and the man stood alone.

Ann flew at him. "Father," she cried. "You're back again, father."

She went into his arms and the man, looking over her shoulder, suddenly saw the man with the beard.

"Yes, Ann," he said, "I am back again."

His face hardened as Carter took a step toward them.

"You here," he snapped. "I might have known. Where there's anything afoot you're always around."

Laughter gurgled in the throat of the bearded giant. "So you went adventuring in the dimensions, did you?" he asked, mockery in his voice. "You always wanted to do that, John. The great John Smith, only man to ever go outside the four dimensional continuum."

His laughter seemed to rock the room.

"I suppose you got me out," said Smith, "so you could gloat over me."

The men stood, eyes locked, and Kent sensed between them an antagonism that was almost past understanding.

"I won't thank you for it," said Smith.

"Why, John, I never expected you to," chortled Carter. "I knew you'd hate me for it. I didn't do it for you. I did it for your little girl. She came from Landing City across hundreds of miles of deserts and canals to help you. She came down into Mad-Man's. She's the one I did it for. For her and the two brave men who came with her."

For the first time, apparently, Smith noticed Kent and Charley.

"I do thank you," he said, "for whatever you have done."

"Shucks," said Charley, "it wasn't nothin'. Nothin' at all. I always wanted to see Mad-Man's. Nobody ever came down here and came out sane. Most of them that came down didn't come out at all."

"If it hadn't been for my Ghosts neither would you," Carter reminded him.

"Father," pleaded Ann, "you mustn't be like this. Uncle brought you back. He was the only man who could have. If it hadn't been for him, you would still be out in the extra-dimension."

"What was it like, John?" asked Carter. "Dark and nothing to see?"

"As a matter of fact," said Smith, "that is exactly what it was."

"That's what you thought," jeered Carter. "Because you had no sense of perception to see or hear or make any contacts or associations in that world. Did you actually think your pitiful little human senses would serve you in a place like that?"

"What do you know about it?" snarled Smith.

"The Ghosts," said Carter. "You must not forget. The Ghosts tell me everything."

Carter looked around the room. "And now," he said, "I fear that you must go." He looked at Ann. "I did what you wanted me to do, didn't I?"

She nodded. "You are turning us out?" she asked.

"Call it that if you wish," said Carter. "I have work to do. A great deal of work to do. One of the reasons I came to Mad-Man's was to be alone."

"Now look here, mister," said Carter bluntly. "It's a long pull up Mad-Man's. A longer pull back to our igloo. You aren't turning us out without a chance to rest, are you?"

"He's crazy," said Smith. "He's always been crazy. He's sane only half of the time. Don't pay any attention to him."

Carter paid Smith no attention. He addressed Charley. "You won't have to walk back," he said. "My rocket ship is out there. Take it." He chuckled. "You needn't bother bringing it back. I'll give it to you."

"But, uncle," cried Ann. "What about yourself?"

"Don't worry about me," Carter told her. "I won't need it. The Ghosts can take me any place I want to go upon a moment's notice. I've outgrown your silly rocket ships. I've outgrown a lot of things."

He swept his arm about the room, pointed at the globe of brilliant fire that hung suspended between floor and ceiling.

"Pure energy," he said. "In there atoms are being created. Millions of horsepower are being generated. An efficient, a continual source of power. Enclosed in a sphere of force waves, the only thing that would stand the pressure and temperature inside the sphere."

He ceased speaking, looking around.

"That's only one of the things I've learned," he said. "Only one of the things. The Ghosts are my teachers, but given time I will be their master."

There was a wild light of fanaticism in his eyes.

"Why, man," said Kent, "you will be hailed as the greatest scientist the world has ever known."

The man's eyes seemed to flame. "No, I won't," he said, "because I'm not going to tell the world. Why should I tell the world? What has mankind ever done for me?" His laughter bellowed and reverberated in the domed room. "Find out for yourselves," he shouted. "Go and find out for yourselves. It will take you a million years."

His voice calmed. "The Ghosts are almost immortal," he said. "Not quite—almost. Before I am through with this, I will be immortal. There is a way. I almost have it now. I will become a Ghost—a super-Ghost—a creature of pure force. And when that happens, the Ghosts and I will forsake this worn-out world. We will go out into the void and build a new world, a perfect world. We will live through all eternity and watch and laugh at the foolish strugglings of little people. Little people like mankind."

The four of them stared at him.

"You don't mean this, Howard," protested Smith. "You can't mean it."

The wild light was gone from Carter's eyes. His voice boomed with mockery. "You don't think so, John?" he asked.

He reached into his shirt front, pulled out something that shone in the light of the radium bulbs. It was a key, attached to a string hung around his neck. He pulled the loop over his head, handed the key to Kent.

"The key to the rocket ship," he said. "The fuel tanks are nearly full. You fly her at a 30-degree angle out of here to miss the cliffs."

Kent took the key, turned it awkwardly in his hands.

Carter bowed ceremoniously to them, still with that old trace of mockery. "I hope you have a fine trip," he said.

Slowly they turned away, heading for the door.

Carter called after them.

"And you might tell anyone you see not to try to come into Mad-Man's. Tell them something unpleasant might happen."

Charley turned around. "Mister," he said, "I think you're batty as a bed-bug."

"Charley," declared Carter, "you aren't the first one to say that to me. And maybe . . . well, sometimes, I think, maybe you are right."

The sturdy rocket ship blasted its way across the red deserts. Far below, the criss-crossing of the canals, more deeply red, were etched like fiery lines.

"Lad," said Charley to Kent, "there's another story to tell the boys. Another yarn about Harry, the Hermit."

"They won't believe it," Kent declared. "They'll listen and then go out and retell it and make it a little better. And someone else will make it better yet. All we can do, Charley, is to give rise to another, an even greater, Harry, the Hermit."

Ann, sitting beside her father, smiled at them. "Just a couple of myth-makers," she said.

Charley studied the terrain beneath them, combed his beard. "You know," he said, "I still think that bird back there was off his nut. He'll try makin' himself into a Ghost—and just be an ordinary Earth kind of ghost. The kind that just ain't."

A Ghost suddenly materialized, shimmered faintly in the rocket cabin.

And for the first time known to man, perhaps for the first time in all history, the Ghost spoke, spoke with a voice they all recognized, the voice of the man back in Mad-Man's, that voice with its old mockery.

"So you think so, do you?" said the Ghost.

Then he faded from their view.

WORLDS WITHOUT END

---

*"Worlds Without End" was originally published in the winter 1956–
1957 issue of* Future Science Fiction. *At that time, the magazine
was edited by Robert W. Lowndes, who had been purchasing stories
from Clifford D. Simak since World War II. However, Lowndes, was
not Cliff's preferred editor; John W. Campbell Jr., who ran* Astounding Science Fiction, *had that distinction before the war and then
Horace Gold, who created* Galaxy Magazine. *But Lowndes was the
one who got this story about the corruption of a long-established organization.*

—dww

I

She did not look like the kind of person who would want to take
the Dream. Although, Norman Blaine reflected, one could never
tell.

He wrote the name she had given him down on the scratch
pad, instead of putting it on the application blank, he wrote it
slowly, deliberately, to give himself time to think, for there was
something here that was puzzling.

Lucinda Silone.

Peculiar name, he thought. Not like a real name. More like a stage name taken to cover up plain Susan Brown, or ordinary Betty Smith, or some other common run of name.

He wrote it slowly so that he could think, but he couldn't think too well. There were too many other things cluttering up his brain: The shakeup rumor that had whispered its way for days back and forth within the Center, his own connection with that rumor, and the advice that had been given him—there was something funny about the job. The advice was: don't trust Farris (as if he needed that advice!)—look it over well if it is offered you. It was all kindly-meant advice, but not very helpful.

And there was the lapel-clinging Buttonholer who had caught him in the parking lot that morning and had clung onto him when he tried to push him off; there was Harriet Marsh, with whom he had a date this very night.

Now, finally, this woman across the desk from him.

Although it was foolish, Blaine told himself—to think a thing like that, to tie her up with all the other thoughts that were bumping together like driftwood in his brain. For there could be no connection—there simply couldn't be.

She was Lucinda Silone, she'd said. Something about the name and something, as well, about the way she said it—the little lilting tones meant consciously to give it grace and make it sparkle—set tiny alarm bells ringing in his brain.

"You're with Entertainment." He said it casually, very much off-hand; this was a trick question and one that must be rightly put.

"Why, no," she replied, "I'm not."

Listening to the way she said it, Blaine could find nothing wrong. Her voice held a touch of fluttery happiness that betrayed pleasure at his thinking she must be Entertainment. And that was just as it should be. It was exactly the way that most of the others answered—flattered at the implication that they belonged to the fabulous Entertainment guild.

He gave her her money's worth. "I would have guessed you were."

He looked directly at Lucinda Silone, watching the expression on her face, but seeing all the other good points, too. "We get good at judging people here," he said. "We aren't often wrong."

She didn't wince. There was no reaction—no start of guilt, no flutter of confusion.

Her hair was honey color, her eyes were china blue, and her skin so milky white that one looked a second time to make sure that it was real.

We don't get many like this one, thought Blaine. *The old and sick and the disappointed. The desperate ones and those who know frustration.*

"You're mistaken, Mr. Blaine," she said. "I am Education."

He wrote *Education* on the scratch pad, and said, "It may have been the name. It's a very good name. Easy to say. Musical. It would go well on the stage."

He looked up from the pad and said, smiling—making himself smile against the inexplicable tension that was rising in him: "Although it was not the name alone; I am sure of that."

She didn't smile and he wondered swiftly if he had been awkward. He snapped the words he'd said in quick review across his mind and decided that he'd not been awkward. When you were director of Fabrication, you were not an awkward man. You knew how to handle people; you had to know how to handle them. And you knew, as well, how to handle yourself—how to make your face say one thing while your mind might be thinking something else.

No, his words had been a compliment, and not too badly put. She should have smiled. That she had failed to smile might mean something—or it mightn't mean a thing, except that she was clever. Norman Blaine had no doubt that Lucinda Silone was clever, and as cool a customer as he had ever seen.

Although coolness in itself was not too unusual. You got the cool ones, too—the cool and calculating—the ones who had figured it all out well ahead of time and knew what they were doing. And there were others, too, who had cut off all retreat behind them.

"You wish a Sleep," he said.

She nodded.

"And a Dream?"

"And a Dream," she said.

"You've thought it out quite thoroughly, I suppose. You wouldn't come, of course, if you had any doubts."

"I've thought it through," she told him, "and I have no doubts."

"You still have time. You'll have time to change your mind up to the final moment. We're most anxious that you get that fact fixed firmly in your mind."

"I'll not change my mind," she said.

"We still prefer to assume you may. We do not try to change your mind, but we insist upon complete understanding upon your part that a change is possible. You are under no obligation to us. No matter how far we've gone, there still is no obligation. The Dream may have been fabricated and processed; you may have paid your fee; you may already have entered the receptacle—there's still time to change your mind. The Dream will then be destroyed, your fee will be returned, and the record will be expunged. So far as we are then concerned, we will have never seen you."

"I quite understand," she said.

He nodded quietly. "We'll proceed on that understanding."

He picked up his pencil and wrote her name and classification on the application blank. "Age?"

"Twenty nine."

"Married?"

"No."

"Children?"

"None."

"Nearest of kin?"

"An aunt."

"Name?"

She gave him the name and he wrote it down, with address, age and classification of the aunt.

"Any others?"

"None at all."

"Your parents?"

Her parents had been dead for years, she said; she was an only child. She gave her parents' names, their classifications, their ages at the time of death, their last place of residence, their place of burial.

"You'll check on all of this?" she asked.

"We check on everything."

Here was the place where most of the applicants—even those who had nothing in their life to hide—would show some nervousness, would frantically start checking back along their memories to unearth some possible, long-forgotten incident which might turn up in the course of investigation to embarrass or impede them.

Lucinda Silone was not nervous; she sat there, waiting for the other questions.

Norman Blaine asked them: The number of her guild, her card number, her immediate superior, last medical exam, physical or psychic defects or ailments—all the other trivia which went into the details of daily life.

Finally he was finished and laid the pencil down. "Still no doubts?"

She shook her head.

"I keep harking back to that," said Blaine, "to make absolutely certain we have a willing client; otherwise we have no legal status. But aside from that, there is the matter of ethics . . ."

"I understand," she said, "that you are very ethical."

It might have been mockery; if so, it was very clever mockery. He tried to decide if it were or not, but he wasn't sure.

He let it drop. "We have to be," he told her. "Here is a setup which, to survive, must be based on the highest code of ethics. You give your body into our hands for our safekeeping over a number of years. What is more, you give your mind over to us, to a lesser extent. We gain much intimate knowledge of your life in the course of our work with you. To continue in the job we're doing, we must enjoy the complete confidence not only of our clients, but of the general public. The slightest breath of scandal . . ."

"There has never been a scandal?"

"In the early days, there were a few. They've been forgotten now, or we hope they have. It was those early scandals which made our guild realize how important it was that we keep ourselves free of any professional taint. A scandal in any of the other guilds is no more than a legal matter which can be adjudicated in the courts and then forgiven and forgotten. But with us there'd be no forgiving or forgetting; we'd never live it down."

Sitting there, Norman Blaine thought of his pride in the work he did—a bright and shining pride, a comfortable and contented pride in a job well done. And this feeling was not confined to he himself alone, but was held by everyone at Center. They might be flippant when they talked among themselves, but the pride was there, hidden deep beneath the flippancy and the workaday approach.

"You almost sound," she said, "like a dedicated people."

Mockery again, he wondered. Or was it flattery to match his own. He smiled a little at it. "Not dedicated," he said. "At least, we never think of ourselves as dedicated."

And that was not quite right, he knew, for there were times when every one of them must have thought of themselves as dedicated. It was not a thing, of course, that one could say aloud—but the thought was there.

It was a strange situation, he thought—the pride of work, the fierce loyalty to the guild itself, and, then, the cutthroat competition, and the vicious Center politics which existed in the midst of that pride and loyalty.

Take Roemer for example. John Roemer, after years of work, was on his way out. That had been the talk for days—the open secret which had been whispered through the Center. Farris had something to do with it, Lew Giesey was involved in some way, and there were others who were mentioned. Blaine himself, for example, had been mentioned as one of the men who might be chosen to step up into Roemer's position. Thank goodness, he had steered clear of Center politics all these years. There was too much headache in Center politics. Norman Blaine's work had been enough for him.

Although it would be fine, he thought, if he were picked to take over Roemer's job. It was higher up the ladder; the pay was better; and maybe if he got more money he could talk Harriet into giving up her newspaper job and . . .

He pulled himself back to the job at hand.

"There are certain considerations which you should take into account," he told the woman across the desk. "You should realize all the implications of what your decision means before you go ahead. You must realize that once you go to sleep, you will awaken in a culture different than your own. The planets will not stand still while you sleep; they will advance—or at least we hope they will. Much will be different. Styles will change, in clothing and in manners. Thought and speech and perspective—all will change. You will awaken an alien in a world that has left you far behind; you will be old fashioned.

"There will be public issues of which there now is not the faintest inkling. Governments may have evolved, and customs will be different. What is illegal today may have become quite acceptable; what is acceptable and legal today may have become outrageous or illegal then. Your friends will all be dead . . ."

"I have no friends," Lucinda Silone said.

He disregarded her and went on: "What I am trying to

impress upon you is that once you wake you cannot step from here straight back into the world, for it will be your world no longer. Your world will have died many years before; you will have to be readjusted, will have to take a course in reorientation. In certain instances, depending upon the awakened person to some extent, to the cultural changes to an even greater extent, this matter of reorientation may take quite some time. For we must give you not only the facts of the changes which have occurred while you were asleep—we must gain your acceptance of those changes. Until you have readjusted not only your data, but your culture as well, we cannot let you go. To live a normal life in that world in which you wake you must accept it as if you had been born into it—you must become, in fact, part of it. And that must often be a long and painful process."

"I realize all that," she said; "I'm ready to abide by all the conditions you lay down."

She had not hesitated once. Lucinda Silone had shown no regret or nervousness. She was as cool and calm as when she'd walked into the office.

"Now," Blaine said, "the reason."

"The reason?"

"The reason why you wish to take the Sleep; we must know."

"You'll investigate that, too?"

"We shall; we must be sure, you see. There are many reasons—many more than you'd think there'd be."

He kept on talking, to give her a chance to steel herself and tell him the reason. More often than not this was the hardest thing of all that a client faced. "There are those," he said, "who take the Sleep because they have a disease which at the moment is incurable. They do not contract for a Sleep of any specified length, but only till the day when a cure has been discovered.

"Then there are those who wish to wait out the time against the return of a loved one who is traveling to the stars—waiting out on Earth the subjective time of the faster-than-light flights.

And there are those who wish to sleep out an investment which they are sure, given time, will make them a fortune. Usually we try to talk them out of it; we call in our economists, who try to show them . . ."

She interrupted him. "Would ennui be enough?" she asked. "Just simple ennui?"

He wrote *ennui* for the reason and shoved the application to one side. "You can sign it later."

"I can sign it now."

"We'd prefer you wait a little."

Blaine fiddled with the pencil, trying to think it out—wondering why this client should disturb him so. Lucinda Silone was wrong and he couldn't place the wrongness; yet, he knew he should be able to, for he met all sorts of clients.

"If you wish," he said, "we could discuss the Dream. Usually we don't but . . ."

"Let's discuss it," she said.

"A Dream is not necessary," he told her. "There are those who take the Sleep without one. I don't wish to appear to be arguing against a Dream; in many cases it appears to me to be preferable. You would not be conscious of the time—an hour or a century is no longer than a second. You go to sleep; then you wake, and it is as if there had been no time at all . . ."

"I want a Dream," she said.

"In that case, we are glad to serve you. Have you thought what kind?"

"A friendly dream. A restful one and friendly."

"No excitement? No adventure?"

"Some; perhaps, it might get monotonous otherwise. But genteel, if you please."

"A polite society, perhaps," suggested Blaine. "Let's say, one much concerned with manners."

"And no competition, if you can manage it; no rushing about to beat out someone else."

"An old, established home," continued Blaine. "Good position in the community, high family traditions; sufficient income to banish money worries."

"It sounds a bit archaic."

"It's the kind of Dream you asked for."

"Of course," she said. "What am I thinking of? It will be lovely. It's the sort of thing, the sort . . ." she laughed. "The sort of thing you dream of."

He laughed with her.

"You like it? We can change it, bring it up to date."

"Don't you dare, it's just what I want."

"You'll want to be young, I suppose, younger than twenty-nine—sixteen or seventeen."

She nodded.

"And pretty, of course, you would be beautiful despite anything we did."

She did not answer.

"Plenty of admirers," he said. "We could put in lots of them."

She nodded.

"Sexual adventures?"

"A few, don't overdo it, though."

"We'll keep it dignified," he promised. "You'll have no regrets; we'll give you a Dream you'll need not be ashamed of—one you can look back upon with a lot of happiness. There naturally will have to be some disappointments, a few heartaches; happiness can't run on forever without getting stale. There must be something, even in a Dream, upon which you can establish comparative values."

"I'll leave that all to you."

"All right, then, we'll get to work on it. Could you come back, say in three days' time? We'll have it roughed out then and we can go over it together. It may take half a dozen—well, let us call them fittings, before we have what you want."

Lucinda Silone rose and held out her hand. Her clasp was firm and friendly. "I'll stop at the cashier's and pay the fee," she said. "And thanks, so very much."

"There's no need to pay the fee this soon."

"I'll feel better when I do."

Norman Blaine watched her go, then sat back down again. The intercom buzzed. "Yes, Irma."

His secretary said, "Harriet called. You were with the client, and couldn't be disturbed; she left a message."

"What did she want?"

"Just to let you know she can't have dinner with you tonight. She said something about an assignment, some big bug from Centauri."

He said: "Irma, let me give you a tip. Never fall in love with Communications. You can't depend on them."

"You keep forgetting, Mr. Blaine; I married Transportation."

"So I do," said Blaine.

"George and Herb are out here waiting. They've been slapping one another on the back and rolling on the floor. Take them off my hands before I go stark raving."

"Send them in," he said.

"Are they all right?"

"George and Herb?"

"Who else?"

"Certainly, Irma; it's just the way they work."

"It's a comfort to know that," she said, "I'll shoo them in."

He settled back and watched the two come in. They sprawled themselves in chairs.

George shied a folder at him. "The Jenkins Dream; we got it all worked out."

"He's a jerk who wants to hunt big game," said Herb; "we cooked up some dillies for him."

"We made it authentic," George declared with pride; "we didn't skip a thing. We put him in the jungle, and we put in mud and insects and the heat; we crammed the place with ravenous nightmares. There's something thirsting for his blood behind every bush."

"It's no hunt," said Herb; "it's a running battle. When he isn't scared, he's jumpy. Damned if I can figure out a guy like that."

"It takes all kinds," said Blaine.

"Sure; and we get them all."

"Some day," Blaine told them drily, "you guys will lay it on so thick you'll get booted to Conditioning."

"They can't do that," said Herb. "You got to have a medical degree to get into Conditioning. And George and me, we couldn't bandage a finger the way it should be done."

George shrugged. "We haven't a thing to worry about; Myrt takes care of that. When we go too hog wild, she tames it down."

Blaine laid the folder to one side. "I'll feed it in before I leave tonight." He picked up the pad. "I have something different here. You'll have to slick down your hair and get on good behavior before I turn you loose on it."

"The one who just went out?"

Blaine nodded.

"I could cook up a Dream for her," said Herb.

"She wants peace and dignity," Blaine informed them. "Genteel society. A sort of modern version of mid-nineteenth century Old Plantation days. No rough stuff; just magnolia and white columns; horses in the bluegrass."

"Likker, " said Herb. "Oceans of likker. Bourbon and mint leaves and . . ."

"Cocktails," Blaine told him, "and not too many of them."

"Fried chicken," said George, getting into the act. "Watermelon. Moonlight. River boats. Lemme at it."

"Not so fast; you have the wrong approach. Slow and easy. Tame down. Imagine slow music. A sort of eternal waltz."

"We could put in a war," said Herb; "they fought polite in those days. Sabers and all dressed up in fancy uniforms."

"She doesn't want a war."

"You gotta have *some* action."

"No action—or very little of it. No worry; no competition. Gentility . . ."

"And us," lamented George, "all spattered up with jungle mud."

The intercom buzzed. "The b.a. wants to see you," Irma said.

"O.K., tell him . . ."

"He wants to see you now."

"Oh, oh," said George.

"I always liked you, Norm," said Herb.

"All right," said Blaine. "Tell him I'll be right up."

"After all these years," Herb said, sadly. "Cutting throats and stabbing backs to get ahead and now it comes to this."

George drew his forefinger across his throat and made a hissing sound, like a blade slashing into flesh.

They were very funny.

II

Lew Giesey was the business agent of the Dream guild. For years he had run it with an iron fist and disarming smile. He was loyal and he demanded loyalty; he dealt out sharp, decisive discipline as quickly as he rewarded praise.

He worked in an ornate office, but behind a battered desk to which he clung stubbornly, despite all efforts to provide him with a better one. To him, the desk must have been a symbol—or a reminder—of the bitter struggle to attain his station. He had started with that desk in the early days; it had followed him from office to office as he fought his bare-knuckled way ahead, up the table of organization to the very top. The desk was scarred and battered, unlike the man himself. It was almost as if the desk, in the course of years, might have intervened itself to take the blows aimed at the man behind it.

But there had been one blow which it could not take for him. For Lou Giesey sat in his chair behind the desk and he was quite dead. His head had fallen forward on his chest and his forearms still rested on the chair's arms and his hands still clutched the wood.

The room was at utter peace and so, it seemed as well, the man behind the desk. There was a quietness in the room, as if respite had come from all the years of struggle and of planning. It rested now with a sense of urgency, as if it might have known that the respite could not last for long. In a little while, another man would come and sit behind the desk—perhaps a different one, for no other man would want Giesey's battered desk—and the struggle and the turmoil would start up again.

Norman Blaine stopped when he was halfway between the door and desk; it was the quietness of the room, as well as the head sunk upon the chest, that told him what had happened.

He stopped and listened to the soft whirring of the clock upon the wall, a sound usually lost until this moment in this place. He heard the almost-inaudible flutter of a typewriter from across the hall, the far-off, muffled rumble of wheels rushing along the highway that ran past the Center.

He thought, with one edge of his mind: *Death and peace and quiet, the three of them together, companions hand in hand.* Then his mind recoiled upon itself and built up into a tight coil spring of horror.

Blaine took a slow step forward, then another one, walking across the carpeting that allowed no footfall sound. He had not as yet realized the full impact of what had happened there—that moments before the business agent had asked to speak to him; that he was the one to find Giesey dead; that his presence in the office might lead to suspicion of him.

He reached the desk and the phone was there in front of him, on one corner of the desk. He lifted the receiver and when the switchboard voice came, he said: "Protection, please."

He heard the clicking as the signal was set up. "Protection."

"Farris, please."

Blaine started to shake, then—the muscles in his forearm jumping, others twitching in his face. He felt breathlessness rising in him, his chest constricting, a choking in his throat, and his mouth suddenly dry and sticky. He gritted his teeth and stopped the jumping muscles.

"Farris speaking."

"Blaine. Fabrication."

"Oh, yes, Blaine. What can I do for you?"

"Giesey called me up to see him; when I got here he was dead."

There was a pause—not too long a pause. Then: "You're sure he's dead."

"I haven't touched him. He's sitting in his chair; he looks dead to me."

"Anyone else know?"

"No one. Darrell is out in the reception room, but . . ."

"You didn't yell out that he was dead."

"Not a word; I picked up the phone and called you."

"Good boy! That's using your head. Stay right there; don't tell anyone, don't let anyone in; don't touch anything. We're on our way."

The connection clicked and Norman Blaine put the receiver back into the cradle.

The room was still at rest, squeezing out of the next few moments all the rest it could. Soon the fury would take up again; Paul Farris and his goons would come bursting in.

Blaine stood by the corner of the desk, uncertainly—waiting, too. And now that he had the time to think, now that the shock had partially worn away and the acceptance of the fact began to seep into his mind, new ideas came creeping in to plague him.

He had found Giesey dead, but would they believe that Blaine had found him dead? Would they ask Blaine how he could prove that he had found Lew Giesey dead?

What did he want to see you for? they'd ask. How often had Giesey called you in before? Do you have any idea why he called you in this time? Praise? Reprimand? Caution? Discussion of new techniques? Trouble in your department, maybe? Some deviation in your work. How's your private life? Some indiscretion that you had committed?

He sweated, thinking of the questions.

For Farris was thorough. You had to be thorough and unrelenting—and tough—to head up Protection. You were hated from the start, and fear was a necessary factor to counteract the hatred.

Protection was necessary. The guild was an unwieldy organization for all its tight efficiency, and it must be kept in line. Intrigue must be rooted out. Deviationism—dickering with other unions—must be run down and have an end put to it. There must be no wavering in the loyalty of any members; and to effect all this, there was need of an iron hand.

Blaine reached out to clutch at the desk, then remembered that Farris had told him not to touch a thing.

He pulled his hand back, let it hang by his side, and that seemed awkward and unnatural. He put it in his pocket, and that seemed awkward, too. He put both his hands behind his back and clasped them, then teetered back and forth.

He fidgeted.

He swung around to look at Giesey, wondering if the head still rested on the chest, if the hands still gripped the chair arms. For a moment, Norman Blaine built up in his mind the little speculative fiction that Lew Giesey would not be dead at all, but would have raised his head and be looking at him. And if that were so, Blaine wondered how he would explain.

He needn't have wondered; Giesey still was dead.

And now, for the first time, Norman Blaine began to see the man in relation to the room—not as a single point of interest, but as a man who sat in a chair, with the chair resting on the carpeting and the carpeting covering the floor.

Giesey's uncapped pen lay upon the desk in front of him, resting where it had stopped after rolling off a sheaf of papers. Giesey's spectacles lay beside the pen; off to one side was a glass with a little water left in the bottom of it; beside it stood the stopper of the carafe from which Giesey must recently have poured himself a drink.

And on the floor, beside Lew Giesey's feet, was a single sheet of paper.

Blaine stood there, staring at the paper, wondering what it was. It was a form of some sort, he could see, and there was writing on it. He edged around the desk to get a better look at it, egged on by an illogical curiosity.

He bent low to read the writing, and a name came up and struck him in the face. *Norman Blaine!*

He bent swiftly and scooped the paper off the carpet. It was an appointment form, dated the day before yesterday and it appointed Norman Blaine as Administrator of Records, Dream Department, effective as of midnight of this day. It was duly signed and stamped as having been recorded.

John Roemer's job, Blaine thought, the job that they had whispered about for weeks throughout the Center.

He had a fleeting moment of triumph. They'd picked him. He had been the man for the job! But there was more than triumph. He not only had the job, but he had the answers to the questions they would ask.

Why were you called in? they'd ask. Now he could answer them. With this paper in his pocket, he would have the answer.

But he didn't have much time.

He laid the paper on the desk and folded it one third over, forcing himself to take the time to do it neatly. Then, just as neatly, he folded the other one third over and thrust it in his pocket. Then he turned again to face the door and waited.

The next moment, Paul Farris and a half dozen of his goons came stamping in.

III

Farris was a smooth operator. He was a top-notch policeman and had the advantage of looking like a college instructor. He was not a big man; he wore his hair slicked down, and his eyes were weak and wavery back of the spectacles.

He settled himself comfortably in the chair behind his desk and laced his hands over his belly. "I'll have to ask you some questions," he told Blaine. "Just for the record, naturally. The death is an open-and-shut one of suicide. Poison. We won't know what kind until Doc gets the test run through."

"I understand," said Blaine.

And thought: *I understand, all right. I know just how you work. Lull a man to sleep, then belt him in the guts.*

"You and I have worked together for a long time," said Farris. "Not together, exactly, but under the same roof and for the same purpose. We've got along fine; I know that we will continue in exactly the same way."

"Why, certainly," said Blaine.

"This appointment form," said Farris; "you say you got it in an inter-office envelope."

Blaine nodded. "It was in my basket this morning, I suppose. I didn't get around to going through the stuff until rather late."

Which was true enough, he hadn't gone through the basket until 10 o'clock or so. And another thing—there was no record of inter-office mail.

And still another thing: Maintenance came around and emptied the waste baskets at precisely 11:30; it was now a quarter of one, and anything that had been in his basket had long since been burned.

"And you just put the form in your pocket and forgot about it?"

"I didn't forget about it; I had an applicant about that time.

Then, when the applicant left, two of the fabricators came in. I was going over a point or two with them when Giesey called and asked me to come up. "

Farris nodded. "You think he wanted to talk with you about your new position?"

"That was what I thought."

"Had he talked about it before? Did you know that it was coming?"

Norman Blaine shook his head. "It was a complete surprise."

"A happy one, of course?"

"Naturally. It's a better job. Better pay. A man wants to get ahead."

Farris looked thoughtful. "Didn't it strike you as a rather strange procedure to get an appointment—particularly to a key position—in an inter-office envelope?"

"Of course it did; I wondered about it at the time."

"But you did nothing about it?"

"I have told you," Blaine said, "I was busy. And what would you suggest that I should have done?"

"Nothing," Farris told him.

"That is what I thought," said Blaine. He thought: *Make something out of it, if you can.*

He felt a brief elation and fought it down. It was too soon, he knew.

At the moment there wasn't a thing that Farris could do—not a single thing. The appointment was in order, properly signed and executed. As of the coming midnight he, Norman Blaine, would be administrator of records, taking over from Roemer. Only the delivery of the appointment was not in order, but there was no way in the world that Farris could prove that Blaine had not received it in the inter-office mail.

He wondered, briefly, what might have happened if Giesey had not died. Would the appointment have come through, or would it have been quashed somewhere along the line? Would some pressure have been brought to bear to give the position to someone else?

Farris was saying, "I knew the change was going to be made. Roemer was getting—well, just a little difficult. It had come to my attention, and I spoke to Giesey about it. So had several others. We talked about it some; he mentioned you as among several men who could be trusted, but that was all he said."

"You didn't know he had decided?"

Farris shook his head. "No, but I'm glad he picked you for the post. You're the kind of man I like to work with, realistic. We'll get along. We'd better talk about it."

"Any time," said Blaine.

"If you have the time, how about dropping in on me tonight? Any time at all, I'll be home all evening. You know where I live?"

Blaine nodded and got to his feet.

"Don't worry about this business," Farris said. "Lew Giesey was a good man, but there are other good men. We all thought a lot of him. I know it must have been a shock, walking in on him that way."

He hesitated for a moment, then: "And don't worry about any change in your appointment. I'll speak to whomever replaces Giesey."

"Any idea who it'll be?"

Farris' eyelids flicked just once, then his eyes were hard and steady, wavery no longer. "No idea," he said, brusquely. "The executive board will name the man. I have no idea who they'll put the finger on."

The hell you don't, thought Blaine.

"You're sure about it being suicide?"

"Certain," Farris said. "Giesey had a heart history, he was worried."

He rose and reached for his cap, put it on. "I like a man who thinks fast on his feet. Keep thinking on your feet, Blaine. We'll get along."

"I'm sure we will."

"Don't forget about tonight."

"I'll be seeing you," Blaine told him.

IV

The Buttonholer had seized upon Norman Blaine that morning, after he had parked his car, just when he was leaving the lot. How the man had gotten in, Blaine could not imagine, but there he was, waiting for a victim. "Just a second, sir," he said.

Blaine swung around toward him. The man took a quick step forward, put out both his hands and clasped Blaine's lapels firmly. Blaine backed away, but the man's fingers held their grip and halted him.

"Let me go," Blaine said, but the man told him, "Not until I've had a word with you. You work at the Center and you're just the man I want to talk with. Because if I can make you understand—why, then, sir, I know that there is hope.

"Hope," he said, a fine spray of saliva flying from between his lips—"hope that we can make the people understand the viciousness of Dreams. Because they are vicious, sir, they undermine the moral fiber of the people. They hold the opportunity for quick escape from the troubles and the problems which develop character. With the Dreams, there is no need for a man to face his troubles—he can run away from them, he can seek a forgetfulness in Dreams. I tell you, sir, it is the damnation of our culture."

Remembering it now, Norman Blaine still felt the cold, quiet whiteness of the anger that had enveloped him.

"Let loose of me," he'd said. There must have been something in his tone which warned the Buttonholer, for the man let loose his grip and backed away. And Blaine, lifting his arm to wipe his face upon his coat sleeve, watched him back away, then finally turn and run.

It had been the first time he'd ever been seized upon by a Buttonholer, although he had heard of them often and had laughed them off.

Now, thinking back upon it, he was surprised at the impact of his encounter with a Buttonholer—his horror that here, finally, he had physical evidence that there were persons in the world who doubted the sincerity and the purpose of the Dreams.

He jerked himself away from his reverie; there were other, more important things with which to concern himself. Giesey's death and the sheet of paper he had found upon the floor—the strange conduct of Farris. *Almost,* he thought, *as if there were a conspiracy between the two of us—as if he and I had been involved in some gigantic plot, now coming to fruition.*

He sat quietly behind his desk and tried to think it out.

Given a moment to consider, he was certain that he would not have snatched the paper off the floor; given another moment for consideration, even after having seen what it was, he was certain that he would have dropped it back on the floor again. But there had been no time at all. Farris and his goons were already on their way and Blaine had stood defenseless in the office with a dead man, without an adequate explanation of why he should be there, without an adequate answer to any of the questions that they were sure to ask him.

The paper had given him a reason for being in the office, had given him the answer to the questions, had forestalled many other questions that would have been asked if he had not had the answer to the first ones.

Farris had said suicide.

Would it have been suicide or murder, Blaine wondered, if he had not had the paper in his pocket? If he had remained defenseless, would his luckless position have been used to explain Giesey's death?

Farris had said he liked a man who could think standing on his feet. And there was no doubt he did. For Farris himself was a man who could think standing on his feet, who could improvise and trim his course with each passing situation.

And he was not a man to trust.

Blaine wondered if the appointment still would have come through if he'd not been there to pick it off the carpet. Certainly he was not the sort of man Paul Farris would have picked to take over Roemer's job. Would Farris, finding the appointment on the floor, have destroyed it and forged another, appointing someone more to his liking to the post?

And, another question: What was the importance of the job? Why did it matter, or seem to matter so much, who was appointed to it? No one had said, of course, that it was important; but Farris had been interested and Paul Farris never was interested in unimportant things.

Could the appointment, in some way, have been linked with Lew Giesey's death? Blaine shook his head. There was no way that one could answer.

The important thing was that he had the appointment—that Giesey's death had not prevented its delivery, that for the moment at least Farris was willing to let the situation ride.

But, Norman Blaine warned himself, he could not afford to take Farris at face value. As steward of the guild, Paul Farris was a police official with a loyal corps of men, with wide discretion in carrying out his functions, politically-minded and unscrupulous, busily carving out a niche large enough to fit full-scale ambition.

More than likely Giesey's death fitted in with this ambition. It was not beyond reason that Farris might, in some small and hidden way, have contributed—if, in fact, he had not engineered it.

Suicide, he had said. Poison. Worried. Heart history. Easy words to say. Watch your step, Blaine told himself. Take it easy. Make no sudden moves. And be ready to duck. Especially—be ready to duck.

He sat quietly, letting the turmoil of speculation run out of his mind. *No use thinking of it,* he told himself. *No use at all right now.* Later, when and if he had some facts to go on—then would be the time to think.

He glanced at the clock and it was three fifteen. Too early to go home.

And there was work to do. Tomorrow he'd be moving up to another office, but today there still was work to do.

He picked up the Jenkins folder and looked at it. A big game hunt, the two zany fabricators had said. We gave him the works, they'd said, or words to that effect.

He flipped the folder open and ran through the first few pages, shuddering just a little.

No accounting for tastes, he thought.

He remembered Jenkins—a great, massive brute of a man who had bellowed out a flow of language that had made the office quake.

Well, maybe he can take it, Blaine thought. *Anyhow, it is what he asked for.*

He tucked the folder under his arm and went out into the reception room.

Irma said, "We just heard the word."

"About Giesey, you mean."

"No, we heard that earlier. We all felt badly; I guess everybody liked him. But I mean the word about you. It's all over now. Why didn't you tell us right away? We think it's wonderful."

"Why, thank you, Irma."

"We'll miss you, though."

"That is good of you."

"Why did you keep it secret? Why didn't you let us know?"

"I didn't know myself until this morning; I guess I got too busy. Then Giesey called."

"There were goons all over the place, going through the waste baskets. I think they even went through your desk. What was the matter with them?"

"Just curious." Blaine went out into the hall and the chill of fear crept up his spine with every step he took.

He had known it before, of course, with Farris' crack about thinking on one's feet, but this put the clincher on it. This left no doubt at all that Farris knew he'd lied.

Maybe there was some merit in it, after all, though. His lie and bluff put him, momentarily, into Farris' class—made Blaine the kind of man the goon leader was able to understand, the kind of man he could do business with.

But could he keep up the bluff? Could he be tough enough?

Keep cool, Blaine, he told himself. *No sudden moves. Ready to duck, although you can't let them know you are. Poker face,* he told himself—*the kind of face you use when you face an applicant.*

He tramped on and the coldness wore away.

Going down the stairs into Myrt's room, the old magic gripped him once again.

There she sat—the great machine of dreams, the ultimate in the fabrication of the imaginative details of man's wildest fantasies.

He stood in the silence of the place and felt the majesty and peace, the almost-tenderness, that he always felt—as if Myrt were some sort of protective mother-goddess to which one might flee for understanding and unquestioning refuge.

He tucked the folder more tightly under his arm and walked softly across the floor, fearing to break the hush of the place with an awkward or a heavy footfall.

He mounted the stairs that led to the great keyboard, and sat down in the traveling seat which would move at the slightest touch to any part of the coding panels. He clamped the open folder on a clipboard in front of him and reached out to the query lever. He pressed it, and an indicator winked a flashing green. The machine was clear, he could feed in his data.

He punched in the identification and then he sat in silence—as he often sat in silence there.

This he would miss, Blaine knew, when he moved up to that other job. Here he was like a priest, a sort of communicant with a force that he reverenced, but could not understand—not in its entirety. For no man could know the structure of the dream machine in its entirety. It was too vast and complicated a mechanism to be fixed in any mind.

It was a computer with magic built into it, and freed from the utter, straight-line logic of other, less fabulous computers. It dealt in fantasy rather than in fact—it was a gigantic plot machine that wove out of punched-in symbols and equations the strange stories of many different lives. It took in code and equations and it dished out dreams!

Blaine started to punch in the data from the folder sheets, moving swiftly about the face of the coding panel in the traveling chair. The panel began to twinkle with many little lights and from the dream machine came the first faint sounds of tripping relays, the hum of power stirring through the mechanisms, the click of control counters, the faint, far-off chattering of memory files being probed, and the purr of narrative sequence channels getting down to work.

He worked on in a tense, closed-in world of concentration, setting up the co-ordinates from sheet after sheet. Time came to an end and there was no other world than the panel with its myriad keys, and trips and buttons, and its many flashing lights.

Finally he was done, the last sheet fluttered down to the floor from the empty clipboard. Time took up again and the room came into being. Norman Blaine sat limply, shirt soaked with perspiration, hair damp against his forehead, hands resting in his lap.

The machine was thundering now. Lights flashed by the thousands, some of them winking steadily, others running bright little sequences like lazy lightning flashes. The sound of power surged within the room, filling it to bursting, and yet beneath the hum of power could be heard the busy thumps and clicks and the erratic insane chattering of racing mechanisms.

Wearily Blaine got out of the chair and picked up the fallen sheets, bundling them together, helter-skelter, without regard to numbering, back into the folder.

He walked to the far end of the machine and stood staring for a moment at the glass-protected cabinet where tape was spinning on a reel. He watched the spinning tape, fascinated, as always, by the thought that upon the tape was impressed the seeming life of a dream that might last a century or a thousand years—a dream built with such sheer story-telling skill that it would never pall, but would be fresh and real until the very last.

He turned away and walked to the stairway, went halfway up, then turned and looked back.

It was his last dream, he knew, the last he'd ever punch; tomorrow he'd be on another job. He raised his arm in half salute.

"So long, Myrt," he said.

Myrt thundered back at him.

V

Irma had left for the day and the office was empty, but there was a letter, addressed to Blaine, propped against the ash tray on his desk. The envelope was bulky and distorted when he picked it up, it jangled.

Norman Blaine ripped it open and a ring, crowded full of keys, fell out of it and clattered on the desk. A sheet of paper slipped halfway out and stuck.

He pushed the keys to one side, took out the sheet of paper and unfolded it. There was no salutation. The note began abruptly: *I called to turn over the keys, but you were out and your secretary didn't know when you would be back. There seemed no point in staying. If you should want to see me later, I am at your service. Roemer.*

He let the note fall out of his hand and flutter to the desk. He picked up the keys and tossed them up and down, listening to them jangle, catching them in his palm.

What would happen to John Roemer now, he wondered. Had a place been made for him, or hadn't Giesey gotten around to appointing him to some other post? Or had Giesey intended that the man be out entirely? That seemed unlikely, for the guild took care of its own; it did not, except under extreme provocation, throw a man out on his own.

And, for that matter, who would take over the direction of Fabrication? Had Lew Giesey died before he could make an appointment? George or Herb—either one of them—would be in line, but they hadn't said a word. They would have said something, Blame was sure, if they had been notified.

He picked up the sheet of paper and read the note again. It was noncommittal, completely deadpan; there was nothing to be learned from it.

He wondered how Roemer might feel about being summarily replaced, but there was no way of knowing; the note certainly gave no clue. And *why* had he been replaced? There had been rumors, all sorts of rumors, about a shakeup in the Center, but the rumors had stopped short of the reasons for the shakeup.

It seemed a little strange—this leaving of the keys, the transfer of authority symbolized by the leaving of the keys. It was as if Roemer had thrown them on Blaine's desk, said: "There they are, boy; they're all yours," and then had left without another word.

Just a little burned up, perhaps. Just a little hurt.

But the man had come in person. Why? Under ordinary circumstances, Blaine knew, Roemer would have stayed to break in the man who was to succeed him, then would have gone up to Records. But Roemer would have stayed on until his successor knew the ropes.

These were not ordinary circumstances. Come to think of it, they seemed to be turning out to be most extraordinary.

It was a fouled-up mess, Norman Blaine told himself. Going through regular channels, it would have been all right—a normal operation, the shifts made without disruption. But the appointment had not gone through channels; and had Blaine not been the one to find Lew Giesey dead, had he not seen the paper on the floor, the appointment might not have gone through at all.

But the job was his—he'd stuck out his neck to get it and it was his. It was not something he had sought, but now that he had it, he'd keep it. It was a step up the ladder; it was advancement. It paid better, had more prestige, and put him closer to the top—third from the top, in fact, for the chain of command ran: business agent, Protection, and then Records.

He'd tell Harriet tonight—but, no, he kept forgetting; he'd not see Harriet tonight.

He put the keys in his pocket and picked up the note again. *If you should want to see me later, I am at your service.*

Protocol? he wondered. Or was there something that he might need to know? Something that needed telling?

Could it be that Roemer had come to tell him something and then had lost his nerve?

Blaine crumpled the note and hurled it to the floor. He wanted to get out, get away from Center, get out where he could try to think it out, plan what he was to do. He should clean out his desk, he knew, but it was late—far past quitting tune. And there was his date with Harriet—no, damn it, he kept forgetting. Harriet had called and said she couldn't make it.

There'd be time tomorrow to clean out his desk. He took his hat and coat and went out to the parking lot.

An armed guard had replaced the regular attendant at the entrance to the lot. Blaine showed his identification.

"All right, sir," said the guard. "Keep an eye peeled, though. A suspendee got away."

"Got away?"

"Sure; just woke a week or two ago."

"He can't get far," said Elaine. "Things change; he'll give himself away. How long was he in Sleep?"

"Five hundred years, I think."

"Things change a lot in five hundred years. He hasn't got a chance."

The guard shook his head. "I feel sorry for him. Must be tough, waking up like that."

"It's tough, all right. We try to tell them, but they never listen."

"Say," said the guard, "you're the one who found Giesey."

Blaine nodded.

"Was it the way they tell it? Was he dead when you got there?"

"He was dead."

"Murdered?"

"I don't know."

"It does beat hell. You get up to the top, then *pouf*. . ."

"It does beat hell," agreed Blaine.

"You never know."

"No, you never do." Blaine hurried off.

He drove out of the lot and swung onto the highway. Dusk was just beginning and the road was almost deserted.

Norman Blaine drove slowly, watching the autumn countryside slide past. The first lamps glimmered from the windows of the villas set upon the hills; there was the smell of burning leaves and of the slow, sad dying of the year.

Thoughts flitted at him, like the skimming birds hurrying to a night-time tree, but he batted them away—the Buttonholer who had grabbed him—what Farris might suspect or know and what he might intend to do—why John Roemer had called personally to deliver the keys, and then had decided not to wait—why a suspendee should escape.

And that last one was a funny deal; it was downright crazy, when you thought about it. What could possibly be gained by such an escape, such a fleeing out into an alien world for which one was not prepared? It would be like going to an alien planet all alone without adequate briefing. It would be like walking onto a job with which one had no acquaintance and trying to bluff one's way.

I wonder why, he thought. *I wonder why he did it.*

He brushed the thought away; there was too much to think of. He'd have to get it straightened out before he could think it through. He could not allow himself to get the thoughts all cluttered up.

He reached out to the dash and turned on the radio.

A commentator was saying: " . . . who know their political history can recognize the crisis points that now are becoming more clearly defined. For more than five hundred years, the government, in actuality, has been in the hands of the Central Labor Union. Which is to say that the government is rule by committee, with each of the guilds and unions represented on the central group. That such a group should be able to continue in control for five full centuries—for the last 60 years in openly admitted control—is not so much to be attributed to wisdom, forebearance, or patience, as to a fine balance of power which has obtained within the body at all times. Mutual distrust and fear have at no time allowed any one union or guild or any combination to become dominant. As soon as one group threatened to become so, the personal ambitions of other groups operated to undermine the ascendant group.

"But this, as everyone must recognize, is a situation which has lasted longer than could normally have been expected. For years the stronger unions have been building up their strength—and not trying to use it. You may be sure that none of them will attempt to use their strength until they're absolutely sure of themselves. Just where any of them stand, strength-wise, is impossible to say, for it is not good strategy that any union should let its strength be known. The day cannot be too far distant when there must be a matching of this strength. The situation, as it stands, must seem intolerable to some of the stronger unions with ambitious leaders . . ."

Blaine turned off the radio and was astonished at the solemn peace of the autumn evening. It was all old stuff, anyway. So long as he could remember, there had been commentators talking thus. There were eternal rumors which at one time would name Transportation as the union that would take over, and at another time would hint at Communications, and at still another time would insist—just as authoritatively—that Food was the one to watch.

Dreams, he told himself smugly, were beyond that kind of politics. The guild—his guild—stood for public service. It was represented on Central, as was its right and duty, but it had never played at politics.

It was Communications that was always stirring up a fuss with articles in the papers and blatting commentators. If he didn't miss his guess, Blaine told himself, Communications was the worst of all—in there every minute waiting for its chance. Education, too; Education was always fouling up the detail, and what a bunch of creeps!

He shook his head, thinking of how lucky he was to be with Dreams—not to have to feel a sense of guilt when the rumors came around. You could be sure that Dreams never would be mentioned; of all the unions, Dreams was the only one that could stand up straight and tall.

He'd argued with Harriet about Communications, and at times she had gotten angry with him; she seemed to have the stubborn notion that Communications was the union which had the best public service record and the cleanest slate.

It was natural, of course, Blaine admitted, that one should think his own particular union was all right. Unions were the only loyalty to which a man could cling. Once, long ago, there had been nations and the love of one's own nation was known as patriotism. But now the unions had taken their place.

He drove into the valley that wound among the hills, and finally turned off the highway and followed the winding road that climbed into the hills.

Dinner would be waiting and Ansel would be cross (he was a cranky robot at the best). Philo would be waiting for him at the gate and they'd ride in together.

He passed Harriet's house and stared briefly at it, set well back among the trees, but there were no lights. Harriet wasn't home. An assignment, she had said; an interview with someone.

He turned in at his own gate and Philo was there, barking out his heart. Norman Blaine slowed the car and the dog jumped in, reached up to nuzzle his master's cheek just once, then settled sedately in the seat while they wheeled around the drive to stop before the house.

Philo leaped out quickly and Blaine got out more slowly. It had been a tiring day, he told himself. Now that he was home, he suddenly was tired.

He stood for a moment, looking at the house. It was a good house, he thought; a good place for a family—if he ever could persuade Harriet to give up her news career.

A voice said: "All right. You can turn around now. And take it easy; don't try any funny stuff."

Slowly Blaine turned. A man stood beside the car in the gathering dusk. He held a glinting object in his hand and he said, "There's nothing to be afraid of; I don't intend you any harm. Just don't get gay about it."

The man's clothes were wrong; they seemed to be some sort of uniform. And his words were wrong. The inflection was a bit off color, concise and crisp, lacking the slurring of one word into another which marked the language. And the phrases—*funny stuff; don't get gay.*

"This is a gun I have. No monkey business, please."

Monkey business.

"You are the man who escaped," said Blaine.

"That I am."

"But how . . ."

"I rode all the way with you. Hung underneath the car; those dumb cops didn't think to look."

The man shrugged. "I regretted it once or twice. You drove further than I hoped. I almost let go a time or two. "

"But me? Why did you . . ."

"Not you, mister; anyone at all. It was a way to hide—a means to get away."

"I don't read you," Blaine told him. "You could have made a clean break; you could have let go at the gate. The car was going slow then. You could have sneaked away right now. I'd never noticed you."

"And been picked up as soon as I showed myself. The clothes are a giveaway. So is my speech. Then there's my eating habits, and maybe even the way I walk. I would stick out like a bandaged thumb."

"I see," said Blaine. "All right, then; put up the gun. You must be hungry. We'll go in and eat."

The man put away the gun. He patted his pocket. "I still have it, and I can get it fast. Don't try any swifties."

"O.K.," said Blaine. "No swifties." Thinking: Picturesque. *Swifties.* Never heard the word. But it had a meaning; there could be no doubt of that.

"By the way, how did you get that gun?"

"That's something," said the man, "I'm not telling you."

VI

His name, the fugitive said, was Spencer Collins. He'd been

in suspension for five hundred years; he'd come out of it just a month before. Physically, he said, he was as good a man as ever—fifty-five, and well preserved. He'd paid attention to himself all his life—had eaten right, hadn't gone without sleep, had exercised both mind and body, knew something about psychosomatics.

"I'll say this for your outfit," he told Blaine, "you know how to take care of a sleeper's body. I was a little gaunt when I came out; a little weak; but there'd been no deterioration."

Norman Blaine chuckled. "We're at work at it constantly. I don't know anything about it, of course, but the biology boys are at it all the time—it's a continuing problem with them. A practical problem. During your five hundred years you probably were shifted a dozen times or more—to a better receptacle each time, with improvements in the operation. You got the benefit of the new improvements as soon as we worked them out."

Collins had been a professor of sociology, he said, and he'd evolved a theory. "You'll excuse me if I don't go into what it was."

"Why certainly," said Blaine.

"It's not of too much interest except to the academic mind. I presume you're not an academic mind."

"I suppose I'm not."

"It involved long-term social development," Collins told him. "I figured that five hundred years should show some indication of whether I had been right or wrong. I was curious. It's rough to figure out a thing, then up and die without ever knowing if it comes true or not."

"I can understand."

"If you doubt me in any detail you can check the record."

"I don't doubt a word of it," said Blaine.

"You are used to screwball cases."

"Screwball?"

"Loopy. Crazy."

"I see many screwball cases," Blaine assured him.

But nothing quite so screwball as this, he thought. Nothing quite so crazy as sitting on the patio beneath the autumn stars, on his own home acres, talking to a man five centuries out of time. If he were in Readjustment, of course, he'd be accustomed to it, would not think it strange at all; Readjustment worked continually with cases just like this.

Collins was fascinating. His inflection betrayed the change in the spoken language, and there were those slang words always cropping up—idioms of the past that had somehow missed fire and found no place within the living language, although many others had survived.

At dinner there had been dishes the man had tackled with distrust, others that he'd eaten with disgust showing on his face, yet too polite to refuse them outright—determined, perhaps, to do his best to fit into the culture in which he found himself.

There were certain little mannerisms and affectations that seemed pointless now; performed too often, they could become distinctly irritating. These were actions like stroking his chin when he was thinking, or popping joints by pulling at his fingers. That last one, Blaine told himself, was unnerving and indecent. Perhaps in the past it had not been ill-bred to fiddle with one's body. He'd have to look that one up, he told himself, or maybe ask someone. The boys in Readjustment would know—they'd know a lot of things.

"I wonder if you'd tell me," Blaine asked,—"this theory of yours. Did it work out the way you thought it would?"

"I don't know. You'll agree, perhaps, that I've scarcely been in a position to find out."

"I suppose that's true. But I thought you might have asked."

"I didn't ask," said Collins.

They sat in the evening silence, looking out across the valley.

"You've come a long way in the last five hundred years," Collins finally said. "When I went to sleep, we were speculating on the stars and everyone was saying that the light speed limit had us licked on that. But today . . ."

"I know," said Blaine. "Another five hundred years . . ."

"You could go on forever and forever—sleep a thousand years and see what had happened. Then another . . ."

"It wouldn't be worth it."

"You're telling me," said Collins.

A nighthawk skimmed above the trees and planed into the sky in jerky, fluttering motions, busy catching insects. "That doesn't change," said Collins. "I can remember nighthawks . . ."

He paused, then asked, "What are you going to do with me?"

"You're my guest."

"Until the keepers come."

"We'll talk about it later; you are safe tonight."

"There is one thing you've been wondering about; I've watched it gnawing at you."

"Why you ran away."

"That is it," said Collins.

"Well?"

"I chose a dream," said Collins, "such as you might expect. I asked a professorial retreat—a sort of idealized monastery where I could spend my time in study, where I could live with other men who could talk my language. I wanted peace—a walk along a quiet river, a good sunset, simple food, time for reading and for thinking . . ."

Blaine nodded appreciatively. "A good choice, Collins; there should be more like it."

"I thought so, too," said Collins. "It was what I wanted."

"It proved enjoyable?"

"I wouldn't know."

"Wouldn't know?"

"I never got it."

"But the Dream was fabricated . . ."

"I got a different dream."

"There was some mistake."

"No mistake," said Collins; "I am sure there wasn't."

"When you ask a certain dream," Blaine began, speaking stiffly, but Collins cut him short. "There was no mistake, I tell you. The dream was substituted."

"How could you know that?"

"Because the dream they gave me wasn't one that anyone would ask for. Not even one that ever would be thought of. It was one that was deliberately tailored for some reason I can't figure out. It was a different world."

"An alien world!"

"Not alien; it was Earth, all right—but a different culture. I lived five hundred years in that world, every minute of five hundred years. The dream pattern was not shortened as I understand they often are, telescoping a thousand years of Sleep into a normal lifetime. I got the works, the full five hundred years. I know what the score is when I tell you that it was a deliberately fashioned dream—no mistake at all—but fashioned for a purpose."

"Now let's not rush ahead so fast," protested Blaine. "Let us take it easy. The world had a different culture?"

"It was a world," said Collins, "in which the profit motive had been eliminated, in which the concept of profit never had been thought of. It was the same world that we have, but lacking in all the factors and forces which in our world stem from the profit motive. To me, of course, it was utterly fantastic, but to the natives of the place—if you can call them that—it seemed the normal thing."

He watched Blaine closely. "I think you'll agree," he said, "that no one would want to live in a world like that. No one would ask a Dream like that."

"Some economist, perhaps . . ."

"An economist would know better. And, aside from that, there was a terribly consistent pattern to the dream that no one without prior knowledge could ever figure out to put into a dream."

"Our machine . . ."

"Your machine would have no more prior knowledge than

you yourself. No more, at least, than your best economist. And another thing—that machine is illogical; that's the beauty of it. It needn't think in logic. It shouldn't, because that would spoil the Dream. A Dream should not be logical."

"And yours was logical?"

"Very logical," said Collins. "You can figure out the factors hell to breakfast and you can't tell what will happen until you see a thing in action. That is logic for you."

He rose and walked across the patio, then walked back again, stood facing Blaine. "That's why I ran away. There's something dirty going on; I can't trust that gang of yours."

"I don't know," said Blaine. "I simply do not know."

"I can clear out if you want me to; no need to get yourself messed up in a deal like this. You took me in and fed me, gave me clothes, and you listened to me. I don't know how far I can get, but . . ."

"No," said Blaine, "you're staying here. This is something that needs investigation, and I may need you later on. Keep out of sight. Don't mind the robots. We can trust them; they won't talk."

"If they smell me out," said Collins, "I'll manage to get off your land before they nab me. Caught, I'll keep my mouth shut."

Norman Blaine rose slowly and held out his hand. Collins took it in a swift, sure grip. "It's a deal."

"It's a deal," echoed Blaine.

VII

At night, the Center was a place of ghosts, its deserted corridors ringing with their emptiness. Men worked throughout the building, Blaine knew—the Readjustment force; the Conditioners; the Tank Room gang, but there was no sign of them.

A robot guard stepped out of his embrasure. "Who goes there?"

"Blaine. Norman Blaine."

The robot stood for a second, whirring gently, searching through its memory banks to find the name of Blaine. "Identification," it said.

Blaine held up his identification disk. "Pass, Blaine," the robot said, then tried an amenity. "Working late?"

"Something I forgot," Blaine told it.

He went along the corridor and took the elevator, got out at the sixth.

Another robot stopped him. He identified himself.

"You're on the wrong floor, Blaine."

"New appointment." He showed the robot the form.

"All right, Blaine," it said.

Blaine went along the corridor and found the door to Records. He tried six keys before he hit the right one and the door swung open.

He closed the door behind him and waited until he could see a little before he found the light switch.

There was a front office; off it, a door led into the record stacks. What he sought should be here somewhere, Blaine told himself. Myrt would have finished it hours before—the Jenkins dream of big game hunting in the steaming jungle.

It would not have been filed as yet, might not be filed at all, for Jenkins would be coming in to take the Sleep in just a day or two. Perhaps there was a rack somewhere where the dreams-to-be-called-for were placed against their use.

He walked around a desk and looked about the room. Filing cabinets, more desks, a testing cubicle, a drink and lunch dispenser, and a rack in which were stacked half a dozen reels.

He walked swiftly to the rack and picked up the first reel. He found the Jenkins Dream five reels down and stood with it in his hand, wondering just how insane a man could get.

Collins must be mistaken, or there had been some mistake—or it was all a lie, directed to what purpose he had no idea. It simply couldn't be, Blaine told himself, that a dream would be deliberately substituted.

But he had come this far. Thus far he had made a fool out of himself . . .

He shrugged; he might just as well go all the way now that he was here.

Reel in hand, Norman Blaine walked into the testing cubicle and closed the door behind him. He inserted the reel and set the time at thirty minutes; then he put the cap upon his head and lay down upon the bed. Reaching out, he turned on the mechanism.

There was a faint whirring of the mechanism. Something puffed into his face and the whirr was gone; the cubicle was gone and Blaine stood in a desert, or what seemed to be a desert.

The landscape was red and yellow; there was a sun, and heat rose up from sand and rocks to strike him in the face. He raised his head to stare out at the horizons and saw that they lay far distant, for the land was flat. A lizard ran, squeaking, from the shade of one rock to the shadow of another. Far in the hot silk-blue of the sky a bird was circling.

He saw that he stood upon a road of sorts; it wound across the desert's face until it was lost in the heat-wavers that rose up from the tortured ground. And far off on the road a black speck travelled slowly.

He looked around for shade and there was no shade, nothing big enough to cast a shadow for anything bigger than the scuttling, squeaking lizard.

Blaine lifted his hands and looked at them; they were tanned so deeply, that for a moment, he thought that they were black. He wore a pair of ragged trousers, chewed off between knee and ankle, and a tattered shirt, plastered to his back with sweat. He wore no shoes, and wondered about that until he lifted his feet and saw the horn-like callouses that had grown upon them to protect them from the heat and rocks.

Wondering dimly what he might be doing here, what he had been doing a moment before, what he was supposed to do, Norman Blaine stood and stared off across the desert. There was not a thing to see—just the red and yellow and the sand and heat.

He shuffled his feet in the sand, digging holes with his toes, then smoothing them out again with the flat of his calloused feet. Then the memory of who he was, and what he had meant to do, came seeping slowly back. It came in snatches and in driblets, and a great deal of it did not seem to make much sense.

He had left his home village that morning to travel to a city. There was some important reason why he should make the trip, although for the life of him he could not think of the reason. He had come from thataway and he was going thisaway; he wished that he could at least remember the name of his home village. It would be embarrassing if he met someone who asked him where he hailed from, and he could not tell them. He wished, too, that he could remember the name of the city he was going to, but that didn't matter quite so much. After a time, he'd get there and learn the name.

He started down the road, going thisaway, and he seemed to remember that he had a long way to travel yet. Somehow or other, he'd fooled around and lost a lot of time; it behooved him to get a hustle on if he expected to reach the city before nightfall.

He saw the black dot moving on the road and now it seemed much closer.

He was not afraid of the black dot and that was encouraging, he told himself. But when he tried to figure out why it should be so encouraging, Blaine simply couldn't say.

And because he had wasted a lot of time and had a long way yet to go, he broke into a trot. He legged it down the road as fast as he could go, despite the roughness of the trail and the hotness of the sun. As he ran he slapped his pockets and found that in one of them he carried certain objects. He knew immediately that the objects were of more than ordinary value; in a little while, he'd know what the objects were.

The black dot drew nearer; finally, it was close enough so that Blaine could see it was a large cart with wooden wheels. It was drawn by a fly-blown camel; a man sat upon the seat of the cart, beneath a tattered umbrella that, at one time, might have been colorful but now was leached by the sun to a filthy gray.

He approached the cart, still running, and finally drew abreast of it. The man yelled something at the camel, which stopped.

"You took your time," he said. "Now get up here; get a wiggle on."

"I was detained," said Blaine.

"You were detained," sneered the other man, and thrust the reins at Blaine, jumping off the cart.

Blaine yelled at the camel and slapped him with the reins; he wondered what in hell was going on, and he was back in the cubicle again. His shirt was stuck against his back with perspiration, and he could feel the heat of the desert sun fading from his face.

He lay for a long moment, gathering his wits, reorienting himself. Beside him the reel moved slowly, bunching up the tape against the helmet slot. Blaine reached out a hand and stopped it, slowly spun it backwards to take up the tape.

Then the horror of it dawned upon him, and for a moment he was afraid that he might cry out; but the cry died in his throat and he lay there motionless, frozen with the realization of what had happened.

He swung his feet off the cot and jerked the reel from its holder, stripping the tape out of the helmet. He turned the reel on its side and read the number and the name. The name was Jenkins, and the number was the identifying code he'd punched into the dream machine that very afternoon. There could be no mistake about it. The reel held the Jenkins dream. It was the reel that would be sent down in another day or two, when Jenkins came to take the Sleep.

And Jenkins, who had hankered for a big-game hunting trip, who had wanted to spend the next two hundred years on a shooting orgy, would find himself standing in a red and yellow desert on a track that could be called a road only by the utmost courtesy; in the distance he would see a moving dot, that would turn out later to be a camel and a cart.

He'd find himself in a desert with ragged pants and tattered shirt and with something in his pocket of more than ordinary value—but there would be no jungles and no veldt; there'd be no guns and no safari. There'd be no hunting trip at all.

How many others? Blaine asked himself. *How many others failed to get the dream they wanted?* And what was more: *Why had they failed to get the dream they wanted?*

Why had the dreams been substituted?

Or *had* they been substituted? Had Myrt—

He shook his head at that one. The great machine did what it was told. It took in the symbols and equations and it chattered and it clanked and thundered, and it spun the dream that was asked of it.

Substitution was the only answer, for the dreams were monitored in this very cubicle. No dream went out until someone had checked to see that it was the dream ordered by the Sleeper.

Collins had lived out five hundred years in a world which lacked the profit concept. And the red and yellow desert—what kind of world was that? Norman Blaine had not been there long enough to know; but there was one thing he did know—that, like Collins' world, the Jenkins world was one no one would ask to live in.

The cart had wooden wheels and had been pulled by camel-power; that might mean that it was a world in which the idea of mechanized transportation never had been thought of. But it might, as well, be any one of a thousand other kinds of cultures.

Blaine opened the door of the cubicle and went out. He put the reel back in the rack and stood for a moment in the center of the icy room. After a moment, he realized that it was not the room that was icy, but himself.

This afternoon, when he had talked with Lucinda Silone, Blaine had thought of himself as a dedicated person, had thought of the Center and the guild as a place of dedication. He had talked unctuously of the fact there must be no taint upon the guild, that it must at all times perform its services so as to merit the confidence of anyone who might apply for Sleep.

And where was that dedication now? Where was the public confidence?

How many others had been given substituted dreams? How long had this been going on? Five hundred years ago, Spencer Collins had been given a dream that was not the dream he wanted. So the tampering had been going on five hundred years, at least.

And how many others in the years to come?

Lucinda Silone—what kind of dream would she get? Would it be the mid-nineteenth century plantation or some other place? How many of the dreams that Blaine had helped in fabricating had been changed?

He thought of the girl who had sat across the desk from him that morning—the honey color hair and the blue eyes, the milky whiteness of her skin, the way she talked, the things she had said, and the others that she had not said.

She, too, he thought.

And there was an answer to that. He moved swiftly toward the door.

VIII

He climbed the steps and rang the bell; a voice told him to come in.

Lucinda Silone sat in a chair beside a window. There was only one light—a dim light—in the far corner of the room, so that she sat in shadow. "Oh, it's you," she said. "You do the investigating, too."

"Miss Silone . . ."

"Come in and have a seat. I'm quite willing to answer any questions; you see, I am still convinced . . ."

"Miss Silone," said Blaine, "I came to tell you not to take the Sleep. I came to warn you; I have . . ."

"You fool," she said. "You utter, silly fool."

"But . . ."

"Get out of here," she told him.

"But it's . . ."

She rose out of her chair and there was scorn in every line of her. "So I can't take a chance. Go ahead; tell me it's dangerous. Go on and tell me it's a trick. You fool—I knew all that before I ever came."

"You knew . . ."

They stood for a moment in tense silence, each staring at the other. "And now *you* know." And she said something else he had thought himself not half an hour before: "How about that dedication now?"

"Miss Silone, I came to tell you . . ."

"Don't tell anyone," she said. "Go back home and forget you know it; you'll be more comfortable that way. Not dedicated, maybe, but much more comfortable. And you'll live a good deal longer."

"There is no need to threaten . . ."

"Not a threat, Blaine; just a tip. If word should get to Farris that you know, you could count your life in hours. And I could see that the tip got round to Farris. I know just the way to do it."

"But Farris . . ."

"He's dedicated, too?"

"Well, no, perhaps not. I don't . . ."

The thought was laughable. Paul Farris dedicated!

"When I come back to Center," she said, speaking evenly and calmly, "we'll proceed just as if this had never happened. You'll make it your personal business to see that my Sleep goes through, without a hitch. Because if you don't, word will get to Farris."

"But why is it so important that you take the Sleep, knowing what you do?"

"Maybe I'm Entertainment," she said. "You rule out Entertainment, don't you? You asked me if I was Entertainment and you were very foxy while you were doing it. You fob off Entertainment because you're afraid they'll steal your Dreams for solidiographs. They tried to do it once, and you've been jumpy ever since."

"You're not Entertainment."

"You thought so this morning. Or was that all an act?"

"It was an act," Blaine admitted miserably.

"But this tonight isn't an act," she said coldly, "because you're scared as you've never been before. Well, keep on being scared. You have a right to be."

She stood for a moment, looking at him in disgust. "And now get out."

IX

Philo did not meet him at the gate, but ran out of a clump of shrubbery, barking in high welcome, when he swung the car around the circle drive and stopped before the house. "Down, Philo," Blaine told him. "Down."

He climbed out of the car and Philo moved, quietly now, to stand beside him; in the quietness of the night, he could hear the click of the dog's toenails upon the bluestone walk. The house stood large and dark, although a light burned beside the door. He wondered how it was that houses and trees always seemed larger in the night, as if with the coming of the dark they took on new dimensions.

A stone crunched underneath a footstep and he swung around. Harriet stood on the path. "I was waiting for you," she said. "I thought you'd never come. Philo and I were waiting, and . . ."

"You gave me a start," he told her. "I thought that you were working."

She moved swiftly forward and the light from the entrance lamp fell across her face. She was wearing a low-cut dress that sparkled in the light, and a sparkling veil was flung across her head so that it seemed she was surrounded by a thousand twinkling stars. "There was someone here," she told him.

"Someone . . ."

"I drove up the back way. There was a car out front, and Philo was barking. I saw three of them come out the door, dragging a fourth. He was fighting and struggling, but they hurried him along and pushed him in the car. Philo was nipping at them, but they paid him no attention, they were in such a hurry. I thought at first it might be you, but then I saw it wasn't. The three were dressed like goons and I was a little frightened. I sped up and drove past and tore out on the highway, as fast as I could go, and . . ."

"Now, wait a minute," Blaine cautioned. "You're going too fast; take your time and tell me . . ."

"Then, later, I drove back, without my lights, and parked the car at my place. I came across the woods and I've been waiting for you."

She paused, breathless with her rush of words.

He reached out, put his fingers underneath her chin, tipped up her face and kissed her.

She brushed his hand away. "At a time like this," she said.

"Any time, at all."

"Norm, are you in trouble? Is someone after you?"

"There may be several who are after me."

"And you stand around and slobber over me."

"I just happened to think," he said, "of what I have to do."

"What do you have to do?"

"Go see Farris. He invited me; I forgot until just now."

"But you forget. I said goons . . ."

"They weren't goons. They were dressed to look like goons."

For now, suddenly, Norman Blaine saw it as a single unit with a single purpose—saw at last the network of intrigue and of purpose that he had sought since that morning.

First, there had been the Buttonholer who had collared him; then Lucinda Silone who had wished a dream of dignity and peace; and after that, Lew Giesey, dead behind his battered desk—and finally the man who had spent five hundred years in a culture that had not discovered profit.

"But Farris . . ."

"Paul Farris is a friend of mine."

"He is no one's friend."

"Just like that," said Blaine, thrusting out two fingers, pressed very close together.

"I'd be careful just the same."

"Since this afternoon, Farris and I are conspiratorial pals. We are in a deal together; Giesey died . . ."

"I know. What has that to do with this sudden friendship?"

"Before he died, Giesey put an appointment through. I'm moving up to Records."

"Oh, Norm. I'm so glad!"

"I had hoped you'd be."

"Then what is it all about?" she asked. "Tell me what is going on. Who was that man the goons dragged out of here?"

"I told you—they weren't goons."

"Who was the man. Don't try to duck the question."

"An escapee. A man who ran away from Center."

"And you were helping him."

"Well, no . . ."

"Norm, why should anyone want to escape from Center? Have you got folks locked up?"

"This one was an awakened suspendee . . ."

He knew he'd said too much, but it was too late. He saw the glint in her eyes—the look he'd grown to know. "It's not a story," he said. "If you use this . . ."

"That's what you think."

"This was in confidence."

"Nothing's in confidence; you can't talk to News in confidence."

"You'd just be guessing."

"You'd better tell me now," she said. "I can find out, anyhow."

"That old gag!"

"You may as well go ahead and tell me. It'll save me a lot of trouble, and you'll know I have it straight."

"Not another word."

"All right, smart guy," she said.

She stood on tiptoe, kissed him swiftly, then ducked away.

"Harriet!" he cried, but she had stepped back into the shadow of the shrubbery and was gone. He took a quick step forward, then halted. There was no use going after her. He could never find or catch her, for she knew the gardens and the woods that stretched between their houses full as well as he did.

Now he'd let himself in for it. By morning, the story would be in the papers.

He knew that Harriet had meant exactly what she said. Damn

the woman. Fanatical, he told himself. Why couldn't she see things in their right perspective? Her loyalty to Communications was utterly fantastic.

And yet it was no more so than Norman Blaine's to Dreams. What had the commentator said when he'd been driving home? The unions were building up their strength, and it was this very fanatic loyalty—his to Dreams, Harriet's to Communications—which was the basis of that growing strength.

He stood in the puddle of light before the door and shivered at the thought of the story with 96-point headlines screaming from Page One.

Not a breath of scandal, he had said that afternoon. For Dreams was built on public confidence; any hint of scandal would bring it tumbling down. And here was scandal—or something that could be made to sound very much like scandal.

There were two things he could do. He could try to stop Harriet—how, he did not know. Or he could unmask this intrigue for what it really was—a plot to eliminate Dreams in the struggle for power, a move in that Central Labor struggle about which the commentator had held forth so pontifically.

Now Blaine was sure that he knew how it all tied up, was sure that he could trace the major plot-lines that ran through these fantastic happenings. But if he meant to prove what he suspected, he didn't have much time. Harriet was already off on a hunt for the facts of which he'd given her a hint. Perhaps she'd not have them for the morning editions, but by evening the story would be broken.

And before that happened, Dreams must have its story to combat the flying rumors.

There was one fact he had to verify. A man should know his history, Blaine told himself. It should not be a thing to be looked up in books, but carried in one's head, a ready tool for use.

Lucinda Silone had said she was Education and she would have told the truth. That was something which could be checked, one of the facts that would be checked automatically. Spencer

Collins was Education, too. A professor of sociology, he had said, who had evolved a theory.

There was something in the history of the guilds concerning Dreams and Education, something about a connection that had once existed between them—and it might apply.

He went swiftly up the walk and through the hall, trudging down the hall to the study, with Philo following after. He thumbed up the switch and went quickly to the shelves. He ran a finger along a row of books until he found the one he wanted.

At the desk, he turned on the lamp and ran quickly through the pages. He found what he wanted—the fact he'd known was there, read long ago and forgotten, dimmed out by the years of never being needed.

X

Farris' house was surrounded by a great metallic wall, too high to jump, too smooth to climb. A guard was posted at the gate and another at the door.

The first guard frisked Blaine; the second demanded identification. When he was satisfied, he called a robot to take the visitor to Farris.

Paul Farris had been drinking. The bottle on the table beside his chair was better than half empty. "You took your time in coming," he growled.

"I got busy."

"Doing what, my friend?"

Farris pointed at the bottle. "Help yourself. There are glasses in the rack."

Blaine poured out liquor until the glass was almost full. He said casually, "Giesey was murdered, wasn't he?"

The liquor in Farris' glass slopped slightly, but there was no other sign. "The verdict was suicide."

"There was a glass on the desk," said Blaine. "He'd just had a drink out of the carafe; there was poison in the water."

"Why don't you tell me something I don't know?"

"And you're covering up for someone."

"Could be," Farris said. "Could be, too, it's none of your damn business."

"I was just thinking. Education . . ."

"What's that!"

"Education has been carrying a knife for us for a long time now. I looked up the history of it. Dreams started as a branch of Education, a technique for learning while you were asleep. But we got too big for them, and we got some new ideas—a thousand years ago. So we broke away, and . . ."

"Now, wait a minute; say that slow, again."

"I have a theory."

"You have a head, too, Blaine. A good imagination. That's what I said this afternoon; you think standing."

Farris lifted his glass and emptied it in a single gulp. "We'll stick the knife into them," he said, dispassionately. "Clear up to their gizzard."

Still dispassionately, he hurled the glass against the wall. It exploded into dust. "Why the hell couldn't someone have thought of that to start with? It would have made it simple . . . Sit down, Blaine. I think we got it made."

Blaine sat down and suddenly was sick—sick at the realization that he had been wrong. It was not Education which had engineered the murder. It had been Paul Farris—Farris and how many others? For no one man—even with the organization the goon leader had at his command—could have worked on a thing like this alone.

"One thing I want to know," said Farris. "How did you get that appointment? You didn't get it the way you said; you weren't meant to get it."

"I found it on the floor; it fell off Giesey's desk."

There was no need of lying any longer, of lying or pretending. There was no further need of anything; the old pride and loyalty were gone. Even as Norman Blaine thought about it, the bitterness sank deeper into his soul; the futility of all the years was a torture grate that rasped across raw flesh.

Farris chuckled. "You're all right," he said. "You could have kept your mouth shut and made it stick. It takes guts to do a thing like that. We can work together."

"It still is sticking," Blaine told him sharply. "Take it away from me if you think you can."

This was sheer bravado and bitterness, a feeble hitting back, and Blaine wondered why he did it, for the job meant nothing now.

"Take it easy," Farris said. "You're keeping it. I'm glad it worked out as it did. I didn't think you had it in you, Blaine; I guess that I misjudged you."

He reached for the bottle. "Hand me another glass."

Blaine handed him another glass and Farris filled both. "How much do you know?"

Blaine shook his head. "Not too much. This business of the dream substitution . . ."

"You hit it on the head," said Farris; "that's the core of it. We'd had to fill you in before too long, so I might as well fill you in right now."

He settled back comfortably in his chair. "It started long ago, and it has been carried on with tight security for more than seven hundred years. It had to be a long-range project, you understand, for few dreams last less than a hundred years and many last much longer. At first, the work was carried on slowly and very cautiously; in those days, the men in charge had to feel their way along. But in the last few hundred years it has been safe to speed it up. We've worked through the greater part of the program first laid out, and are taking care of some of the supplementary angles that have been added since. Less than another hundred years and we will be ready—we could be ready any time, but we'd like to wait another hundred years. We have worked up techniques from what we've already done that are plain impossible to believe. But they'll work; we have firsthand evidence that they are workable."

Blaine was cold inside, cold with the shock of disillusion.

"All the years," he said.

Farris laughed. "You're right. All the years. And all the others thought that we were lily pure. We were at pains to make them think we were; such quiet people. We were quiet from the very start, while the others bunched their muscles, shouted. One by one they learned the lesson we had known from the very first—that you keep your mouth shut, that you do not show your strength. You wait until the proper time."

"The others learned, eventually. They took their lessons hard, but they finally learned the facts of politics—too late. Even before there was a Central Union, Dreams saw what was coming and planned. We sat quietly in the corner and kept our hands neatly folded in our laps; we bowed our heads a little and kept our eyes half closed—a pose of utter meekness. Most of the time, the others didn't even know that we were around. We are so small and quiet, you see. Everyone is watching Communications or Transportation or Food or Fabrication, because they are the big boys. But they should be watching Dreams, for Dreams is the one that has it."

"Just one thing," said Blaine. "Two things, maybe. How do you know the substitute dreams run true? All the genuine ones we make are pure fantasy; they couldn't really happen the way we fabricate them."

"That," Farris told him, "is the one thing that has us on the ropes. When we can explain that one, we'll have everything. Back at the beginning there were experiments. Dreams tried it out on their own personnel—ones who volunteered, for short periods, five years or ten. And the dreams didn't come out the way they were put in.

"When you give a dream a logical basis, instead of wish-fulfillment factors, it follows the lines of logic. When you juggle cultural factors, the patterns run true—well, maybe not true, but different than you thought they would. When you feed in illogic, you get a jumble of illogic; but when you feed in logic, the logic takes over and it shapes the dream. Our study of logic dreams leads us to believe that they follow lines of true development. Unforeseen trends show up, governed by laws and circumstances we could not have guessed—and those trends work out to logical conclusions."

There was fear in the man—a fear that must have lain deep in the minds of many men throughout seven hundred years. "Is it just pretend? Or do those dreams actually exist? Are there such other worlds somewhere? And if they are, do we create them? Or do we merely tap them?"

"How do you know about the dreams?" asked Blaine. "The Sleepers wouldn't tell you; if they did, you couldn't believe . . ."

Farris laughed. "That's the easy part. We have a two-way helmet. A feed-in to establish the pattern and to set up the factors, a sort of introduction to set the dream going. It operates for a brief period, then cuts out and the dream is on its own. But we have a feed-back built into the helmet, and the dream is put on tape. We study it as it comes in; we don't have to wait. We have stacks of tape. We have at our fingertips the billions of factors that go into many thousand different cultures. We have a history of the never-was, and of the might-have-been, and perhaps the yet-to-come."

Dreams is the one that has it, he had said. They had stacks of tape from seven hundred years of dreams. They had millions of man-hours experience—first-hand experience—in cultural patterns that had never happened. Some of them could not have happened; others of them might have come within a hair-breadth of happening—and there were many of them, perhaps, that could be made to happen.

From those tapes they had learned lessons outside the curriculum of human experience. Economics, politics, sociology, philosophy, psychology—in all facets of human effort they held all the trumps. They could pull out economic dazzlers to blind the people; they could employ political theory that would be sure to win hands down; they had psychological tricks that would stop all the other unions dead.

They'd played dumb for years sitting meekly in the corner, hands folded in their lap, being very quiet. And all the time they had been fashioning a weapon for use at its proper time.

And the dedication, Blaine thought, the human dedication. The pride and comfort of a job well done. The warmth of accomplishment and service—the close human fellowship.

For years the tapes had rolled, recording the feed-back, while men and women—who had come in trusting confidence to seek fairylands of their imagination—plodded drearily through logic dreams that were utterly fantastic.

Farris' voice had gone on and on and now it came back to him.

" . . . Giesey was going soft on us. He wanted to replace Roemer with someone who would see it his way. And he picked you, Blaine—of all men, he picked you."

He laughed again, uproariously. "It does beat hell how mistaken one can be."

"Yes, it does," agreed Blaine.

"So we had to kill him before the appointment could go through; but you beat us to it, Blaine. You're a fast man on your feet. How did you know about it? How did you know what to do?"

"Never mind."

"The timing," said Farris. "The timing was perfect."

"You've got it all doped out."

Farris nodded. "I talked to Andrews. He'll go along; he doesn't like it, of course, but there's nothing he can do."

"You're taking a long chance, Farris, telling me all this."

"Not a chance; you are one of us. You can't get out of it. If you say a word, you wreck the guild—and you won't have a chance to say a word. From this moment, Blaine, there's a gun against your back; there'll be someone watching all the time.

"Don't try to do it, Blaine; I like you. I like the way you operate. That Education angle is pure genius. You play along with us, and it'll be worth your while. There's nothing you *can* do but play along with us; you're in it, clear up to your chin. As the head of Records, you have custody of all the evidence, and you can't write off that fact . . . Go on, man; finish up that drink."

"I'd forgotten it," said Blaine.

He flicked the glass and the liquor splashed out, into Farris' face. As if it were the same motion, Blaine's fingers left the glass, let it drop, and reached for the liquor bottle.

Paul Farris came to his feet, blinded, hands clawing at his face. Blaine rose with him, bottle arcing, and his aim was good. The bottle crashed on the goon leader's skull and the man went down upon the carpeting, with snakes of blood oozing through his hair.

For a second Norman Blaine stood there. The room and the man upon the floor suddenly were bright and sharp, each feature of the place and the shape upon the carpeting burning themselves into his consciousness. He lifted his hand and saw that he still grasped the bottle's neck with its jagged, broken edges. He hurled it from him and ran, hunched against the expected bullet, straight toward the window. He leaped and rolled himself into a ball even as he leaped, arms wrapped around his face. He crashed into the glass, heard the faint *ping* of its explosion, and then was through and falling.

He lit on the gravel path and rolled until thick shrubbery stopped him, then crawled swiftly toward the wall. But the wall was smooth, he remembered—not one to be climbed. Smooth and high and with only one gate. They would hunt him down and kill him. They'd shake him out like a rabbit in a brushpile. He didn't have a chance.

He didn't have a gun and he'd not been trained to fight. All that he could do was hide and run; even so, he couldn't get away, for there wasn't much to hide in and there wasn't far to run. *But I'm glad I did it,* he told himself.

It was a blow against the shame of seven hundred years, a reassertion of the old, dead dedication. The blow should have been struck long ago; it was useless now, except as a symbol that only Norman Blaine would know.

He wondered how much such symbolism might count in this world around him.

Blaine heard them running now, and shouting; he knew it would not be long. He huddled in the bushes and tried to plan what he should do, but everywhere he ran into blank walls and there was nothing he could do.

A voice hissed at him, a whisper from the wall. Blaine started, pressing himself further back into the clump of bushes.

"Psst, " said the voice once again.

A trick, he thought, wildly. *A trick to lure me out.* Then he saw the rope, dangling from the wall, where it was lighted by the broken window.

"Psst," said the voice.

Blaine took the chance. He leaped from the bushes and across the path toward the wall. The rope was real and was anchored. Spurred by desperation, Blaine went up it like a monkey, flung out an arm across the top of the wall and hauled himself upward. A gun cracked angrily; a bullet hit the wall and ricocheted, wailing, out into the night.

Without thinking of the danger, he hurled himself off the wall. He struck hard ground that drove the breath from him and he doubled up with agony, retching, gasping to regain his breath, while stars wheeled with tortuous deliberation in the center of his brain.

He felt hands lifting him and carrying him and heard the slamming of a door, then the flow of speed as a car howled through the night.

XI

A face was talking to him and Norman Blaine tried to place it; he knew that he'd seen it once before. But he couldn't recognize it; he shut his eyes, tried to find soft, cool blackness. The blackness was not soft, but harsh and painful; he opened his eyes again.

The face still was talking to him and it had shoved itself up close to him. He felt the fine spray of the other's saliva fly against his face. Once before, when a man had talked to Blaine, this had happened. That morning at the parking lot a man had buttonholed him. And here he was again, with his face thrust close and the words pouring out of him.

"Cut it out, Joe," said another voice. "He's still half out. You hit him too hard; he can't understand you."

And Blaine knew that voice too. He put out his hand, pushed the face away, and hauled himself to a sitting position, with a rough wall against his back.

"Hello, Collins," he said to the second voice. "How did you get here?"

"I was brought," said Collins.

"So I heard."

Blaine wondered where he was: An old cellar, apparently—a fit place for conspirators. "Friends of yours?" he asked.

"It turns out that they are."

The face of the Buttonholer popped up once again.

"Keep him away from me," said Blaine.

Another voice told Joe to get away. And he knew that voice, too. Joe's face left.

Blaine put up his arm and wiped his own face. "Next," he said, "I'll find Farris here."

"Farris is dead," said Collins.

"I didn't think you had the guts," said Lucinda Silone.

He turned his head against the roughness of the wall and he saw them now, standing to one side of him—Collins and Lucinda and Joe and two others that he did not know.

"He won't laugh again," said Blaine. "I smashed the laugh off him."

"Dead men never laugh," said Joe.

"I didn't hit him very hard."

"Hard enough."

"How do you know?"

"We made sure," said Lucinda.

He remembered her from the morning, sitting across the desk from him, and the calmness of her. She still was calm. She was one, Blaine thought, who could make sure—very sure—that a man was dead.

It would not have been too hard to do. Blaine had been seen going over the wall and there would have been a chase. While the guard poured out after him it would have been a fairly simple matter to slip into the house and make entirely certain that Farris was dead.

He reached up a hand and felt the lump on his head, back of the ear. They had made certain of him, too, he thought—certain that he would not wake too soon and that he'd make no trouble. He stumbled to his feet and stood shakily, putting out a hand against the wall to support himself.

He looked at Lucinda. "Education," he said, and he looked at Collins and said, "You too."

And he looked at the rest of them, from one to another. "And you?" he asked. "Every one of you?"

"Education has known It for a long time," Lucinda told him. "For a century or more. We've been working on you; and this time, my friend, we have Dreams nailed down."

"A conspiracy," said Blaine, grim laughter in his throat. "A wonderful combination—Education and conspiracy. And the Buttonholers. Oh, God, don't tell me the Buttonholers!"

She held her chin just a little tilted and her shoulders were straight. "Yes, the Buttonholers, too."

"Now," Blaine told her, "I've heard everything." He flicked a questioning thumb at Collins.

"A man," said the girl, "who took a Dream before we ever knew; who took you at the outward value that you give yourselves. We got to him . . ."

"Got to him!"

"Certainly. You don't think that we're without—well, you might call them representatives, at Center."

"Spies."

"All right; call them spies."

"And I—where do I work in? Or did I just stumble in the way?"

"You in the way? Never! You were so conscientious, dear. So smug and self-satisfied, so idealistic."

So he'd not been entirely wrong, then. It *had* been an Education plot—except that the plot had run headlong into a Center intrigue and he'd been caught squarely in the middle. And oh, the beauty of it, he thought—the utter, fouled-up beauty of it! You couldn't have worked a tangled mass like this up intentionally if you'd spent a lifetime at it.

"I told you, pal," said Collins, "that there was something wrong. That the dream was made to order for a certain purpose."

Purpose, Blaine thought. The purpose of collecting data from hypothetical civilizations, from imaginary cultures, of having first-hand knowledge as to what would happen under many possible conditions; to collect and co-ordinate that data and pick from it the factors that could be grafted onto the present culture; to go about the construction of a culture in a cold-blooded, scientific manner, as a carpenter might set out to build a hen-coop. And the lumber and the nails used in that hen-coop culture would have been fabricated from the stuff of dreams dreamt by reluctant dreamers.

And the purpose of Education in exposing the plot? Politics, perhaps. For the union which could unmask such duplicity would gain much in the way of public admiration, would thus be strengthened for the coming showdown. Or perhaps the purpose might be more idealistic, honestly motivated by a desire to thwart a scheme which would most surely put one union in unquestioned domination of all the rest of them.

"Now what?" Blaine asked.

"They want me to bring a complaint," said Collins.

"And you are going to do it."

"I suppose I shall."

"But why you? Why now? There were others with substituted dreams; you were not the first. Education must have sleepers planted by the hundreds."

He looked at the girl. "You applied," he said; "you tried to plant yourself."

"Did I?" she asked.

And had she? Or had her application been aimed at him—for now it was clear that he had been selected as one weak link in Dreams. How many other weak links, now and in the past, had Education used? Had her application been a way to contact him, a means of applying some oblique pressure to make him do a thing that Education might want someone like him to do?

"We are using Collins," said Lucinda, "because he is the first independent grade A specimen we have found, who is untainted with the brush of Education espionage. We used our own sleepers to build up the evidence, but we could not produce in court evidence collected by admitted spies. But Collins is clean; he took the sleep before we even suspected what was going on."

"He is not the first; there have been others. Why haven't you used them?"

"They were not available."

"Not . . ."

"Dreams could tell what happened. Perhaps you might know what happened to them, Mr. Blaine."

He shook his head. "But why am I here? You certainly don't expect me to testify. What made you grab me off?"

"We saved your neck," said Collins; "you keep forgetting that."

"You may leave," Lucinda told him, "any time you wish."

"Except," Joe said, "you are a hunted man. The goons are looking for you."

"If I were you," said Collins, "I do believe I'd stay."

They thought they had him. He could see they thought so— had him tied and haltered, had him in a corner where he would have to do anything they said. A cold, hard anger grew inside of him—that anyone should think so easily to trap a man of Dreams and bend him to their will.

Norman Blaine took a slow step forward, away from the wall, and stood unsupported in the dim-lit cellar. "Which way out?" he asked.

"Up those steps," said Collins.

"Can you make it?" Lucinda asked.

"I can make it."

He walked unsteadily toward the stairs, but each step seemed to be a little surer and he knew he'd make it, up the stairs and out into the coolness of the night. Suddenly he yearned for the first breath of the cool, night air, to be out of this dank hole that smelled of dark conspiracy.

He turned and faced them, where they stood like big-eyed ghosts against the cellar wall. "Thanks for everything," he said.

He stood there for another instant, looking back at them. "For *everything,*" he repeated.

Then he turned and climbed the stairs.

XII

The night was dark, though dawn could not be far off. The moon had set, but the stars burned like steady lamps and a furtive dawn-wind had come up to skitter down the street.

He was in a little village, Blaine saw—one of the many shopping centers scattered across the countryside, with its myriad shop fronts and their glowing night lights.

He walked away from the cellar opening, lilting his head so the wind could blow against it. The air was clean and fresh after the dankness of the cellar; he gulped in great breaths of it, and it seemed to clear his head of fog and put new strength into his legs.

The street was empty; he trudged along it, wondering what he should do next. Obviously, he had to do something. The move was up to him. He couldn't be found, come morning, still wandering the streets of this shopping center.

He must find some place to hide from the hunting goons!

But there was no way in which he could hide from them. They'd be relentless in their search for Blaine. He had killed their leader—or had seemed to kill him—and that was a precedent they could not allow to go unpunished.

There'd be no public hue or outcry, for the Farris killing could not be advertised; but that would not mean the search would be carried on with any less ferocity. Even now they would be hunting for him, even now they would have covered all his likely haunts and contacts. He could not go home, or to Harriet's home, or to any of the other places—

Harriet's home!

Harriet was not home; she was off somewhere, tracking down a story that he must somehow stop. There was a greater factor here than his personal safety. There was the honor and the integrity of the Dream guild; if any of its honor and integrity were left.

But there was, Norman Blaine told himself. It still was left in the thousands of workers, and in the departmental heads who had never heard of substituted dreams. The basic purpose of the guild still remained what it had been for a thousand years, so far as the great majority of its members were concerned. To them the flame of service, the pride and comfort of that service, and the dedication to it burned as bright and clear as it ever had.

But not for long; not for many hours. The first headline in a paper, the first breath of whispered scandal, and the bright, clear light of purpose would be a smoky flare, glaring redly in the murk of shame.

There was a way—there had to be a way—to stop it. There must be a way in which the Dream guild could be saved. And if there were a way, he must be the one to find it; of them all, Blaine was the only one who knew the imminence of dishonor.

The first step was to get hold of Harriet, to talk with her, to make her see the right and wrong.

The goons were hunting for him, but they would be on their own; they could not enlist the help of any other union. It should be safe to phone.

Far up the street, he saw a phone booth sign and he headed there, hurrying along, his footsteps ringing sharply in the morning chill.

He dialed the number of Harriet's office.

No, the voice said, she wasn't there. No, he had no idea. Should he have her call back if she happened to come in.

"Never mind," said Blaine.

He called another number.

"We're closed," a voice told him; "there's no one here at all."

He called another and there was no answer.

Another. "There ain't no one here, mister. We closed up hours ago. It's almost morning now."

She wasn't at her office; she wasn't at her favorite night spots.

Home, perhaps?

He hesitated for a moment, then decided it wasn't safe to call her there. The goons, in defiance of all Communications regulations, would have her home line tapped, and his home line as well.

There was that little place out by the lake where they'd gone one afternoon. *Just a chance,* he told himself.

He looked up the number, dialed it. "Sure she's here," said the man who answered.

He waited.

"Hello, Norm," she said, and he could sense the panic in her voice, the little quick catch in her breath.

"I have to talk with you."

"No," she said. "No. What do you mean by calling? You can't talk with me. The goons are hunting you . . ."

"I've got to talk to you; that story . . ."

"I've got the story, Norm."

"But you have to listen to me. The story's wrong. It's not the way you have it; that's not the way it was at all."

"You better get away, Norm. The goons are everywhere . . ."

"Damn the goons," he said.

"Goodbye, Norm," she said; "I hope you get away."

The line was dead.

He sat stunned, staring at the phone.

I hope you get away. Goodbye, Norm. I hope you get away.

She had been frightened when he'd called. She wouldn't listen; she was sorry, now, that she had ever known him—a man disgraced, a killer, hunted by the goons.

She had the story, she had told him; and that was all that mattered. A story wormed out of the whispered word, out of a gin and tonic or a Scotch and soda. The old, wise story garnered from many confidences, from knowing the right people, from having many pipelines.

"Ugly," he said.

So she had the story and would write it soon and it would be splashed in garish lettering for the world to read.

There must be a way to stop it—there had to be a way to stop it.

There was a way to stop it!

He shut his eyes and shivered, suddenly cold with the horror. "No, no," he said.

But it was the only answer. Blaine got up, groped his way out of the booth, and stood in the loneliness of the empty sidewalk, with the splashes of light thrown across the concrete from the many shop fronts with the first dawn wind stirring in the sky above the roofs.

A car came creeping down the street, with its lights off, and he did not see it until it was almost opposite him. The driver stuck out his head. "Ride, mister?"

He jumped, startled by the car and the voice. His muscles bunched but there was no place to go, no place to duck, nowhere to hide. They had him cold, he knew. He wondered why they didn't shoot.

The back door popped open. "Get in here," said Lucinda Silone. "Don't stand and argue. Get in, you crazy fool."

He moved swiftly, leaped into the car and slammed the door.

"I couldn't leave you out there naked," said the girl. "The way you are, the goons would have you before the sun was up."

"I have to go to Center," Blaine told her. "Can you take me there?"

"Of all the places . . ."

"I have to go," he said; "if you won't take me . . ."

"We can take you."

"We can't take him and you know it," said the driver.

"Joe, the man wants to go to Center."

"It's a stupid business," said Joe. "What does he want to go to Center for? We can hide him out. We . . ."

"They won't be looking for me there," said Blaine. "That's the last place in the world they'd expect to find me."

"You can't get in . . ."

"I can get him in," Lucinda said.

XIII

They came around a curve and were confronted by the road block. There was no time to stop, no room to turn around and flee. "Get down!" yelled Joe.

The motor howled in sudden fury at an accelerator jammed tight against the boards. Blaine reached out an arm and pulled Lucinda to him, hurling both of them off the seat and to the floor.

Metal screamed and grated as the car slammed into the block. Out of the corner of his eye, Norman Blaine saw timber go hurtling past the window. Something else smashed into a window and they were sprayed with glass.

The car bucked and slewed, then was through. One tire was flat, thumping and pounding on the pavement.

Blaine reached up a hand and grasped the back of the seat. He hauled himself up, pulling Lucinda with him.

The hood of the machine, sprung loose, canted upward, blocking out the driver's vision of the road. The metal of the hood was twisted and battered, flapping in the wind. "Can't hold it long," Joe grunted, fighting the wheel.

He turned his head, a swift glance back at them, then swung it back again. Half of Joe's face, Blaine saw, was covered with blood from a cut across the temple.

A shell exploded off to one side of them. Flying, jagged metal slammed into the careening car.

Hand mortars—and the next one would be closer!

"Jump!" yelled Joe.

Blaine hesitated, and a swift thought flashed in his mind. He couldn't jump; he couldn't leave this man alone—this Buttonholer by the name of Joe. He had to stick with him. After all, this was his fight much more than it was Joe's.

Lucinda's fingers bit into his arm. "The door!"

"But Joe . . ."

"The door!" she screamed at him.

Another shell exploded, in front of the car and slightly to one side. Blaine's hand found the button of the door and pressed. The door snapped open, retracting back into the body. He hurled himself at the opening.

His shoulder slammed into concrete and he skidded along it; then the concrete ended, and he fell into nothingness. He landed in water and thick mud and fought his way up out of it, sputtering and coughing, dripping slime and muck.

His head buzzed madly and there was a dull ache in his neck. One shoulder, where he'd hit and skidded on the concrete, seemed to be on fire. He smelled the acrid odor of the muck, the mustiness of decaying vegetation, and the wind that blew down the roadside ditch was so cold it made him shiver.

Far up the road, another shell exploded, and in the flash of light he saw metallic objects flying out into the dark. Then a column of flame flared up and burned, like a lighted torch.

There went the car, he thought.

And there went Joe as well—the little man who'd waylaid him in the parking lot that morning, a little Buttonholer for whom he'd felt anger and disgust. But a man who'd died, who had been willing to die, for something that was bigger than himself.

Blaine floundered up the ditch, stooping low to keep in the cover of the reeds that grew along its edges. "Lucinda!"

There was a floundering in the water ahead. He wondered briefly at the thankfulness of relief that welled up inside of him.

She had made it, then; she was safe, here in the ditch— although to be in the ditch was only temporary safety. They might have been seen by the watching goons. They had to get away, as swiftly as they could.

The flare of the burning car was dying down and the ditch was darker now. He floundered ahead, trying to be as quiet as possible.

She was waiting for him, crouched against the bank. "All right?" he whispered and she nodded at him, her face making the quick motion in the darkness.

She lifted an arm and pointed; there, seen through the tight-growing reeds of the marsh beyond the ditch, was Center, a great building that towered against the first light of morning in the eastern sky. "We're almost there," she told him softly.

She led the way slowly along the ditch and off into the marsh, following a watery runway that ran through the thick cover of sedges and rushes. "You know where you are going?"

"Just follow me," she told him.

He wondered vaguely how many others might have followed this hidden path across the marsh—how many times she herself might have followed it. Although it was hard to think of her as she was now, dirty with muck and slime, wading through the water. Behind them they still could hear the shouts of the squad of goons that had been stationed at the block.

The goons had gone all out, he thought, setting up a block on a public highway. Someone could get into a lot of trouble for a stunt like that.

He'd told Lucinda that the goons would never dream of his going back to Center. But he had been wrong; apparently they had expected he'd try to make it back to Center. And they'd been set and waiting for him. Why?

Lucinda had halted in front of the mouth of a three-foot drain pipe, emerging from the bank just above the waterway. A tiny trickle of water ran out of it and dripped into the swamp. "How are you at crawling?"

"I can do anything," he told her.

"It's a long ways."

He glanced up at the massive Center which, from where he stood, seemed to rise out of the marsh. "All the way?"

"All the way," she said.

She lifted a muddy hand and brushed back a strand of hair, leaving a streak of mud across her face. He grinned at the sight of her—sodden and bedraggled, no longer the cool, unruffled creature who had sat across the desk from him. "If you laugh out loud," she said, "I swear I'll smack you one."

She braced her elbows on the lip of the pipe and hauled herself upward, wriggling into the pipe. She gained the pipe and went forward on hands and knees.

Blaine followed. "You know your way around," he whispered, the pipe catching up the whisper and magnifying it, bouncing it back and forth in an eerie echo.

"We had to, we fought a vicious enemy."

They crawled and crept in silence, then, for what seemed half of eternity. "Here," said Lucinda. "Careful."

She reached back a hand and guided him forward in the darkness. A glow of feeble light came from a break in the side of the pipe, where a chunk of the tile had been broken or had fallen out. "Tight squeeze," she told him.

He watched her wriggle through and drop from sight.

Blaine followed cautiously. A broken spear of the tile bit into his back and ripped his shirt, but he forced his body through and dropped.

They stood in a dim-lit corridor. The air smelled foul and old; the stones dripped with dampness. They came to stairs and climbed them, went along another corridor for a ways, then climbed again.

Then, suddenly, there were no dripping stones and dankness, but a familiar hall of marble, with the first-floor murals shining on the walls above the gleaming bronze of elevator doors.

There were robots in the hall; suddenly, the robots all were looking at them and starting to walk toward them.

Lucinda backed against the wall.

Blaine grabbed at her wrist.

"Quick," he said. "Back the way . . ."

"Blaine," said one of the advancing robots. "Wait a minute, Blaine."

He swung around and waited. All the robots stopped. "We've been waiting for you," said the robot spokesman. "We were sure you'd make it."

Blaine jerked at Lucinda's wrist. "Wait," she whispered. "There's something going on here."

"Roemer said you would come back," the robot said. "He said that you would try."

"Roemer? What has Roemer got to do with it?"

"We are with you," said the robot. "We threw out all the goons. Please allow me, sir."

The doors of the nearest elevator were slowly sliding back.

"Let's go along," Lucinda said. "It sounds all right to me."

They stepped into the elevator, with the robot spokesman following.

The car shot up and stopped. The door opened and they stepped out, between two solid lines of robots, flanking their path from the elevator to the door marked Records.

A man stood in the door, a great foursquare, dark-haired man whom Norman Blaine had seen before on a few occasions. A man who had written: *If you should want to see me later, I am at your service.*

"I heard about it, Blaine," said Roemer. "I hoped you'd try to make it back; I figured you were that kind of man."

Blaine stared back at him haggardly. "I'm glad you think so, Roemer. Five minutes from now . . ."

"It had to be someone," said Roemer. "Don't think about it too much. It simply had to come."

Blaine walked on leaden feet between the file of robots, brushed past Roemer at the door.

The phone was on the desk and Norman Blaine lowered himself into the chair before it. Slowly he reached out his hand.

No! No! There must be another way. There must be another, better way to beat them—Harriet with her story; and the goons who were hunting him; and the plot with its roots reaching back through seven hundred years. Now he could make it stick—with Roemer and the robots he could make it stick. When he'd first thought of it, he had not been sure he could. His only thought then, he remembered, had been to get back to Center somehow, to get into this office and try to hold the place long enough, so he could not be stopped from doing what he meant to do.

He had expected to die here, behind some desk or chair, with a goon bullet in his body, and a shattered door through which the goons had finally burst their way.

There had to be another way—but there was no other way. There was only one way—the bitter fruit of seven hundred years of sitting quietly in the corner, with hands folded in one's lap, and poison in one's brain. He lifted the receiver out of the cradle and held it there, looking across the desk at Roemer.

"How did you do it?" he asked. "These robots? Why did you do it, John?"

"Giesey's dead," said Roemer; "so is Farris. No one has been appointed to their posts. Chain of command, my friend. Business agent, Protection, Records—you're the big boss now; you've been the head of Dreams since the moment Farris died."

"Oh, my God," said Blaine.

"The robots are loyal," Roemer went on. "Not to any man; not to any one department. They are conditioned to be loyal to Dreams. And you, my friend, are Dreams. For how long, I don't know; but at the moment you are Dreams."

They stared at one another for a long moment.

"The authority is yours," said Roemer; "go ahead and make your call."

So that was why, Blaine thought, *the goons assumed I would return.* That was why they'd set up the road block, not on one road only, perhaps, but on all of them—so that he could not get back and take over before someone could be named.

I should have thought of it, he told himself. *I knew it. I thought of it this very afternoon, how I was third in line—*

The operator was saying: "Number, please. Number, please. What number do you wish, please."

Blaine gave the number and waited.

Lucinda had laughed at him and said: "You are a dedicated man." Perhaps not those words exactly but that had been what she meant. Mocking him with his dedication; prodding him to see what he would do. A dedicated man, she'd said. And now, here finally, was the price of dedication.

"News" said a voice. "This is Central News."

"I have a story for you."

"Who is speaking, please?"

"Norman Blaine. I am Blaine, of Dreams."

"Blaine?" A pause. "You said your name was Blaine?"

"That's right."

"We have a story here," said Central News, "from one of our branches. We've been checking it. We held it up, in fact, to check it . . ."

"Put me on transcription. I want you to get this right; I don't want to be misquoted."

"You're on transcription sir."

"Then here you are . . ."

Then here you are.

Here is the end of it—

"Go ahead, Blaine."

Blaine said, "Here it is, then. For seven hundred years, the

Dreams guild has been carrying out a series of experiments aimed at the study of parallel cultures . . ."

"That is what the story we have says, sir; you are sure that that is right?"

"You disbelieve it?"

"No, but . . ."

"It's true. We've worked on it for seven hundred years—under strict security because of certain continuing situations which made it seem unwise to say anything about it . . ."

"The story I have here . . ."

"Forget the story that you have!" Blaine shouted. "I don't know what it's all about; I called you up to tell you that we're giving it away. Do you understand that? *We're giving it away.* Within the next few days, we plan to make all our data available to a commission we'll ask to be set up. Its membership will be chosen from the various unions, to assess the data and decide where use may best be made of it."

"Blaine. Wait a minute, Blaine."

Roemer reached out for the phone. "Let me finish it; you're beat out. Take it easy now. I will handle it."

He lifted the receiver, smiling. "They'll want your authority, and all the rest of it."

He smiled again. "This was what Giesey wanted, Blaine. That's why Farris made him fire me; that's why Farris killed him . . ."

Roemer spoke into the phone. "Hello, sir. Blaine had to leave; I'll fill in the rest . . ."

The rest? There wasn't any more. Couldn't they understand? He'd made it very simple.

Dreams was giving up its one last chance at greatness. It was all Dreams had, and Norman Blaine had given it away. He had beaten Harriet and Farris and the hunting goons, but it was a bitter, empty victory.

It saved the pride of Dreams; and that was all it saved.

Something—some thought, some impulse, made him lift his head, almost as if someone had called to him from across the room.

Lucinda stood beside the door, looking at him, with a gentle smile upon her mud-streaked face, and her eyes were deep and soft. "Can't you hear them cheering?" she asked. "Can't you hear the whole world cheering you? It's been a long time, Norman Blaine, since the whole world cheered together!"

BARB WIRE BRINGS BULLETS!

Clifford D. Simak sent a story named "Blood Buys Barb Wire" to Charles Tilden in late May 1945, and it appeared, under a new title, in the November 1945 issue of Ace-High Western Stories, *where it was the lead story. I particularly like this tale because it evokes the feelings of being always outdoors, of living in the wind and, often, in the rain.*

And it's the only traditional western tale I've ever seen that contains the word robot, no doubt a slip-up on Cliff's part. . . .

—dww

Chapter One
Fighting Odds—Three to One

Charley Cornish read trouble in the grim faces of the trio as they came slowly towards him. Bracing his back against the bar, he knew the thing he'd fought against had come, the thing he'd run a race with time against had happened. Here was the fate of Anderson out on the Yellowstone and the end of Melvin in the Bighorn foothills—the thing that had whisked those two into an eternity of silence was walking toward him in the tramping boots and the hard, set faces. Steve knew this was the showdown.

And just when he was on the verge of sending in an order that would make old man Jacobs' eyes pop out of the dried-up skull that was his face.

Cornish's eyes flicked swiftly to one side, saw the bottle standing on the bar. He knew that he could reach it with one swift motion if need be. But he hoped he wouldn't be forced to such action.

The three stopped in front of him and stood silently, menacing shapes looming in the saloon's twilight shadow, and behind him Cornish heard the wheezing breath of Steve, the bartender.

The tall, raw-boned giant in front was Titus, foreman of the Tumbling K.

And the scowling man must be Squint Douglas, who went everywhere with Titus. But the third man, with the flaming mop of red hair writhing from beneath his pushed back hat, was a total stranger.

"You're Cornish?" asked Titus.

Cornish nodded.

"You sell barb wire?" asked Titus.

Cornish forced a grin upon his lips. "You gents in the market? No better wire to be had anywhere."

Titus interrupted him. "We don't like barb wire," he said.

"Now," said Cornish, smoothly, "that's a matter of opinion. Boys over on Cottonwood creek figure it is just the thing."

"I told you," snarled Titus, "that we don't like no kind of wire."

Cornish sucked in his breath. "Well, gents, that's just too bad!"

His hand shot out for the bottle as Titus took the first step forward, swung it high above his head as Titus took the second. It whistled in the air as the angular foreman closed in on him, struck as groping fingers touched his shirt, struck and exploded with a dull, thudding sound, spraying broken glass and a spume of whiskey.

Titus slumped against Cornish's knees, then slid to the floor.

Squint Douglas was coming in, a charging bull, with his face twisted into a mask of mingled anger and surprise. Behind him was the red-haired man, open mouth bawling something that failed to penetrate the roaring thunder of excitement that surged through Cornish's mind.

Squint's fist was a black ball aiming at his face and almost unconsciously Cornish swung up with his right hand to fend it off—a hand still clutching the broken whiskey bottle. Squint screamed as the jagged glass scraped across his face. He staggered backward blood streaming down his beard.

Cornish hurled the broken bottle at the red-haired man. The bottle slammed against the wall and smashed like a hundred tinkling bells all ringing at once.

Cornish picked up a chair and waited. Squint was crawling along the floor, whimpering. Blood ran down his beard and ripped onto the sawdust. The red-haired man was fumbling at his belt, fumbling in haste, his eyes smoky with fear and hatred.

"Give it here," snapped a voice and Cornish flicked his eyes toward the bar.

Steve, the bartender, leaned across it and in his hand he held a heavy six-gun that pointed straight at the red-haired man.

"Toss it to me," said Steve, "and take it easy when you do it. You hombres can wrestle around all that you've a mind to, but it just ain't fair to be using guns."

The red-haired man growled at him. "Keep out of this, Steve."

"The hell I will," said Steve. "Three to one is bad enough without dragging out your irons."

Cornish poised the chair, watching the man's gun slide out, watching the cunning fox look that slid across his face.

Slowly the gun came out, rasping on the leather, inch by inch. Then the man's arm jerked swiftly and Cornish stepped toward him, with the chair above his head. The gun exploded in a coughing gush of flame and the chair was coming down. It smashed and splintered against the flesh and bone beneath it. One leg came off and spun along the floor, kicking up a spray of sawdust. A rung came loose and clattered to the boards.

Cornish stepped back, with the wreckage of the chair dangling in his hands. The red-haired man reeled to his feet, stood unsteadily, rocking on his heels. Cornish stepped in, swung the chair again. The man dropped like a pole-axed ox.

Cornish stopped, picked up the gun and tossed it across the bar to Steve.

Squint clawed his way erect beside the bar, stood clinging to it with one hand, while he wiped the blood out of his eyes with the other.

"Why the hell," demanded Steve, "don't you go ahead and finish off the dirty coyotes? They came in asking for it."

Cornish shook his head.

"Guess they had enough."

But even as he spoke, he saw Squint's hand streaking for the holster, saw the glint of metal flashing in the light.

Cornish flung the battered chair with all his might, then lunged to one side. The gun roared and a window crashed with a muted sound as the bullet smashed the glass.

The chair slammed into Squint and staggered him, sent him reeling back along the bar. Cornish dived, arms looping for the legs of the reeling man. One arm missed, but the other caught and he hugged the legs against his chest, carried the yelling Squint to the floor with him.

Quickly Cornish sprang to his feet. He saw his antagonist rising in front of him. Blued steel flashed in a vicious arc and Cornish ducked, caught the blow of the smashing six-gun on his shoulder, swung his right with the hunched power of a pivoting heel behind it. His fist scraped Squint's elbow, angled down against the ribs, skidded across them, slammed into the stomach. He heard the whoosh of the breath going out of the man before him.

Cornish leaned against the bar, gasping for breath.

The doorway, he saw, was crowded with watching faces, while others peered through the windows, men pushing one another to get a better look. News of the fight in the Longhorn bar apparently had spread rapidly through the little town of Silver Bow.

Titus had crawled against the bar and propped himself against it. The red-haired man lay still in the center of the room.

Squatted on top of the bar, Steve was talking to Titus.

"Make one move for that gun, Titus, and I'll put one through your brisket."

The bartender blew fiercely through his nostrils.

"This fight," he announced to the crowd, "has been fair so far and I'm plumb set on seeing that it keeps on being fair."

Cornish pushed himself away from the bar, picked up another chair, spoke to Squint Douglas.

"I don't just fight for fun," he said. "Don't fight often, but when I do, I fight for keeps. What's your pleasure, Squint?"

Squint stared sourly at him, dabbing at his bloody beard.

He didn't answer Cornish, spoke to Titus instead. "Let's get going, Jim."

Slowly Titus heaved himself erect, stooped to pick up his hat. He socked it on his head and tottered to the door.

"Maybe," suggested Steve, "some of you gents would get Red out of here. He clutters up the place."

Two volunteers came in, lifted the unconscious man and carried him out. The others streamed into the saloon.

Steve hopped off the bar, stood back of it.

"Drinks are on the house," he said.

Slowly, Cornish swung around, walked to a card table in the back of the room, sat down on a chair. Suddenly he felt tired.

The thing that he feared had come and he'd won the first round, but this, he knew, was no more than a mere beginning. After this the Tumbling K would be out for blood. The trio who had walked in the door a while ago had meant to rough him up, to scare him out of town. Next time they would play for keeps.

Maybe Anderson out in the Yellowstone country had won the first round, too. But Anderson had disappeared. Back in Jacobs' office, there was little doubt as to what had finally happened.

Most of the crowd had drifted away—only a few had gone up to the bar. Even one on the house had been no attraction when staying there and drinking might have been construed as approval of what had happened to the three men from the Tumbling K.

Got the town in the hollow of their hand, thought Cornish bitterly. One big cow outfit rules the whole damn country. Even those nesters out on the Cottonwood had been scared to death. It had taken some fast talking to make them even admit that they wanted barb wire.

One man came slowly from the bar, drink in hand, crossed the room and stood in front of Cornish's table.

"You don't scare easy, son," he said.

"Hell, no," said Cornish, shortly. "There were only three of them."

The man turned around and went back to the bar.

One by one they drifted away and the room was empty.

Steve came out from behind the bar and sat down across from Cornish.

"You stuck out your neck," said Cornish. "You shouldn't have done that, using the gun on them."

Steven laughed a little bitterly.

"I'm sick of the job, anyhow," he said. "Time to be moving on."

He drummed his fingers along the table.

"First time anyone stood up to the Tumbling K," he said. "First time anyone ever pushed them around a little. They won't like it, Charley. They'll come loaded for bear next time. You better buckle on a gun."

Cornish shook his head. "My job is selling wire," he said.

"Not fighting. Besides, I won't be around long. The nesters are having a meeting tonight at Russell's."

"To decide whether they'll buy the wire or not?"

"That's the idea. And they better buy it, or they won't be here next year. Without the wire, the Tumbling K will push their stock down into the valley and every nester will be starved out."

The bartender shook his head. "There'll be fresh blood on the wire," he said slowly.

Cornish got up, walked to the bar and came back with a bottle and two glasses.

"Feel like I need that one on the house," he said.

"I shouldn't have offered it to them," Steve declared, moodily. "Look at the ones that turned it down. Spooked of their own shadows, that's what's the matter with them. The Tumbling K gang has run this town too long. Every one of them jumps ten feet high whenever Titus snaps the whip."

"Titus just the foreman, ain't he?"

"That's everything he is," said Steve. "Fellow by the name of Armstrong, Cornelius Armstrong, owns the spread. Ain't here except a week or two each summer. Lives somewhere in the east."

"Titus just as good as owns it, then, so far as running it is concerned."

Steve gulped his drink and nodded. "That's the way it is, Charley. And he'd cut his own grandma's throat if it put ten dollars in his pocket."

Cornish downed his own drink and got up.

"I owe you for one chair," he said.

"Ah, forget it," snapped Steve.

He twirled the glass in his hand, considering. "It was worth a chair," he decided, "to see them three bullies get the hell beat out of them."

Chapter Two
Hanging by Moonlight

The campfire glowed brightly in the dusk, a speck that stood out like a too-low star in the gentle swells of the heaving prairie.

Cornish saw it first when he was a mile or two away, lost it when the trail dipped down into a swale. And he wondered who would be building a campfire out there when town was so close and darkness was just falling.

The dusk was deeper and the fire glowed brighter when he topped the next swell, and riding across the level land, he saw the canted top of the small covered wagon that stood beside the fire— the covered wagon with the canvas gleaming rosy-white in the reflection of the leaping flames, the scraggy shape of two old crow-baits grazing at their picket pins, the hunched, black figure of a man with a tattered hat bending over the frying pan and coffee pot.

The man hailed him as he drew opposite the fire. Cornish swung the horse off the trail, trotted it toward the wagon.

The man straightened up beside the fire and Cornish saw that he was as much a crowbait as the horses. His clothes were little more than rags that hung about his scrawny frame, his hat was something that any other man would have thrown away many years before. The haggardness of his face showed through the ragged, unkempt beard that hung almost to his chest.

"Good evening," said Cornish.

"The peace of the Lord be on you," the scarecrow replied.

Startled, Cornish sat in the saddle, staring at the man.

"A preacher?" he asked.

"That's right, my friend. I carry the Word to strange corners of the earth."

"Nothing strange about this corner of the earth," protested Cornish.

"Any place that has not heard the Word is strange," the old man told him. "This Silver Bow, now, it has no church?"

Cornish shook his head. "I don't believe it has. Five saloons, but not a single church."

"And no man of God?"

"That's right," said Cornish. "Not a single preacher."

"Then," declared the scarecrow, "it is the place for me."

"What denomination?" asked Cornish.

The old man made a gesture that was almost contempt. "I just heard the call and went. I said to myself, if old Joe Wicks can do anything that will please the Lord, he'll bust a gut a-trying."

Loco, thought Cornish. Loco as a pet coon.

"And you, my friend," the old man asked. "What might be your calling?"

"Me?" said Cornish. "I'm just a barb wire salesman."

"You'll be riding back this way?"

Cornish nodded.

"Going to a meeting down in Cottonwood valley. Make me or break me."

"Wonder would you do something for me," asked the preacher.

"If I can, I will," said Cornish.

"Keep an eye peeled for a little bucket, will you? Must of bounced out of the wagon. Looked all over and I can't find it. Used it to cook my oatmeal in."

"Sure will."

"Wouldn't want to step down and have a cup of coffee?"

"Can't stop," said Cornish.

He reined the horse around. Back on the trail, he looked behind him, saw the ragged old man standing outlined against the fire, with one arm raised in farewell.

Cornish kept watch for the bucket that had fallen from the wagon, but his thoughts were on other thing, were running along the trail ahead of him to the meeting down at Russell's cabin, where the nesters of Cottonwood valley would decide whether or not they would buy the wire to fence in their valley against the ranging herds of the Tumbling K.

Swiftly Cornish ran over in his mind the men he could depend on. Billings and Hobbs and probably Goodman. Russell was for it, but not as enthusiastic as he might be. Old Bert Hays was against it because he said it would only stir up trouble with the Tumbling K. And a lot of the men would listen to what Bert had to say.

Molly might have helped, but she wouldn't listen to him, Cornish thought. She had a way with Bert. Orneriest man in the whole dang valley, his neighbors said of Bert, but that gal of his'n can twist him around her finger.

Selling wire was tough work—and dangerous, at least out here where the big cattle outfits regarded wire as the devil's doings, looked upon it as something that barred the way to watering places, cut off pasturage they had called their own by the right of usage. Wire was the thing that would doom free range and the cattlemen weren't having any of it when they could do anything about it.

Sometimes they did unpleasant things, thought Cornish. Unpleasant things had happened to Anderson and Melvin. And not only them alone, but other barb wire men who had run up against the antagonism of the cattle barons.

The horse trotted down a slope and Cornish heard the sound of trickling water—a little unnamed stream that ran into the Cottonwood five miles or so below.

The trail leveled off and ran beside the stream. Bunches of cottonwoods loomed up, their bushy tops black against the stars. The horse's hoofs clopped through the trail dust with a muffled, drumming thud. On the hills above a coyote yapped and far off an owl chuckled over some quiet joke.

A dark shape moved beside a cottonwood and Cornish pulled the horse to a halt, half swung across the trail.

"Make a move," said a voice from the shadow, "and I'll plug you sure as hell."

For a moment dark panic swirled inside Cornish's brain, then smoothed out. No use of running. No use of trying to fight back, for he had no gun. Just wait and see what happened.

Horses moved from beneath the cottonwood and blocked the trail. Metal gleamed in the starlight and the men were black shapes watching him.

"Going to a meeting?" one of them asked and Cornish, remembering the voice back in the saloon, recognizing the angular shadow that sat upon the horse, knew that it was Titus. The other two riders sat silently.

Titus chuckled viciously. "There ain't going to be no meeting, Cornish."

"Nice of you," said Cornish, "to ride out and tell me."

"You're too damn smart," snarled Titus. "We'll take that out of you."

"With a rope," said one of the other men as he moved behind Cornish and forced his hands behind his back.

"Steady," snapped Titus. "Stay right where you are."

His gun made a threatening motion.

The ropes bit into Cornish's wrists, bit and burned with the savage strength of the man who pulled them tight and tied them.

"Titus," said Cornish, half in a whisper.

"Yes," said Titus, "but it won't do you any good to squall. We're going to haul you up and leave you hanging there. You can crawl all you want to and it won't help you none."

Cornish fought for calmness, made his tongue move in a mouth that suddenly was dry as cotton.

"You can hang me," he said, "and a dozen others like me, Titus, but you won't stop the wire. It's coming, sure as God made green apples, it's coming out into this country to hold your cows where they belong. It's going to mark the land that's yours and the land that's the other fellow's and when it comes guns won't be worth a damn against it."

A harsh, biting loop was flung out of the darkness behind him, brushed his face and settled on his shoulders.

"You talk too much," rasped Titus savagely.

The rope jerked tight and for a single instant Cornish felt the blind rush of overwhelming fear. His muscles tensed and his feet moved swiftly, but the gun that Titus held jammed itself into his belly and he stopped, stood rigid—rigid with a night-born terror talking in the wind-rustling of the cottonwood above him, in the murmur of the creek that hurried down its stream bed.

He clamped his teeth and felt the muscles of his jaws go stiff. He wouldn't talk, he wouldn't beg or whine. That was what these men wanted—a show before they hanged him. A little laughter before they strung him up.

The rope jerked tight again for an instant, eased up for a second and then tightened into a steady pull that was tugging at his body. They had thrown the rope over the lowest limb of the cottonwood, he knew, and were holding it taut.

A voice asked. "Shall we let 'er rip?"

Titus holstered his gun. "Swing him up," he said.

The rope tightened with a savage yank and Cornish tried to cry out as a band of fire burned around his throat, as his neck and shoulder muscles screamed with wrenching pain—but his tongue was leaden and there was no breath to yell with and the world was spinning in a giddy dance of stars and tree tops.

His unbound feet danced on empty air and he strained for an instant to tear his hands free of the rope that held them, his body twitching and quivering, mind fighting against the strangling black mist that rolled in from the stars. His lungs burned and his mouth gulped air that could not reach the lungs.

The mists of darkness rolled in wispily and clung to him and seeped into his mind, so that his thoughts were dull and he knew that his body was twirling slowly on the rope that held it off the ground.

The stars blinked out and the wind in the cottonwood was a roaring sound that thundered in his brain—a roaring sound that suddenly was staccato, like a series of explosions.

The ground came up and hit him and the rope loosened about his neck and his starving lungs drew in great gulps of air. Slobbering, whimpering, dazed, he crawled along the ground, hitching himself along like a twisting snake, one thought only in his mind—to get away from the tree that had held the rope.

The moaning of the wind in the cottonwoods came back and his eyes came open. He flopped over on his back and saw the stars burning in the sky, burning with an impish, flickering light that made a glittering dance.

A footstep crunched nearby and he tried to crawl, but he was too tired.

A voice said: "Where are you, Charley? Where the hell have you gone to?"

Cornish sat bolt upright and croaked, his battered throat refusing to form words.

The man moved through the night, scuffing through the grass, his figure looming darkly.

"Steve!" croaked Cornish.

The bartender knelt down, loosened the rope, flung it over Cornish's head.

"Nicked one of the dirty sons," he said, "but they got away."

"That was you shooting, then," squeaked Cornish. "Heard something that sounded like shots just before they dropped me."

Steve's knife sawed through the ropes that bound Cornish's hands.

"Yeah," said Steve, "I quit the job. Figured I might as well. Tumbling K boys would be out after my hide for what I done this afternoon."

Cornish massaged his throat, trying to work out the burn and fever where the rope had been.

"Manage it down to the creek?" asked Steve. "Drink of water would do you good."

"Got to get down to the Cottonwood," said Cornish. "Something's happened down there. Titus said there wasn't going to be a meeting."

"Seems you should have had enough for one night," protested Steve, "without asking for any more."

"They got me sore," Cornish explained. "They tried to rough me up and they tried to hang me. Now there're trying to mess up my wire deal."

"O.K.," agreed Steve. "O.K., I'll let you have my horse to get down there and lend you a gun. And you use that gun—don't hold back a minute if you get backed into a tight."

Cornish rose shakily to his feet. "Guess you're right, Steve. About time to start using a gun."

He headed for the creek. "I'll get that drink," he said.

The bartender's horse was waiting when he came back to the trail.

"Here's the gun," said Steve. "Buckle it around you and keep it handy."

"Guess I owe you some thanks," said Cornish.

"Not a one," protested Steve. "Glad of the fun. Figured I'd better trail along behind you just to sort of check up. Them human rattlers out at the Tumbling K are liable to do most anything. Can't trust them for a minute."

Cornish swung into the saddle, headed down the trail. His throat still burned with a throbbing ache and it was a torture to turn his head. His brain still buzzed with a keening pain and his mouth was dry as the bitter dust that lay along the trail.

But within him a rage was growing—a cold and twisted rage against the Tumbling K, against Titus, against the old system of free range that said a man could keep all the land he could seize and hold.

Once wire fenced in the valley of the Cottonwood, the Tumbling K would be barred from the pasture and the water its herds had used for more than twenty years. Used by custom rather than by right, by six-gun power rather than by legal status.

The nesters hadn't bothered them so much at first, for the punchers still threw the herds down into the valley despite the scattered cabins, bluffing their way in and out with the six-guns they packed. But the wire would make if different. Wire was a definite thing, a deadline, a sign of legal possession—something that marked off one man's land from another man's.

The trail broke free of the shaggy hills, came out into the wide valley of the Cottonwood, forked north and south. Cornish took the south fork.

A mile beyond he drew up before the huddled group of buildings that belonged to old Bert Hays. The place was silent and lightless.

A dog came tearing out of the barn, barking savagely. It reached Cornish's horse and circled it, yapping viciously.

The cabin door slammed open and a man with a rifle stepped out—a man barefooted and clad only in his underwear.

"Hello, Bert," yelled Cornish to make himself heard above the barking of the dog.

The gun muzzle, trained at his head, never wavered.

"So it's you," spat Hays. "Come down to raise some more hell in the valley."

"Come down to see what happened," declared Cornish. "Understand the meeting was called off."

Hays yelled at the dog. "Shut up! Shut up before I take a club to you!"

The dog fell silent, trotted off, tail between its legs, sat down to watch from a safe distance.

Hays spat into the dust. "Yeah, it was called off."

"Called off by the Tumbling K," said Cornish.

"Don't matter who called it off," the nester bellowed. "None of your damn business who called it off. It's been called off. We don't want no wire. That's all you need to know."

Cornish leaned forward in his saddle. "They bluffed you out.

They threatened you and you folded up. Every last one of you put your tail between your legs and crawled."

The old man hauled back the hammer of the rifle. "Cornish," he warned, "I've shot men for less than that."

"You should have started on the Tumbling K," said Cornish.

"All you care about is selling wire," yelled Hays. "You don't care what happens after that. You don't care how many men get shot across that wire after you have sold it."

"They sent three men to run me out of town this afternoon," said Cornish, hotly, "and I ran them out instead. They just tried hanging me and that didn't work either. You're not the only one taking the risk in this deal of ours."

"We're the ones that got to go on living here," yelled Hays. "We're the ones that have to protect that wire after it is up. We decided we'd rather live at peace without no wire."

"Live at peace!" Cornish shouted. "Man, don't you know there'll never be any peace along the Cottonwood until you call the Tumbling K—call them and make it stick. As long as you have the grass and water that they want, wire or no wire, you'll never have any peace. You're going to have to fight and you may as well fight over wire as anything else."

"Get out of here," screamed Hays. "Get out of here before I put a bullet in you!"

A swift figure stepped from the cabin door, reached out a hand, wrenched the rifle away from Hays with one quick motion.

Cornish lifted his hat. "Good evening, Miss Hays," he said.

Her face was a white blur in the starlight, but he could tell from the poise of her body, the tilt of her head, that she was angry.

Her words bit like the swift lash of a snarling whip.

"I'm ashamed of you," she said. "Ashamed of the both of you. Two grown men, standing here, yelling at one another like two alley cats."

"I'm sorry, miss," said Cornish.

"By God, I'm not," Hays bellowed. "He can't come riding in in the middle of the night and tell me my own business. He can't make me buy his fence if I don't want to buy it. He don't care a hang about what happens after the fence is sold . . ."

"Father," yelled Molly Hays. "Father you be still!"

The old man suddenly fell silent. The dog sat watching, ears cocked forward.

"You better go," Molly said to Cornish. "All the others feel the same way my father does. The only way to keep the peace along the Cottonwood is to get along without your wire."

"Jim Titus decided that for you," Cornish told her, bitterly.

Her chin lifted. "It doesn't matter, Mr. Cornish, how we decided it."

There was, he saw, no more to say, nothing more to do.

He lifted his hat again.

"Good evening," he said and swung the horse away, riding toward the trail.

Chapter Three
You've Got to Shoot to Live!

The campfire beside the covered wagon of the traveling preacher was a beacon in the night and Cornish pushed his horse toward it, for the first time realizing that he was ravenously hungry, utterly fagged and filled with a thousand aches and pains.

Pulling up his horse, he wearily got down from the saddle. There were two men sitting in front of the blaze. One of them got up and walked toward him. It was Steve, the bartender.

"How did it go?" asked Steve.

Cornish shook his head. "The whole mess is in the fire. The

Tumbling K has the nesters scared silly. They wouldn't touch any wire with a ten foot pole."

To his nostrils came the aroma of cooking coffee; he saw the battered, blackened pot keeping warm beside the coals. Joe Wicks was already slicing bacon into a pan.

"We sort of sat up for you," Steve explained. "We figured you'd be coming back this way."

"I wondered where you were," said Cornish.

"Saw the fire when I went past the first time," said Steve. "So when you took my horse I just hustled back here. Good a place to wait as any."

Wearily, Cornish sat down before the fire.

"Find my bucket?" asked Joe Wicks.

Cornish shook his head. "Not a sign of it."

He stared into the fire, felt the cold night wind blowing on his back.

Licked, he thought. Licked before I hardly got a start. Tumbling K just waited to see if I could get the nesters interested and then they gummed up the works. Didn't want to mess around none unless it seemed I was getting somewhere. But I didn't have a chance. Not even from the start.

"The only way," he mumbled, "to sell barb wire in this man's country is to lick the Tumbling K."

"You made a good start this afternoon," said Steve from across the fire.

"Sure, I know," said Cornish, bitterly. "I licked three of them in a rough and tumble brawl and no one was more surprised than I was. But it's more than that—a lot more than that."

"I returned," declared Joe Wicks solemnly, *"and saw under the sun, that the race is not to the swift, nor the battle to the strong, neither yet bread to the wise . . ."*

"That's the Bible," explained Steve. "He spouts it all the time, chapter and verse. Never heard the beat of it."

The bacon sputtered in the pan and in the darkness one of the horses pawed the ground. The wind fluttered the canvas top of the wagon, making a noise like beating wings.

Cornish nodded, feeling the warmth of the fire in front of him, smelling the bacon in the pan, hearing the rustle of the wind that walked among the grasses.

"Like her crisp or tender?" asked Joe Wicks.

Cornish did not answer. Both men stared at him. His head hung and his arms drooped across his knees.

"Sound asleep," said Steve.

"Better get him laid out," said Wicks, "before he pitches head first into the fire."

Steve got up, stretched and yawned.

"Look, parson, wouldn't have any drinking liquor around, would you? I left in such a hurry that I didn't bring none."

Wicks hesitated. "Carry a bottle of the stuff," he finally admitted. "Awfully good for snake bites."

"A snake just bit me," Steve told him.

Wicks' beard split with a grin. "Danged if I didn't forget," he said. "One bit me just a while back, too."

Drumming hoofs pounding along the trail jerked Cornish from the blankets. Sitting upright beside the now-cold fire, he saw the rider tearing down toward him, bent low on the horse's neck, urging the animal along with kicking heels and slapping reins.

He rubbed his eyes astonished at what he saw. For the rider was a woman. Her hair was flying in the wind and the gathered up dress fluttered behind her.

"Molly!" he shouted. "Molly, what's wrong?"

He threw off the blankets and scrambled to his feet. The horse shied and the girl pulled up.

On the opposite side of the fire, Steve and Joe Wicks were sitting, rubbing their eyes.

"My father!" screamed Molly Hays. "They shot my father!"

She would have started up again, but Cornish strode out into the trail and seized the horse's bridle.

"Take it easy, Molly," he said. "Tell me what happened. Who was it that shot your father?"

She had been crying, for her face was tear-streaked, and she was ready to cry again.

"It was the Tumbling K," she said. "They drove in a herd this morning—a big herd. Right across our wheat field. My father went out to stop them and they . . . and they . . ."

She swayed in the saddle and Cornish put out an arm to catch her, but she did not fall.

"Where is your father now?"

"I got him to the house, then I rode to get the doctor. That's where I'm going now."

A voice spoke behind Cornish, the cracked voice of Joe Wicks. "Look, miss, you're in no shape to go riding into town. Why don't you let one of us do it?"

"We could take you back to the place," said Steve. "Maybe your father will need you."

She looked at them for a long minute, then slowly nodded.

"Perhaps that's best," she said.

"Cornish will ride into town," said Steve. "Joe and me will take you back."

Cornish held out his arms and she slid into them. He let her gently to the ground and for a moment, swaying, she clung to him. Then she straightened.

Cornish seized the reins, vaulted to the saddle, hesitated for a moment.

"That bunch of cattle?" he asked. "Where are they headed?"

She stared at him for a moment, almost uncomprehending, then she spoke.

"Straight up the valley, heading for the other places."

Cornish's face stiffened into grim lines.

"It's the showdown, then," he said, tersely. "It's the Tumbling

K's ace card. They're moving in. That herd will wipe out every-thing in the entire valley and if the nesters try to stop it, they'll be wiped out, too!"

He swung on the bartender. "Take Miss Hays back, Steve, quick as you can. Then hustle back to town with the wagon. I got an idea . . ."

Cornish kicked the horse into motion, went storming down the trail for Silver Bow.

With Doc Moore started on his way toward the Hays place, Cor-nish rode to the town's lone hotel.

The street was quiet, almost deserted. A dog sitting in front of the Longhorn bar snapped lazily at flies. The black plume of smoke from a train that had left the station a few minutes before still trailed across the sky.

At the hotel desk a man with a gray hat and expensively cut suit was pounding on the floor with a gold-headed cane.

His voice, high and querulous, rang through the lobby.

"It's an outrage. No bath. Why don't you people get up to date out here? I've been on a long and dusty train ride and I want a bath. Not an hour from now. Right now!"

"I'm sorry, Mr. Armstrong," whined the clerk. "I'll have some water heated right away, but it will take a while. Half an hour at least."

"Don't people ever bathe out here?" snapped the man.

The clerk didn't answer and the man went on: "There was no one to meet me at the station. Fine state of affairs. And they knew I was coming, too. Did you see any of them around?"

"Titus and some of the other boys were in yesterday," the clerk told him, "but I haven't seen a sign of them today."

The man turned away from the desk. Cornish stepped for-ward.

"I'll carry Mr. Armstrong's bags," he offered. "I was going up, anyhow."

Armstrong turned to face him and Cornish noted the pinched, squeezed face of a New England businessman. Lips thin and colorless, eyes the drab color of gray slate.

"Er—thank you, sir," Armstrong said.

"Not at all," said Cornish. "Glad to help you. What room, Jake?"

"Seventeen," said the desk man, tossing him the key.

Cornish led the way up the flight of stairs, set down the bags and opened the door, then carried the bags inside.

Armstrong fumbled in his pocket. "Perhaps you'd have a drink on me?"

Cornish shook his head.

"Not a drink, Armstrong. Just a talk."

Armstrong's eyebrows went up and the colorless lips pulled straighter.

"I can't imagine . . ."

"You own the Tumbling K," said Cornish.

"Yes, I do."

"Know what's going on?"

Armstrong's face tightened, went a shade more chalky.

"Look here, young man. I don't know what you're driving at . . ."

"Murder," said Cornish, tightly. "Or it will be before the thing is finished. Titus is driving a herd up the Cottonwood. Not across it, or into it, but straight up it."

"The Cottonwood," said Armstrong. "Let's see—that's where the nesters are."

"So you knew about the nesters."

"Naturally. Titus keeps me well informed."

"And you knew what Titus planned to do?"

"Scarcely what he planned to do. I intimated to him that he could feel free to take whatever action he thought prudent."

"I suppose it's prudent to destroy the crops of all those people who are trying to make homes in the valley. Destroy their crops and kill any of them that try to make a fight."

Armstrong flicked a dust spot from his sleeve.

"Frankly, I would say we'd be doing them a favor. This isn't farming land, it's range land. Farmers would starve to death. A good year now and then, maybe, but not often enough to make both ends meet. They've been brought here by the false idea that they can make a living. It's the government that's to blame, really, for opening up the land."

His eyes narrowed until they were gray slits. "I can't imagine, young man, why you should be so interested. Are you one of these—er—nesters?"

Cornish laughed shortly. "No. I sell barb wire."

Armstrong stiffened. "Barb wire!"

"I see you've heard about me, too," said Cornish. "Did you advise Titus to proceed prudently with me?"

Armstrong pounded the floor angrily with his cane.

"I've never seen much impudence!" he shouted.

"Mister," said Cornish, "you ain't seen nothing yet. If you figure you're coming out here to ramrod this war . . ."

"I don't know anything about a war," Armstrong shouted at him. "I always come out here every summer, for at least a week or two."

"O.K.," snapped Cornish. "O.K., if that's the way you want it, but let me tell you something. Your men are messing up a deal of mine. I've spent a lot of time selling wire to those nesters out there and I'm not letting you and your Tumbling K ruin all the work I've done . . ."

A step sounded in the corridor outside and Cornish spun around to face the door.

Squint Douglas stood just inside the room, feet spread, hand poised above his gun.

"So," he said, and the drawn out word was a challenge and a shout of triumph.

Cornish jerked back his hand until his fingers touched the grip of the Colt that Steve had loaned him.

For a long moment the two men stood facing one another, each unmoving, eyes narrowed against the light, waiting for the slightest move to send them into action.

"All right, Squint," said Cornish. "Go ahead and make your play."

Squint stood as if rooted to the floor, like a man suddenly stricken into stone.

"You're just a yellow rat," Cornish snarled. "Yellow to the core. You'd hang me when I didn't have a chance. You'd tackle me when you had a couple of men to help you. But you won't shoot it out when the breaks are even."

The twisted grin that twitched at Squint's ugly face warned Cornish even before he heard the step behind him and he instinctively jerked his body to one side. The whizzing cane missed his head by a fraction of an inch, slammed into his shoulder so hard that he buckled at the knees.

Through pain-dazed eyes, Cornish saw Squint's gun coming out of leather, saw the leer of triumph that spread across his face. Knocked off balance by the blow from Armstrong's cane, Cornish clawed desperately for the Colt hanging at his hip, found it even as the blast from Squint's gun filled the room to bursting with a monstrous clap of thunder.

The bullet brushed Cornish's cheek, slammed into a bedpost behind him, breaking out a shower of splinters.

Squint's gun crashed again and Cornish felt the sting of lead slash across his ribs, heard the bullet smash into the mirror that hung upon the wall.

Then his own gun was tilting in his hand and his finger was closing on the trigger. The run roared and slammed against his wrist and Cornish knew he would not have to shoot again.

In the doorway, Squint stood with a blue hole in his forehead, stood for an instant before he toppled forward, dead.

Cornish straightened from his crouch, stood looking at Armstrong through the stinging powder smoke that befogged the room.

Armstrong's pale lips moved thinly. "You killed him!"

Cornish snarled back, motioned with his gun toward Squint's lifeless body on the floor.

"That's what I was trying to tell you, Armstrong. That is what I meant. The Tumbling K had better not try to stop me selling wire."

Cornish moved toward the door, gun dangling in his hand. He stepped across Squint, but turned before he left.

"Next time," he told Armstrong, "when two men shoot it out don't go mixing in with that cane of yours."

A crowd had gathered in the lobby downstairs and Cornish halted on the stairs, looking at the faces that stared up at him. Blank faces—some of them the faces of the men who had refused to drink at the Longhorn bar when Steve had set them up.

"I just killed Squint," said Cornish, almost conversationally. "Anyone know of anything they'd like to do about it?"

None of them did, apparently. They parted and made a lane for him and he walked out onto the porch, crossed the sidewalk, vaulted to the saddle, went pounding down the street.

The wagon stood in front of the Hays' place at the south end of Cottonwood valley and Steve was lounging against one wheel when Cornish rode up.

"You look all out of breath," said Steve.

Cornish didn't answer, jerked his thumb toward the house.

"How about it?"

"Doc says we got to take old Bert to town where he can keep a close watch on him. We'll fix up a bed inside the wagon and have to travel slow."

"Look," said Cornish, "I got into a brush with Squint, had to shoot him."

"Dead, I hope," said Steve.

Cornish nodded. "The fat's really in the fire, Steve. Do you want to stick with me?"

"Ain't got another blessed thing to do," said Steve. "Look at that there wheat field. Cows plumb spoiled it. Makes you hot inside just to think of it."

"Soon as you get to town," said Cornish, "get the barb wire I got stored in the railroad warehouse. I got enough to throw across the valley and stop those cows. Then come back as fast as you can. Head for the Narrows. Know where they are?"

Steve nodded. "East place to string a fence. Not more'n half a mile and trees you can use for posts."

"That's the idea. And another thing. Can I keep your gun awhile? Had to leave so quick I couldn't get my own."

"Sure," said Steve. "Joe's got lots of them. Damnest preacher ever I see. Got a bottle cached out and an arsenal of guns. Always figured preachers were downright peaceable."

Cornish swung his horse around, headed for the valley.

Looking back, he saw Molly Hays standing in the doorway, watching after him.

Chapter Four
Stop Titus!

Cornish squatted on his heels in the shade of a tree and rolled himself a smoke. Far below lay the valley of the Cottonwood, a burnished strip of green that ran between ochre-yellow hills. And spread across the valley, in a straggling line, thin in some places, bunched and fat in others, was the Tumbling K herd.

Cornish struck the match against his thumbnail and lighted the smoke.

Smart, he told himself. Smart as wolves. Letting the cattle move up the valley slowly, not pushing things too hard, not forcing a quick decision. Giving the nesters plenty of time to think it over, time to figure out what a range war meant. Let one family pile its possessions on a wagon and start moving out and the whole valley would follow, one by one, realizing that a divided force could not stand against the ranchers' march.

Smart and cold-blooded.

Smoking quietly, he considered. The cattle would not reach the Narrows before dark, moving at the rate they were. That gave him time to string the wire under the cover of darkness, to talk the nesters over to the possibility of defending those thin strands of steel—a chance to make them see that wire gave them a chance to make a stand, to break the Tumbling K.

Carefully he crushed out the cigarette, remounted the horse and moved along the hills.

The sun had started down the western slope of the sky when he reached the Narrows, where the valley narrowed to a half mile throat between hundred foot bluffs cut by deep ravines gashing down to the valley floor. Sparse clumps of trees ran across the valley and for a moment, sitting his horse, he mapped out the fence line mentally, sketching it from tree to tree.

He clucked to the horse and started down one of the gullies that led into the valley.

A mile above the Narrows lay the Russell place and as he rode toward it, Cornish saw that at least a dozen horses stood slack hipped in front of the cabin, while men sat about on the doorstep and other perched on the corral fence.

They watched him silently as he rode up, none of them offering greeting.

"Howdy, men," he said.

They stared back stolidly, almost angrily.

John Russell rose slowly from the doorstep, advanced a few paces toward him.

"Cornish," he said, gruffly, "you're not wanted here."

"Still scared?" asked Cornish, softly.

Russell bristled. "Not scared. Just sensible. What's the use of fighting when the Tumbling K will buy us out."

"Buy you out?"

"Sure, we talked with Titus. He made us an offer."

"You're wrong," Cornish declared. "They aren't buying you out, they're buying you off. Paying you nuisance money to get rid of you without too much trouble."

"We're taking it," snapped Russell. "We're selling out!"

"So you're moving on," said Cornish. "You're licked and moving on. You'll look for a place as good as this and you may never find it. You'll live out of a wagon and you'll be without a home. You'll go back to being wagon men again."

A great black-bearded man stepped up alongside Russell, face sullen and angry.

"What would you have us do?" he asked and a threat ran through his words.

"I'm offering you a way to stop the Tumbling K," said Cornish. "I'm bringing out a load of wire. String it across the Narrows and stand back of it with guns. Serve notice on the Tumbling K that any man or critter that touches that wire is fair game."

"And you'll grab a gun and stand there with us?" asked Russell, almost sarcastically.

"Damn right I will!" Cornish snapped out.

The black-bearded man slowly shook his head.

"Ain't no good," he said.

"Billings," demanded Cornish, "can you think of a better way?"

Russell's hand dipped down deliberately, hauled out the six-gun that he wore.

"Get going, Cornish," he said, "before I let you have it. We don't want to see any more of you or your damned barb wire. If it hadn't been for your barb wire talk we'd kept on peaceable. It was you that go the mess stirred up."

Cornish flicked his eyes from face to face, read the same answer in all of them. Slowly, he wheeled the horse about and rode away, back toward the Narrows.

So this is the end of it, he thought. What was the use of trying to fight when the men you fought for didn't want to fight—when all they wanted to do was run off with their tails between their legs.

He could well understand their not wanting to fight, not wanting to subject their families to the terrors of range war—the burning cabin and the gutted buildings, the flaming haystacks and the swift shot in the dark, the man coming home draped across the saddle.

But there had to be a time when men would fight. There had to be something that was worth fighting for. And the valley of the Cottonwood, he told himself, must be one of those things, one of those principles, one of those rights for which men always had been willing to haul out their guns.

The horse climbed slowly up the gully that led to the heights above the Narrows. Cornish, slumped in the saddle, thinking, rocked with the horse's careful pace along the rocky slope.

At first the sound meant nothing—a sharp, short pinging sound that was dimmed by distance—just another sound with the shrill singing of the insects in cliff-side bushes, the chatter of a squirrel down among the cedars.

Then it came again and he jerked erect.

A shot!

The sound came again, the sharp, spiteful spitting of a high power rifle—and on its heels the crash of whipping six-guns.

Cornish yelled at the horse and the animal plunged up the trail, sending a shower of pebbles rattling down the gully.

The guns were an empty rattle in the wind as Cornish topped the bluffs and the horse lengthened out into a racing gallop.

A mile beyond, as they topped a ridge, Cornish saw the wagon, saw the riders who raced beside it with their smoking six-guns.

Joe Wicks stood in the wagon's front, beard flying in the wind, whip lashing at the crowbait team. The tattered canvas looked like shredded sails, jerking on the bows set in the wagon's bed and the team was running like scared rabbits.

The wheels hit a hidden rock and the wagon lurched, sailed for a good six feet with all four wheels off the ground, struck the ground and bounced soggily. The team kept on running as Joe Wicks yelled and shrieked.

Crouched beside Wicks, smoking rifle leveled, squatted Steve. Beside Steve was another figure—gingham and golden hair, and as Cornish watched in frozen wonder the girl raised a gun and fired.

The horse was plunging down the slope and Cornish yelled— a savage yell jerked from the bottom of his lungs.

Ahead of him the six-guns yammered as the riders rushed the wagon and the two rifles talked back huskily. One of the bows holding up the canvas buckled, hit and splintered by a bullet.

Cornish stiffened himself in the saddle, brought up his gun and fired.

Splinters flew from the wagon box and a bullet, glancing off a tire, whined its way into the sky.

The rifles crashed with a steady tempo and powder-smoke swirled like a crazy cloud above the bouncing wagon.

Out ahead of him, Cornish saw a horse going down, its rider flying above its head. The man struck the ground and rolled like a rubber ball, then he was on his feet again, clutching for his second gun. A rifle hammered and the man went over, as if a mighty fist had struck him and slammed him back into the earth.

Suddenly the two remaining horsemen wheeled about, frightened horses fighting at the bits. Cornish gritted his teeth, fired his last shot. One of the horses reared, feet pawing empty air, then tumbled screaming to the ground as its hind legs gave way beneath it.

The wagon thundered past, screeching and groaning, while Steve and Molly Hays crouched with silent guns.

Fumbling, swearing to himself, Cornish spilled cartridges with clumsy fingers reloading on the run.

The man whose horse had fallen was up and running for a cedar brake. The other rider had wheeled about, was waiting with lifted gun, his horse dancing sidewise with mincing steps. A great, tall man, angular and powerful, who sat the saddle with an easy grace.

Titus! He was waiting there on his mincing horse and with his gun all ready. For fists had failed and a rope had failed—and now it was the gun.

Rage steeled Cornish as he raised his gun, tried to hold it true against the motion of his horse. And even as he raised it, Titus' arm came down in a slow, smooth sweep and his gun spat fire.

The bullet whistled past Cornish's head with a dull and wicked hum and the gun winked again. Cornish's horse jumped, stung by the lead that raked along its withers and slammed with a drilling whistle into the stirrup leather, flicking Cornish's boot.

Close, now, thought Cornish. Almost too close to miss. Titus' gun flamed anew and Cornish worked the trigger. The blasts came almost as one and as the sound exploded in his ears, Cornish felt himself flying from the saddle of the racing horse.

Dully he felt the impact of his body striking ground, he felt himself descending into a roaring pit that was filled with flame that seemed to have no heat, but was a howling maelstrom of red, then winked into black ash.

Out of the silence came a sharp whiplash of sound. Cornish stirred, felt the life running back into his body, smelled the grass and earth, knew the warmth of the westering sun shining on his back.

The sound came again, the rasping crack of a distant rifle. Then another sound, nearer at hand, the rolling chortle of a churning six-gun.

Cornish was lying on his face and now he tried to roll over. The pain, which before that had been a dull, throbbing ache he scarcely noticed, mounted to a screaming thing. Cornish gasped and fell back on his face again, lay quivering to the pounding agony that thundered in his left shoulder.

For the first time he became conscious of the gun still clutched in his right hand—his grip must have frozen to it when Titus had shot him. He twisted his head to one side and moved his right hand up into the range of vision. He tilted his wrist to see that the muzzle was clear and not clogged by earth.

The rifle spanged and down the hillside Cornish saw the instinctive, nervous crouch of a man squatting behind a clump of cedars.

The man was not Titus. He was dumpy and broad, whereas Titus was gaunt and angular. It must be, he reasoned, the man whose horse he'd shot. The fellow, he remembered, had run for the cedar brake.

The rifle talked again and Cornish saw the cedars jerk and shake to the passage of the bullet that thudded into the hillside above the man in a shower of torn-up sod. The rifleman, whoever it was, knew where the man was hiding, probably was deliberately shooting to cover every angle of the hideout.

The man huddled tighter against the ground and again the cedars jerked as another bullet tore its way through the shield of green.

There was no sign of Titus. Yet Titus had to be there. Perhaps crouching behind some bush, hidden in some hollow, waiting for a chance at the hidden rifleman who had to be one of the three who had been riding in the barb wire-laden wagon.

Carefully, Cornish twisted his body about to bring his gun arm into play. Grimly he lined his sights on the man behind the cedars.

But he did not pull the trigger, although his finger tightened. It was almost as if something that walked the earth had stopped for a moment and told him not to shoot. Something that would not let him shoot a man with his back toward him. Then, too, there was Titus to consider. As long as Titus thought that he was dead, Titus wouldn't shoot.

Out by the cedars, the man was crawling, inching his way along, crawling up the hill. Then, suddenly, he exploded from the ground and was upright, running, head down, long legs working like driving pistons, angling up the hill, ducking and dodging to confuse the hidden rifle.

A single driving thought snapped into Cornish's mind, brought him to his feet in a blur of stumbling pain.

The man must not get away. If he did, the Tumbling K would know the story of the barb wire. And if the Tumbling K knew about the wire, its riders would sweep the valley clean in one swift stroke.

The hidden rifle chugged and a tiny fountain of dirt and grass gushed into the air wide of the running man.

The man ducked swiftly, ran like a startled rabbit, then jerked to a halt, straightened with a snarl upon his face, gun snapping up to point at Cornish.

Gritting his teeth, Cornish fought to keep his feet, fought to stand on the hill that was buckling and rolling. The man before him went around in circles and the scene was hazy.

Cornish tried to lift his gun and the gun was heavy in his grasp. And even as he tried to lift it, he knew that it was no go, that he couldn't shoot it out, not with the way the ground crawled beneath his feet and the way his eyes refused to focus.

The gun in front of him was a red eye winking in the haze and he felt the stir of buzzing lead snarling past his face.

His own gun was bucking in his hand, but he knew the shots were wild. His knees buckled and he took a slow step forward to regain his balance, watching the snarl on the misty face behind the winking gun of his antagonist.

Then the man's face froze and his body stiffened. From across the gully came the crashing snarl of the heavy rifle. The man sagged in the middle, jack-knifing like a rusty and reluctant hinge. The gun slid from nerveless fingers and the knees gave way and the man was down, a huddled figure in the wind-whipped grass.

Awkwardly, Cornish holstered his gun, tried to wipe away the mist that clung against his face, saw the fluttering blue of the gingham dress running down the opposite slope.

"Molly!" he croaked.

He went down the hill to meet her on unsteady legs, his bullet-smashed shoulder a roaring pain that filled half his brain with the howl of monstrous winds.

Near the bottom of the slope, she caught him, a reeling robot of a man. He leaned against her, amazed at the strength that held him up, that guided him to a place upon the ground.

"Titus!" he croaked.

"Titus got away."

"Molly."

"Hold still," she snapped at him. "I've got to get this blood stopped."

"Molly, you got to warn the nesters. Titus will wipe them out. He won't wait for nothing now that he knows about the wire."

"Soon as I get you fixed up," she said.

"Steve?"

"Stringing wire," she said. "I made them do it. I'm no good at building fence, but I can use a gun."

"You stayed back to keep those two pinned down?"

"That's right," she said, "but I didn't do so good. Titus got away."

Chapter Five
More Blood for the Wire

The match snicked against the stone and Cornish held it cupped in his one good hand. Squatting in the gully, he held the tiny flame close above the ground, moved it slowly to find the narrow-tired track of the wagon that had gone before him.

There it was, a deep rut in the earth, with the ragged edges of it still crumbling. Slowly he moved the match and saw the other marks, the skidding hoof-marks of horses fighting against the neck-yoke to hold the dead weight of the load on the downhill grade.

Cornish tossed the match away and got to his feet, staring out into the vast bowl of darkness that was Cottonwood valley.

The wagon had come this way and somewhere down there in the darkness, working their way slowly across the Narrows, were Joe Wicks and Steve, stringing out the wire. Two men who had no interest in barb wire or nesters, laboring in the night to work out the valley's destiny.

And was there any use, Cornish wondered—any use at all of stringing out that wire now that Titus had carried back the word?

Cornish shook his head, blundered down the trail, careful in the dark, left arm and shoulder swaddled in the white petticoat bandage that Molly Hays had fashioned. A target in the dark that the Tumbling K could aim at.

Stones rolled beneath his boots and he fought to keep his balance. Once his bandaged shoulder scraped against a tree and he doubled up with the pain lancing through his body.

Here, beneath the trees, the night was dark as pitch, although the valley ahead was faintly lighted by the shine of stars in the cloudless sky.

At the foot of the gully, he found the beginning of the fence, three strands of wire wrapped and stapled around a scrub white oak. One hand upon the strand, he followed it across the undulating terrain of the valley, a deep pride quickening in him at the feel of stretching steel. For although some of the intervals between the trees were long, the strands were taut and sang an excited song when he tapped his gun against them.

Up ahead, he knew, Steve and Joe were stringing the three strands simultaneously, using the wagon as a stringer and a stretcher. His feet hit something in the dark and he stumbled over it. Desperately he threw himself to land on his good shoulder, save the shattered left. Wind knocked out of him, he struggled to his feet, sought the thing that tripped him. It was the abandoned core of one of the spools of wire.

At the fence again, he found the splice in the wire and wondered. One of the men stringing that wire up ahead was a man who knew barb wire and it couldn't be Steve. Steve had spent his life behind the bars throughout the West. It must be Wicks.

Standing beside the fence, he listened, and there was no sound of hammering, no buzzing in the wire as there would have been if it were being worked with at the other end.

Terror welled up in him and he hurried along the fence, crossing the swells, stumbling down into a thicket.

Out of the trees a dark figure rose and words came through the night.

"Stand right where you are and h'ist up your paws."

Cornish skidded to a stop, raised his right hand high.

The man came warily toward him. "What's the matter with the other hand?" he asked.

"Shot," said Cornish, flatly.

"Cornish!" the other man whispered fiercely. "Damn my eyes if it ain't the boy hisself."

He moved forward and the starlight fell across the silvered beard, the slouchy, battered hat.

"Joe Wicks!"

"Hush yourself," Wicks cautioned. "We are lying low. One of them damned Tumbling K riders just scouted through."

"More than likely looking to see if there was any fence," said Cornish. "Titus got away and told them about the wire."

"He'd better not come messin' around," Wicks said fiercely, "or we'll blow his bloody guts out."

Cornish stared at him. "You don't sound like a preacher, Joe."

Joe spat and to Cornish came the smell of whiskey breath.

"Ain't no preacher," Wicks declared. "Never was no preacher. All of that was just a disguise. Me, I'm working for the same outfit you are."

"Ajax!"

"Exactly," said Wicks. "Seems there were too many accidents a-happening to the fellers selling wire, too many of them dropping out of sight and turning up missing. So they sent me out here to keep an eye on you. And when I got here I found hell starting in full swing, so I did the best I could."

He spat again. "Reckon we got a chance to stop them?"

"If the nesters will back us up," said Cornish. "Molly went down to warn them."

"Great gal," declared Wicks. "Got a lot of guts. Left her old man in the doctor's care and came along with us. Said if outsiders, meaning us and you, could stand up to the Tumbling K, it was the least that she could do."

Another figure came stealing through the trees. "The rider just went back," he said. "We'd better start with that wire again, pronto."

Steve came through the darkness, peered at Cornish.

"Figured you was dead," he said. "Titus knocked you out of the saddle slick and clean."

Wicks chuckled thinly. "Takes more than a little lead to stop an Ajax man."

They stood together in the darkness, listening to the high, thin whine of the wind moving in the trees and walking through the grass. From the bluffs to the west an owl laughed irrationally. The stars were a glittering net strung across the sky.

"Hey, Joe," whispered Steve. "Haul out that bottle. When a man's come back from the dead, we gotta drink to it."

Wicks shuffled his feet, dug into his back pocket. The hiss of glass sliding on denim came softly through the night.

"Quiet!" snapped Cornish. "Listen!"

They stood like frozen men in an attitude of attention. Faintly at first it came, then louder . . . the thunder of horses' hoofs sweeping up the valley.

Steve's voice almost sobbed. "It's them! And we ain't got the wire strung!"

Cornish, listening, felt the cold weight of defeat dropping down upon him. Those hoofbeats were too far to the east . . . they would miss the fence entirely, would go on up the valley to catch the hesitating nesters before they had a chance to fight.

"We have to turn them," he yelled and started to run. Steve clumped after him.

"What are you doing?" he shrieked at Cornish. "Come back, you fool! They will run you down."

"We got to turn them," gasped Cornish. "We have to get east of them and open up on them."

He was out of the trees and running in the open, teeth clenched against the pain that lanced through his shoulder with every jarring step. Running a race with hoofbeats that thundered through the night, running a race with the sound of fury that was storming up the valley.

Behind him he heard the thumping of Steve's feet and the quick, short breaths of the racing Wicks.

The ground opened beneath his feet and he was skidding down the banks of the Cottonwood, down into the water, wading across the stream, the water reaching to his waist, the suck of treacherous sands clutching at his feet.

He reached the opposite bank and clambered up in a shower of mud and crumbling clay, flopped face down in the grass and listened—and knew that they had won. The horses were west of the stream and they had outflanked them.

Slowly, confidently, his hand went back to the holster, pulled out the six-gun.

"Start shooting soon as you can see them," he whispered. "Drive them into the fence."

Steel gleamed in the starlight as Steve lifted out his gun and Joe Wicks, settling his body prone in the grass, was chuckling as he pushed his rifle forward.

Shadows suddenly were moving on the opposite bank, shadows that were silent except for the drum of hoofs, shadows highlighted by the gleam of stars on glittering rifle barrels.

Shouts rang out across the stream and the drum of hoofs was broken, became a threshing sound of snarled and frightened horses, like the writhing struggles of a wounded beast of prey.

Above the sound of hoofs came another sound, the thump and rumble of swiftly rolling wheels, the clank and jangle of a bouncing wagon bed. Out of the darkness loomed a whiteness like a dancing ghost, a blooming whiteness that jigged and tapped a rigadoon. Straight for the creek it came, then swerved and lumbered along the bank.

"It's them damn crowbaits of mine," yelled Wicks. "Running away, by jingo! I would of swore they didn't have it in them."

Six-guns crashed wickedly across the creek and bullets chugged angrily into the ground and whistled through the grass where the three men crouched. But above the crash of guns, above the stamp and scream of frightened horses, above the thump of the running wagon, came another sound—a threadlike sound that wove its way between the other noises—the high-pitched singing of unwinding stands of wire.

"We just put on some new spools when we had to quit," said Steve. "That there team is unraveling them at a right smart clip."

The wagon swept past on the opposite bank, the two crow-baits humping like animals gone crazy, the spools spinning on the upright stringer improvised on the wagon box.

Crouched low, gun held between his knees, Cornish worked with his one good hand, clicking cartridges into the cylinder. To his left Wicks' rifle churned with a steady rhythm, while down the creek, Steve slung a stream of lead into the swirling shadows.

Tumbling K guns answered back, spitting muzzles flickering like dancing fireflies in the star-lit night. Bullets ripped past with an angry sound, questing death winging through the dark, hissing in the grass.

Suddenly Wicks screamed and staggered upward, a bear-like figure fumbling on wilting knees. The gun dropped from his hand and rattled down the creek bank and Wicks, doubling over, plunged after it, hit the stream with a splash and lay there, a sprawled and misty figure against the starry gleam of water.

Cornish staggered down the creek bank, bent above Wicks' huddled figure. Even as his good hand reached out to clutch him, Cornish knew that Wicks was dead, that there was no life in that limp-sack body. Sobbing in his throat, he hauled Wicks from the water, laid him on his back, straightened a knee that was bent beneath him. The man looked up at him out of vacant eyes that held the gleam of stars.

Steve came striding down the bank.

"They hit the wire," he said. "Ran into it full tilt. That will hold them for a while."

Cornish nodded dumbly. "I heard them hit," he said.

He straightened up and saw that Steve was staring at the limp body sprawled on the sand.

"It's Wicks," said Cornish. "They got him just before they went into the fence."

He passed a hand before his eyes. "Remember, Steve, you said there'd be blood upon the wire?"

A running horse came toward the creek, galloping wildly, then sheered off and went down the valley. Listening, the two in the stream bed could hear the empty slap-slap of flapping stirrups and they knew that the saddle of the running horse was empty.

A single rifle bellowed through the dark. An angry yell went up and a six-gun barked. The rifle answered back and another one joined in. Six-guns rattled and a man screamed, a racking scream that shuddered through the sky and ended in a gurgle.

"The nesters!" yelled Steve.

"It's about time," Cornish said, bitterly, "that they were buying in."

Steve looked at him searchingly. "It means we've won," he reminded Cornish.

Cornish nodded. Yes, it meant he'd won. It meant that the order would go back to Illinois and the eyes would pop out of the dried-up skull that was Jacobs' face. It meant that wire would ring the valley and cut up the fields and pastures. It meant that the Tumbling K would have to settle down and be content with what it had instead of running wild on the lands of other men.

For with nester rifles backing up the fence, the Tumbling K was through. It had made its play and lost. Its hole card had been too low.

But curiously it didn't matter, now. For Wicks was dead and blood was on the wire. Wire cost too much, he thought. All over the west it's costing more than it may be worth. For every rod of fence is paid for in blood and lives. For fence is revolution and revolutions don't come without someone getting hurt.

He heard the splashing in the water and turned, saw Steve wading out and climbing the opposite bank. He opened his mouth to call to him but the man was gone.

To the west, along the fence, the rifles growled and snarled and six-guns hammered with sudden hateful chatter.

Cornish turned slowly, walking away from Wicks, following

Steve across the stream. Halfway across the creek he heard the running feet on the bank above him. Then the man was hurtling over the edge and plunging down the bank to hit the water with a soggy splash.

Sputtering and spitting water he struggled to his feet, stood knee-deep in the stream, staring straight at Cornish. Tall, angular—a giant looming in the night.

Cornish stared back, frozen.

"So it's you!" rasped Titus.

His hand was pistoning for his belt as Cornish drove forward, forcing his body through the resisting water with a strength he did not know he had. Diving for the legs of the man before him.

Starlight flashed on the weapon as it cleared the holster and at that moment, Cornish hit—his good right shoulder ramming into Titus' knees, arm wrapping around the boots and clamping tight with a vicious wrench.

The gun flamed in a crash of thunder as Titus went over, slamming against the bank.

Cornish flung himself forward, a snarl rising in his throat. Titus' foot came up and back, then shot forward in a vicious jab. Cornish tried to duck, but he was too late. The driving boot caught him in the chest and set him reeling back, feet sliding.

Titus was crouching, hand groping blindly for the gun that had fallen from his grasp, making whining noises of haste and exasperation in his throat.

Cornish swept his own hand back to the waiting holster . . . and the gun was gone! The holster flapped empty at his side.

Cornish walked slowly forward, cautiously, fist ready.

Suddenly Titus' body straightened.

Cornish brought his fist up fast, felt the jolt of it hitting flesh and bone, sensed the shiver that went through Titus' body as the big man staggered back.

Cornish swung again and yet again, blows that started from

his boot-tops and landed with an impact that made his arm a dead thing from the elbow down—blows that staggered Titus and kept him off his balance and drove him, step by step, ruthlessly and relentlessly, back toward the water.

It was not anger that drove Cornish—nor fear—nor confidence—but a plain and simple logic that it was his only chance, that he had to finish Titus fast or himself be finished.

Feet in the water, Titus tottered, hands clawing at the air in front of him, groggy with the blows that had battered at his body. Deliberately, mercilessly, Cornish aimed at his chin.

The blow smacked hollowly and Titus sank into the water with a splash.

Cornish let his arm fall to his side, felt the stinging of the cuts along his knuckles, felt the dull, dead ache that ran through the punished muscles.

"More blood for the wire," thought Cornish, dully.

Slowly, painfully, he turned his back upon the stream and clambered up the bank.

Far to the west came the dull beat of hoofs, but otherwise than that the valley was silent. The guns were quiet and the men had gone. Tumbling K was beaten.

Cornish stumbled forward.

"Cornish!"

"Here I am," he answered weakly.

He saw Molly coming through the gloom and stopped and waited for her.

From the look on her face and her outstretched arms, Cornish knew his fight had not been in vain.

SECOND CHILDHOOD

Originally published in the February 1951 issue of Galaxy Science Fiction, *"Second Childhood" may be the culmination of the list of second thoughts Clifford D. Simak had about the concept of immortality. And it makes suicide look like a good idea, if only one could do it. . . .*

—*dww*

You did not die.

There was no normal way to die.

You lived as carelessly and as recklessly as you could and you hoped that you would be lucky and be accidently killed.

You kept on living and you got tired of living.

"God, how tired a man can get of living!" Andrew Young said.

John Riggs, chairman of the immortality commission, cleared his throat.

"You realize," he said to Andrew Young, "that this petition is a highly irregular procedure to bring to our attention."

He picked up the sheaf of papers off the table and ruffled through them rapidly.

"There is no precedent," he added.

"I had hoped," said Andrew Young, "to establish precedent."

Commissioner Stanford said, "I must admit that you have made a good case, Ancestor Young. Yet you must realize that this commission has no possible jurisdiction over the life of any person, except to see that everyone is assured of all the benefits of immortality and to work out any kinks that may show up."

"I am well aware of that," answered Young, "and it seems to me that my case is one of the kinks you mention."

He stood silently, watching the faces of the members of the board. They are afraid, he thought. Every one of them. Afraid of the day they will face the thing I am facing now. They have sought an answer and there is no answer yet except the pitifully basic answer, the brutally fundamental answer that I have given them.

"My request is simple," he told them, calmly. "I have asked for permission to discontinue life. And since suicide has been made psychologically impossible, I have asked that this committee appoint a panel of next-friends to make the necessary and some-what distasteful arrangements to bring about the discontinuance of my life."

"If we did," said Riggs, "we would destroy everything we have. There is no virtue in a life of only five thousand years. No more than in a life of only a hundred years. If Man is to be immortal, he must be genuinely immortal. He cannot compromise."

"And yet," said Young, "my friends are gone."

He gestured at the papers Riggs held in his hands. "I have them listed there," he said. "Their names and when and where and how they died. Take a look at them. More than two hun-dred names. People of my own generation and of the generations closely following mine. Their names and the photo-copies of their death certificates."

He put both of his hands upon the table, palms flat against the table, and leaned his weight upon his arms.

"Take a look at how they died," he said. "Every one involves accidental violence. Some of them drove their vehicles too fast and, more than likely, very recklessly. One fell off a cliff when he reached down to pick a flower that was growing on its edge. A case of deliberately poor judgment, to my mind. One got stinking drunk and took a bath and passed out in the tub. He drowned . . ."

"Ancestor Young," Riggs said sharply, "you are surely not implying these folks were suicides."

"No," Andrew Young said bitterly. "We abolished suicide three thousand years ago, cleared it clean out of human minds. How could they have killed themselves?"

Stanford said, peering up at Young, "I believe, sir, you sat on the board that resolved that problem."

Andrew Young nodded. "It was after the first wave of suicides. I remember it quite well. It took years of work. We had to change human perspective, shift certain facets of human nature. We had to condition human reasoning by education and propaganda and instill a new set of moral values. I think we did a good job of it. Perhaps too good a job. Today a man can no more think of deliberately committing suicide than he could think of overthrowing our government. The very idea, the very word is repulsive, instinctively repulsive. You can come a long way, gentlemen, in three thousand years."

He leaned across the table and tapped the sheaf of papers with a lean, tense finger.

"They didn't kill themselves," he said. "They did not commit suicide. They just didn't give a damn. They were tired of living . . . as I am tired of living. So they lived recklessly in every way. Perhaps there always was a secret hope that they would drown while drunk or their car would hit a tree or . . ."

He straightened up and faced them. "Gentlemen," he said. "I am 5,786 years of age. I was born at Lancaster, Maine, on the planet Earth on September 21, 1968. I have served humankind well in those fifty-seven centuries. My record is there for you to see. Boards, commissions, legislative posts, diplomatic missions. No one can say that I have shirked my duty. I submit that I have paid any debt I owe humanity . . . even the well-intentioned debt for a chance at immortality."

"We wish," said Riggs, "that you would reconsider."

"I am a lonely man," replied Young. "A lonely man and tired. I have no friends. There is nothing any longer that holds my interest. It is my hope that I can make you see the desirability of assuming jurisdiction in cases such as mine. Someday you may find a solution to the problem, but until that time arrives, I ask you, in the name of mercy, to give us relief from life."

"The problem, as we see it," said Riggs, "is to find some way to wipe out mental perspective. When a man lives as you have, sir, for fifty centuries, he has too long a memory. The memories add up to the disadvantage of present realities and prospects for the future."

"I know," said Young. "I remember we used to talk about that in the early days. It was one of the problems which was recognized when immortality first became practical. But we always thought that memory would erase itself, that the brain could accommodate only so many memories, that when it got full up it would dump the old ones. It hasn't worked that way."

He made a savage gesture. "Gentlemen, I can recall my childhood much more vividly than I recall anything that happened yesterday."

"Memories are buried," said Riggs, "and in the old days, when men lived no longer than a hundred years at most, it was thought those buried memories were forgotten. Life, Man told himself, is a process of forgetting. So Man wasn't too worried over memories when he became immortal. He thought he would forget them."

"He should have known," argued Young. "I can remember my father, and I remember him much more intimately than I will remember you gentlemen once I leave this room. . . . I can remember my father telling me that, in his later years, he could recall things which happened in his childhood that had been forgotten all his younger years. And that, alone, should have tipped us off. The brain buries only the newer memories deeply . . . they are not available; they do not rise to bother one, because they are not sorted or oriented or correlated or whatever it is that the brain may do with them. But once they are all nicely docketed and filed, they pop up in an instant."

Riggs nodded agreement. "There's a lag of a good many years in the brain's bookkeeping. We will overcome it in time."

"We have tried," said Stanford. "We tried conditioning, the same solution that worked with suicides. But in this, it didn't work. For a man's life is built upon his memories. There are certain basic memories that must remain intact. With conditioning, you could not be selective. You could not keep the structural memories and winnow out the trash. It didn't work that way."

"There was one machine that worked," Riggs put in. "It got rid of memories. I don't understand exactly how it worked, but it did the job all right. It did too good a job. It swept the mind as clean as an empty room. It didn't leave a thing. It took all memories and it left no capacity to build a new set. A man went in a human being and came out a vegetable."

"Suspended animation," said Stanford, "would be a solution. If we had suspended animation. Simply stack a man away until we found the answer, then revive and recondition him."

"Be that as it may," Young told them, "I should like your most earnest consideration of my petition. I do not feel quite equal to waiting until you have the answer solved."

Riggs said, harshly, "You are asking us to legalize death."

Young nodded. "If you wish to phrase it that way. I'm asking it in the name of common decency."

Commissioner Stanford said, "We can ill afford to lose you, Ancestor."

Young sighed. "There is that damned attitude again. Immortality pays all debts. When a man is made immortal, he has received full compensation for everything that he may endure. I have lived longer than any man could be expected to live and still I am denied the dignity of old age. A man's desires are few, and quickly sated, and yet he is expected to continue living with desires burned up and blown away to ash. He gets to a point where nothing has a value . . . even to a point where his own personal values are no more than shadows. Gentlemen, there was a time when I could not have committed murder . . . literally could not have forced myself to kill another man . . . but today I could, without a second thought. Disillusion and cynicism have crept in upon me and I have no conscience."

"There are compensations," Riggs said. "Your family . . ."

"They get in my hair," said Young disgustedly. "Thousands upon thousands of young squirts calling me Grandsire and Ancestor and coming to me for advice they practically never follow. I don't know even a fraction of them and I listen to them carefully explain a relationship so tangled and trivial that it makes me yawn in their faces. It's all new to them and so old, so damned and damnably old to me."

"Ancestor Young," said Stanford, "you have seen Man spread out from Earth to distant stellar systems. You have seen the human race expand from one planet to several thousand planets. You have had a part in this. Is there not some satisfaction . . ."

"You're talking in abstracts," Young cut in. "What I am concerned about is myself . . . a certain specific mass of protoplasm shaped in biped form and tagged by the designation, ironic as it may seem, of Andrew Young. I have been unselfish all my life. I've asked little for myself. Now I am being utterly and entirely selfish and I ask that this matter be regarded as a personal problem rather than as a racial abstraction."

"Whether you'll admit it or not," said Stanford, "it is more than a personal problem. It is a problem which some day must be solved for the salvation of the race."

"That is what I am trying to impress upon you," Young snapped. "It is a problem that you must face. Some day you will solve it, but until you do, you must make provisions for those who face the unsolved problem."

"Wait a while," counseled Chairman Riggs. "Who knows? Today, tomorrow."

"Or a million years from now," Young told him bitterly and left, a tall, vigorous-looking man whose step was swift in anger where normally it was slow with weariness and despair.

There was yet a chance, of course.

But there was little hope.

How can a man go back almost six thousand years and snare a thing he never understood?

And yet Andrew Young remembered it. Remembered it as clearly as if it had been a thing that had happened in the morning of this very day.

It was a shining thing, a bright thing, a happiness that was brand-new and fresh as a bluebird's wing of an April morning or a shy woods flower after sudden rain.

He had been a boy and he had seen the bluebird and he had no words to say the thing he felt, but he had held up his tiny fingers and pointed and shaped his lips to coo.

Once, he thought, I had it in my very fingers and I did not have the experience to know what it was, nor the value of it. And now I know the value, but it has escaped me—it escaped me on the day that I began to think like a human being. The first adult thought pushed it just a little and the next one pushed it farther and finally it was gone entirely and I didn't even know that it had gone.

He sat on the chair on the flagstone patio and felt the Sun upon him, filtering through the branches of trees misty with the breaking leaves of Spring.

Something else, thought Andrew Young. Something that was not human—yet. A tiny animal that had many ways to choose, many roads to walk. And, of course, I chose the wrong way. I chose the human way. But there was another way. I know there must have been. A fairy way—or a brownie way, or maybe even pixie. That sounds foolish and childish now, but it wasn't always.

I chose the human way because I was guided into it. I was pushed and shoved, like a herded sheep.

I grew up and I lost the thing I held.

He sat and made his mind go hard and tried to analyze what it was he sought and there was no name for it. Except happiness. And happiness was a state of being, not a thing to retain and grasp.

But he could remember how it felt. With his eyes open in the present, he could remember the brightness of the day of the past, the clean-washed goodness of it, the wonder of the colors that were more brilliant than he ever since had seen—as if it were the first second after Creation and the world was still shiningly new.

It was that new, of course. It would be that new to a child.

But that didn't explain it all.

It didn't explain the bottomless capacity for seeing and knowing and believing in the beauty and the goodness of a clean new world. It didn't explain the almost non-human elation of knowing that there were colors to see and scents to smell and soft green grass to touch.

I'm insane, Andrew Young said to himself. Insane, or going insane. But if insanity will take me back to an understanding of the strange perception I had when I was a child, and lost, I'll take insanity.

He leaned back in his chair and let his eyes go shut and his mind drift back.

He was crouching in a corner of a garden and the leaves were drifting down from the walnut trees like a rain of saffron gold. He lifted one of the leaves and it slipped from his fingers, for his hands were chubby still and not too sure in grasping. But he tried again and he clutched it by the stem in one stubby fist and he saw that it was not just a blob of yellowness, but delicate, with many little veins. When he held it so that the Sun struck it, he imagined that he could almost see through it, the gold was spun so fine.

He crouched with the leaf clutched tightly in his hand and for a moment there was a silence that held him motionless. Then he heard the frost-loosened leaves pattering all around him, pattering as they fell, talking in little whispers as they sailed down through the air and found themselves a bed with their golden fellows.

In that moment he knew that he was one with the leaves and the whispers that they made, one with the gold and the autumn sunshine and the far blue mist upon the hill above the apple orchard.

A foot crunched stone behind him and his eyes came open and the golden leaves were gone.

"I am sorry if I disturbed you, Ancestor," said the man. "I had an appointment for this hour, but I would not have disturbed you if I had known."

Young stared at him reproachfully without answering.

"I am kin," the man told him.

"I wouldn't doubt it," said Andrew Young. "The Galaxy is cluttered up with descendants of mine."

The man was very humble. "Of course, you must resent us sometimes. But we are proud of you, sir. I might almost say that we revere you. No other family—"

"I know," interrupted Andrew Young. "No other family has any fossil quite so old as I am."

"Nor as wise," said the man.

Andrew Young snorted. "Cut out that nonsense. Let's hear what you have to say and get it over with."

The technician was harassed and worried and very frankly puzzled. But he stayed respectful, for one always was respectful to an ancestor, whoever he might be. Today there were mighty few left who had been born into a mortal world.

Not that Andrew Young looked old. He looked like all adults, a fine figure of a person in the early twenties.

The technician shifted uneasily. "But, sir, this . . . this . . ."

"Teddy bear," said Young.

"Yes, of course. An extinct terrestrial subspecies of animal?"

"It's a toy," Young told him. "A very ancient toy. All children used to have them five thousand years ago. They took them to bed."

The technician shuddered. "A deplorable custom. Primitive."

"Depends on the viewpoint," said Young. "I've slept with them many a time. There's a world of comfort in one, I can personally assure you."

The technician saw that it was no use to argue. He might as well fabricate the thing and get it over with.

"I can build you a fine model, sir," he said, trying to work up some enthusiasm. "I'll build in a response mechanism so that it can give simple answers to certain keyed questions and, of course, I'll fix it so it'll walk, either on two legs or four . . ."

"No," said Andrew Young.

The technician looked surprised and hurt. "No?"

"No," repeated Andrew Young. "I don't want it fancied up. I want it a simple lump of make-believe. No wonder the children of today have no imagination. Modern toys entertain them with a bag of tricks that leave the young'uns no room for imagination. They couldn't possibly think up, on their own, all the screwy things these new toys do. Built-in responses and implied consciousness and all such mechanical trivia. . . ."

"You just want a stuffed fabric," said the technician, sadly, "with jointed arms and legs."

"Precisely," agreed Young.

"You're sure you want fabric, sir? I could do a neater job in plastics."

"Fabric," Young insisted firmly, "and it must be scratchy."

"Scratchy, sir?"

"Sure. You know. Bristly. So it scratches when you rub your face against it."

"But no one in his right mind would want to rub his face . . ."

"I would," said Andrew Young. "I fully intend to do so."

"As you wish, sir," the technician answered, beaten now.

"When you get it done," said Young, "I have some other things in mind."

"Other things?" The technician looked wildly about, as if seeking some escape.

"A high chair," said Young. "And a crib. And a wooly dog. And buttons."

"Buttons?" asked the technician. "What are buttons?"

"I'll explain it all to you," Young told him airily. "It all is very simple."

It seemed, when Andrew Young came into the room, that Riggs and Stanford had been expecting him, had known that he was coming and had been waiting for him.

He wasted no time on preliminaries or formalities.

They know, he told himself. They know, or they have guessed. They would be watching me. Ever since I brought in my petition, they have been watching me, wondering what I would be thinking, trying to puzzle out what I might do next. They know every move I've made, they know about the toys and the furniture and all the other things. And I don't need to tell them what I plan to do.

"I need some help," he said, and they nodded soberly, as if they had guessed he needed help.

"I want to build a house," he explained. "A big house. Much larger than the usual house."

Riggs said, "We'll draw the plans for you. Do anything else that you—"

"A house," Young went on, "About four or five times as big as the ordinary house. Four or five times normal scale, I mean. Doors twenty-five to thirty feet high and everything else in proportion."

"Neighbors or privacy?" asked Stanford.

"Privacy," said Young.

"We'll take care of it," promised Riggs. "Leave the matter of the house to us."

Young stood for a long moment, looking at the two of them. Then he said, "I thank you, gentlemen. I thank you for your helpfulness and your understanding. But most of all I thank you for not asking any questions."

He turned slowly and walked out of the room and they sat in silence for minutes after he was gone.

Finally, Stanford offered a deduction: "It will have to be a place that a boy would like. Woods to run in and a little stream to fish in and a field where he can fly his kites. What else could it be?"

"He's been out ordering children's furniture and toys," Riggs agreed. "Stuff from five thousand years ago. The kind of things he used when he was a child. But scaled to adult size."

"Now," said Stanford, "he wants a house built to the same proportions. A house that will make him think or help him believe that he is a child. But will it work, Riggs? His body will not change. He cannot make it change. It will only be in his mind."

"Illusion," declared Riggs. "The illusion of bigness in relation to himself. To a child, creeping on the floor, a door is twenty-five to thirty feet high, relatively. Of course the child doesn't know that. But Andrew Young does. I don't see how he'll overcome that."

"At first," suggested Stanford, "he will know that it's illusion, but after a time, isn't there a possibility that it will become reality so far as he's concerned? That's why he needs our help. So that the house will not be firmly planted in his memory as a thing that's merely out of proportion . . . so that it will slide from illusion into reality without too great a strain."

"We must keep our mouths shut." Riggs nodded soberly. "There must be no interference. It's a thing he must do himself . . . entirely by himself. Our help with the house must be the help of an unseen, silent agency. Like brownies, I think the term was that he used, we must help and be never seen. Intrusion by anyone would introduce a jarring note and would destroy illusion and that is all he has to work on. Illusion pure and simple."

"Others have tried," objected Stanford, pessimistic again. "Many others. With gadgets and machines . . ."

"None has tried it," said Riggs, "with the power of mind alone. With the sheer determination to wipe out five thousand years of memory."

"That will be his stumbling block," said Stanford. "The old, dead memories are the things he has to beat. He has to get rid of them . . . not just bury them, but get rid of them for good and all, forever."

"He must do more than that," said Riggs. "He must replace his memories with the outlook he had when he was a child. His mind must be washed out, refreshed, wiped clean and shining and made new again . . . ready to live another five thousand years."

The two men sat and looked at one another and in each other's eyes they saw a single thought—the day would come when they, too, each of them alone, would face the problem Andrew Young faced.

"We must help," said Riggs, "in every way we can and we must keep watch and we must be ready . . . but Andrew Young cannot know that we are helping or that we are watching him. We must anticipate the materials and tools and the aids that he may need."

Stanford started to speak, then hesitated, as if seeking in his mind for the proper words.

"Yes," said Riggs. "What is it?"

"Later on," Stanford managed to say, "much later on, toward the very end, there is a certain factor that we must supply. The one thing that he will need the most and the one thing that he cannot think about, even in advance. All the rest can be stage setting and he can still go on toward the time when it becomes reality. All the rest may be make-believe, but one thing must come as genuine or the entire effort will collapse in failure."

Riggs nodded. "Of course. That's something we'll have to work out carefully."

"If we can," Stanford said.

The yellow button over here and the red one over there and the green one doesn't fit, so I'll throw it on the floor and just for the fun of it, I'll put the pink one in my mouth and someone will find me with it and they'll raise a ruckus because they will be afraid that I will swallow it.

And there's nothing, absolutely nothing, that I love better than a full-blown ruckus. Especially if it is over me.

"Ug," said Andrew Young, and he swallowed the button.

He sat stiff and straight in the towering high chair and then, in a fury, swept the oversized muffin tin and its freight of buttons crashing to the floor.

For a second he felt like weeping in utter frustration and then a sense of shame crept in on him.

Big baby, he said to himself.

Crazy to be sitting in an overgrown high chair, playing with buttons and mouthing baby talk and trying to force a mind conditioned by five thousand years of life into the channels of an infant's thoughts.

Carefully he disengaged the tray and slid it out, cautiously shinnied down the twelve-foot-high chair.

The room engulfed him, the ceiling towering far above him.

The neighbors, he told himself, no doubt thought him crazy, although none of them had said so. Come to think of it, he had not seen any of his neighbors for a long spell now.

A suspicion came into his mind. Maybe they knew what he was doing, maybe they were deliberately keeping out of his way in order not to embarrass him.

That, of course, would be what they would do if they had realized what he was about. But he had expected . . . he had expected . . . that fellow, what's his name? . . . at the commission, what's the name of that commission, anyhow? Well, anyway, he'd expected a fellow whose name he couldn't remember from a commission the name of which he could not recall to come snooping around, wondering what he might be up to, offering to help, spoiling the whole setup, everything he'd planned.

I can't remember, he complained to himself. I can't remember the name of a man whose name I knew so short a time ago as yesterday. Nor the name of a commission that I knew as well as I know my name. I'm getting forgetful. I'm getting downright childish.

Childish?

Childish!

Childish and forgetful.

Good Lord, thought Andrew Young, that's just the way I want it.

On hands and knees he scrabbled about and picked up the buttons, put them in his pocket. Then, with the muffin tin underneath his arm, he shinnied up the high chair and, seating himself comfortably, sorted out the buttons in the pan.

The green one over here in this compartment and the yellow one . . . oops, there she goes onto the floor. And the red one in with the blue one and this one . . . this one . . . what's the color of this one? Color? What's that?

What is what?

What—

"It's almost time," said Stanford, "and we are ready, as ready as we'll ever be. We'll move in when the time is right, but we can't move in too soon. Better to be a little late than a little early. We have all the things we need. Special size diapers and—"

"Good Lord," exclaimed Riggs, "it won't go that far, will it?"

"It should," said Stanford. "It should go even further to work right. He got lost yesterday. One of our men found him and led him home. He didn't have the slightest idea where he was and he was getting pretty scared and he cried a little. He chattered about birds and flowers and he insisted that our man stay and play with him."

Riggs chuckled softly. "Did he?"

"Oh, certainly. He came back worn to a frazzle."

"Food?" asked Riggs. "How is he feeding himself?"

"We see that there's a supply of stuff, cookies and such-wise, left on a low shelf, where he can get at them. One of the robots cooks up some more substantial stuff on a regular schedule and leaves it where he can find it. We have to be careful. We can't mess around too much. We can't intrude on him. I have a feeling he's almost reached an actual turning point. We can't afford to upset things now that he's come this far."

"The android's ready?"

"Just about," said Stanford.

"And the playmates?"

"Ready. They were less of a problem."

"There's nothing more that we can do?"

"Nothing," Stanford said. "Just wait, that's all. Young has carried himself this far by the sheer force of will alone. That will is gone now. He can't consciously force himself any further back. He is more child than adult now. He's built up a regressive momentum and the only question is whether that momentum is sufficient to carry him all the way back to actual babyhood."

"It has to go back to that?" Riggs looked unhappy, obviously thinking of his own future. "You're only guessing, aren't you?"

"All the way or it simply is no good," Stanford said dogmatically. "He has to get an absolutely fresh start. All the way or nothing."

"And if he gets stuck halfway between? Half child, half man, what then?"

"That's something I don't want to think about," Stanford said.

—

He had lost his favorite teddy bear and gone to hunt it in the dusk that was filled with elusive fireflies and the hush of a world quieting down for the time of sleep. The grass was drenched with dew and he felt the cold wetness of it soaking through his shoes as he went from bush to hedge to flowerbed, looking for the missing toy.

It was necessary, he told himself, that he find the nice little bear, for it was the one that slept with him and if he did not find it, he knew that it would spend a lonely and comfortless night. But at no time did he admit, even to his innermost thought, that it was he who needed the bear and not the bear who needed him.

A soaring bat swooped low and for a terrified moment, catching sight of the zooming terror, a blob of darkness in the gathering dusk, he squatted low against the ground, huddling against the sudden fear that came out of the night. Sounds of fright bubbled in his throat and now he saw the great dark garden as an unknown place, filled with lurking shadows that lay in wait for him.

He stayed cowering against the ground and tried to fight off the alien fear that growled from behind each bush and snarled in every darkened corner. But even as the fear washed over him, there was one hidden corner of his mind that knew there was no need of fear. It was as if that one area of his brain still fought against the rest of him, as if that small section of cells might know that the bat was no more than a flying bat, that the shadows in the garden were no more than absence of light.

There was a reason, he knew, why he should not be afraid—a good reason born of a certain knowledge he no longer had. And that he should have such knowledge seemed unbelievable, for he was scarcely two years old.

He tried to say it—two years old.

There was something wrong with his tongue, something the matter with the way he had to use his mouth, with the way his lips refused to shape the words he meant to say.

He tried to define the words, tried to tell himself what he meant by two years old and one moment it seemed that he knew the meaning of it and then it escaped him.

The bat came again and he huddled close against the ground, shivering as he crouched. He lifted his eyes fearfully, darting glances here and there, and out of the corner of his eye he saw the looming house and it was a place he knew as refuge.

"House," he said, and the word was wrong, not the word itself, but the way he said it.

He ran on trembling, unsure feet and the great door loomed before him, with the latch too high to reach. But there was another way, a small swinging door built into the big door, the sort of door that is built for cats and dogs and sometimes little children. He darted through it and felt the sureness and the comfort of the house about him. The sureness and the comfort—and the loneliness.

He found his second-best teddy bear, and, picking it up, clutched it to his breast, sobbing into its scratchy back in pure relief from terror.

There is something wrong, he thought. Something dreadfully wrong. Something is as it should not be. It is not the garden or the darkened bushes or the swooping winged shape that came out of the night. It is something else, something missing, something that should be here and isn't.

Clutching the teddy bear, he sat rigid and tried desperately to drive his mind back along the way that would tell him what was wrong. There was an answer, he was sure of that. There was an answer somewhere; at one time he had recognized the need he felt and there had been no way to supply it—and now he couldn't even know the need, could feel it, but he could not know it.

He clutched the bear closer and huddled in the darkness, watching the moonbeam that came through a window, high above his head, and etched a square of floor in brightness.

Fascinated, he watched the moonbeam and all at once the terror faded. He dropped the bear and crawled on hands and knees, stalking the moonbeam. It did not try to get away and he reached its edge and thrust his hands into it and laughed with glee when his hands were painted by the light coming through the window.

He lifted his face and stared up at the blackness and saw the white globe of the Moon, looking at him, watching him. The Moon seemed to wink at him and he chortled joyfully.

Behind him a door creaked open and he turned clumsily around.

Someone stood in the doorway, almost filling it—a beautiful person who smiled at him. Even in the darkness he could sense the sweetness of the smile, the glory of her golden hair.

"Time to eat, Andy," said the woman. "Eat and get a bath and then to bed."

Andrew Young hopped joyfully on both feet, arms held out— happy and excited and contented.

"Mummy!" he cried. "Mummy . . . Moon!"

He swung about with a pointing finger and the woman came swiftly across the floor, knelt and put her arms around him, held him close against her. His cheek against hers, he stared up at the Moon and it was a wondrous thing, a bright and golden thing, a wonder that was shining new and fresh.

On the street outside, Stanford and Riggs stood looking up at the huge house that towered above the trees.

"She's in there now," said Stanford. "Everything's quiet so it must be all right."

Riggs said, "He was crying in the garden. He ran in terror for the house. He stopped crying about the time she must have come in."

Stanford nodded. "I was afraid we were putting it off too long, but I don't see now how we could have done it sooner. Any outside interference would have shattered the thing he tried to do. He had to really need her. Well, it's all right now. The timing was just about perfect."

"You're sure, Stanford?"

"Sure? Certainly I am sure. We created the android and we trained her. We instilled a deep maternal sense into her personality. She knows what to do. She is almost human. She is as close as we could come to a human mother eighteen feet tall. We don't know what Young's mother looked like, but chances are he doesn't either. Over the years his memory has idealized her. That's what we did. We made an ideal mother."

"If it only works," said Riggs.

"It will work," said Stanford, confidently. "Despite the shortcomings we may discover by trial and error, it will work. He's been fighting himself all this time. Now he can quit fighting and shift responsibility. It's enough to get him over the final hump, to place him safely and securely in the second childhood that he had to have. Now he can curl up, contented. There is someone to look after him and think for him and take care of him. He'll probably go back just a little further . . . a little closer to the cradle. And that is good, for the further he goes, the more memories are erased."

"And then?" asked Riggs worriedly.

"Then he can proceed to grow up again."

They stood watching, silently.

In the enormous house, lights came on in the kitchen and the windows gleamed with a homey brightness.

I, too, Stanford was thinking. Some day, I, too. Young has pointed the way, he has blazed the path. He had shown us, all the other billions of us, here on Earth and all over the Galaxy, the way it can be done. There will be others and for them there will be more help. We'll know then how to do it better.

Now we have something to work on.

Another thousand years or so, he thought, and I will go back, too. Back to the cradle and the dreams of childhood and the safe security of a mother's arms.

It didn't frighten him in the least.

BEACHHEAD

This story originally appeared in the July 1951 issue of Fantastic
Adventures *as "You'll Never Go Home Again." But the author's
journals suggest that Cliff Simak sent it to his agent under the title
"Beachhead," and that's how it appeared in subsequent anthologies.
Thus, the story was first copyrighted under the former name, but its
appearance here is under that second name.*

"This looks like an interesting world," the anthropologist said.

—dww

There was nothing, absolutely nothing, that could stop a human
planetary survey party. It was a specialized unit created for and
charged with one purpose only—to establish a bridgehead on an
alien planet, to blast out the perimeters of that bridgehead and
establish a base where there would be some elbow-room. Then
hold that elbow-room against all comers until it was time to go.

After the base was once established, the brains of the party got
to work. They turned the place inside out. They put it on tape
and captured it within the chains of symbols they scribbled in
their field books. They pictured it and wrote it and plotted it and
reduced it to a neat assembly of keyed and symbolic facts to be
inserted in the galactic files.

If there was life, and sometimes there was, they prodded it to
get reaction. Sometimes the reaction was extremely violent, and

other times it was much more dangerously subtle. But there were ways in which to handle both the violent and the subtle, for the legionnaires and their robots were trained to a razor's edge and knew nearly all the answers.

There was nothing in the galaxy, so far known, that could stop a human survey party.

Tom Decker sat at ease in the empty lounge and swirled the ice in the highball glass, well contented, watching the first of the robots emerge from the bowels of the cargo space. They dragged a conveyor belt behind them as they emerged, and Decker, sitting idly, watched them drive supports into the ground and rig up the belt.

A door clicked open back of Decker and he turned his head.

"May I come in, sir?" Doug Jackson asked.

"Certainly," said Decker.

Jackson walked to the great curving window and looked out. "What does it look like, sir?" he asked.

Decker shrugged. "Another job," he said. "Six weeks. Six months. Depends on what we find."

Jackson sat down beside him. "This one looks tough," he said. "Jungle worlds always are a bit meaner than any of the others."

Decker grunted at him. "A job. That's all. another job to do. Another report to file. Then they'll either send out an exploitation gang or a pitiful bunch of bleating colonists."

"Or," said Jackson, "they'll file the report and let it gather dust for a thousand years or so."

"They can do anything they want," Decker told him. "We turn it in. What someone else does with it after that is their affair, not ours."

They sat quietly watching the six robots roll out the first of the packing cases, rip off its cover and unpack the seventh robot, laying out his various parts neatly in a row in the tramped-down, waist-high grass. Then, working as a team, with not a single fumble, they put No. 7 together, screwed his brain case into his metal skull, flipped up his energizing switch and slapped the breastplate home.

No. 7 stood groggily for a moment. He swung his arms uncertainly, shook his head from side to side. Then, having oriented himself, he stepped briskly forward and helped the other six heave the packing box containing No. 8 off the conveyor belt.

"Takes a little time this way," said Decker, "but it saves a lot of space. Have to cut our robot crew in half if we didn't pack them at the end of every job. They stow away better."

He sipped at his highball speculatively. Jackson lit a cigarette.

"Someday," said Jackson, "we're going to run up against something that we can't handle."

Decker snorted.

"Maybe here," insisted Jackson, gesturing at the nightmare jungle world outside the great curved sweep of the vision plate.

"You're a romanticist," Decker told him shortly. "In love with the unexpected. Besides that, you're new. Get a dozen trips under your belt and you won't feel this way."

"It could happen," insisted Jackson.

Decker nodded, almost sleepily. "Maybe," he said. "Maybe it could, at that. It never has, but I suppose it could. And when it does, we take it on the lam. It's no part of our job to fight a last ditch battle. When we bump up against something that's too big to handle, we don't stick around. We don't take any risks."

He took another sip.

"Not even calculated risks," he added.

The ship rested on the top of a low hill, in a small clearing masked by tall grass, sprinkled here and there with patches of exotic flowers. Below the hill a river flowed sluggishly, a broad expanse of chocolate-colored water moving in a sleepy tide through the immense vine-entangled forest.

As far as the eye could see, the jungle stretched away, a brooding darkness that even from behind the curving quartz of the vision plate seemed to exude a heady, musty scent of danger that swept up over the grass-covered hilltop. There was no sign of life, but one knew, almost instinctively, that sentiency lurked in the buried pathways and tunnels of the great tree-land.

Robot No. 8 had been energized and now the eight split into two groups, ran out two packing cases at a time instead of one. Soon there were twelve robots, and then they formed themselves into three working groups.

"Like that," said Decker, picking up the conversation where they had left it lying. He gestured with his glass, now empty. "No calculated risks. We send the robots first. They unpack and set up their fellows. Then the whole gang turns to and uncrates the machinery and sets it up and gets it operating. A man doesn't even put his foot on the ground until he has a steel ring around the ship to give him protection."

Jackson sighed. "I guess you're right," he said. "Nothing can happen. We don't take any chances. Not a single one."

"Why should we?" Decker asked. He heaved himself out of the chair, stood up and stretched. "Got a thing or two to do," he said. "Last minute checks and so on."

"I'll sit here for a while," said Jackson. "I like to watch. It's all new to me."

"You'll get over it," Decker told him. "In another twenty years."

In his office, Decker lifted a sheaf of preliminary reports off his desk and ran through them slowly, checking each one carefully, filing away in his mind the basic facts of the world outside.

He worked stolidly, wetting a big, blunt thumb against his outthrust tongue to flip the pages off the top of the next stack and deposit them, in not so neat a pile, to his right, face downward.

Atmosphere—Pressure slightly more than Earth. High in oxygen.

Gravity—A bit more than Earth.

Temperature—Hot. Jungle worlds always were. There was a

breeze outside now, he thought. Maybe there'd be a breeze most of the time. That would be a help.

Rotation—Thirty-six hour day.

Radiation—None of local origin, but some hard stuff getting through from the sun.

He made a mental note: Watch that.

Bacterial and virus count—As usual. Lots of it. Apparently not too dangerous. Not with every single soul hypoed and immunized and hormoned to his eyebrows. But you never can be sure, he thought. Not entirely sure. No calculated risks, he had told Jackson. But here was a calculated risk and one you couldn't do a single thing about. If there was a bug that picked you for a host and you weren't loaded for bear to fight him, you took him on and did the best you could.

Life factor—Lot of emanation. Probably the vegetation, maybe even the soil, was crawling with all sorts of loathsome life. Vicious stuff, more than likely. But that was something you took care of as a matter of routine. No use taking any chances. You went over the ground even if there was no life—just to be sure there wasn't.

A tap came on the door and he called out for the man to enter.

It was Captain Carr, commander of the Legion unit.

Carr saluted snappily. Decker did not rise. He made his answering salute a sloppy one on purpose. No use, he told himself, letting the fellow establish any semblance of equality, for there was no such equality in fact. A captain of the Legion simply did not rank with the commandant of a galactic survey party.

"Reporting, sir," said Carr. "We are ready for a landing."

"Fine, Captain. Fine."

What was the matter with the fool? The Legion always was ready, always would be ready—that was no more than tradition. Why, then, carry out such an empty, stiff formality?

But it was the nature of a man like Carr, he supposed. The Legion, with its rigid discipline, with its ancient pride of service and tradition, attracted men like Carr, was a perfect finishing school for accomplished martinets.

Tin soldiers, Decker thought, but accomplished ones. As hard-bitten a gang of fighting men as the galaxy had ever known. They were drilled and disciplined to a razor's edge, serum- and hormone-injected against all known diseases of an alien world, trained and educated in alien psychology and strictly indoctrinated with high survival characteristics which stood up under even the most adverse circumstances.

"We shall not be ready for some time, Captain," Decker said. "The robots have just started their uncrating."

"Very well," said Carr. "We await your orders, sir."

"Thank you, Captain," Decker told him, making it quite clear that he wished he would get out. But when Carr turned to go, Decker called him back.

"What is it, sir?" asked Carr.

"I've been wondering," said Decker. "Just wondering, you understand. Can you imagine any circumstances which might arise that the Legion could not handle?"

Carr's expression was a pure delight to see. "I'm afraid, sir, that I don't understand your question."

Decker sighed. "I didn't think you would," he said.

Before nightfall, the full working force of robots had been uncrated and had set up some of the machines, enough to establish a small circle of alarm posts around the ship.

A flame thrower burned a barren circle on the hilltop, stretching five hundred feet around the ship. A hard-radiations generator took up its painstaking task, pouring pure death into the soil. The toll must have been terrific. In some spots the ground virtually boiled as the dying life forms fought momentarily and fruitlessly to escape the death that cut them down.

The robots rigged up huge batteries of lamps that set the hill-top ablaze with a light as bright as day, and the work went on.

As yet, no human had set foot outside the ship.

Inside the ship, the robot stewards set up a table in the lounge so that the human diners might see what was going on outside the ship.

The entire company, except for the legionnaires, who stayed in quarters, had gathered for the meal when Decker came into the room.

"Good evening, gentlemen," he said.

He strode to the table's head and the others ranged themselves along the sides. He sat down and there was a scraping of drawn chairs as the others took their places.

He clasped his hands in front of him and bowed his head and parted his lips to say the customary words. He halted even as he was about to speak, and when the words did come they were different from the ones he had said by rote a thousand times before.

"Dear Father, we are Thy servants in an unknown land and there is a deadly pride upon us. Teach us humility and lead us to the knowledge, before it is too late, that men, despite their far traveling and their mighty works, still are as children in Thy sight. Bless the bread we are about to break, we beg Thee, and keep us forever in Thy compassion. Amen."

He lifted his head and looked down the table. Some of them, he saw, were startled. The others were amused.

They wonder if I'm cracking, he thought. They think the Old Man is breaking up. And that may be true, for all I know. Although I was all right until this afternoon. All right until young Doug Jackson . . .

"Those were fine words, lad," said Old MacDonald, the chief engineer. "I thank you for them, sir, and there is them among us who would do well to take some heed upon them."

Platters and plates were being passed up and down the table's length and there was the commonplace, homely clatter of silverware and china.

"This looks like an interesting world," said Waldron, the anthropologist. "Dickson and I were up in observation just before the sun set. We thought we saw something down by the river. Some sort of life."

Decker grunted, scooping fried potatoes out of a bowl onto his plate. "Funny if we don't run across a lot of life here. The radiation wagon stirred up a lot of it when it went over the field today."

"What Waldron and I saw," said Dickson, "looked humanoid."

Decker squinted at the biologist. "Sure of that?" he asked.

Dickson shook his head. "The seeing was poor. Couldn't be absolutely sure. Seemed to me there were two or three of them. Matchstick men."

Waldron nodded. "Like a picture a kid would draw," he said. "One stroke for the body. Two strokes each for arms and legs. A circle for a head. Angular. Ungraceful. Skinny."

"Graceful enough in motion, though," said Dickson. "When they moved, they went like cats. Flowed, sort of."

"We'll know plenty soon enough," Decker told them mildly. "In a day or two we'll flush them."

Funny, he thought. On almost every job someone popped up to report he had spotted humanoids. Usually there weren't any. Usually it was just imagination. Probably wishful thinking, he told himself, the yen of men far away from their fellow men to find in an alien place a type of life that somehow seemed familiar.

Although the usual humanoid, once you met him in the flesh, turned out to be so repulsively alien that alongside him an octopus would seem positively human.

Franey, the senior geologist, said, "I've been thinking about those mountains to the west of us, the ones we caught sight of when we were coming in. Had a new look about them. New mountains are good to work in. They haven't worn down. Easier to get at whatever's in them."

"We'll lay out our first survey lines in that direction," Decker told him.

Outside the curving vision plate, the night was alive with the blaze of the batteries of lights. Gleaming robots toiled in shining gangs. Ponderous machines lumbered past. Smaller ones scurried like frightened beetles. To the south, great gouts of flame leaped out and the sky was painted red with the bursts of a squad of flame throwers going into action.

"Chewing out a landing field," said Decker. "A tongue of jungle juts out there. Absolutely level ground. Like a floor. Won't take a great deal of work to turn it into a field."

The stewards brought coffee and brandy and a box of good cigars. Decker and his men settled back into their chairs, taking life easy, watching the work going on outside the ship.

"I hate this waiting," Franey said, settling down comfortably to his cigar.

"Part of the job," said Decker. He poured more brandy into his coffee.

By dawn the last machines were set up and either had been moved out to their assigned positions or were parked in the motor pool. The flamers had enlarged the burned-over area and three radiation wagons were busy on their rounds. To the south, the airfield had been finished and the jets were lined up and waiting in a plumb-straight row.

Some of the robots, their work done for the moment, formed themselves in solid ranks to form a solid square, neat and orderly and occupying a minimum of space. They stood there in the square, waiting against the time when they would be needed, a motor pool of robots, a reservoir of manpower.

Finally the gangplank came down and the legionnaires marched out in files of two, with clank and glitter and a remorseless precision that put machines to shame. There were no banners and there were no drums, for these are useless things and the

Legion, despite its clank and glitter, was an organization of ruthless efficiency.

The column wheeled and became a line and the line broke up and the platoons moved out toward the planet-head. There, machines and legionnaires and robots manned the frontier Earth had set up on an alien world.

Busy robots staked out and set up an open-air pavilion of gaudily-striped canvas that rippled in the breeze, placed tables and chairs beneath its shade, moved in a refrigerator filled with beer and with extra ice compartments.

It finally was safe and comfortable for ordinary men to leave the shelter of the ship.

Organization, Decker told himself—organization and efficiency and leaving not a thing to chance. Plug every loophole before it became a loophole. Crush possible resistance before it developed as resistance. Gain absolute control over a certain number of square feet of planet and operate from there.

Later, of course, there were certain chances taken; you just couldn't eliminate them all. There would be field trips and even with all the precautions that robot and machine and legionnaire could offer, there would be certain risks. There would be aerial survey and mapping, and these, too, would have elements of chance, but with these elements reduced to the very minimum.

And always there would be the base, an absolutely safe and impregnable base to which a field party or a survey flight could retreat, from which reinforcements could be sent out or counter-action taken.

Foolproof, he told himself. As foolproof as it could be made.

He wondered briefly what had been the matter with him the night before. It had been that young fool, Jackson, of course—a capable biochemist, possibly, but certainly the wrong kind of man for a job like this. Something had slipped up; the screening board should have stopped a man like Jackson, should have spotted his emotional instability. Not that he could do any actual harm, of course, but he could be upsetting. An irritant, thought Decker, that is what he is. Just an irritant.

Decker laid an armload of paraphernalia on the long table underneath the gay pavilion. From it he selected a rolled-up sheet of map paper, unrolled it, spread it flat and thumb-tacked it at four corners. On it a portion of the river and the mountains to the west had been roughly penciled in. The base was represented by an X'ed-through square—but the rest of it was blank.

But it would be filled in; as the days went by it would take on shape and form.

From the field to the south a jet whooshed into the sky, made a lazy turn and straightened out to streak toward the west. Decker walked to the edge of the pavilion's shade and watched it as it dwindled out of sight. That would be Jarvis and Don-nelly, assigned to the preliminary survey of the southwest sector between the base and the western mountains.

Another jet rose lazily, trailing its column of exhaust, gathered speed and sprang into the sky. Freeman and Johns, he thought.

Decker went back to the table, pulled out a chair and sat down. He picked up a pencil and tapped it idly on the almost-blank map paper. Behind his back he heard another jet whoom upward from the field.

He let his eyes take in the base. Already it was losing its raw, burned-over look. Already it had something of the look of Earth about it, of the efficiency and common sense and get-the-job-done attitude of the men of Earth.

Small groups of men stood around talking. One of them, he saw, was squatted on the ground, talking something over with three squatting robots. Others walked around, sizing up the situation.

Decker grunted with satisfaction. A capable gang of men, he thought. Most of them would have to wait around to really get down to work until the first surveys came in, but even while they waited they would not be idle.

They'd take soil samples and test them. The life that swarmed in the soil would be captured and brought in by grinning robots, and the squirming, vicious things would be pinned down and investigated—photographed, X-rayed, dissected, analyzed, observed, put through reaction tests. Trees and plants and grasses would be catalogued and attempts made to classify them. Test pits would be dug for a look at soil strata. The river's water would be analyzed. Seines would dredge up some of the life they held. Wells would be driven to establish water tables.

All of this here, at the moment, while they waited for the first preliminary flights to bring back data that would pin-point other areas worthy of investigation.

Once those reports were in, the work would be started in dead earnest. Geologists and mineral men would probe into the planet's hide. Weather observation points would be set up. Botanists would take far-ranging check samples. Each man would do the work for which he had been trained. Field reports would pour back to the base, there to be correlated and fit into the picture.

Work then, work in plenty. Work by day and night. And all the time the base would be a bit of Earth, a few square yards held inviolate against all another world might muster.

Decker sat easily in his chair and felt the breeze that came beneath the canvas, a gentle breeze that ruffled through his hair, rattled the papers on the table and twitched the tacked-down map. It was pleasant here, he thought. But it wouldn't stay pleasant long. It almost never did.

Someday, he thought, I'll find a pleasant planet, a paradise planet where the weather's always perfect and there is food for the picking of it and natives that are intelligent to talk with and companionable in other ways, and I will never leave it. I'll refuse to leave when the ship is ready to blast off. I'll live out my days in a fascinating corner of a lousy galaxy—a galaxy that is gaunt with hunger and mad with savagery and lonely beyond all that may be said of loneliness.

He looked up from his reverie and saw Jackson standing at the pavilion's edge, watching him.

"What's the matter, Jackson?" Decker asked with sudden bitterness. "Why aren't you—"

"They're bringing in a native, sir," said Jackson, breathlessly. "One of the things Waldron and Dickson saw."

The native was humanoid, but he was not human.

As Waldron and Dickson had said, he was a matchstick man, a flesh and blood extension of a drawing a four-year-old might make. He was black as the ace of spades, and he wore no clothing, but the eyes that looked out of the pumpkin-shaped head at Decker were bright with a light that might have been intelligence.

Decker tensed as he looked into those eyes. Then he looked away and saw the men standing silently around the pavilion's edge, silent and waiting, tense as he was.

Slowly Decker reached out his hand to one of the two headsets of the mentograph. His fingers closed over it and for a moment he felt a vague, but forceful, reluctance to put it on his head. It was disturbing to contact, or attempt to contact, an alien mind. It gave one a queasy feeling in the pit of the stomach. It was a thing, he thought, that Man never had been intended to do—an experience that was utterly foreign to any human background.

He lifted the headset slowly, fitted it over his skull, made a sign toward the second set.

For a long moment the alien eyes watched him, the creature standing erect and motionless.

Courage, thought Decker. Raw and naked courage, to stand there in this suddenly unfamiliar environment that had blossomed almost overnight on familiar ground, to stand there motionless and erect, surrounded by creatures that must look as if they had dropped from some horrible nightmare.

The humanoid took one step closer to the table, reached out a hand and took the headset. Fumbling with its unfamiliarity, he clamped it on his head. And never for a moment did the eyes waver from Decker's eyes, always alert and watchful.

Decker forced himself to relax, tried to force his mind into an attitude of peace and calm. That was a thing you had to be careful of. You couldn't scare these creatures—you had to lull them, quiet them down, make them feel your friendliness. They would be upset, and a sudden thought, even a suggestion of human brusqueness would wind them up tighter than a drum.

There was intelligence here, he told himself, being careful to keep his mind unruffled, a greater intelligence than one would think, looking at the creature. Intelligence enough to know that he should put on the headset, and guts enough to do it.

He caught the first faint mental whiff of the matchstick man, and the pit of his stomach contracted suddenly and there was an ache around his chest. There was nothing in the thing he caught, nothing that could be put into words, but there was an alienness, as a smell is alien. There was a non-human connotation that set one's teeth on edge. He fought back the gagging blackness of repulsive disgust that sought to break the smooth friendliness he held within his mind.

"We are friendly," Decker forced himself to think. "We are friendly. We will not harm you. We will not harm—"

"You will never leave," said the humanoid.

"Let us be friends," thought Decker. "Let us be friends. We have gifts. We will help you. We will—"

"You should not have come," said the matchstick thought. "But since you are here, you can never leave."

Humor him, thought Decker to himself. Humor him.

"All right, then," he thought. "We will stay. We will stay and we will be friendly. We will stay and teach you. We will give you the things we have brought for you and we will stay with you."

"You will not leave," said the matchstick man's thought, and there was something so cold and logical and matter-of-fact about the way the thought was delivered that Decker suddenly was cold.

The humanoid meant it—meant every word he said. He was not being dramatic, nor was he blustering—but neither was he bluffing. He actually thought that the humans would not leave, that they would not live to leave the planet.

Decker smiled softly to himself.

"You will die here," said the humanoid thought.

"Die?" asked Decker. "What is die?"

The matchstick man's thought was pure disgust. Deliberately, he reached up, took off the headset and laid it carefully back upon the table.

Then he turned and walked away, and not a man made a move to stop him.

Decker took off his headset and slammed it on the table top.

"Jackson," he said, "pick up that phone and tell the Legion to let him through. Let him leave. Don't try to stop him."

He sat limply in his chair and looked at the ring of faces that were watching him.

Waldron asked, "What is it, Decker?"

"He sentenced us to death," said Decker. "He said that we would not leave the planet. He said that we would die here."

"Strong words," said Waldron.

"He meant them," Decker said.

He lifted a hand, flipped it wearily. "He doesn't know, of course," he said. "He really thinks that he can stop us from leaving. He thinks that we will die."

It was an amusing situation, really. That a naked humanoid should walk out of the jungle and threaten to do away with a human survey party, that he should really think that he could do it. That he should be so positive about it.

But there was not a single smile on any of the faces that looked at Decker.

"We can't let it get us," Decker said.

"Nevertheless," Waldron declared, "we should take all precautions."

Decker nodded. "We'll go on emergency alert immediately," he said. "We'll stay that way until we're sure . . . until we're . . ."

His voice trailed off. Sure of what? Sure that an alien savage who wore no clothing, who had not a sign of culture about him, could wipe out a group of humans protected by a ring of steel, held within a guard of machines and robots and a group of fighting men who knew all there was to know concerning the refinements of dealing out swift and merciless extermination to anything that moved against them?

Ridiculous!

Of course it was ridiculous!

And yet the eyes had held intelligence. The being had not only intelligence, but courage. He had stood within a circle of—to him—alien beings, and he had not flinched. He had faced the unknown and said what there was to say, and then had walked away with a dignity any human would have been proud to wear. He must have guessed that the alien beings within the confines of the base were not of his own planet, for he had said that they should not have come, and his thought had implied that he was aware they were not of this world of his. He had understood that he was supposed to put on the headset, but whether that was an act more of courage than of intelligence one would never know—for you could not know if he had realized what the headset had been for. Not knowing, the naked courage of clamping it to his head was of an order that could not be measured.

"What do you think?" Decker asked Waldron.

"We'll have to be careful," Waldron told him evenly. "We'll have to watch our step. Take all precautions, now that we are warned. But there's nothing to be scared of, nothing we can't handle."

"He was bluffing," Dickson said. "Trying to scare us into leaving."

Decker shook his head. "I don't think he was," he said. "I tried to bluff him and it didn't work. He's just as sure as we are."

The work went on. There was no attack.

The jets roared out and thrummed away, mapping the land. Field parties went out cautiously. They were flanked by robots and by legionnaires and preceded by lumbering machines that knifed and tore and burned a roadway through even the most stubborn of the terrain they went up against. Radio weather stations were set up at distant points, and at the base the weather tabulators clicked off on tape the data that the stations sent back.

Other field parties were flown into the special areas pinpointed for more extensive exploration and investigation.

And nothing happened.

The days went past.

The weeks went past.

The machines and robots watched and the legionnaires stood ready, and the men hurried with their work so they could get off the planet.

A bed of coal was found and mapped. An iron range was discovered. One area in the mountains to the west crawled with radioactive ores. The botanists found twenty-seven species of edible fruit. The base swarmed with animals that had been trapped as specimens and remained as pets.

And a village of the matchstick men was found.

It wasn't much of a place. Its huts were primitive. Its sanitation was nonexistent. Its people were peaceful.

Decker left his chair under the striped pavilion to lead a party to the village.

The party entered cautiously, weapons ready but being very careful not to move too fast, not to speak too quickly, not to make a motion that might be construed as hostile.

The natives sat in their doorways and watched them. They did not speak and they scarcely moved a muscle. They simply watched the humans as they marched to the center of the village.

There the robots set up a table and placed a mentograph upon it. Decker sat down in a chair and put one of the headsets on his skull. The rest of the party waited off to one side. Decker waited at the table.

They waited for an hour and not a native stirred. None came forward to put on the other headset.

Decker took off the headset wearily and placed it on the table.

"It's no use," he said. "It won't work. Go ahead and take your pictures. Do anything you wish. But don't disturb the natives. Don't touch a single thing."

He took a handkerchief out of his pocket and mopped his steaming face.

Waldron came and leaned on the table. "What do you make of it?" he asked.

Decker shook his head. "It haunts me," he said. "There's just one thing that I am thinking. It must be wrong. It can't be right. But the thought came to me, and I can't get rid of it."

"Sometimes that happens," Waldron said. "No matter how illogical a thing may be, it sticks with a man, like a burr inside his brain."

"The thought is this," said Decker. "That they have told us all they have to tell us. That they have nothing more they wish to say to us."

"That's what you thought," said Waldron.

Decker nodded. "A funny thing to think," he said. "Out of a clear sky. And it can't be right."

"I don't know," said Waldron. "Nothing's right here. Notice that they haven't got a single iron tool. Not a scrap of metal in evidence at all. Their cooking utensils are stone, a sort of funny stuff like soapstone. What few tools they have are stone. And yet they have a culture. And they have it without metal."

"They're intelligent," said Decker. "Look at them watching us. Not afraid. Just waiting. Calm and sure of themselves. And that fellow who came into the base. He knew what to do with the headset."

Waldron sucked thoughtfully at a tooth. "We'd better be getting back to base," he said. "It's getting late." He held his wrist in front of him. "My watch has stopped. What time do you have, Decker?"

Decker lifted his arm and Waldron heard the sharp gasp of his indrawn breath. Slowly Decker raised his head and looked at the other man.

"My watch has stopped, too," he said, and his voice was scarcely louder than a whisper.

For a moment they were graven images, shocked into immobility by a thing that should have been no more than an inconvenience. Then Waldron sprang erect from the table, whirled to face the men and robots.

"Assemble!" he shouted. "Back to the base. Quick!"

The men came running. The robots fell into place. The column marched away. The natives sat quietly in their doorways and watched them as they left.

Decker sat in his camp chair and listened to the canvas of the pavilion snapping softly in the wind, alive in the wind, talking and laughing to itself. A lantern, hung on a ring above his head, swayed gently, casting fleeting shadows that seemed at times to be the shadows of living, moving things. A robot stood stiffly and quietly beside one of the pavilion poles.

Stolidly, Decker reached out a finger and stirred the little pile of wheels and springs that lay upon the table.

Sinister, he thought. Sinister and queer.

The guts of watches, lying on the table. Not of two watches

alone, not only his and Waldron's watches, but many other watches from the wrists of other men. All of them silent, stilled in their task of marking time.

Night had fallen hours before, but the base still was astir with activity that was at once feverish and furtive. Men moved about in the shadows and crossed the glaring patches of brilliance shed by the batteries of lights set up by the robots many weeks before. Watching the men, one would have sensed that they moved with a haunting sense of doom, would have known as well that they knew, deep in their inmost hearts, that there was no doom to fear. No definite thing that one could put a finger on and say, this is the thing to fear. No direction that one might point toward and say, doom lies here, waiting to spring upon us.

Just one small thing.

Watches had stopped running. And that was a simple thing for which there must be some simple explanation.

Except, thought Decker, on an alien planet no occurrence, no accident or incident, can be regarded as a simple things for which a simple explanation must necessarily be anticipated. For the matrix of cause and effect, the mathematics of chance, may not hold true on an alien planet as they hold true on Earth.

There was one rule, Decker thought grimly. One rule: Take no chances. That was the one safe rule to follow, the only rule to follow.

Following it, he had ordered all field parties back to base, had ordered the crew to prepare the ship for emergency take-off, had alerted the robots to be ready at an instant to get the machines aboard. Even to be prepared to desert the machines and leave without them if circumstances should dictate that this was necessary.

Having done that, there was no more to do but wait. Wait until the field parties came back from their advance camps. Wait until some reason could be assigned to the failure of the watches.

It was not a thing, he told himself, that should be allowed to panic one. It was something to recognize, not to disregard. It was a circumstance that made necessary a certain number of precautions, but it was not a situation that should make one lose all sense of proportion.

You could not go back to Earth and say, "Well, you see, our watches stopped and so . . ."

A footstep sounded and he swung around in his chair. It was Jackson.

"What is it, Jackson?" Decker asked.

"The camps aren't answering, sir," said Jackson. "The operator has been trying to raise them and there is no answer. Not a single peep."

Decker grunted. "Take it easy," he said. "They will answer. Give them time."

He wished, even as he spoke, that he could feel some of the assurance that he tried to put into his voice. For a second, a rising terror mounted in his throat and he choked it back.

"Sit down," he said. "We'll sit here and have a beer and then we'll go down to the radio shack and see what's doing."

He rapped on the table. "Beer," he said. "Two beers."

The robot standing by the pavilion pole did not answer.

He made his voice louder. The robot did not stir.

Decker put his clenched fists upon the table and tried to rise, but his legs were suddenly cold and had turned unaccountably to water, and he could not raise himself.

"Jackson," he panted, "go and tap that robot on the shoulder. Tell him we want beer."

He saw the fear that whitened Jackson's face as he rose and moved slowly forward. Inside himself, he felt the terror start and worry at his throat.

Jackson stood beside the robot and reached out a hesitant hand, tapped him gently on the shoulder, tapped him harder— and the robot fell flat upon its face!

Feet hammered across the hard-packed ground, heading for the pavilion.

Decker jerked himself around, sat foursquare and solid in his chair, waiting for the man who ran.

It was MacDonald, the chief engineer.

He halted in front of Decker and his hands, scarred and grimy with years of fighting balky engines, reached down and gripped the boards of the table's edge. His seamy face was twisted as if he were about to weep.

"The ship, sir. The ship . . ."

Decker nodded, almost idly. "I know, Mr. MacDonald. The ship won't run."

MacDonald gulped. "The big stuff's all right, sir. But the little gadgets . . . the injector mechanism . . . the—"

He stopped abruptly and stared at Decker. "You knew," he said. "How did you know?"

"I knew," said Decker, "that someday it would come. Not like this, perhaps. But in any one of several ways. I knew that the day would come when our luck would run too thin. I talked big, like the rest of you, of course, but I knew that it would come. The day when we'd covered all the possibilities but the one that we could not suspect, and that, of course, would be the one that would ruin us."

He was thinking, the natives had no metal. No sign of any metal in their village at /Sall. Their dishes were soapstone, and they wore no ornaments. Their implements were stone. And yet they were intelligent enough, civilized enough, cultured enough, to have fabricated metal. For there was metal here, a great deposit of it in the western mountains. They had tried perhaps, many centuries ago, had fashioned metal tools and had them go to pieces underneath their fingers in a few short weeks.

A civilization without metal. A culture without metal. It was unthinkable. Take metal from a man and he went back to the caves. Take metal from a man and he was earthbound, and his bare hands were all he had.

Waldron came into the pavilion, walking quietly in the silence. "The radio is dead," he said, "and the robots are dying like flies. The place is littered with them, just so much scrap metal."

Decker nodded. "The little stuff, the finely fabricated, will go first," he said. "Like watches and radio innards and robot brains and injector mechanisms. Next, the generators will go and we will have no lights or power. Then the machines will break down and the Legion's weapons will be no more than clubs. After that, the big stuff, probably."

"The native told us," Waldron said, "when you talked to him. 'You will never leave,' he said."

"We didn't understand," said Decker. "We thought he was threatening us and we knew that we were too big, too well guarded for any threat of his to harm us. He wasn't threatening us at all, of course. He was just telling us."

He made a hopeless gesture with his hands. "What is it?"

"No one knows," said Waldron quietly. "Not yet, at least. Later, we may find out, but it won't help us any. A microbe, maybe. A virus. Something that eats iron after it has been subjected to heat or alloyed with other metals. It doesn't go for iron ore. If it did, that deposit we found would have been gone long ago."

"If that is true," said Decker, "we've brought it the first square meal it's had in a long, long time. A thousand years. Maybe a million years. There is no fabricated metal here. How would it survive? Without stuff to eat, how would it live?"

"I wouldn't know," said Waldron. "It might not be a metal-eating organism at all. It might be something else. Something in the atmosphere."

"We tested the atmosphere."

But, even as the words left his mouth, Decker saw how foolish they were. They had tested the atmosphere, but how could they have detected something they had never run across before? Man's yardstick was limited—limited to the things he knew about, limited by the circle of his own experience. He guarded himself against the obvious and the imaginable. He could not guard himself against the unknowable or the unimaginable.

Decker rose and saw Jackson still standing by the pavilion pole, with the robot stretched at his feet.

"You have your answer," he told the biochemist. "Remember that first day here? You talked with me in the lounge."

Jackson nodded. "I remember, sir."

And suddenly, Decker realized, the entire base was quiet.

A gust of wind came out of the jungle and rattled the canvas.

Now, for the first time since they had landed, he caught in the wind the alien smell of an alien world.

SUNSPOT PURGE

According to his journal, Clifford D. Simak sent this story to
Astounding Science Fiction *in January 1940, and it was accepted
less two weeks later by John W. Campbell Jr., the editor who molded
that magazine into one of the great forces in science fiction. His quick
reaction speaks to a ringing endorsement. Campbell sent Cliff a check
for $87.50 and published the story in the November 1940 issue of
his magazine. In this tale, Cliff combined his coinciding newspaper
background with the time travel idea from his very first published
story, "The World of the Red Sun." But in later years, he would
describe "Sunspot Purge," along with "Madness from Mars," as "truly
horrible examples of an author's fumbling agony in the process of
finding himself." Since both of those stories carry the effectively por-
trayed emotional weight that Cliff had been seeking to bring to science fiction, I find that I do not fully agree with his self-analysis; and
I believe that I am only seconding Campbell's opinion. After all, he
backed up his acceptance of the story with money. Nor was Cliff's
own assessment one of unalloyed disaster. Immediately following the
quoted passage, he continued with this: "It is possible the discerning
reader may discover in them some of the seeds of later writing, but I
cringe at their being read."*

*And in the back of my mind, I wonder how much this story
resulted from Cliff's perceptions about World War II, which was more
than a year old when Cliff wrote this story (although the United*

States had not yet been dragged into it). Many commentators have come to believe that the "City" stories, which would begin to be written only a few years after "Sunspot Purge," owed at least a portion of their genesis to Cliff's reactions to the war; and it seems to me that such might explain the pessimism so evident here.

—dww

I was sitting around, waiting for the boy to bring up the first batch of papers from the pressroom. I had my feet up on the desk, my hat pulled down over my eyes, feeling pretty sick.

I couldn't get the picture of the fellow hitting the sidewalk out of my mind. Twenty stories is a long way to jump. When he'd hit he'd just sort of spattered and it was very messy.

The fool had cavorted and pranced around up on that ledge since early morning, four long hours, before he took the dive.

Herb Harding and Al Jarvey and a couple of other *Globe* photographers had gone out with me, and I listened to them figure out the way they'd co-operate on the shots. If the bird jumped, they knew they'd each have just time enough to expose one plate. So they got their schedules worked out beforehand.

Al would take the first shot with the telescopic lens as he made the jump. Joe would catch him halfway down. Harry would snap him just before he hit, and Herb would get the moment of impact on the sidewalk.

It gave me the creeps, listening to them.

But anyhow, it worked and the *Globe* had a swell sequence panel of the jump to go with my story.

We knew the *Standard,* even if it got that sidewalk shot, wouldn't use it, for the *Standard* claimed to be a family newspaper and made a lot of being a sheet fit for anyone to read.

But the *Globe* would print anything—and did. We gave it to 'em red-hot and without any fancy dressing.

"The guy was nuts," said Herb, who had come over and sat down beside me.

"The whole damn world is nuts," I told him. "This is the sixth bird that's hopped off a high building in the last month. I wish they'd put me down at the obit desk, or over on the markets, or something. I'm all fed up on gore."

"It goes like that," said Herb. "For a long time there ain't a thing worth shooting. Then all hell breaks loose."

Herb was right. News runs that way—in streaks. Crime waves and traffic-accident waves and suicide waves. But this was something different. It wasn't just screwballs jumping off high places. It was a lot of other things.

There was the guy who had massacred his family and then turned the gun on himself. There was the chap who'd butchered his bride on their honeymoon. And the fellow who had poured gasoline over himself and struck a match.

All such damn senseless things.

No newsman in his right mind objects to a little violence, for that's what news is made of. But things were getting pretty thick; just a bit revolting and horrifying. Enough to sicken even a hard-working legman who isn't supposed to have any feelings over things like that.

Just then the boy came up with the papers, and, if I say so myself, that story of mine read like a honey. It should have. I had been thinking it up and composing it while I watched the bird teetering around up on that ledge.

The pictures were good, too. Great street-sale stuff. I could almost see old J.R. rubbing his hands together and licking his lips and patting himself on the back for the kind of a sheet we had.

Billy Larson, the science editor, strolled over to my desk and draped himself over it. Billy was a funny guy. He wore big, horn-rimmed spectacles, and he wiggled his ears when he got excited, but he knew a lot of science. He could take a dry-as-dust scientific paper and pep it up until it made good reading.

"I got an idea," he announced.

"So have I," I answered. "I'm going down to the Dutchman's and take me on a beer. Maybe two or three."

"I hope," piped Herb, "that it ain't something else about old Doc Ackerman and his time machine."

"Nope," said Billy, "it's something else. Doc's time machine isn't so hot any more. People got tired of reading about it. I guess the old boy has plenty on the ball, but what of it? Who will ever use the thing? Everyone is scared of it."

"What's it this time?" I asked.

"Sunspots," he said.

I tried to brush him off, because I wanted that beer so bad I could almost taste it, but Billy had an idea, and he wasn't going to let me get away before he told me all about it.

"It's pretty well recognized," he told me, "that sunspots do affect human lives. Lots of sunspots and we have good times. Stocks and bonds are up, prices are high. Trade is good. But likewise, we have an increased nervous tension. We have violence. People get excited."

"Hell starts to pop," said Herb.

"That's exactly it," agreed Billy. "Tchijevsky, the Russian scientist, pointed it out thirty years ago. I believe he's the one that noted increased activity on battle fronts during the first World War occurring simultaneously with the appearance of large spots on the Sun. Back in 1937, the sit-down strikes were ushered in by one of the most rapid rises in the sunspot curve in twenty years."

I couldn't get excited. But Billy was all worked up about it. That's the way he is—enthusiastic about his work.

"People have their ups and downs," he said, a fanatic light creeping into his eyes, the way it does when he's on the trail of some idea to make *Globe* readers gasp.

"Not only people, but peoples—nations, cultures, civilizations. Go back through history and you can point out a parallelism in the cycles of sunspots and significant events. Take 1937, for example, the year they had the sit-down strikes. In July of that year the sunspot cycle hits its maximum with a Wolfer index of 137.

"Scientists are pretty sure periods of excitement are explained by acute changes in the nervous and psychic characters of humanity which take place at sunspot maxima, but they aren't sure of the reasons for those changes."

"Ultraviolet light," I yawned, remembering something I had read in a magazine about it.

Billy wiggled his ears and went on: "Most likely ultraviolet has a lot to do with it. The spots themselves aren't strong emission centers for ultraviolet. But it may be the very changes in the Sun's atmosphere which produce the spots also result in the production of more ultraviolet.

"Most of the ultraviolet reaching Earth's atmosphere is used up converting oxygen into ozone, but changes of as much as twenty percent in its intensity are possible at the surface.

"And ultraviolet produces definite reaction in human glands, largely in the endocrine glands."

"I don't believe a damn word of it," Herb declared flatly, but there was no stopping Billy.

He clinched his argument: "Let's say, then, that changes in sunshine, such as occur during sunspot periods, affect the physiological character and mental outlook of all the people on Earth. In other words, human behavior corresponds to sunspot cycles.

"Compare Dow Jones averages with sunspots and you will find they show a marked sympathy with the cycles—the market rising with sunspot activity. Sunspots were riding high in 1928 and 1929. In the autumn of 1929 there was an abrupt break in sunspot activity and the market crashed. It hit bedrock in 1932 and 1933, and so did the sunspots. Wall Street follows the sunspot cycle."

"Keep those old sunspots rolling," I jeered at him, "and we'll have everlasting prosperity. We'll simply wallow in wealth."

"Sure," said Herb, "and the damn fools will keep jumping off the buildings."

"But what would happen if we reversed things—made a law against sunspots?" I asked.

"Why, then," said Billy, solemn as an owl, "we'd have terrible depressions."

I got up and walked away from him. I had got to thinking about what I had seen on the sidewalk after the fellow jumped, and I needed that beer.

Jake, one of the copy boys, yelled at me just as I was going out the door.

"J.R. wants to see you, Mike."

So I turned around and walked toward the door behind which J.R. sat rubbing his hands and figuring out some new stunts to shock the public into buying the *Globe*.

"Mike," said J.R. when I stepped into his office, "I want to congratulate you on the splendid job you did this morning. Mighty fine story, my boy, mighty fine."

"Thanks, J.R.," I said, knowing the old rascal didn't mean a word of it.

Then J.R. got down to business.

"Mike," he said, "I suppose you've been reading this stuff about Dr. Ackerman's time machine."

"Yeah," I told him, "but if you think you're going to send me out to interview that old publicity grabber, you're all wrong. I saw a guy spatter himself all over Fifth Street this morning, and I been listening to Billy Larson telling about sunspots, and I can't stand much more. Not in one day, anyhow."

Then J.R. dropped the bombshell on me.

"The *Globe*," he announced, "has bought a time machine."

That took me clear off my feet.

The *Globe*, in my time, had done a lot of wacky things, but this was the worst.

"What for?" I asked weakly, and J.R. looked shocked; but he recovered in a minute and leaned across the desk.

"Just consider, Mike. Think of the opportunities a time

machine offers a newspaper. The other papers can tell them what has happened and what is happening, but, by Godfrey, they'll have to read the *Globe* to know what is going to happen."

"I have a slogan for you," I said. "Read the News Before It Happens."

He didn't know if I was joking or was serious and waited for a minute before going on.

"A war breaks out," he said. "The other papers can tell what is happening at the moment. We can do better than that. We can tell them what will happen. Who will win and lose. What battles will be fought. How long the war will last—"

"But, J.R.," I yelled at him, "you can't do that! Don't you see what a hell of a mess you'll make of things. If one side knew it was going to lose—"

"It doesn't apply merely to wars," said J.R. "There's sports. Football games. Everybody is nuts right now to know if Minnesota is going to lick Wisconsin. We jump into our time machine, travel ahead to next Saturday. Day before the game we print the story, with pictures and everything."

He rubbed his hands and purred.

"I'll have old Johnson down at the *Standard* eating out of my hand," he gloated. "I'll make him wish he never saw a newspaper. I'll take the wind out of his sails. I'll send my reporters out a day ahead—"

"You'll have every bookie on your neck," I shouted. "Don't you know there's millions of dollars bet every Saturday on football games? Don't you see what you'd do? You'd put every jackpot, every betting window out of business. Tracks would close down. Nobody would spend a dime to see a game they could read about ahead of time. You'd put organized baseball and college football, boxing, everything else out of business. What would be the use of staging a prize fight if the public knew in advance who was going to win?"

But J.R. just chortled gleefully and rubbed his hands.

"We'll publish stock-market quotations for the coming month on the first of every month," he planned. "Those papers will sell for a hundred bucks apiece."

Seeing him sitting there gave me a sinking feeling in the pit of my stomach. For I knew that in his hands rested a terrible power, a power that he was blind to or too stubborn to respect.

The power to rob every human being on Earth of every bit of happiness. For if a man could look ahead and see some of the things that no doubt were going to happen, how could he be happy?

Power to hurl the whole world into chaos. Power to make and break any man, or thing, or institution that stood before him.

I tried another angle.

"But how do you know the machine will work?"

"I have ample proof," said J.R. "The other papers ridiculed Dr. Ackerman, while we presented his announcement at face value. That is why he is giving us an exclusive franchise to the purchase and use of his invention. It's costing us plenty of money—a barrel of money—but we're going to make two barrels of money out of it."

I shrugged my shoulders.

"O.K.," I said. "Go ahead. I don't see why the hell you called me in."

"Because," beamed J.R., "you're going to make the first trip in the time machine!"

"What!" I yelled.

J.R. nodded. "You and a photographer. Herb Harding. I called you in first. You leave tomorrow morning. Five hundred years into the future for a starter. Get pictures. Come back and write your story. We'll spring it in the Sunday paper. Whole front-page layout. What does the city look like five hundred years from now? What changes have been made? Who's mayor? What are the women wearing in the fall of 2450?"

He grinned at me.

"And you might say, too, that the *Standard* no longer is published. Whether it's the truth or not, you know. Old Johnson will go hog wild when he reads that in your story."

I could have refused, of course, but if I had, he would have sent somebody else and tied the can on me. Even in 1950, despite a return to prosperity that beggared the flushest peak of 1929, good jobs in the newspaper field were not so easy to pick up.

So I said I'd go, and half an hour later I found myself getting just a bit excited about being one of the first men to travel into time. For I wouldn't be the very first. Doc Ackerman had traveled ahead a few years in his own machine, often enough and far enough to prove the thing would work.

But the prospect of it gave me a headache when I tried to reason it out. The whole thing sounded wacky to me. Not so much the idea that one could really travel in time, for I had no doubt one could. J.R. wasn't anybody's fool. Before he sunk his money in that time machine he would have demanded ironclad, gilt-edged proof that it would operate successfully.

But the thing that bothered me was the complications that might arise. The more I thought of it, the sicker and more confused I got.

Why, with a time machine a reporter could travel ahead and report a man's death, get pictures of his funeral. Those pictures could be taken back in time and published years before his death. That man, when he read the paper, would know the exact hour that he would die, would see his own face framed within the casket.

A boy of ten might know that some day he would be elected president of the United States simply by reading the *Globe*. The present president, angling for a third term, could read his own political fate if the *Globe* chose to print it.

A man might read that the next day he would meet death in a traffic accident. And if that man knew he was going to die, he would take steps to guard against it. But could he guard against it? Could he change his own future? Or was the future cast in a rigid mold? If the future said something was going to happen, was it absolutely necessary that it must happen?

The more I thought about it, the crazier it sounded. But somehow I couldn't help but think of it. And the more I thought about it, the worse my head hurt.

So I went down to the Dutchman's.

Louie was back of the bar, and when he handed me my first glass of beer, I said to him: "It's a hell of a world, Louie."

And Louie said to me: "It sure as hell is, Mike."

I drank a lot of beer, but I didn't get drunk. I stayed cold sober. And that made me sore, because I figured that by rights I should take on a load. And all the time my head swam with questions and complicated puzzles.

I would have tried something stronger than beer, but I knew if I mixed drinks I'd get sick, so finally I gave up.

Louie asked me if there was something wrong, and I said no, there wasn't, but before I left I shook hands with Louie and said good-by. If I had been drunk, Louie wouldn't have thought a thing of it, but I could see he was surprised I acted that way when he knew I was sober as the daylight.

Just as I was going out the door I met Jimmy Langer coming in. Jimmy worked for the *Standard* and was a good newspaperman, but mean and full of low-down tricks. We were friends, of course, and had worked on lots of stories together, but we always watched one another pretty close. There was never any telling what Jimmy might be up to.

"Hi, Jimmy," I said.

And Jimmy did a funny thing. He didn't say a word. He just looked right at me and laughed into my face.

It took me so by surprise I didn't do anything until he was inside the Dutchman's, and then I walked down the street. But at the corner I stopped, wondering if I hadn't better go back and punch Jimmy's nose. I hadn't liked the way he laughed at me.

The time-machine device was installed in a plane because, Doc Ackerman told us, it wouldn't be wise to try to do much traveling at ground level. A fellow might travel forward a hundred years or so and find himself smack in the middle of a building. Or the ground might rise or sink and the time machine would be buried or left hanging in the air. The only safe way to travel in time, Doc warned us, was to do it in a plane.

The plane was squatting in a pasture a short distance from Doc's laboratories, situated at the edge of the city, and a tough-looking mug carrying a rifle was standing guard over it. That plane had been guarded night and day. It was just too valuable a thing to let anyone get near it.

Doc explained the operation of the time machine to me.

"It's simple," he said. "Simple as falling off a log."

And what he said was true. All you had to do was set the indicator forward the number of years you wished to travel. When you pressed the activator stud you went into the time spin, or whatever it was that happened to you, and you stayed in it until you reached the proper time. Then the mechanism acted automatically, your time speed was slowed down, and there you were. You just reversed the process to go backward.

Simple. Simple, so Doc said, as falling off a log. But I knew that behind all that simplicity was some of the most wonderful science the world had ever known—science and brains and long years of grueling work and terrible disappointment.

"It will be like plunging into night," Doc told me. "You will be traveling in time as a single dimension. There will be no heat, no air, no gravitation, absolutely nothing outside your plane. But the plane is insulated to keep in the heat. In case you do get cold, just snap on those heaters. Air will be supplied, if you need it, by the oxygen tanks. But on a short trip like five hundred years you probably won't need either the heaters or the oxygen. Just a few minutes and you'll be there."

J.R. had been sore at me because I had been late. Sore, too, because Herb had one of the most beautiful hangovers I have ever laid eyes on. But he'd forgotten all about that now. He was hopping up and down in his excitement.

"Just wait," he chortled. "Just wait until Johnson sees this down at the *Standard*. He'll probably have a stroke. Serve him right, the stubborn old buzzard."

The guard, standing just outside the door of the ship, was shuffling his feet. For some reason the fellow seemed nervous.

Doc croaked at him. "What's the matter with you, Benson?"

The guy stammered and shifted his rifle from one hand to another. He tried to speak, but the words just dried up in his mouth. Then J.R. started some more of his gloating and we forgot about the guard.

Herb had his cameras stowed away and everything was ready. J.R. stuck out his fist and shook hands with me and Herb, and the old rascal was pretty close to tears.

Doc and J.R. got out of the ship, and I followed them to the door. Before I closed and sealed it I took one last look at the city skyline. There it shimmered, in all its glory, through the blue haze of an autumn day. Familiar towers, and to the north the smudge of smoke that hung over the industrial district.

I waved my hand at the towers and said to them: "So long, big boys. I'll be seeing you five hundred years from now."

The skyline looked different up there in the future. I had expected it to look different because in five hundred years some buildings would be torn down and new ones would go up. New architectural ideas, new construction principles over the course of five centuries will change any city skyline.

But it was different in another way than that.

I had expected to see a vaster and a greater and more perfect city down below us when we rolled out of our time spin, and it was vaster and greater, but there was something wrong.

It had a dusty and neglected look.

It had grown in those five hundred years, there was no doubt of that. It had grown in all directions, and must have been at least three times as big as the city Herb and I had just left behind.

Herb leaned forward in his seat.

"Is that really the old burg down there?" he asked. "Or is it just my hangover?"

"It's the same old place," I assured him. Then I asked him. "Where did you pick up that beauty you've got?"

"I was out with some of the boys," he told me. "Al and Harry. We met up with some of the *Standard* boys and had a few drinks with them later in the evening."

There were no planes in the sky and I had expected that in 2450 the air would fairly swarm with them. They had been getting pretty thick even back in 1950. And now I saw the streets were free of traffic, too.

We cruised around for half an hour, and during that time the truth was driven home to us. A truth that was plenty hard to take.

That city below us was a dead city! There was no sign of life. Not a single automobile on the street, not a person on the sidewalks.

Herb and I looked at one another, and disbelief must have been written in letters three feet high upon our faces.

"Herb," I said, "we gotta find out what this is all about."

Herb's Adam's apple jiggled up and down his neck.

"Hell," he said. "I was figuring on dropping into the Dutchman's and getting me a pick-up."

It took almost an hour to find anything that looked like an airport, but finally I found one that looked safe enough. It was overgrown with weeds, but the place where the concrete runways had been was still fairly smooth, although the concrete had been broken here and there, and grass and weeds were growing through the cracks.

I took her down as easy as I could, but even at that we hit a place where a slab of concrete had been heaved and just missed a crackup.

The old fellow with the rifle could have stepped from the pages of a history of early pioneer days except that once in a while the pioneers probably got a haircut.

He came out of the bushes about a mile from the airport, and his rifle hung cradled in his arm. There was something about him that told me he wasn't one to fool with.

"Howdy, strangers," he said in a voice that had a whiny twang.

"By Heaven," said Herb, "it's Daniel Boone himself."

"You jay birds must be a right smart step from home," said the old guy, and he didn't sound as if he'd trust us very far.

"Not so far," I said. "We used to live here a long time ago."

"Danged if I recognize you." He pushed back his old black felt hat and scratched his head. "And I thought I knew everybody that ever lived around here. You wouldn't be Jake Smith's boys, would you?"

"Doesn't look like many people are living here any more," said Herb.

"Matter of fact, there ain't," said Daniel Boone. "The old woman was just telling me the other day we'd have to move so we'd be nearer neighbors. It gets mighty lonesome for her. Nearest folks is about ten miles up thataway."

He gestured to the north, where the skyline of the city loomed like a distant mountain range, with gleaming marble ramparts and spires of mocking stone.

"Look here," I asked him. "Do you mean to say your nearest neighbor is ten miles away?"

"Sure," he told me. "The Smiths lived over a couple of miles to the west, but they moved out this spring. Went down to the south. Claimed the hunting was better there."

He shook his head sadly. "Maybe hunting is all right. I do a lot of it. But I like to do a little farming, too, And it's mighty hard to break new ground. I had a right handsome bunch of squashes and carrots this year. 'Taters did well, too."

"But at one time a lot of people lived here," I insisted. "Thousands and thousands of people. Probably millions of them."

"I heard tell of that," agreed the old man, "but I can't rightfully say there's any truth in it. Must've been a long time ago. Somebody must have built all them buildings—although what for I just can't figure out."

The *Globe* editorial rooms were ghostly. Dust lay everywhere, and a silence that was almost as heavy as the dust.

There had been some changes, but it was still a newspaper office. All it needed was the blur of voices, the murmur of the speeding presses to bring it to life again.

The desks still were there, and chairs ringed the copy table.

Our feet left trails across the dust that lay upon the floor and raised a cloud that set us both to sneezing.

I made a beeline for one dark corner of the room; there I knew I would find what I was looking for.

Old bound files of the paper. Their pages crackled when I opened them, and the paper was so yellowed with age that in spots it was hard to read.

I carried one of the files to a window and glanced at the date. September 14, 2143. Over three hundred years ago!

A banner screamed: "Relief Riots in Washington."

Hurriedly we leafed through the pages. And there, on the front pages of those papers that had seen the light more than three centuries before, we read the explanation for the silent city that lay beyond the shattered, grime-streaked windows.

"Stocks Crash to Lowest Point in Ten Years!" shrieked one banner. Another said: "Congress Votes Record Relief Funds." Still another: "Taxpayers Refuse to Pay." After that they came faster and faster. "Debt Moratorium Declared"; "Bank Holiday Enforced"; "Thousands Starving in Cleveland"; "Jobless March on Washington"; "Troops Fight Starving Mobs"; "Congress Gives Up, Goes Home"; "Epidemic Sweeping East"; "President Declares National Emergency"; "British Government Abdicates"; "Howling Mob Sweeping Over France"; "U.S. Government Bankrupt."

In the market and financial pages, under smaller heads, we read footnotes to those front-page lines. Story after story of business houses closing their doors, of corporations crashing, reports on declining trade, increasing unemployment, idle factories.

Civilization, three hundred years before, had crashed to ruin under the very weight of its own superstructure. The yellowed files did not tell the entire story, but it was easy to imagine.

"The world went nuts," said Herb.

"Yeah," I said. "Like that guy who took the dive."

I could see it all as plain as day. Declining business, increasing unemployment, heavier taxation to help the unemployed and buy back prosperity, property owners unable to pay those taxes. A vicious circle.

Herb was rummaging around back in the dimness by the filing cabinet. Presently he came out into the light again, all covered with dust.

"There're only twenty or thirty years of files," he said, "and we got the newest one. But I found something else. Back behind the cabinet. Guess it must have fallen back there and nobody ever bothered to clean it out."

He handed it to me—an old and crumpled paper, so brittle with age I was afraid it might crumble to dust in my very hands.

"There was quite a bit of rubble back of the cabinet," said Herb. "Some other papers. Old, too, but this one was the oldest."

I looked at the date. April 16, 1985.

That yellowed paper was almost five hundred years old! It had come off the press less than thirty-five years after Herb and I had taken off with the time machine!

Lying behind the filing cabinet all those years. The cabinet was large and heavy to move, and janitors in newspaper offices aren't noted for outstanding tidiness.

But there was something bothering me. A little whisper way back in my head, somewhere down at the base of my brain, that kept telling me there was something I should remember.

I tossed the old paper on a desk and walked to a window. Most of the glass was broken out, and what wasn't broken out was coated so thick with grime you couldn't see through it. I looked out through the place where there wasn't any glass.

There the city lay—almost as I remembered it. There was Jackson's tower, the tallest in the city back in 1950, but now dwarfed by three or four others. The spire of the old cathedral was gone, and I missed that, for it had been a pretty thing. I used to sit and watch it from this very window through the mist of early-spring rain or through the ghostly white of the winter's first snowfall. I missed the spire, but Jackson's tower was there, and so were a lot of other buildings I could place.

And every one of them looked lonely. Lonely and not quite understanding—like a dog that's been kicked out of a chair he thinks of as his own. Their windows gaping like dead eyes. No cheerful glow of light within them. Their colors dulled by the wash of seasons that had rolled over them.

This was worse, I told myself, than if we'd found the place all smashed to hell by bombs. Because, brutal as it is, one can understand a bombed city. And one can't understand, or feel comfortable in a city that's just been left behind to die.

And the people!

Thinking about them gave me the jitters. Were all the people like old Daniel Boone? We had seen how he and his family lived, and it wasn't pretty. People who had backed down the scale of progress. People who had forgotten the printed word, had twisted the old truths and the old history into screwy legends.

It was easy enough to understand how it had happened. Pull

the economic props from under a civilization and there's hell to pay. First you have mad savagery and even madder destruction as class hatred flames unchecked. And when that hatred dies down after an orgy of destruction there is bewilderment, and then some more savagery and hatred born of bewilderment.

But, sink as low as he may, man always will climb again. It's the nature of the beast. He's an ornery cuss.

But man, apparently, hadn't climbed again. Civilization, as Herb and I knew it, had crashed all of three hundred years before—and man still was content to live in the shadow of his former greatness, not questioning the mute evidences of his mighty past, uninspired by the soaring blocks of stone that reared mountainous above him.

There was something wrong. Something devilish wrong.

Dust rose and tickled my nose, and suddenly I realized my throat was hot and dry. I wanted a beer, if I could only step down the street to the Dutchman's—

Then it smacked me straight between the eyes, the thing that had been whispering around in the back of my head all day.

I remembered Billy Larson's face and the way his ears wiggled when he got excited and how hopped up he had been about a sunspot story.

"By Heaven, Herb, I got it," I yelled, turning from the window.

Herb's mouth sagged, and I knew he thought that I was nuts.

"I know what happened now," I said. "We have to get a telescope."

"Look here, Mike," said Herb, "if you feel—"

But I didn't let him finish.

"It's the sunspots," I yelled at him.

"Sunspots?" he squeaked.

"Sure," I said. "There aren't any."

My hunch had been right.

There weren't any sunspots. No black dots on that great ball of flame.

It had taken two days before we found a pair of powerful field glasses in the rubbish of what once had been a jewelry store. Most of the stores and shops were wiped clean. Raided time after time in the violence which must have followed the breakdown of government, they later would have been looted systematically.

"Herb," I said, "there must have been something in what Billy said. Lots of sunspots and we have good times. No sunspots and we have bad times."

"Yeah," said Herb, "Billy was plenty smart. He knew his science, all right."

I could almost see Billy, his ears wiggling, his eyes glowing, as he talked to me that morning.

Wall Street followed the sunspot cycle, he had said. Business boomed when sunspots were riding high, went to pot when they blinked out.

I remembered asking him what would happen if someone passed a law against sunspots. And now it seemed that someone had!

It was hard to believe, but the evidence was there. The story lay in those musty files up in the *Globe* office. Stories that told of the world going mad when business scraped rock bottom. Of governments smashing, of starving hordes sweeping nation after nation.

I put my head down between my hands and groaned. I wanted a glass of beer. The kind Louie used to push across the bar, cool and with a lot of foam on top. And now there wasn't any beer. There hadn't been for centuries. All because of sunspots!

Ultraviolet light. Endocrine glands and human behavior. Words that scientists rolled around in their mouths and nobody paid much attention to. But they were the things that had played the devil with the human race.

Herb chuckled behind me. I swung around on him, my nerves on edge.

"What's the matter with you?" I demanded.

"Boy," said Herb, "this Wash Tubbs can get himself into some of the damnedest scrapes!"

"What you got there?" I asked, seeing he was reading a paper.

"Oh, this," he said. "This is that old paper we found up at the office. The one published in '85. I'm going to take it back and give it to J.R. But right now I'm reading the funnies—"

I grunted and hunkered down, turning my mind back to the sunspots. It sounded wacky, all right, but that was the only explanation.

It didn't seem right that a body of matter ninety-three million miles away could rule the lives of mankind—but, after all, all life depended on the Sun. Whiff out the Sun and there wouldn't be any life. Those old savages who had worshiped the Sun had the right idea.

Say, then, that sunspots had gone out of style. What would happen? Exactly what those files back at the *Globe* office had shown.

Depression, ever deepening. Business failures, more and more men out of work, taxes piling higher and higher as a panicky government fought to hold off the day of reckoning.

I heard Herb making some strangling sounds and swung around again. I was getting annoyed with Herb.

But the look on Herb's face halted the words that were bubbling on my lips. His face was stark. It was white as a sheet and his eyes were frozen wide.

He shoved the paper at me, babbling, a shaking finger pointing at a small item.

I grabbed the sheet and squinted to make out the faded type. Then I read, slowly, but with growing horror:

LANGER DIES

"James Langer, convicted in 1951 of tampering with the time machine in which Mike Hamilton and Herb Harding, *Globe* newsmen, set out on a flight into the future the preceding year, died in Rocky Point prison today at the age of sixty-five.

"Langer, at his trial, confessed he had bribed the guard placed in charge of the machine, to allow him to enter the plane in which it was installed. There, he testified, he removed that portion of the mechanism which made it possible for the machine to move backward in time.

"Langer, at that time, was an employee of the *Standard*, which went out of business a few years later.

"National indignation aroused by the incident resulted in the passage by Congress of a law prohibiting further building or experimentation with time machines. Heartbroken, Dr. Ambrose Ackerman, inventor of the machine, died two weeks after the trial."

I sat numb for a few minutes, my hand tightening in a terrible grip upon the paper, grinding its yellowed pages into flaking shreds.

Then I looked at Herb, and as I looked into his fear-stricken face I remembered something.

"So," I said, and I was so mad that I almost choked.

"So, you just had a few drinks with the boys that night before we left. You just met up with some *Standard* boys and had a few."

I remembered the way Jimmy Langer had laughed in my face as I was leaving the Dutchman's. I remembered how nervous the guard had been that morning.

"You didn't spill your guts, did you?" I rasped.

"Look, Mike—" said Herb, getting up off the ground.

"You got drunk, damn you," I yelled at him, "and your brains ran right out of your mouth. You told that *Standard* crowd everything you knew. And Old Man Johnson sent Langer out to do the dirty work."

I was mad, mad clear down to the soles of my boots.

"Damn you, Mike—" said Herb, and right then I let him have it. I gave him a poke that shook him clear down to the ground, but he came right back at me. Maybe he was mad, too.

He clipped me alongside the jaw and I plastered him over the eye, and after that we went at it hammer and tongs.

Herb wasn't any slouch with his dukes, and he kept me pretty busy. I gave him everything I had, but he always came back for more, and he pasted me a few that set my head to ringing.

But I didn't mind—all I wanted was to give Herb a licking he'd remember right down to the day he breathed his last.

When we quit it was just because neither one of us could fight another lick. We lay there on the ground, gasping and glaring at one another. One of Herb's eyes was closed, and I knew I had lost a couple of teeth and my face felt like it bad been run through a meat grinder.

Then Herb grinned at me.

"If I could have stayed on my feet a bit longer," he gasped, "I'd have murdered you."

And I grinned back at him.

Probably we should have stayed back in 2450. We had a chance back there. Old Daniel Boone didn't know too much, but at least he was civilized in a good many ways. And no doubt there still were books, and we might have been able to find other useful things.

We might have made a stab at rebuilding civilization, although the cards would have been stacked against us. For there's something funny about that sunspot business. When the sunspots stopped rearing around out on the Sun, something seemed to have run out of men—the old double-fisted, hell-for-leather spirit that had taken them up through the ages.

But we figured that men would make a come-back. We were pretty sure that somewhere up in the future we'd find a race that had started to climb back.

So we went ahead in time. Even if we couldn't go back, we could still go ahead.

We went five hundred years and found nothing. No trace of Daniel Boone's descendants. Maybe they'd given up raising squashes and had moved out where the hunting was better. The city still stood, although some of the stones had crumbled and some of the buildings were falling to pieces.

We traveled another five hundred years, and this time a horde of howling savages, men little more advanced than the tribes which roamed over Europe in the old Stone Age, charged out of the ruins at us, screaming and waving clubs and spears.

We just beat them to the plane.

In two thousand years the tribe had disappeared, and in its place we saw skulking figures that slunk among the mounds that once had been a city. Things that looked like men.

And after that we found nothing at all. Nothing, that is, except a skeleton that looked like it might once have been a human being.

Here at last we stop. There's no use of going farther, and the gas in the tank of our plane is running low.

The city is a heap of earthy mounds, bearing stunted trees. Queer animals shuffle and slink over and among the mounds. Herb says they are mutations—he read about mutations somewhere in a book.

To the west stretch great veldts of waving grass, and across the river the hills are forested with mighty trees.

But Man is gone. He rose, and for a little while he walked the Earth. But now he's swept away.

Back in 1950, Man thought he was the whole works. But he wasn't so hot, after all. The sunspots took him to the cleaners. Maybe it was the sunspots in the first place that enabled him to rise up on his hind legs and rule the roost. Billy said that sunspots could do some funny things.

But that doesn't matter now. Man is just another has-been.

There's not much left for us to do. Just to sit and think about J.R. rubbing his hands together. And Billy Larson wiggling his ears. And the way Jimmy Langer laughed that night outside the Dutchman's place.

Right now I'd sell my soul to walk into the Dutchman's place and say to Louie: "It's a hell of a world, Louie."

And hear Louie answer back: "It sure as hell is, Mike."

DROP DEAD

"Drop Dead" first appeared in the July 1956 issue of Galaxy Science Fiction. *It's enough to give a space explorer ulcers.*

—*dww*

The critters were unbelievable. They looked like something from the maudlin pen of a well-alcoholed cartoonist.

One herd of them clustered in a semicircle in front of the ship, not jittery or belligerent—just looking at us. And that was strange. Ordinarily, when a spaceship sets down on a virgin planet, it takes a week at least for any life that might have seen or heard it to creep out of hiding and sneak a look around.

The critters were almost cow-size, but nohow as graceful as a cow. Their bodies were pushed together as if every blessed one of them had run full-tilt into a wall. And they were just as lumpy as you'd expect from a collision like that. Their hides were splashed with large squares of pastel color—the kind of color one never finds on any self-respecting animal: violet, pink, orange, chartreuse, to name only a few. The overall effect was of a checkerboard done by an old lady who made crazy quilts.

And that, by far, was not the worst of it.

From their heads and other parts of their anatomy sprouted a weird sort of vegetation, so that it appeared each animal was hiding, somewhat ineffectively, behind a skimpy thicket. To compound the situation and make it completely insane, fruits and vegetables—or what *appeared* to be fruits and vegetables—grew from the vegetation.

So we stood there, the critters looking at us and us looking back at them, and finally one of them walked forward until it was no more than six feet from us. It stood there for a moment, gazing at us soulfully, then dropped dead at our feet.

The rest of the herd turned around and trotted awkwardly away, for all the world as if they had done what they had come to do and now could go about their business.

Julian Oliver, our botanist, put up a hand and rubbed his balding head with an absentminded motion.

"Another whatisit coming up!" he moaned. "Why couldn't it, for once, be something plain and simple?"

"It never is," I told him. "Remember that bush out on Hamal V that spent half its life as a kind of glorified tomato and the other half as grade-A poison ivy?"

"I remember it," Oliver said sadly.

Max Weber, our biologist, walked over to the critter, reached out a cautious foot and prodded it.

"Trouble is," he said, "that Hamal tomato was Julian's baby and this one here is mine."

"I wouldn't say entirely yours," Oliver retorted. "What do you call that underbrush growing out of it?"

I came in fast to head off an argument. I had listened to those two quarreling for the past twelve years, across several hundred light-years and on a couple dozen planets. I couldn't stop it here, I knew, but at least I could postpone it until they had something vital to quarrel about.

"Cut it out," I said. "It's only a couple of hours till nightfall and we have to get the camp set up."

"But this critter," Weber said. "We can't just leave it here."

"Why not? There are millions more of them. This one will stay right here and even if it doesn't—"

"But it dropped dead!"

"So it was old and feeble."

"It wasn't. It was right in the prime of life."

"We can talk about it later," said Alfred Kemper, our bacteri-ologist. "I'm as interested as you two, but what Bob says is right. We have to get the camp set up."

"Another thing," I added, looking hard at all of them. "No matter how innocent this place may look, we observe planet rules. No eating anything. No drinking any water. No wandering off alone. No carelessness of any kind."

"There's nothing here," said Weber. "Just the herds of critters. Just the endless plains. No trees, no hills, no nothing."

He really didn't mean it. He knew as well as I did the reason for observing planet rules. He only wanted to argue.

"All right," I said, "which is it? Do we set up camp or do we spend the night up in the ship?"

That did it.

We had the camp set up before the sun went down and by dusk we were all settled in. Carl Parsons, our ecologist, had the stove together and the supper started before the last tent peg was driven.

I dug out my diet kit and mixed up my formula and all of them kidded me about it, the way they always did.

It didn't bother me. Their jibes were automatic and I had automatic answers. It was something that had been going on for a long, long time. Maybe it was best that way, better than if they'd disregarded my enforced eating habits.

I remember Carl was grilling steaks and I had to move away so I couldn't smell them. There's never a time when I wouldn't give my good right arm for a steak or, to tell the truth, any other kind of normal chow. This diet stuff keeps a man alive all right, but that's about the only thing that can be said of it.

I know ulcers must sound silly and archaic. Ask any medic and he'll tell you they don't happen any more. But I have a riddled stomach and the diet kit to prove they sometimes do. I guess it's what you might call an occupational ailment. There's a lot of never-ending worry playing nursemaid to planet survey gangs.

After supper, we went out and dragged the critter in and had a closer look at it.

It was even worse to look at close than from a distance.

There was no fooling about that vegetation. It was the real McCoy and it was part and parcel of the critter. But it seemed that it only grew out of certain of the color blocks in the critter's body.

We found another thing that practically had Weber frothing at the mouth. One of the color blocks had holes in it—it looked almost exactly like one of those peg sets that children use as toys. When Weber took out his jackknife and poked into one of the holes, he pried out an insect that looked something like a bee. He couldn't quite believe it, so he did some more probing and in another one of the holes he found another bee. Both of the bees were dead.

He and Oliver wanted to start dissection then and there, but the rest of us managed to talk them out of it.

We pulled straws to see who would stand first guard and, with my usual luck, I pulled the shortest straw. Actually there wasn't much real reason for standing guard, with the alarm system set to protect the camp, but it was regulation—there had to be a guard.

I got a gun and the others said good night and went to their tents, but I could hear them talking for a long time afterward. No matter how hardened you may get to this survey business, no matter how blasé, you hardly ever get much sleep the first night on any planet.

I sat on a chair at one side of the camp table, on which burned a lantern in lieu of the campfire we would have had on any other planet. But here we couldn't have a fire because there wasn't any wood.

I sat at one side of the table, with the dead critter lying on the other side of it and I did some worrying, although it wasn't time for me to start worrying yet. I'm an agricultural economist and I don't begin my worrying until at least the first reports are in.

But sitting just across the table from where it lay, I couldn't help but do some wondering about that mixed-up critter. I didn't get anywhere except go around in circles and I was sort of glad when Talbott Fullerton, the Double Eye, came out and sat down beside me.

Sort of, I said. No one cared too much for Fullerton. I have yet to see the Double Eye I or anybody else ever cared much about.

"Too excited to sleep?" I asked him.

He nodded vaguely, staring off into the darkness beyond the lantern's light.

"Wondering," he said. "Wondering if this could be the planet."

"It won't be," I told him. "You're chasing an El Dorado, hunting down a fable."

"They found it once before," Fullerton argued stubbornly. "It's all there in the records."

"So was the Gilded Man. And the Empire of Prester John. Atlantis and all the rest of it. So was the old Northwest Passage back on ancient Earth. So were the Seven Cities. But nobody ever found any of those places because they weren't there."

He sat with the lamplight in his face and he had that wild look in his eyes and his hands were knotting into fists, then straightening out again.

"Sutter," he said unhappily, "I don't know why you do this—this mocking of yours. Somewhere in this universe there is immortality. Somewhere, somehow, it has been accomplished. And the human race must find it. We have the space for it now—all the space there is—millions of planets and eventually other galaxies. We don't have to keep making room for new generations, the way we would if we were stuck on a single world or a single solar system. Immortality, I tell you, is the next step for humanity!"

"Forget it," I said curtly, but once a Double Eye gets going, you can't shut him up.

"Look at this planet," he said. "An almost perfect Earth-type planet. Main-sequence sun. Good soil, good climate, plenty of water—an ideal place for a colony. How many years, do you think, before Man will settle here?"

"A thousand. Five thousand. Maybe more."

"That's right. And there are countless other planets like it, planets crying to be settled. But we won't settle them, because we keep dying off. And that's not all of it . . ."

Patiently, I listened to all the rest—the terrible waste of dying—and I knew every bit of it by heart. Before Fullerton, we'd been saddled by one Double Eye fanatic and, before him, yet another. It was regulation. Every planet-checking team, no matter what its purpose or its destination, was required to carry as supercargo an agent of Immortality Institute.

But this kid seemed just a little worse than the usual run of them. It was his first trip out and he was all steamed up with idealism. In all of them, though, burned the same intense dedication to the proposition that Man must live forever and an equally unyielding belief that immortality could and would be found. For had not a lost spaceship found the answer centuries before—an unnamed spaceship on an unknown planet in a long-forgotten year!

It was a myth, of course. It had all the hallmarks of one and all the fierce loyalty that a myth can muster. It was kept alive by Immortality Institute, operating under a government grant and billions of bequests and gifts from hopeful rich and poor—all of whom, of course, had died or would die in spite of their generosity.

"What are you looking for?" I asked Fullerton, just a little wearily, for I was bored with it. "A plant? An animal? A people?"

And he replied, solemn as a judge: "That's something I can't tell you."

As if I gave a damn!

But I went on needling him. Maybe it was just something to while away my time. That and the fact that I disliked the fellow. Fanatics annoy me. They won't get off your ear.

"Would you know it if you found it?"

He didn't answer that one, but he turned haunted eyes on me.

I cut out the needling. Any more of it and I'd have had him bawling.

We sat around a while longer, but we did no talking.

He fished a toothpick out of his pocket and put it in his mouth and rolled it around, chewing at it moodily. I would have liked to reach out and slug him, for he chewed toothpicks all the time and it was an irritating habit that set me unreasonably on edge. I guess I was jumpy, too.

Finally he spit out the mangled toothpick and slouched off to bed.

I sat alone, looking up at the ship, and the lantern light was just bright enough for me to make out the legend lettered on it: *Caph VII—Ag Survey 286,* which was enough to identify us anywhere in the Galaxy.

For everyone knew Caph VII, the agricultural experimental planet, just as they would have known Aldebaran XII, the medical research planet, or Capella IX, the university planet, or any of the other special departmental planets.

Caph VII is a massive operation and the hundreds of survey teams like us were just a part of it. But we were the spearheads who went out to new worlds, some of them uncharted, some just barely charted, looking for plants and animals that might be developed on the experimental tracts.

Not that our team had found a great deal. We had discovered some grasses that did well on one of the Eltanian worlds, but by and large we hadn't done anything that could be called distinguished. Our luck just seemed to run bad—like that Hamal poison ivy business. We worked as hard as any of the rest of them, but a lot of good that did.

Sometimes it was tough to take—when all the other teams brought in stuff that got them written up and earned them bonuses, while we came creeping in with a few piddling grasses or maybe not a thing at all.

It's a tough life and don't let anyone tell you different. Some of the planets turn out to be a fairly rugged business. At times, the boys come back pretty much the worse for wear and there are times when they don't come back at all.

But right now it looked as though we'd hit it lucky—a peaceful planet, good climate, easy terrain, no hostile inhabitants and no dangerous fauna.

Weber took his time relieving me at guard, but finally he showed up.

I could see he still was goggle-eyed about the critter. He walked around it several times, looking it over.

"That's the most fantastic case of symbiosis I have ever seen," he said. "If it weren't lying over there, I'd say it was impossible. Usually you associate symbiosis with the lower, more simple forms of life."

"You mean that brush growing out of it?"

He nodded.

"And the bees?"

He gagged over the bees.

"How are you so sure it's symbiosis?"

He almost wrung his hands. "I *don't* know," he admitted.

I gave him the rifle and went to the tent I shared with Kemper. The bacteriologist was awake when I came in.

"That you, Bob?"

"It's me. Everything's all right."

"I've been lying here and thinking," he said. "This is a screwy place."

"The critters?"

"No, not the critters. The planet itself. Never saw one like it. It's positively naked. No trees. No flowers. Nothing. It's just a sea of grass."

"Why not?" I asked. "Where does it say you can't find a pasture planet?"

"It's too simple," he protested. "Too simplified. Too neat and packaged. Almost as if someone had said 'let's make a simple planet, let's cut out all the frills, let's skip all the biological experiments and get right down to basics. Just one form of life and the grass for it to eat.'"

"You're way out on a limb," I told him. "How do you know all this? There may be other life-forms. There may be complexities we can't suspect. Sure, all we've seen are the critters, but maybe that's because there are so many of them."

"To hell with you," he said and turned over on his cot.

Now there's a guy I liked. We'd been tent partners ever since he'd joined the team better than ten years before and we got along fine.

Often I had wished the rest could get along as well. But it was too much to expect.

The fighting started right after breakfast, when Oliver and Weber insisted on using the camp table for dissecting. Parsons, who doubled as cook, jumped straight down their throats. Why he did it, I don't know. He knew before he said a word that he was licked, hands down. The same thing had happened many times before and he knew, no matter what he did or said, they would use the table.

But he put up a good battle. "You guys go and find some other place to do your butchering! Who wants to eat on a table that's all slopped up?"

"But, Carl, where can we do it? We'll use only one end of the table."

Which was a laugh, because in half an hour they'd be sprawled all over it.

"Spread out a canvas," Parsons snapped back.

"You can't dissect on a canvas. You got to have—"

"Another thing. How long do you figure it will take? In a day or two, that critter is going to get ripe."

It went on like that for quite a while, but by the time I started up the ladder to get the animals, Oliver and Weber had flung the critter on the table and were at work on it.

Unshipping the animals is something not exactly in my line of duty, but over the years I'd taken on the job of getting them unloaded, so they'd be there and waiting when Weber or some of the others needed them to run off a batch of tests.

I went down into the compartment where we kept them in their cages. The rats started squeaking at me and the zartyls from Centauri started screeching at me and the punkins from Polaris made an unholy racket, because the punkins are hungry all the time. You just can't give them enough to eat. Turn them loose with food and they'd eat themselves to death.

It was quite a job to get them all lugged up to the port and to rig up a sling and lower them to the ground, but I finally finished it without busting a single cage. That was an accomplishment. Usually I smashed a cage or two and some of the animals escaped and then Weber would froth around for days about my careless-ness.

I had the cages all set out in rows and was puttering with canvas flies to protect them from the weather when Kemper came along and stood watching me.

"I have been wandering around," he announced. From the way he said it, I could see he had the wind up.

But I didn't ask him, for then he'd never have told me. You had to wait for Kemper to make up his mind to talk.

"Peaceful place," I said and it was all of that. It was a bright, clear day and the sun was not too warm. There was a little breeze and you could see a long way off. And it was quiet. Really quiet. There wasn't any noise at all.

"It's a lonesome place," said Kemper.

"I don't get you," I answered patiently.

"Remember what I said last night? About this planet being too simplified?"

He stood watching me put up the canvas, as if he might be considering how much more to tell me. I waited.

Finally, he blurted it. "Bob, there are no insects!"

"What have insects—"

"You know what I mean," he said. "You go out on Earth or any Earthilke planet and lie down in the grass and watch. You'll see the insects. Some of them on the ground and others on the grass. There'll be all kinds of them."

"And there aren't any here?"

He shook his head. "None that I could see. I wandered around and lay down and looked in a dozen different places. Stands to reason a man should find some insects if he looked all morning. It isn't natural, Bob."

I kept on with my canvas and I don't know why it was, but I got a little chilled about there not being any insects. Not that I care a hoot for insects, but as Kemper said, it was unnatural, although you come to expect the so-called unnatural in this planet-checking business.

"There are the bees," I said.

"What bees?"

"The ones that are in the critters. Didn't you see any?"

"None," he said. "I didn't get close to any critter herds. Maybe the bees don't travel very far."

"Any birds?"

"I didn't see a one," he said. "But I was wrong about the flowers. The grass has tiny flowers."

"For the bees to work on."

Kemper's face went stony. "That's right. Don't you see the pattern of it, the planned—"

"I see it," I told him.

He helped me with the canvas and we didn't say much more. When we had it done, we walked into camp.

Parsons was cooking lunch and grumbling at Oliver and

Weber, but they weren't paying much attention to him. They had the table littered with different parts they'd carved out of the critter and they were looking slightly numb.

"No brain," Weber said to us accusingly, as if we might have made off with it when he wasn't looking. "We can't find a brain and there's no nervous system."

"It's impossible," declared Oliver. "How can a highly organized, complex animal exist without a brain or nervous system?"

"Look at that butcher shop!" Parsons yelled wrathfully from the stove. "You guys will have to eat standing up!"

"Butcher shop is right," Weber agreed. "As near as we can figure out, there are at least a dozen different kinds of flesh—some fish, some fowl, some good red meat. Maybe a little lizard, even."

"An all-purpose animal," said Kemper. "Maybe we found something finally."

"If it's edible," Oliver added. "If it doesn't poison you. If it doesn't grow hair all over you."

"That's up to you," I told him. "I got the cages down and all lined up. You can start killing off the little cusses to your heart's content."

Weber looked ruefully at the mess on the table.

"We did just a rough exploratory job," he explained. "We ought to start another one from scratch. You'll have to get in on that next one, Kemper."

Kemper nodded glumly.

Weber looked at me. "Think you can get us one?"

"Sure," I said. "No trouble."

It wasn't.

Right after lunch, a lone critter came walking up, as if to visit us. It stopped about six feet from where we sat, gazed at us soulfully, then obligingly dropped dead.

During the next few days, Oliver and Weber barely took time out to eat and sleep. They sliced and probed. They couldn't believe half the things they found. They argued. They waved their scalpels in the air to emphasize their anguish. They almost broke down and wept. Kemper filled box after box with slides and sat hunched, half petrified, above his microscope.

Parsons and I wandered around while the others worked. He dug up some soil samples and tried to classify the grasses and failed, because there weren't any grasses—there was just one type of grass. He made notes on the weather and ran an analysis of the air and tried to pull together an ecological report without a lot to go on.

I looked for insects and I didn't find any except the bees and I never saw those unless I was near a critter herd. I watched for birds and there were none. I spent two days investigating a creek, lying on my belly and staring down into the water, and there were no signs of life. I hunted up a sugar sack and put a hoop in the mouth of it and spent another two days seining. I didn't catch a thing—not a fish, not even a crawdad, not a single thing.

By that time, I was ready to admit that Kemper had guessed right.

Fullerton walked around, too, but we paid no attention to him. All the Double Eyes, every one of them, always were looking for something no one else could see. After a while, you got pretty tired of them. I'd spent twenty years getting tired of them.

The last day I went seining, Fullerton stumbled onto me late in the afternoon. He stood up on the bank and watched me working in a pool. When I looked up, I had the feeling he'd been watching me for quite a little while.

"There's nothing there," he said.

The way he said it, he made it sound as if he'd known all along there was nothing there and that I was a fool for looking.

But that wasn't the only reason I got sore.

Sticking out of his face, instead of the usual toothpick, a stem of grass and he was rolling it around in his lips chewing it the way he chewed the toothpicks.

"Spit out that grass!" I shouted at him. "You fool, spit it out!"

His eyes grew startled and he spit out the grass.

"It's hard to remember," he mumbled. "You see, it's my first trip out and—"

"It could be your last one, too," I told him brutally. "Ask Weber sometime, when you have a moment, what happened to the guy who pulled a leaf and chewed it. Absent-minded, sure. Habit, certainly. He was just as dead as if he'd committed suicide."

Fullerton stiffened up.

"I'll keep it in mind," he said.

I stood there, looking up at him, feeling a little sorry that I'd been so tough with him.

But I had to be. There were so many absent-minded, well-intentioned ways a man could kill himself.

"You find anything?" I asked.

"I've been watching the critters," he said. "There was something funny that I couldn't quite make out at first . . ."

"I can list you a hundred funny things."

"That's not what I mean, Sutter. Not the patchwork color or the bushes growing out of them. There was something else. I finally got it figured out. *There aren't any young.*"

Fullerton was right, of course. I realized it now, after he had told me. There weren't any calves or whatever you might call them. All we'd seen were adults. And yet that didn't necessarily mean there *weren't* any calves. It just meant we hadn't seen them. And the same, I knew, applied as well to insects, birds and fish. They all might be on the planet, but we just hadn't managed to find them yet.

And then, belatedly, I got it—the inference, the hope, the half-crazy fantasy behind this thing that Fullerton had found, or imagined he'd found.

"You're downright loopy," I said flatly.

He stared back at me and his eyes were shining like a kid's at Christmas.

He said: "It had to happen sometime, Sutter, somewhere."

I climbed up the bank and stood beside him. I looked at the

net I still held in my hands and threw it back into the creek and watched it sink.

"Be sensible," I warned him. "You have no evidence. Immortality wouldn't work that way. It couldn't. That way, it would be nothing but a dead end. Don't mention it to anyone. They'd ride you without mercy all the way back home."

I don't know why I wasted time on him. He stared back at me stubbornly, but still with that awful light of hope and triumph on his face.

"I'll keep my mouth shut," I told him curtly. "I won't say a word."

"Thanks, Sutter," he answered. "I appreciate it a lot."

I knew from the way he said it that he could murder me with gusto.

We trudged back to camp.

The camp was all slicked up.

The dissecting mess had been cleared away and the table had been scrubbed so hard that it gleamed. Parsons was cooking supper and singing one of his obscene ditties. The other three sat around in their camp chairs and they had broken out some liquor and were human once again.

"All buttoned up?" I asked, but Oliver shook his head.

They poured a drink for Fullerton and he accepted it, a bit ungraciously, but he did take it. That was some improvement on the usual Double Eye.

They didn't offer me any. They knew I couldn't drink it.

"What have we got?" I asked.

"It could be something good," said Oliver. "It's a walking menu. It's an all-purpose animal, for sure. It lays eggs, gives milk, makes honey. It has six different kinds of red meat, two of fowl, one of fish and a couple of others we can't identify."

"Lays eggs," I said. "Gives milk. Then it reproduces."

"Certainly," said Weber. "What did you think?"

"There aren't any young."

Weber grunted. "Could be they have nursery areas. Certain places instinctively set aside in which to rear their young."

"Or they might have instinctive birth control," suggested Oliver. "That would fit in with the perfectly balanced ecology Kemper talks about."

Weber snorted. "Ridiculous!"

"Not so ridiculous," Kemper retorted. "Not half so ridiculous as some other things we found. Not one-tenth as ridiculous as no brain or nervous system. Not any more ridiculous than my bacteria."

"Your bacteria!" Weber said. He drank down half a glass of liquor in a single gulp to make his disdain emphatic.

"The critters swarm with them," Kemper went on. "You find them everywhere throughout the entire animal. Not just in the bloodstream, not in restricted areas, but in the entire organism. And all of them the same. Normally it takes a hundred different kinds of bacteria to make a metabolism work, but here there's only one. And that one, by definition, must be general purpose—it must do all the work that the hundred other species do."

He grinned at Weber. "I wouldn't doubt but right there are your brains and nervous systems—the bacteria doubling in brass for both systems."

Parsons came over from the stove and stood with his fists planted on his hips, a steak fork grasped in one hand and sticking out at a tangent from his body.

"If you ask me," he announced, "there ain't no such animal. The critters are all wrong. They can't be made that way."

"But they are," said Kemper.

"It doesn't make sense! One kind of life. One kind of grass for it to eat. I'll bet that if we could make a census, we'd find the critter population is at exact capacity—just so many of them to the acre, figured down precisely to the last mouthful of grass. Just enough for them to eat and no more. Just enough so the grass won't be overgrazed. Or undergrazed, for that matter."

"What's wrong with that?" I asked, just to needle him.

I thought for a minute he'd take the steak fork to me.

"What's *wrong* with it?" he thundered. "Nature's never static, never standing still. But here it's standing still. Where's the competition? Where's the evolution?"

"That's not the point," said Kemper quietly. "The fact is that that's the way it is. The point is *why?* How did it happen? How was it planned? *Why* was it planned?"

"Nothing's planned," Weber told him sourly. "You know better than to talk like that."

Parsons went back to his cooking. Fullerton had wandered off somewhere. Maybe he was discouraged from hearing about the eggs and milk.

For a time, the four of us just sat.

Finally Weber said: "The first night we were here, I came out to relieve Bob at guard and I said to him . . ."

He looked at me. "You remember, Bob?"

"Sure. You said symbiosis."

"And now?" asked Kemper.

"I don't know. It simply couldn't happen. But if it did—if it *could*—this critter would be the most beautifully logical example of symbiosis you could dream up. Symbiosis carried to its logical conclusion. Like, long ago, all the life-forms said let's quit this feuding, let's get together, let's cooperate. All the plants and animals and fish and bacteria got together—"

"It's far-fetched, of course," said Kemper. "But, by and large, it's not anything unheard of, merely carried further, that's all. Symbiosis is a recognized way of life and there's nothing—"

Parsons let out a bellow for them to come and get it, and I went to my tent and broke out my diet kit and mixed up a mess of goo. It was a relief to eat in private, without the others making cracks about the stuff I had to choke down.

I found a thin sheaf of working notes on the small wooden crate I'd set up for a desk. I thumbed through them while I ate.

They were fairly sketchy and sometimes hard to read, being smeared with blood and other gook from the dissecting table. But I was used to that. I worked with notes like that all the blessed time. So I was able to decipher them.

The whole picture wasn't there, of course, but there was enough to bear out what they'd told me and a good deal more as well.

For examples, the color squares that gave the critters their crazy-quiltish look were separate kinds of meat or fish or fowl or unknown food, whatever it might be. Almost as if each square was the present-day survivor of each ancient symbiont—if, in fact, there was any basis to this talk of symbiosis.

The egg-laying apparatus was described in some biologic detail, but there seemed to be no evidence of recent egg production. The same was true of the lactation system.

There were, the notes said in Oliver's crabbed writing, five kinds of fruit and three kinds of vegetables to be derived from the plants growing from the critters.

I shoved the notes to one side and sat back on my chair, gloating just a little.

Here was diversified farming with a vengeance! You had meat and dairy herds, fish pond, aviary, poultry yard, orchard and garden rolled into one, all in the body of a single animal that was a complete farm in itself!

I went through the notes hurriedly again and found what I was looking for. The food product seemed high in relation to the gross weight of the animal. Very little would be lost in dressing out.

That is the kind of thing an ag economist has to consider. But that isn't all of it, by any means. What if a man couldn't eat the critter? Suppose the critters couldn't be moved off the planet because they died if you took them from their range?

I recalled how they'd just walked up and died; that in itself was another headache to be filed for future worry.

What if they could only eat the grass that grew on this one planet? And if so, could the grass be grown elsewhere? What kind of tolerance would the critter show to different kinds of climate? What was the rate of reproduction? If it was slow, as was indicated, could it be stepped up? What was the rate of growth?

I got up and walked out of the tent and stood for a while, outside. The little breeze that had been blowing had died down at sunset and the place was quiet. Quiet because there was nothing but the critters to make any noise and we had yet to hear them make a single sound. The stars blazed overhead and there were so many of them that they lighted up the countryside as if there were a moon.

I walked over to where the rest of the men were sitting.

"It looks like we'll be here for a while," I said. "Tomorrow we might as well get the ship unloaded."

No one answered me, but in the silence I could sense the half-hidden satisfaction and the triumph. At last we'd hit the jackpot! We'd be going home with something that would make those other teams look pallid. *We'd* be the ones who got the notices and bonuses.

Oliver finally broke the silence. "Some of our animals aren't in good shape. I went down this afternoon to have a look at them. A couple of the pigs and several of the rats."

He looked at me accusingly.

I flared up at him. "Don't look at me! I'm not their keeper. I just take care of them until you're ready to use them."

Kemper butted in to head off an argument. "Before we do any feeding, we'll need another critter."

"I'll lay you a bet," said Weber.

Kemper didn't take him up.

It was just as well he didn't, for a critter came in, right after breakfast, and died with a *savoir faire* that was positively marvelous. They went to work on it immediately.

Parsons and I started unloading the supplies. We put in a busy day. We moved all the food except the emergency rations we left in the ship. We slung down a refrigerating unit Weber had been yelling for, to keep the critter products fresh. We unloaded a lot of equipment and some silly odds and ends that I knew we'd have no use for, but that some of the others wanted broken out. We put up tents and we lugged and pushed and hauled all day. Late in the afternoon, we had it all stacked up and under canvas and were completely bushed.

Kemper went back to his bacteria. Weber spent hours with the animals. Oliver dug up a bunch of grass and gave the grass the works. Parsons went out on field trips, mumbling and fretting.

Of all of us, Parsons had the job that was most infuriating. Ordinarily the ecology of even the simplest of planets is a complicated business and there's a lot of work to do. But here was almost nothing. There was no competition for survival. There was no dog eat dog. There were just critters cropping grass.

I started to pull my report together, knowing that it would have to be revised and rewritten again and again. But I was anxious to get going. I fairly itched to see the pieces fall together— although I knew from the very start some of them wouldn't fit. They almost never do.

Things went well. Too well, it sometimes seemed to me.

There were incidents, of course, like when the punkins somehow chewed their way out of their cage and disappeared.

Weber was almost beside himself.

"They'll come back," said Kemper. "With that appetite of theirs, they won't stay away for long."

And he was right about that part of it. The punkins were the hungriest creatures in the Galaxy. You could never feed them enough to satisfy them. And they'd eat anything. It made no difference to them, just so there was a lot of it.

And it was that very factor in their metabolism that made them invaluable as research animals.

The other animals thrived on the critter diet. The carnivorous ones ate the critter-meat and the vegetarians chomped on critter-fruit and critter-vegetables. They all grew sleek and sassy. They seemed in better health than the control animals, which continued their regular diet. Even the pigs and rats that had been sick got well again and as fat and happy as any of the others.

Kemper told us, "This critter stuff is more than just a food. It's a medicine. I can see the signs: 'Eat Critter and Keep Well!'"

Weber grunted at him. He was never one for joking and I think he was a worried man. A thorough man, he'd found too many things that violated all the tenets he'd accepted as the truth. No brain or nervous system. The ability to die at will. The lingering hint of wholesale symbiosis. And the bacteria.

The bacteria, I think, must have seemed to him the worst of all.

There was, it now appeared, only one type involved. Kemper had hunted frantically and had discovered no others. Oliver found it in the grass. Parsons found it in the soil and water. The air, strangely enough, seemed to be free of it.

But Weber wasn't the only one who worried. Kemper worried, too. He unloaded most of it just before our bedtime, sitting on the edge of his cot and trying to talk the worry out of himself while I worked on my reports.

And he'd picked the craziest point imaginable to pin his worry on.

"You can explain it all," he said, "if you are only willing to concede on certain points. You can explain the critters if you're willing to believe in a symbiotic arrangement carried out on a planetary basis. You can believe in the utter simplicity of the ecology if you're willing to assume that, given space and time enough, anything can happen within the bounds of logic.

"You can visualize how the bacteria might take the place of brains and nervous systems if you're ready to say this is a bacterial world and not a critter world. And you can even envision the bacteria—all of them, every single one of them—as forming one gigantic linked intelligence. And if you accept that theory, then the voluntary deaths become understandable, because there's no actual death involved—it's just like you or me trimming off a hangnail. And if this is true, then Fullerton has found immortality, although it's not the kind he was looking for and it won't do him or us a single bit of good.

"But the thing that worries me," he went on, his face all knotted up with worry, "is the seeming lack of anything resembling a defense mechanism. Even assuming that the critters are no more than fronting for a bacterial world, the mechanism should be there as a simple matter of precaution. Every living thing we know of has some sort of way to defend itself or to escape potential enemies. It either fights or runs and hides to preserve its life."

He was right, of course. Not only did the critters have no defense, they even saved one the trouble of going out to kill them.

"Maybe we are wrong," Kemper concluded. "Maybe life, after all, is not as valuable as we think it is. Maybe it's not a thing to cling to. Maybe it's not worth fighting for. Maybe the critters, in their dying, are closer to the truth than we."

It would go on like that, night after night, with Kemper talking around in circles and never getting anywhere. I think most of the time he wasn't talking to me, but talking to himself, trying by the very process of putting it in words to work out some final answer.

And long after we had turned out the lights and gone to bed, I'd lie on my cot and think about all that Kemper said and I thought in circles, too. I wondered why all the critters that came in and died were in the prime of life. Was the dying a privilege that was accorded only to the fit? Or were all the critters in the prime of life? Was there really some cause to believe they might be immortal?

I asked a lot of questions, but there weren't any answers.

We continued with our work. Weber killed some of his animals and examined them and there were no signs of ill effect from the critter diet. There were traces of critter bacteria in their blood, but no sickness, reaction or antibody formation. Kemper kept on with his bacterial work. Oliver started a whole series of experiments with the grass. Parsons just gave up.

The punkins didn't come back and Parsons and Fullerton went out and hunted for them, but without success.

I worked on my report and the pieces fell together better than I had hoped they would.

It began to look as though we had the situation well nailed down.

We were all feeling pretty good. We could almost taste that bonus.

But I think that, in the back of our minds, all of us were wondering if we could get away scot free. I know I had mental fingers crossed. It just didn't seem quite possible that something wouldn't happen.

And, of course, it did.

We were sitting around after supper, with the lantern lighted, when we heard the sound. I realized afterward that we had been hearing it for some time before we paid attention to it. It started so soft and so far away that it crept upon us without alarming us. At first, it sounded like a sighing, as if a gentle wind were blowing through a little tree, and then it changed into a rumble, but a far-off rumble that had no menace in it. I was just getting ready to say something about thunder and wondering if our stretch of weather was about to break when Kemper jumped up and yelled.

I don't know what he yelled. Maybe it wasn't a word at all. But the way he yelled brought us to our feet and sent us at a dead run for the safety of the ship. Even before we got there, in the few seconds it took to reach the ladder, the character of the sound had changed and there was no mistaking what it was—the drumming of hoofs heading straight for camp.

They were almost on top of us when we reached the ladder

and there wasn't time or room for all of us to use it. I was the last
in line and I saw I'd never make it and a dozen possible escape
plans flickered through my mind. But I knew they wouldn't
work fast enough. Then I saw the rope, hanging where I'd left it
after the unloading job, and I made a jump for it. I'm no rope-
climbing expert, but I shinnied up it with plenty of speed. And
right behind me came Weber, who was no rope-climber, either,
but who was doing rather well.

I thought of how lucky it had been that I hadn't found the
time to take down the rig and how Weber had ridden me unmer-
cifully about not doing it. I wanted to shout down and point it
out to him, but I didn't have the breath.

We reached the port and tumbled into it. Below us, the stampeding critters went grinding through the camp. There seemed to
be millions of them. One of the terrifying things about it was how
silently they ran. They made no outcry of any kind; all you could
hear was the sound of their hoofs pounding on the ground. It seemed
almost as if they ran in some blind fury that was too deep for outcry.

They spread for miles, as far as one could see on the star-lit
plains, but the spaceship divided them and they flowed to either
side of it and then flowed back again, and beyond the spaceship
there was a little sector that they never touched. I thought how
we could have been safe staying on the ground and huddling in
that sector, but that's one of the things a man never can foresee.

The stampede lasted for almost an hour. When it was all
over, we came down and surveyed the damage. The animals in
their cages, lined up between the ship and the camp, were safe.
All but one of the sleeping tents were standing. The lantern still
burned brightly on the table. But everything else was gone. Our
food supply was trampled in the ground. Much of the equipment was lost and wrecked. On either side of the camp, the
ground was churned up like a half-plowed field. The whole
thing was a mess.

It looked as if we were licked.

The tent Kemper and I used for sleeping still stood, so our notes were safe. The animals were all right. But that was all we had—the notes and animals.

"I need three more weeks," said Weber. "Give me just three weeks to complete the tests."

"We haven't got three weeks," I answered. "All our food is gone."

"The emergency rations in the ship?'

"That's for going home."

"We can go a little hungry."

He glared at us—at each of us in turn—challenging us to do a little starving.

"I can go three weeks," he said, "without any food at all."

"We could eat critter," suggested Parsons. "We could take a chance."

Weber shook his head. "Not yet. In three weeks, when the tests are finished, then maybe we will know. Maybe we won't need those rations for going home. Maybe we can stock up on critters and eat our heads off all the way to Caph."

I looked around at the rest of them, but I knew, before I looked, the answer I would get.

"All right," I said. "We'll try it."

"It's all right for you," Fullerton retorted hastily. "You have your diet kit."

Parsons reached out and grabbed him and shook him so hard that he went cross-eyed. "We don't talk like that about those diet kits."

Then Parsons let him go.

We set up double guards, for the stampede had wrecked our warning system, but none of us got much sleep. We were too upset.

Personally, I did some worrying about why the critters had stampeded. There was nothing on the planet that could scare them. There were no other animals. There was no thunder or lightning—as a matter of fact, it appeared that the planet might have no boisterous weather ever. And there seemed to be nothing in the critter makeup, from our observation of them, that would set them off emotionally.

But there must be a reason and a purpose, I told myself. And there must be, too, in their dropping dead for us. But was the purpose intelligence or instinct?

That was what bothered me most. It kept me awake all night long.

At daybreak, a critter walked in and died for us happily.

We went without our breakfast and, when noon came, no one said anything about lunch, so we skipped that, too.

Late in the afternoon, I climbed the ladder to get some food for supper. There wasn't any. Instead, I found five of the fattest punkins you ever laid your eyes on. They had chewed holes through the packing boxes and the food was cleaned out. The sacks were limp and empty. They'd even managed to get the lid off the coffee can somehow and had eaten every bean.

The five of them sat contentedly in a corner, blinking smugly at me. They didn't make a racket, as they usually did. Maybe they knew they were in the wrong or maybe they were just too full. For once, perhaps, they'd gotten all they could eat.

I just stood there and looked at them and I knew how they'd gotten on the ship. I blamed myself, not them. If only I'd found the time to take down the unloading rig, they'd never gotten in. But then I remembered how that dangling rope had saved my life and Weber's and I couldn't decide whether I'd done right or wrong.

I went over to the corner and picked the punkins up. I stuffed three of them in my pockets and carried the other two. I climbed down from the ship and walked up to camp. I put the punkins on the table.

"Here they are," I said. "They were in the ship. That's why we couldn't find them. They climbed up the rope."

Weber took one look at them. "They look well fed. Did they leave anything?"

"Not a scrap. They cleaned us out entirely."

The punkins were quite happy. It was apparent they were glad to be back with us again. After all, they'd eaten everything in reach and there was no further reason for their staying in the ship.

Parsons picked up a knife and walked over to the critter that had died that morning.

"Tie on your bibs," he said.

He carved out big steaks and threw them on the table and then he lit his stove. I retreated to my tent as soon as he started cooking, for never in my life have I smelled anything as good as those critter steaks.

I broke out the kit and mixed me up some goo and sat there eating it, feeling sorry for myself.

Kemper came in after a while and sat down on his cot.

"Do you want to hear?" he asked me.

"Go ahead," I invited him resignedly.

"It's wonderful. It's got everything you've ever eaten backed clear off the table. We had three different kinds of red meat and a slab of fish and something that resembled lobster, only better. And there's one kind of fruit growing out of that bush in the middle of the back . . ."

"And tomorrow you drop dead."

"I don't think so," Kemper said. "The animals have been thriving on it. There's nothing wrong with them."

It seemed that Kemper was right. Between the animals and men, it took a critter a day. The critters didn't seem to mind. They were johnny-on-the-spot. They walked in promptly, one at a time, and keeled over every morning.

The way the men and animals ate was positively indecent. Parsons cooked great platters of different kinds of meat and fish and fowl and what-not. He prepared huge bowls of vegetables. He heaped other bowls with fruit. He racked up combs of honey and the men licked the platters clean. They sat around with belts unloosened and patted their bulging bellies and were disgustingly contented.

I waited for them to break out in a rash or to start turning green with purple spots or grow scales or something of the sort. But nothing happened. They thrived, just as the animals were thriving. They felt better than they ever had.

Then, one morning, Fullerton turned up sick. He lay on his cot flushed with fever. It looked like Centaurian virus, although we'd been inoculated against that. In fact, we'd been inoculated and immunized against almost everything. Each time, before we blasted off on another survey, they jabbed us full of booster shots.

I didn't think much of it. I was fairly well convinced, for a time at least, that all that was wrong with him was overeating.

Oliver, who knew a little about medicine, but not much, got the medicine chest out of the ship and pumped Fullerton full of some new antibiotic that came highly recommended for almost everything.

We went on with our work, expecting he'd be on his feet in a day or two.

But he wasn't. If anything, he got worse.

Oliver went through the medicine chest, reading all the labels carefully, but didn't find anything that seemed to be the proper medication. He read the first-aid booklet. It didn't tell him anything except how to set broken legs or apply artificial respiration and simple things like that.

Kemper had been doing a lot of worrying, so he had Oliver take a sample of Fullerton's blood and then prepared a slide. When he looked at the blood through the microscope, he found that it swarmed with bacteria from the critters. Oliver took some more blood samples and Kemper prepared more slides, just to doublecheck, and there was no doubt about it.

By this time, all of us were standing around the table watching Kemper and waiting for the verdict. I know the same thing must have been in the mind of each of us.

It was Oliver who put it into words. "Who is next?" he asked.

Parsons stepped up and Oliver took the sample.

We waited anxiously.

Finally Kemper straightened.

"You have them, too," he said to Parsons. "Not as high a count as Fullerton."

Man after man stepped up. All of us had the bacteria, but in my case the count was low.

"It's the critter," Parsons said. "Bob hasn't been eating any."

"But cooking kills—" Oliver started to say.

"You can't be sure. These bacteria would have to be highly adaptable. They do the work of thousands of other micro-organisms. They're a sort of handy-man, a jack-of-all-trades. They can acclimatize. They can meet new situations. They haven't weakened the strain by becoming specialized."

"Besides," said Parsons, "we don't cook all of it. We don't cook the fruit and most of you guys raise hell if a steak is more than singed."

"What I can't figure out is why it should be Fullerton," Weber said. "Why should his count be higher? He started on the critter the same time as the rest of us."

I remembered that day down by the creek.

"He got a head start on the rest of you," I explained. "He ran out of toothpicks and took to chewing grass stems. I caught him at it."

I know it wasn't very comforting. It meant that in another week or two, all of them would have as high a count as Fullerton. But there was no sense not telling them. It would have been criminal not to. There was no place for wishful thinking in a situation like that.

"We can't stop eating critter," said Weber. "It's all the food we have. There's nothing we can do."

"I have a hunch," Kemper replied, "it's too late anyhow."

"If we started home right now," I said, "there's my diet kit . . ."

They didn't let me finish making my offer. They slapped me on the back and pounded one another and laughed like mad.

It wasn't that funny. They just needed something they could laugh at.

"It wouldn't do any good," said Kemper. "We've already had it. Anyhow, your diet kit wouldn't last us all the way back home."

"We could have a try at it," I argued.

"It may be just a transitory thing," Parsons said. "Just a bit of fever. A little upset from a change of diet."

We all hoped that, of course.

But Fullerton got no better.

Weber took blood samples of the animals and they bad a bacterial count almost as high as Fullerton's—much higher than when he'd taken it before.

Weber blamed himself. "I should have kept closer check. I should have taken tests every day or so."

"What difference would it have made?" demanded Parsons. "Even if you had, even if you'd found a lot of bacteria in the blood, we'd still have eaten critter. There was no other choice."

"Maybe it's not the bacteria," said Oliver. 'We may be jumping at conclusions. It may be something else that Fullerton picked up."

Weber brightened up a bit. "That's right. The animals still seem to be okay."

They were bright and chipper, in the best of health.

We waited. Fullerton got neither worse nor better.

Then, one night, he disappeared.

Oliver, who had been sitting with him, had dozed off for a moment. Parsons, on guard, had heard nothing.

We hunted for him for three full days. He couldn't have gone far, we figured. He had wandered off in a delirium and he didn't have the strength to cover any distance.

But we didn't find him.

We did find one queer thing, however. It was a ball of some strange substance, white and fresh-appearing. It was about four feet in diameter. It lay at the bottom of a little gully, hidden out of sight, as if someone or something might have brought it there and hidden it away.

We did some cautious poking at it and we rolled it back and forth a little and wondered what it was, but we were hunting Fullerton and we didn't have the time to do much investigating. Later on, we agreed, we would come back and get it and find out what it was.

Then the animals came down with the fever, one after another—all except the controls, which had been eating regular food until the stampede had destroyed the supply. After that, of course, all of them ate critter.

By the end of two days, most of the animals were down.

Weber worked with them, scarcely taking time to rest. We all helped as best we could.

Blood samples showed a greater concentration of bacteria. Weber started a dissection, but never finished it. Once he got the animal open, he took a quick look at it and scraped the whole thing off the table into a pail. I saw him, but I don't think any of the others did. We were pretty busy.

I asked him about it later in the day, when we were alone for a moment. He briskly brushed me off.

I went to bed early that night because I had the second guard. It seemed I had no more than shut my eyes when I was brought upright by a racket that raised goose pimples on every inch of me.

I tumbled out of bed and scrabbled around to find my shoes and get them on. By that time, Kemper had dashed out of the tent.

There was trouble with the animals. They were fighting to break out, chewing the bars of their cages and throwing themselves against them in a blind and terrible frenzy. And all the time they were squealing and screaming. To listen to them set your teeth on edge.

Weber dashed around with a hypodermic. After what seemed

hours, we had them full of sedative. A few of them broke loose and got away, but the rest were sleeping peacefully.

I got a gun and took over guard duty while the other men went back to bed.

I stayed down near the cages, walking back and forth because I was too tense to do much sitting down. It seemed to me that between the animals' frenzy to escape and Fullerton's disappearance, there was a parallel that was too similar for comfort.

I tried to review all that had happened on the planet and I got bogged down time after time as I tried to make the picture dovetail. The trail of thought I followed kept turning back to Kemper's worry about the critters' lack of a defense mechanism.

Maybe, I told myself, they had a defense mechanism, after all—the slickest, smoothest, trickiest one Man ever had encountered.

As soon as the camp awoke, I went to our tent to stretch out for a moment, perhaps to catch a catnap. Worn out, I slept for hours.

Kemper woke me.

"Get up, Bob!" he said. "For the love of God, get up!"

It was late afternoon and the last rays of the sun were streaming through the tent flap. Kemper's face was haggard. It was as if he'd suddenly grown old since I'd seen him less than twelve hours before.

"They're encysting," he gasped. "They're turning into cocoons or chrysalises or . . ."

I sat up quickly. "That one we found out there in the field!"

He nodded.

"Fullerton?" I asked.

"We'll go out and see, all five of us, leaving the camp and animals alone."

We had some trouble finding it because the land was so flat and featureless that there were no landmarks.

But finally we located it, just as dusk was setting in.

The ball had split in two—not in a clean break, in a jagged one. It looked like an egg after a chicken has been hatched.

And the halves lay there in the gathering darkness, in the silence underneath the sudden glitter of the stars—a last farewell and a new beginning and a terrible alien fact.

I tried to say something, but my brain was so numb that I was not entirely sure just what I should say. Anyhow, the words died in the dryness of my mouth and the thickness of my tongue before I could get them out.

For it was not only the two halves of the cocoon—It was the marks within that hollow, the impression of what had been there, blurred and distorted by the marks of what it had become.

We fled back to camp.

Someone, I think it was Oliver, got the lantern lighted. We stood uneasily, unable to look at one another, knowing that the time was past for all dissembling, that there was no use of glossing over or denying what we'd seen in the dim light in the gully.

"Bob is the only one who has a chance," Kemper finally said, speaking more concisely than seemed possible. "I think he should leave right now. Someone must get back to Caph. Someone has to tell them."

He looked across the circle of lantern light at me.

"Well," he said sharply, "get going! What's the matter with you?"

"You were right," I said, not much more than whispering. "Remember how you wondered about a defense mechanism?"

"They have it," Weber agreed. "The best you can find. There's no beating them. They don't fight you. They absorb you. They make you into them. No wonder there are just the critters here. No wonder the planet's ecology is simple. They have you pegged and measured from the instant you set foot on the planet. Take one drink of water. Chew a single grass stem. Take one bite of critter. Do any one of these things and they have you cold."

Oliver came out of the dark and walked across the lantern-lighted circle. He stopped in front of me.

"Here are your diet kit and notes," he said.

"But I can't run out on you!"

"Forget us!" Parsons barked at me. "We aren't human any more. In a few more days . . ."

He grabbed the lantern and strode down the cages and held the lantern high, so that we could see.

"Look," he said.

There were no animals. There were just the cocoons and the little critters and the cocoons that had split in half.

I saw Kemper looking at me and there was, of all things, compassion on his face.

"You don't want to stay," he told me. "If you do, in a day or two, a critter will come in and drop dead for you. And you'll go crazy all the way back home—wondering which one of us it was."

He turned away then. They all turned away from me and suddenly it seemed I was all alone.

Weber had found an axe somewhere and he started walking down the row of cages, knocking off the bars to let the little critters out.

I walked slowly over to the ship and stood at the foot of the ladder, holding the notes and the diet kit tight against my chest.

When I got there, I turned around and looked back at them and it seemed I couldn't leave them.

I thought of all we'd been through together and when I tried to think of specific things, the only thing I could think about was how they always kidded me about the diet kit.

And I thought of the times I had to leave and go off somewhere and eat alone so that I couldn't smell the food. I thought of almost ten years of eating that damn goo and that I could never eat like a normal human because of my ulcerated stomach.

Maybe *they* were the lucky ones, I told myself. If a man got turned into a critter, he'd probably come out with a whole stomach and never have to worry about how much or what he ate. The critters never ate anything except the grass, but maybe, I thought, that grass tasted just as good to them as a steak or a pumpkin pie would taste to me.

So I stood there for a while and I thought about it. Then I took the diet kit and flung it out into the darkness as far as I could throw it and I dropped the notes to the ground.

I walked back into the camp and the first man I saw was Parsons.

"What have you got for supper?" I asked him.

WORRYWART

The title character in "Worrywart" is a copyreader for a big-city newspaper, which was Clifford Simak's first job at the Minneapolis Star, *and he tells us a great deal about that post in this story. And although Cliff quickly moved up to be chief of the copy desk—a position he held for years before being promoted to news editor—I think he really loved being a copyreader: It let him see all the news that came in.*

Of course, the more you know, the more you find to worry about, if you are so inclined.

—dww

Charley Porter is a copyreader on the *Daily Times* and a copyreader is a funny kind of critter. He is a comma watcher and a word butcher and a mighty tide of judgment set against the news. He's a sort of cross between a walking encyclopedia and an ambulatory index.

Occasionally you meet a reporter or an editor or you see their pictures or you hear them spoken of. But you never hear about a copyreader.

The copyreader sits with his fellow copyreaders at a horseshoe-shaped table. If he's an old time copyreader, like Charley is, he wears a green eyeshade and rolls his shirtsleeves up above his elbows.

Inside the curve of the copydesk sits the man who directs the copyreaders. Since the inside of the desk is known as the slot, this man is called the slot man. To the slot man comes the daily flow of news; he passes the copy to the men around the desk and they edit it and write the headlines.

Because there is always copy enough to fill twenty times the allotted space, the copyreader must trim all the stories and see there is no excess wordage in them. This brings him into continuous collision with reporters, who see their ornately worded stories come out chopped and mangled, although definitely more readable.

When work slacks off in the afternoon, the copyreaders break their silence and talk among themselves. They talk about the news and debate what can be done about it. If you listened to them, not knowing who they were, you'd swear you were listening in on some world commission faced by weighty problems on which life or death depended.

For your copyreader is a worrier. He worries because each day he handles the fresh and bleeding incidents that shape the course of human destiny, and there probably is no one who knows more surely nor feels more keenly the knife-edge balance between survival and disaster.

Charley Porter worried more than most. He worried about a lot of things that didn't seem to call for worry.

There was the matter, for instance, of those "impossible" stories happening in sequence. The other men on the copydesk took notice of them after two or three had occurred, and talked about them—among themselves, naturally, for no proper copyreader ever talks to anyone but another copyreader. But they passed them off with only casual mention.

Charley worried about the incidents, secretly, of course, since he could see that none of his fellow copyreaders felt them worthy of really serious worry. After he had done a lot of worrying, he began to see some similarity among them, and that was when he really got down on the floor and wrestled with himself.

First there had been the airliner downed out in Utah. Bad weather held up the hunt for it, but finally air searchers spotted the wreckage strewn over half a mountain peak. Airline officials said there was no hope that any had survived. But when the rescuers were halfway to the wreckage, they met the survivors walking out; every single soul had lived through the crash.

Then there was the matter of Midnight, the 64 to 1 shot, winning the Derby.

And, after that, the case of the little girl who didn't have a chance of getting well. They held a party for her weeks ahead of time so she could have a final birthday. Her picture was published coast to coast and the stories about her made you want to cry and thousands of people sent her gifts and postcards. Then, suddenly, she got well. Not from any new wonder drug or from any new medical technique. She just got well, some time in the night.

A few days later the wires carried the story about old Pal, the coon dog down in Kentucky who got trapped inside a cave. Men dug for days and yelled encouragement. The old dog whined back at them, but finally he didn't whine any more and the digging was getting mighty hard. So the men heaped boulders into the hole they'd dug and built a cairn. They said pious, angry, hopeless words, then went back to their cabins and their plowing.

The next day old Pal came home. He was a walking rack of bones, but he still could wag his tail. The way he went through a bowl of milk made a man feel good just to see him do it. Everyone agreed that old Pal must finally have found a way to get out by himself.

Except that an old dog buried in a cave for days, getting weaker all the time from lack of food and water, doesn't find a way to get out by himself.

And little dying girls don't get well, just like that, in the middle of the night.

And 64 to 1 shots don't win the Derby.

And planes don't shatter themselves among the Utah peaks with no one getting hurt at all.

A miracle, sure. Two miracles, even. But not four in a row and within a few weeks of one another.

It took Charley quite a while to establish some line of similarity. When he did, it was a fairly thin line. But thick enough at least, to justify more worry.

The line of similarity was this: All the stories were "running" or developing stories.

There had been a stretch of two days during which the world waited for the facts of the plane crash. It had been known for days before the race that Midnight would run and that he didn't have a chance. The story of the doomed little girl had been a matter of public interest for weeks. The old coon dog had been in the cave a week or more before the men gave up and went back to their homes.

In each of the stories, the result was not known until some time after the situation itself was known. Until the final fact was actually determined, there existed an infinite number of probabilities, some more probable than others, but with each probability's having at least a fighting chance. When you flip a dime into the air, there always exists the infinitesimal probability, from the moment you flip it until it finally lands heads or tails, that it will land on edge and stay there. Until the fact that it is heads or tails is established, the probability of its landing on edge continues to remain.

And that was exactly what had happened, Charley told himself: the doubt had been flipped four times, and four times running it had stood on edge.

There was one minor dissimilarity, of course . . . the plane crash. It didn't quite fit.

Each event had been a spin of the dime, and while that dime was still in the air, and the public held its breath, a little girl had gotten well, somehow, and a dog had escaped from a cave, somehow, and a 64 to 1 shot had developed whatever short-lived properties of physique and temperament are necessary to make long shots win.

But the plane crash—there had been no thought of it until *after* the fact. By the time the crash came into the public eye, the dime was down, and what had happened on that mountain peak had already happened, and all the hopes and prayers offered for the safety of the passengers were, actually, retroactive in the face of the enormous probability that all had perished.

Please, let the dog escape. Tonight.

Let the little girl get well. Soon.

Let my long shot come in. Next week.

Let the passengers be alive. *Since yesterday.*

Somehow the plane crash worried Charley most of all.

Then, to everyone's surprise, and with no logic whatsoever, the Iranian situation cleared up, just when it began to look as if it might be another Korea.

A few days later Britain announced proudly that it had weathered its monetary storm, that all was well with the sterling bloc, and London would need no further loans.

It took a while for Charley to tie these two stories up with the plane-girl-Derby-hound-dog sequence. But then he saw that they belonged and that was when he remembered something else that might—well, not tie in, exactly—but might have something to do with this extraordinary run of impossibilities.

After work, he went down to the Associated Press office and had an office boy haul out the files, stapled books of carboned flimsies—white flimsies for the A wire, blue flimsies for the B wire, yellow for the sports wire and pink for the market wire. He knew what he was looking for hadn't come over either the market or the sports wire, so he passed them up and went through the A and B wire sheets story by story.

He couldn't remember the exact date the story had come over, but he knew it had been since Memorial Day, so he started with the day after Memorial Day and worked forward.

He remembered the incident clearly. Jensen, the slot man, had picked it up and read it through. Then he had laughed and put it on the spike.

One of the others asked: "What was funny, Jens?"

So Jensen took the story off the spike and threw it over to him. It had gone the rounds of the desk, with each man reading it, and finally it had got back to the spike again.

And that had been the last of it. For the story was too wacky for any newsman to give a second glance. It had all the earmarks of the phony.

Charley didn't find what he was looking for the first day, although he worked well into the evening—so he went back the next afternoon, and found it.

It was out of a little resort town up in Wisconsin, and it told about an invalid named Cooper Jackson who had been bedridden since he was two or three years old. The story said that Cooper's old man claimed that Cooper could foresee things, that he would think of something or imagine something during the evening and the next day it would happen. Things like Linc Abrams' driving his car into the culvert at Trout Run and coming out all right himself, but with the car all smashed to flinders, and like the Reverend Amos Tucker's getting a letter from a brother he hadn't heard from in more than twenty years.

The next day Charley spoke to Jensen.

"I got a few days coming," he said, "from that time I

worked six-day weeks last fall, and I still got a week of last year's vacation you couldn't find the room for . . ."

"Sure, Charley," Jensen said. "We're in good shape right now."

Two days later Charley stepped off the milk-run train in the little resort town in Wisconsin. He went to one of the several cabin camps down on the lake that fronted the town and got himself a small, miserable cabin for which he paid an exorbitant price. And it wasn't until then that he dared let himself think—*really* think—of the reason he had come there.

In the evening he went uptown and spent an hour or two standing around in the general store and the pool room. He came back with the information that he had set out for, and another piece of information he had not been prepared to hear.

The first piece of information, the one he had gone out to get, was that Dr. Erik Ames was the man to see. Doc Ames, it appeared, was not only the doctor and the mayor of the town, but the acknowledged civic leader, sage and father confessor of the whole community.

The second piece of information, one which had served the town as a conversation piece for the last two months, was that Cooper Jackson, after years of keeping to his bed as a helpless invalid, now was on his feet. He had to use a cane, of course, but he got around real well and every day he took a walk down by the lake.

They hadn't said what time of day, so Charley was up early in the morning and started walking up and down the lakeshore, keeping a good lookout. He talked with the tourists who occupied the other cabins and he talked with men who were setting out for a day of fishing. He spent considerable time observing a yellow-winged blackbird that had its nest somewhere in a bunch of rushes on a marshy spit.

Cooper Jackson finally came early in the afternoon, hobbling along on his cane, with a peaked look about him. He walked along the shore for a ways; then sat down to rest on a length of old dead tree that had been tossed up by a storm.

Charley ambled over. "Do you mind?" he asked, sitting down beside him.

"Not at all," said Cooper Jackson. "I'm glad to have you."

They talked. Charley told him that he was a newspaperman up there for a short vacation and how it was good to get away from the kind of news that came over the teletypes, and how he envied the people who could live in this country all the year around.

When he heard Charley was a newspaperman, Cooper's interest picked up like a hound dog cocking its ears. He began to ask all sorts of questions, the kind of questions that everyone asks a newspaperman whenever he can corner one.

What do you think of the situation and what can be done about it and is there any chance of preventing war and what should we do to prevent a war . . . and so on until you think you'll scream.

Except that it seemed to Charley that Cooper's questions were a bit more incisive, backed by a bit more information than were the questions of the ordinary person. He seemed to display more insistence and urgency than the ordinary person, who always asked his questions in a rather detached, academic way.

Charley told him, honestly enough, that he didn't know what could be done to prevent a war, although he said that the quieting of the Iranian situation and the British monetary announcement might go a long way toward keeping war from happening.

"You know," said Cooper Jackson, "I felt the same way, too. That is, after I read the news, I felt that those were two good things to happen."

At this point, perhaps, a couple of things should be considered.

If Charley Porter had been a regular newspaperman instead of copyreader, he might have mentioned the plane wreck and the little girl who hadn't died, and how it was a funny thing about that coon dog getting out of the cave and how he knew of a man who'd made a mint of money riding in on Midnight.

But Charley didn't say these things.

If Charley had been a regular newspaperman, he might have said to Cooper Jackson: "Look here, kid, I'm on to you. I know what you're doing. I got it figured out. Maybe you better straighten me out on a point or two, so I'll have the story right."

But Charley didn't say this. Instead he said that he had heard uptown the night before about Cooper's miraculous recovery, and he was Cooper Jackson, wasn't he?

Yes, Cooper answered, he was Cooper Jackson, and perhaps his recovery was miraculous. No, he said, he didn't have the least idea of how it came about and Doc Ames didn't either.

They parted after an hour or two of talk. Charley didn't say anything about seeing him again. But the next day Cooper came limping down to the beach and headed for the log, and Charley was waiting for him.

That was the day Cooper gave Charley his case history. He had been an invalid, he said, from as far back as he could remember, although his mother had told him it hadn't happened until he was three years old.

He liked to listen to stories, and the stories that his parents and his brothers and sisters told him and read to him were what had kept him alive, he was certain, during those first years. For he made the stories work for him.

He told how he made the characters—Peter Rabbit and the Gingerbread Man and Little Bo Peep and all the rest of them— keep on working overtime after he had heard the stories. He would lie in bed, he said, and relive the stories over and over again.

"But after a while, those stories got pretty threadbare. So I improved on them. I invented stories. I mixed up the characters. For some reason or other Peter Rabbit and the Gingerbread Man always were my heroes. They would go on the strangest odysseys and meet all these other characters, and together they would have adventures that were plain impossible.

"Except," he added, "they never seemed impossible to me."

Finally he had got to be the age where kids usually start off to school. Cooper's Ma had begun to worry about what they should do for his education. But Doc Ames, who was fairly sure Cooper wouldn't live long enough for an education to do him any good, had advised that they teach him whatever he might be interested in learning. It turned out that about all Cooper was interested in was reading. So they taught him how to read. Now he didn't have to have anyone read him stories any more, but could read them for himself. He read *Tom Sawyer* and *Huck Finn* and Lewis Carroll's works and a lot of other books.

So now he had more characters and Peter Rabbit had some rather horrible moments reconciling his world with the world of Tweedledum and Tweedledee and the Mock Turtle. But he finally worked in, and the imagined adventuring got crazier and crazier.

"It's a wonder," said Cooper Jackson, "that I didn't die laughing. But to me it wasn't funny. It was dead serious."

"What do you read now, Cooper?" Charley asked.

"Oh, the newspapers," Cooper said, "and the news magazines and stuff like that."

"That's not what I mean," Charley explained. "What do you read for relaxation? What takes the place of Peter Rabbit?"

Cooper hemmed and hawed a little and finally he admitted it.

"I read science fiction. I ran onto it when someone brought me a magazine six or seven years ago . . . no, I guess it's more like eight."

"I read the stuff myself," said Charley, to put him at his ease.

So they sat the rest of the afternoon and talked of science fiction.

That night Charley Porter lay in his bed in the little lakeshore cabin, staring into the darkness, trying to understand how it must have been for Cooper Jackson, lying there all those years, living with the characters out of children's books and later out of boys' books and then out of science fiction.

He had said that he'd never been in much pain, but sometimes the nights were long and it was hard to sleep, and that was how he'd got started with his imagining. He would imagine things to occupy his mind.

At first, it was just a mental exercise, saying such and such a thing is happening now and going on from there to some other thing that was happening. But after a while he began to see an actual set of characters acting on an imaginary stage, faint and fuzzy characters going through their parts. They were nebulous at first; later on, they became gray, like little skipping ghosts; then they had achieved the sharpness of black and white. About the time he began to deal with *Tom Sawyer* and *Robinson Crusoe,* the characters and background had begun to take on color and perspective.

And from *Huck Finn* and *Robinson Crusoe* and *Swiss Family Robinson,* he had gone on to science fiction.

Good Lord, thought Charley Porter. *He went on to science fiction.*

Take an invalid who had never moved out of his bed, who had never had a formal education, who knew little and cared less about the human viewpoint, give him an overwrought imagination and turn him loose on science fiction—and what have you got?

Charley lay there in the darkness and tried to put himself into the place of Cooper Jackson. He tried to imagine what Cooper might have imagined, what far adventuring he might have embarked upon.

Then let the same invalid suddenly become aware of the world around him, as Cooper had—for now he read the newspapers and the news magazines. Let him see what kind of shape the world was in.

What might happen then?

You're crazy, Charley told himself. But he lay for a long time, looking up into the black, before he went to sleep.

Cooper seemed to like him, and they spent a part of each day together. They talked about science fiction and the news of the day and what should be done to ensure world peace. Charley told him he didn't know what should be done, that a lot of men much smarter than he were working full time on it, and they had found no answer yet.

"Someone," said Cooper, "must do something about it." And the way he said it, you would have sworn that he was going to set out any minute to do that very thing.

So Charley went to call on old Doc Ames.

"I've heard of you," the doctor told him. "Coop was telling me about you just the other day."

"I've been spending a little time with Cooper," Charley said, "and I've wanted to ask him something, but I haven't done it."

"I know. You wanted to ask him about the story that was in the papers here a few months back."

"That's right," Charley agreed. "And I wanted to ask him, too, about how he got up and walked after all those years in bed."

"You're looking for a story?" asked the doctor.

"No," said Charley, "I'm not looking for a story."

"You're a newspaperman."

"I came for a story," Charley told him. "But not any more. Right now I'm . . . well, I'm sort of scared."

"So am I."

"If what I'm thinking is right, it's too big to be a story."

"I hope," said Doc, "that both of us are wrong."

"He's hell bent," Charley went on, "to bring peace to the world. He's asked me about it a dozen times in a dozen different ways. I've told him I don't know, and I don't think there's anyone who does."

"That's the trouble. If he'd just stick to things like that lost

plane out in Utah and the hound dog down in Kentucky, it might
be all right."

"Did he tell you about those things, Doc?"

"No," said Doc, "he didn't really tell me. But he said wouldn't it
be fine if all those people in the plane should be found alive, and he
did a lot of fretting about that poor trapped dog. He likes animals."

"I figure he just practiced up on a few small items," Charley
suggested, "to find if he could do it. He's out for big game now."

Then good, solid, common sense came back to him and he
said: "But, of course, it isn't possible."

"He's got help," said Doc. "Hasn't he told you about the help
he's got?"

Charley shook his head.

"He doesn't know you well enough. I'm the only one he knows
well enough to tell a thing like that."

"He's got help? You mean someone's helping . . . ?"

"Not some*one,*" said Doc. "Some*thing.*"

Then Doc told Charley what Cooper had told him.

It had started four or five years before, shortly after he'd gone
on his science fiction binge. He'd built himself an imaginary ship
that he took out into space. First he'd traveled around our own Solar
System—to Mars and Venus and all the others. Then, tiring of such
backyard stuff, he had built in a gadget that gave his ship speed in
excess of light and had gone out to the stars. He was systematic about
it; you had to say that much for him. He worked things out logically,
and he didn't skip around. He'd land on a certain planet and give that
planet the full treatment before he went on to the next one.

Somewhere along the way, he picked himself up a crew of
companions, most of which were only faintly humanoid, if at all.

And all the time this space-world, this star-world, got clearer
and sharper and more real. It almost got to the point where he
lived in its reality rather than in the reality of the here and now.

The realization that someone else had joined him, that he had
picked up from somewhere a collaborator in his fantasies, began

first as a suspicion, finally solidified into certainty. The fantasies got into the habit of not going as he himself was imagining them; they were modified, and added to, and changed in other ways. Cooper didn't mind though, for generally they were better than anything he could think up by himself—and finally he had grown to know his collaborators—not one of them alone, but three of them, each a separate entity. After the first shocks of recognition, the four of them got along just swell.

"You mean he knows these others—these helpers?"

"He knows them all right," said Doc. "Which doesn't mean, of course, that he has ever seen them or will ever see them."

"You believe this, Doc?"

"I don't know. I don't know. But I do know Coop, and I know that he got up and walked. There is no medical science . . . no *human* medical science . . . that would have made him walk."

"You think these helpers, these collaborators of his, might somehow have cured him?"

"Something did."

"One thing haunts me," said Charley. "Is Cooper Jackson sane?"

"Probably," answered Doc, "he's the sanest man on Earth."

"And the most dangerous."

"That's what worries me. I watch him the best I can. I see him every day . . ."

"How many others have you told?" asked Charley.

"Not a soul," said Doc.

"How many are you going to tell?"

"None. Probably I shouldn't have told you, but you already knew part of it. What are you going to do?"

"I'm going home," said Charley. "I'm going to go home and keep my mouth shut."

"Nothing else?"

"Nothing else. If I were a praying man, I think I'd do some praying."

—

He went home and kept his mouth shut and did a lot of worrying. He wondered whether, praying man or not, he should not try a prayer or two. But when he did, the prayers sounded strange and out of place coming from his lips, so he figured he'd better leave well enough alone.

At times it still seemed impossible. At other times it seemed crystal clear that Cooper Jackson actually could will an event to happen—that by thinking so, he could make it so. But mostly, because he knew too much to think otherwise, Charley knew that the whole thing was true. Cooper Jackson had spent twenty years or so in thinking and imagining, his thoughts and imaginings shaped, not by the course of human events, but by the fantasy of many human minds. He would not think as a normal human being thought, and therein lay both an advantage and a danger.

If he did not think in entirely human channels, he also was not trammeled by the limitations of human thinking; he was free to let his mind wander out in strange directions and bend its energies to strange tasks. His obsession with the necessity of achieving lasting peace was an example of his unhuman attitude; for, while the entire Earth did earnest lip service to the cause of peace, the threat of war had hung over every one so long that its horror had been dulled. But to Cooper Jackson, it was unthinkable that men should slay one another by the millions.

Always Charley came back to those helpers, those three shadowy figures he pictured as standing at Cooper Jackson's shoulder. He assigned them three arbitrary faces, but the faces would not stay as he imagined them. At last he understood that they were things to which you could assign no face.

But the thing that he still worried most about, although he tried not to think of it at all because of its enormity, was the Utah plane crash.

The plane had crashed before Cooper, or anyone else, could

have known it was about to crash. Whatever had happened to the people in the plane had happened *then,* in that one split second when plane and peak had touched—had happened without benefit of the magic of Cooper Jackson's wishful thinking. And to imagine that, without such benefit, the passengers and crew could have escaped unscathed was nothing short of madness. It just couldn't have happened that way.

And that meant that Cooper not only could make something turn out the way he wanted it to turn out, but that he also could go back through time and undo something that was already done! Either that, or he could bring dead people back to life, reassembling their shattered bodies and making them whole again, and that was even madder than to think that his wishful thinking might be retroactive.

Whenever Charley thought about that, the sweat would start out on him and he'd think about Britain and Iran and once again he would see Cooper's face, all puckered up with worry about what the world was coming to.

He watched the news more closely than he had ever watched it, analyzing each unexpected turn in it, searching for the clue that might suggest some harebrained scheme to Cooper Jackson, trying to think the way Cooper might think, but feeling fairly sure that he wasn't even coming close.

He had his bags packed twice to go to Washington—but each time he unpacked them and put away his clothes and shoved the bags back into the closet.

For he realized there was no use going to Washington, or anywhere else for that matter.

"Mr. President, I know a man who can bring peace to the world . . ."

They'd throw him out before he had the sentence finished.

He called Doc Ames, and Doc told him that everything was all right, that Cooper had bought a lot of back-issue science fiction magazines and was going through them, cataloguing story themes and variant ideas. He seemed happy in this pastime and calmer than he'd been for weeks.

When Charley hung up, he found that his hands were shaking and he suddenly was cold all over, for he felt positive that he knew what Cooper was doing with those piles of magazines.

He sat in the one comfortable chair in his rented room and thought furiously, turning over and over the plots that he had run across in his science fiction reading. While there were some that might apply, he rejected them because they didn't fit into the pattern of his fear.

It wasn't until then that he realized he'd been so busy worrying about Cooper that he hadn't been paying attention to the recent magazines. Cold fear gripped him that there might be something in the current issues that might apply most neatly.

He'd have to buy all the magazines he could find, and give them a good, fast check.

But he got busy at one thing and another and it was almost a week before he got around to buying them. By that time his fear had subsided to some extent. Trudging home with the magazines clutched beneath his arm, he decided that he would put aside his worry for one night at least and read for enjoyment.

That evening he settled himself in the comfortable chair and stacked the magazines beside him. He took the first one off the top of the stack and opened it, noting with some pleasure that the lead-off story was by a favorite author.

It was a grim affair about an Earthman holding an outpost against terrific odds. He read the next one . . . about a starship that hit a space warp and got hurled into another universe.

The third was about the Earth being threatened by a terrible war and how the hero solved the crisis by bringing about a condition which outlawed electricity, making it impossible in the Universe. Without electricity, planes couldn't fly and tanks couldn't move and guns couldn't be sighted in, so there was no war.

Charley sat in the chair like a stricken man. The magazine

dropped from his fingers to the floor and he stared across the room at the opposite wall with terror in his eyes, knowing that Cooper Jackson would have read that story, too.

After a while Charley got up and telephoned Doc.

"I'm worried, Charley," Doc told him. "Coop has disappeared."

"Disappeared!"

"We've tried to keep it quiet. Didn't want to stir up any fuss—the way Coop is and all. There might be too many questions."

"You're looking for him?"

"We're looking for him," Doc said, "as quietly as we can. We have scoured the countryside and we've sent out wires to police officials and missing person bureaus."

"You've got to find him, Doc!"

"We're doing all we can." Doc sounded tired and a bit bewildered.

"But where could he have gone?" asked Charley. "He doesn't have any money, does he? He can't stay hiding out too long without . . ."

"Coop can get money any time he wants it. He can get anything he wants any time he wants it."

"I see what you mean," said Charley.

"I'll keep in touch," said Doc.

"Is there anything . . .?"

"Not a thing," said Doc. "Not a thing that anyone can do. We can wait. That's all."

That was months ago, and Charley is still waiting.

Cooper's still missing and there's no trace of him.

So Charley waits and worries.

And the thing he worries about is Cooper's lack of a formal education, his utter lack of certain basic common knowledge.

There is one hope, of course—that Cooper, if and when he decides to act, will make his action retroactive, going back in time to outlaw not electricity itself, but Man's discovery of electricity.

For, disrupting and terrible as that might be, it would be better than the other way.

But Charley's afraid that Cooper won't see the necessity for retroactive action. He's afraid that Cooper won't realize that, when you outlaw electricity, you can't limit it to the current that runs through a wire to light a lamp or turn an engine. When you rule out electricity as a natural phenomenon, you rule out *all* electricity, and that means you rule out an integral part of atomic structure. And that you affect not only this Earth but the entire Universe.

So Charley sits and worries and waits for the flicker of the lamp beside his chair.

Although he realizes, of course, that when it comes there won't be any flicker.

CLIFFORD D. SIMAK, during his fifty-five-year career, produced some of the most iconic science fiction stories ever written. Born in 1904 on a farm in southwestern Wisconsin, Simak got a job at a small-town newspaper in 1929 and eventually became news editor of the *Minneapolis Star-Tribune*, writing fiction in his spare time.

Simak was best known for the book *City*, a reaction to the horrors of World War II, and for his novel *Way Station*. In 1953 *City* was awarded the International Fantasy Award, and in following years, Simak won three Hugo Awards and a Nebula Award. In 1977 he became the third Grand Master of the Science Fiction and Fantasy Writers of America, and before his death in 1988, he was named one of three inaugural winners of the Horror Writers Association's Bram Stoker Award for Lifetime Achievement.

DAVID W. WIXON was a close friend of Clifford D. Simak's. As Simak's health declined, Wixon, already familiar with science fiction publishing, began more and more to handle such things as his friend's business correspondence and contract matters. Named literary executor of the estate after Simak's death, Wixon began a long-term project to secure the rights to all of Simak's stories and find a way to make them available to readers who, given the fifty-five-year span of Simak's writing career, might never have gotten the chance to enjoy all of his short fiction. Along the way, Wixon also read the author's surviving journals and rejected manuscripts, which made him uniquely able to provide Simak's readers with interesting and thought-provoking commentary that sheds new light on the work and thought of a great writer.

THE COMPLETE SHORT FICTION OF CLIFFORD D. SIMAK

FROM OPEN ROAD MEDIA

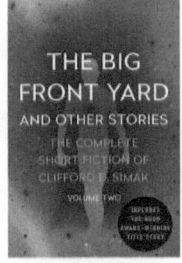
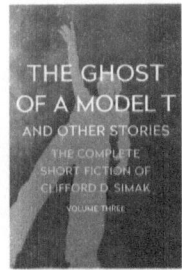

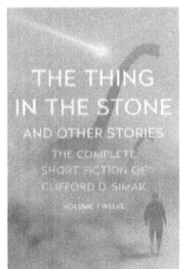

OPEN ROAD

INTEGRATED MEDIA

OPEN ROAD

INTEGRATED MEDIA

Find a full list of our authors and
titles at www.openroadmedia.com

FOLLOW US
@OpenRoadMedia